TRIUMPHANT

Omnibus

Edited by
SPIKE Y JONES
and
FAITH HUNTER

LORE
SEEKERS
PRESS

TRIUMPHANT - ROGUE MAGE OMNIBUS
ISBN 978-1-62268-114-3

Previously published by Lore Seekers Press as seperate e-books:
TRIALS, ISBN: 978-1-62268-112-9, November 2016,
and TRIBULATIONS, ISBN: 978-1-62268-113-6, December 2016.

Library of Congress Control Number: 2017941610

Table of Contents
Rogue Mage Timeline

*Previously published in the *Rogue Mage Role Playing Game.*

Rogue Mage Anthology Vol. I
TRIALS

Introductions for TRIALS

From Spike:

When I was first asked by roleplaying game writer Christina Stiles to work with her on the *Rogue Mage RPG* back in 2007, I'd never heard of New York Times bestselling author Faith Hunter or her *Rogue Mage* trilogy of novels. In fact, nobody had gotten around to coining the "*Rogue Mage* trilogy" term to describe the books at that point, as the third novel hadn't even been released yet. But Christina and I had worked together on a number of projects, and I trusted her judgement and signed on to the project.

After some years of hard work, the roleplaying game was released—as the ROGUE MAGE RPG PLAYER'S HANDBOOK and GAME MASTER'S GUIDE, available in print from Bella Rosa Books and downloadable from Misfit Studios. Then Faith asked me about the next *Rogue Mage* project. Faith had written a couple dozen short-short vignettes as chapter splashes for the game books, and she thought that they could be combined with an equal amount of new material to make an anthology set in the *Rogue Mage* universe, bringing those stories to readers who might not have seen them in the games, while providing new stories to please fans who wanted more. And she wanted me to edit the new material.

One thing led to another, and Rogue Mage: TRIALS and the upcoming companion volume Rogue Mage: TRIBULATIONS are now double the size of that original conception. Along with new Faith Hunter vignettes and short stories, Faith, her agent Lucienne Diver, and I assembled a group of other writers who we felt would enjoy writing in "the Faithiverse." Heck, even I got a chance to contribute, writing a handful of pieces scattered over the two volumes.

There are two things I've really enjoyed about working on these anthologies.

The first are the stories.

Rogue Mage: TRIALS isn't just about the adventures of Thorn St. Croix, "the rogue mage." It's about the entire *Rogue Mage* universe. There are, of course, stories featuring Thorn and the supporting cast of the novels, but also stories set decades, or even millennia, before the stars of the series were born. In fact, instead of the thematic approach that many other short story collections take, the stories in Rogue Mage: TRIALS are arranged chronologically, on a timeline that stretches from a prehistory hinted at in some books of the Bible to a point just months before the start of BLOODRING, the first of the *Rogue Mage* novels. (Rogue Mage:

TRIBULATIONS will feature stories set at the same time as the novels, as well as continuing Thorn St. Croix's saga past the end of the third novel, HOST.)

The stories are set in other parts of the USA, in other countries, on different continents. They feature neomages, of course, but also kylen, humans, and others. There's humour, adventure, tragedy, romance, and a bunch of windows opened into the detailed back-story of the *Rogue Mage* setting. It was a challenge to make these diverse stories come together into a cohesive volume, and a puzzle sometimes figuring out exactly where each piece fit, but I think we managed to make it work.

And the second thing I've enjoyed are the authors.

I didn't know the majority of these writers before we got started, and there were some . . . disagreements between some of us. But in the end I've learned a few things, I think we've forged some relationships that will last, and, most importantly, I hope my editorial efforts have managed to take an assortment of stories that were already good in draft to excellent in print.

In the ROGUE MAGE RPG PLAYER'S HANDBOOK I couldn't imagine what the next project was going to be after that major undertaking. Well, now I'm here on the other side of the next project, and I wonder what we're going to do to top this.

—*Spike Y Jones*

From Faith:

For years I have been asked, "When's the next *Rogue Mage* book?" and, "Is the series really over? It feels unfinished!"

And now I can say: The series isn't dead. Now you have millennia of stories gathered in two volumes, fiction by some fantastic authors and me.

And . . . the series is in your hands, *Rogue Mage* fans. Buy, read, review, and enjoy. And if enough of you still remember and love the series, then there might yet be that long-awaited ending, in serialized novella form. Fingers crossed that you remember and love Thorn St. Croix and the others in her world!

—*Faith Hunter*

Prologue

Stone Walls a Prison Make
circa 3000 BC

Faith Hunter

Batarel lunged at them, his wrists trapped by the silver and gold manacles that secured him to the chamber wall. The cuffs and chains were inscribed with the list of crimes he'd committed, with Scripture, and with the words of the Most High.

The seraphs watched, just beyond the length of the chains, their faces impassive, though Batarel's pain was urging them to help him. His tears smelled of incense and longing.

Itqal stood against the far wall of the cavern. He was here as an observer, watching only, to witness that the three brothers of the condemned carried out the orders of the High Host.

An angel of affection, he was unused to the horror of judgment, but he would do his duty to the Most High and to the High Host.

Even more so, Itqal had been unused to the fury of battle and the anger of its aftermath, but he had been pulled into the war, standing armed, protecting the Most High from the third of the Host who had pulled away, the third who had followed the Red Dragon into sin, who had joined together in rebellion. And though this watcher, Batarel, had not joined Azazel in his uprising, he had observed the atrocities committed by the Dragon and his Dark Host and had done nothing—nothing to help either side. A watcher indeed, and in the worst manner.

Afriel, who stood watchguard over the young in Heaven and on Earth, stepped close to the condemned, sudden tears scoring his perfect face. "I am sorry, my brother. But I saw what happened to the ones under my charge. I saw their remains."

"I harmed none in the infernal war!" Batarel shouted, his chains clanging in a minor key. "I watched only, and only from afar!"

"You speak truth of your part in the rebellion, although you did not call for us when you saw the Dragon gather his forces, and this was held against you in the Court of the High Host. But you are judged not for the war, but for your crimes against mankind," Afriel said, "for your sins. There, on Earth, among the children of men and among your many women, you did not protect the young. Your crimes there cannot be numbered."

"Nooooo . . ." Batarel keened.

"Yes. The Most High has seen." Afriel breathed in the scent of his brother's pain and spoke the words of the incantation. "You have been my brother in the River of Time, but you are my brother no more. I revoke and retract all vows made in the time of your innocence. For your crimes there is no defense." Afriel turned his back and snapped his wings forward over his body, hiding his face.

Batarel screamed in fury, his bell-toned anger the scent of burned stone.

Hadiririon stepped forward, and at his holy glare Batarel lowered his head, gasping, weeping, begging, "You are the beloved angel of God. You are holy. Yet you are here to pass judgment on me for crimes I did not commit."

"No, my brother. Judgment has already been rendered, punishment will be swift. Extend your wings."

"I will not."

"Then we shall do it for you," Hadiririon said. Faster than Itqal could process it, faster than if the other seraph had moved through the River of Time, Hadiririon was beside Batarel, his seraph steel sword raised. At the other side stood Vohal, his sword raised as well. The seraphs gripped the bones beneath the feathers' roots and pulled Batarel's wings straight. Vohal shouted, "All glory to the Most High!" They cut down, each with a single mighty sword stroke, slicing through flesh and bones. Angelic blood sprayed across the cave walls. Batarel screamed.

The seraphs dropped the wings to the floor, the magnificent plumage a carpet of red-stained green. Batarel fell to his knees.

Hiding his emotions, turning his dark eyes away from the bleeding watcher, Itqal pulled his battle-scorched cloak close, shifting his wings and his sword, the blade scraping against the rock wall. "It is done. Seal the cave."

With his words, he and the three seraphs of judgment stepped back and to the other side of the cavern. Although they could see into the cave with ease, the condemned could not see them, could not feel them. He was cut off. He was alone. He was now as he would be, throughout the rest of his eternity, until the end-time judgment by the mankind he had wronged.

The seraphs touched the cave walls with their swords and, as Itqal watched, white light flowed outward from the sword tips in all directions onto the walls, across the cave roof and floor, brighter than the sun. Batarel screamed again, a jarring clash of notes, a song of anguish, of loss. And the light rose and rose, covering the watcher's legs, his torso, his head, growing harder, sealing him in until even the notes of his grief were only a faint vibration in the rock.

The three seraphs of judgment spoke together, repeating the words of the sundering of brotherhood as one. "You have been my brother in the River of Time, but you are my brother no more. I revoke and retract all vows made in the time of your innocence. For your crimes there is no defense. For your crimes there is no defense. For your crimes there is no defense."

The white light solidified, harder than quartz, and the light went out. Batarel's cries were shut off. And the stone began to darken and harden, drawing inward, growing smaller, denser.

Once, long ago, the small chamber had been part of a series of interconnected caverns. Now the cave was to be left sealed until the end of time.

"It is done," Itqal said, "by the words and will of the Most High."

And then, as the four left the dark cavern for the light of the mountainside, the saddest duty was Itqal's to perform. The angel of affection's head tilted to one side, as if listening to a voice whispering from a distance. "There is another. Our brother Kochabiel. Not a watcher—a participant. Again we must fly." The tear that slid down Itqal's cheek was golden in the sun's setting light.

The Honeymoon is Over
June 12, 2011

Faith Hunter

Carl slid his arm around Ella, holding her close, smelling the new perfume she'd bought in a small shop on a side street near their hotel. "Camellia, maybe," he whispered in her ear. "Something soft and floral. Delicate, like you. Hold still," he said, positioning her in front of him and raising the camera. "I want to get this shot of you in that dress, with the Eiffel Tower in the background."

"You have four hours of *me*. Our children will think they came into being by magic—their father was a camera lens. I want shots of *us*." She caught her dress as it billowed out, pulled by the indecisive wind.

"Okay. I'll get that man over there to . . ." his voice trailed off.

"Carl?"

"Damn," he whispered.

Ella followed the aim of the camera, turning around. The grass was baked dry by summer, the sky touched by a few puffy clouds. The Eiffel Tower was the only thing in the background. And Ella followed the lens up, up, to its top. To the bright light that flickered and sparkled. It hadn't been there before, she was sure of it. And then she saw the thing standing on the very top in the center of the too-bright light. Not a man. It was too huge.

"An angel," Carl whispered.

Ella didn't believe in God—or angels. Or at least she hadn't. But that *thing* looked like an oversized man. If a man burned with a halo of pure energy. If a man had wings, glittering wings, outspread, feathered and massive, yet still looking lighter than the clouds. And the man, *the angel*, carried an aura of power so strong she could feel it on her skin like acid, foaming and burning deep; she could taste it when she breathed; the energies blistered like flames, burning like pepper in her nose and on her tongue.

"Let's get closer!" Carl started to jog, his camera still high. Ella followed, uncertain, knowing she was almost forgotten. Falling behind, fighting the fear that was suddenly so strong, so solid and precise.

As she watched, the angel reached to his side and grabbed a sword. He held it aloft, its blade a gold so pure and bright that it captured the sun's rays and threw them back at the sky.

Carl stumbled, his breathing harsh. Ella caught up. The angel turned and looked at them. Right at *them*. Something warm and wet splattered her face, her arm. Startled, Ella looked away from the angel, to her husband of four days.

And she took a half step back, away. She blinked hard, her eyes gritty. Carl was covered in sores—red welts. Some were erupting, bleeding. Her fingers caught her lips. Hot flesh against too hot flesh, fevered. Her arms were blistered, burning. Bleeding. "Carl?" she whispered.

The angel began to speak. "In the Name of the Most High God, I bring a message and judgment. You were given all that you might desire: all the wealth, all the beauty, all the ease. And the Most High blessed you. Yet you turned your back on your fellow man. You turned your back on the Most High, questioning His existence—denying the existence of the Creator God!" His voice rose to a roar, "In His name do I curse you. I curse this city and all who dwell herein. I curse you!"

Ella turned away, and took a step, a single faltering step, before she lost her balance and fell, sideways. It took a long time to fall. In her lost, last moments, her lungs filled. Blood spluttered from her mouth. She was still conscious when she hit the ground. Pain. Blood. Eyes so hot they burned.

From the ground, she watched Carl slide slowly down, blood spreading through his clothes like scarlet sweat. He dropped the camera. It bounced, landed facing the Tower and the Angel of Death who still stood atop it, his sword of judgment raised, as he cursed the Earth.

Finding the Way
5 PA / 2017 AD

Misty Massey

Grog's head was aching, as if a load of bricks had been thrown at him, one at a time but every one with deadly accuracy. Light wormed under his eyelids, sharp as a paring knife. The Angel—was it back? He hadn't heard the tones, but the light was relentless. "No," he groaned. "I can't hear you. I won't hear you." He rolled over, pressing himself closer into the wall. It was Grog's time to rest.

Something hard nudged against his ribs—the toe of a boot. "Get up, brainchow. You can sleep somewhere else." Hands gripped his arms, yanking him to his feet. Men in dark blue jackets crowded the filthy room, yelling that everyone was under arrest and hauling people off the floor. The one holding Grog turned his stony face toward the rest, but his hand was a vise on Grog's elbow.

Grog blinked in confusion. "You're not the Angel," he said.

"Nope, buddy. I'm your worst nightmare if you give me any shit."

Nightmare . . . Grog seemed to remember what that word used to mean. A dream, from which you could wake up. Pastor Daniel had promised he'd be all right once he awakened into his new life. Promised that the signs he was carving into Grog's skin wouldn't hurt for long, that the dust he rubbed into the wounds would transform him into someone special.

But like everyone else back then, he hadn't known anything. None of them saw the Angel, heard its voice, felt the call. They knew enough to scream, though. Scream and scratch and bleed and run away. Only Grog was left, untransformed and alone.

The lawman had nothing to fear from Grog. No point in fighting for his freedom, not when it wasn't really lost. One, two, buckle my shoe, and through the wall he'd go, out of danger and harm's way. Not yet, though. Wait until he was in the car, before they pulled away to lock him up. Better yet, let them take him to the station. It usually took so long he could snatch a couple more hours of sleep, maybe even a meal, out from under the unrelenting gaze of the sun. Once he was fed and rested, he'd slip out at twilight, before the moon took the sun's place hunting for him.

"Spread 'em," the lawman ordered, shoving Grog against a wall and slapping at his pockets. He found the worn leather wallet and opened it. He snorted an ugly laugh.

"The brainchow has ID. Go figure. Gordon Grove, huh?" Without waiting for an answer, the lawman slid a cold metal handcuff onto Grog's right wrist, then pulled it down and brought it to meet his left. Both hands cuffed behind his back, Grog let the man march him outside. The mid-morning sun burned Grog's eyes.

"Watch your head, Gordon," the man said, pushing Grog into the confines of the waiting van. The door thunked closed.

"Grog," he muttered, sliding his body as far down the seat as he could, into the minimal shade. "Gordon's gone."

Other people were already inside the van, some groaning, others quiet. They'd gathered in the crack house to share the escape of whatever drugs they took to forget the horrors of the world around them. They didn't care if one more muttering loonie hunkered down in a corner with them. Not that sleep was easy in places like that. Grog was continually being awakened from one ungentle sleep or another. It was still better than letting the sun find him. The signs the pastor had carved into his skin . . . they burned like acid when he was out in the open. So he was always on the lookout for somewhere to stay hidden.

The only trouble with the junkies was the risk of being rousted by the law like today. That many vulnerable people in one place was too tempting for devil-spawn, and the law didn't like it. Ah well, he knew the process. They'd drive him to a police station, make a record of arresting him, maybe even give him food. When he was a kid, the police used to put people in cages for breaking the law, but since the Plagues began, there weren't enough police left to watch the cages, and no one saw much of a point to holding anyone. Before long they'd kick him out, to start the whole thing over again. With any luck, it'd be twilight by then.

He pressed himself against the wall of the van and closed his eyes, singing to pass the time. "Sting a ling a ding ding," he thought, "sing praises to the Most High for hurting us so. Lay still, it'll only hurt forever."

The ride lasted a minute, or maybe all day. Grog really wasn't sure how time worked anymore. Then the door was opening, and he was being hustled out of the van. They were parked under a metal awning, right outside a concrete-block building. Graffiti covered the walls, bright-colored pictures of winged creatures with fangs tearing into screaming people, and the words "Shoulda known," and "How's that guardian angel look now?" in between. He tilted his head, curious. Had the painter seen real angels when they descended? His Angel hadn't looked like these at all, but since his Angel was a much more terrifying beast, Grog decided the painter was only guessing.

"In the door. Move it, move it."

They shuffled down a short hallway and into a large room filled with desks, although most of them had no one behind them. Chairs were lined along the wall to his left, under a long bulletin board filled with photographs and postings that had probably been out-of-date a year ago. It reminded him of the "Most Wanted" posters he'd seen in the post office as a child.

"Sit in a chair, and wait 'til we call you."

Grog sat down. His stomach growled, and he wondered if he should bother asking for food, or just wait to see if anything was offered.

"Gordon." Someone kicked Grog's feet. "Get up."

They never seemed to understand that Gordon was no longer around, that Grog was all that was left ever since the Angel chose him. Grog followed the lawman to a desk. He turned Grog around and released one hand from the cuffs. Pushing him back forward again, he waved at the chair. Grog sat, and the lawman locked the empty cuff to the arm of the chair.

"Let's see," the man said, as if any of what he did was important. "Name is Gordon Grove. I'm guessing you don't have an address, huh?" Grog shook his head. The man reached into a box on the desk and took out Gordon's wallet. He flipped it open, peering at the old driver's license in its plastic sleeve. "Says here you live in Atlanta."

"Gordon did," Grog said. "He's hiding. In a cloud. The Angel chased him away."

Other people were performing the same dull ritual at other desks around the room. There was a soft hum from the lights on the ceiling, and the irritating scritches of pencils on paper. And something else, another sound. A series of tones, notes chasing each other up and down a line. Almost familiar. Like trumpets. He squinted, trying to shut out the sights around him so he could listen more closely.

"Okay, brainchow, I'll play. Is Gordon's date of birth November 3, 1995?"

"Happy birthday to you, you live in a zoo," Grog sang, then frowned. "No, that's not it."

"That's not your . . . uh, Gordon's birthday?"

Grog shook his head. "It's his birthday."

"Look, if you're gonna answer every question both yes and no, this'll take all night."

"Didn't. The birthday's right, but the song is wrong." He rolled his eyes to the ceiling. "Baa baa black sheep, have a pizza pie . . . nope."

The lawman tapped his pencil against his temple. "Lucky me, I get the weird one." He wrote something down, then took a deep breath. "Next question. What was Gordon doing in the old Moore House? Scoring a hit? Or sleeping one off?"

Grog knew he was supposed to answer, but the sound distracted him. He turned his head, trying to determine which direction the sound came from. "Can't you hear it?"

The lawman sighed. "I don't hear anything."

It was getting louder, more distinct, as if whatever made it was far away but coming closer. It couldn't be, could it? After all this time . . . was the Angel singing at last?

A woman carrying a clipboard walked up to the lawman's side. "Hey, Martin, you got a minute?"

The lawman let his pencil fall to the desk. "Anything to get me out of this," he said. He pointed at Grog. "You, stay here."

They stepped away and spoke together quietly, the lawman occasionally glancing over at Grog. Grog didn't care. The sound was becoming music, the tones sounding more like a voice with every second that passed. But if the Angel was singing, that meant he wanted something. Grog had nothing left to give.

He began to pick at the dead skin at the edges of his fingernails. Somehow the Angel could find him here. He couldn't stay, even if they planned to feed him. He needed to find somewhere dark and unpleasant, somewhere like the junk house. Somewhere the Angel wouldn't think to look for him.

A woman in the waiting area sobbed, calling out someone's name. The lawman nodded his head and returned to where Grog was waiting. Grog rattled the still-cuffed wrist.

"Time for me to go," he said.

"That's right, Gordon. You're getting out of here. Someone's come for you."

The lawman worked for the Angel? Grog's head spun in confusion. "No, no, no," he said, his voice shaking, "Not special. Not different. Just like everyone else."

"That's as may be, son, but at least you have people who care what happens to you. Your guardian."

"Guardian angels watch do keep, but that's not the kind of angel who looks for me." Grog pulled at the cuffs. The sound was loud enough now that everyone should have been able to hear. "The Angel makes everyone tear out their hair and scratch their eyes. There'll be blood and bits on the floor."

"You saw that happen?" The lawman shook his head. "Sorry, kid. Rough break, for sure. Anyway, it's your pastor who's here to get you."

Pastor Daniel. He hadn't seen the pastor since the day the Angel came. The day the pastor's boys held Gordon down on the big altar, and tore his shirt open. The day the pastor cut Gordon's skin in patterns, while Gordon cried. Poured the powder of crushed stones into the wounds while Gordon screamed. Rubbed them, Gordon's blood staining his fingers, until the powder stopped the bleeding and left raised scars all over him. Because he loved Gordon, he said. Because he believed Gordon was meant to be the one to bring them all back to God.

The congregation had watched, listening to Gordon's agony and singing hymns loud enough to drown out his shrieks. And when the Angel at last appeared, singing his mighty song that only Gordon could hear, they'd all gone mad, hurting themselves and each other before running out of the church and into the darkness.

"He made Gordon the symbol," Grog muttered. "Gordon never wanted that."

"Yeah, well, symbol or not, you're leaving with him." The lawman scratched at the corner of his eye with the point of the pencil, leaving dull gray marks on his skin.

The Angel's song thundered in Grog's ears. He closed his eyes, fearing what was to come.

"Gordon."

Pastor Daniel stood next to the desk, smiling down at Grog. His hair was pure white where it had once been brown—thanks to the Angel? The skin around his blue eyes bore scars, and his smile displayed missing teeth. Despite his looks, he radiated strength and wisdom. For an instant, Grog wanted to follow him, do as he said, believe what he told him.

"Gordon, I've been so worried for you, son." He turned to the lawman. "We were baptizing Gordon and he became frightened. He'd seen his mother die during the Plague of Insanity, and the stress of being committed to God was too much for him."

The lawman nodded. "Yeah, he told me. Poor kid." He dragged the pencil across his temple and down to his ear, running the point of it along his ear's inner curves. "Nice that you're here to help him."

"I'm taking him home, where I can keep him safe."

The Angel's song was deafening. A woman at another desk was pulling out her hair, slowly, one strand at a time. Another scratched her wrist viciously, scowling as she dragged her nails along the length of her arm, turning her skin bright red. One of the men who'd ridden in the van with Grog rolled off his chair onto the floor, banging his head against the concrete again and again.

The lawman's face twisted into a grimace. "I just . . . I need . . . you have to sign . . ." he began, but instead of handing the pencil to Pastor Daniel, he slid the point into his ear canal, pushing slowly even while he whimpered in pain. Blood ran down his jawline. With a howl, he snapped the end of the pencil off and fell to the floor, shuddering. The woman with the clipboard cried out, and ran over to help, while the pastor raised his hands to the sky, shouting a prayer.

Time to go. Grog needed to leave the cuffs behind. Only one way to achieve that without the key. It was something he'd learned to do after running from the Angel. He didn't know how it worked or why, and he never liked to do it when people might see. But this was an emergency. If he stayed, the Angel would drive all the people to death, and it would be Grog's fault.

Taking a deep breath, he held it an instant, gathering all the reality of himself into the breath, then let it out. His body lightened, becoming soft as a summer cloud. He cautiously lifted his hand—if he moved too quickly, his clothes would fall off, too, and he didn't want to spend time dressing again. The cuff fell away, clinking against the arm of the chair. With a blink, he let his aspect solidify once more.

Chaos was growing. Blood was flowing. The woman with the clipboard threw herself at the pastor, climbing him and spitting in his face. The pastor fought to free himself, all the while shouting Gordon's name, but whether he wanted Grog to help him or obey, Grog couldn't tell. Not that he intended to do either thing. The Angel had come, which made it the last place Grog wanted to be.

He grabbed Gordon's wallet off the lawman's desk. It was the only thing that was still Gordon's. If Gordon ever came back, he'd want it. Without a backward glance, Grog ran out the door he'd come in, slamming it open hard enough to bounce it off the wall.

Three young men were waiting on the sidewalk, and the biggest one grinned on seeing Grog. He stepped forward, spreading his arms wide as Grog skidded to a stop.

"Gordy!" The young man grabbed for Grog, catching hold of his arm. He pulled him close, wrapping him up in an embrace. "We've been hunting for you."

Pastor Daniel's sons. The ones who'd held Gordon down so the pastor could cut him and hurt him. They had laughed when Gordon screamed. Shadrach, the oldest, squeezed his arm tight around Grog's shoulders. Meshach and Abednego weren't laughing now. Their faces were dark with anger.

"Gordon is gone," Grog said, struggling against Shadrach's hold. "The Angel has come and I have to leave."

"You're not going anywhere." He released Grog, shoving him against the other two brothers. They surrounded him, closing in so tight that Grog couldn't move.

"Dad's so happy," Shadrach said. "He's had us out looking all over the place for you. 'Can't go on without Gordon', he said. 'We need the symbol', he said. 'The only way to convince the people to follow us is to show them the boy'." He slid his fingers into Grog's hair, and pulled it tight, yanking Grog's head back and forcing him to look up. "Maybe now he'll shut the hell up."

"Language, Shad," Meshach warned. "Dad'll be out here any second."

Shadrach rolled his eyes, but he didn't loosen his grip on Grog's hair. He leaned close to Grog's ear. "All this symbol crap is nonsense. You know it. You brought that crazy down, made my dad nuts. If it was up to me, I'd bash your head open against a brick wall and leave you for the flies."

He twisted his hand, pulling Grog's hair so hard he expected it to tear free. "Isn't my call. Dad wants you. And now it occurs to me that you might be an even better symbol if you look more like Christ. Blood on your face, maybe a black eye. And let's not forget some rusty nails through your hands. Dad would love that." He grinned. "It would be my pleasure."

The door slammed open again and Pastor Daniel stepped through. He was missing two shirt buttons, and someone had scratched his face badly. In the room behind him, voices howled in terror. He smiled upon seeing Grog. "Good, you have him."

"Yes, sir," Shadrach said. "Car's waiting." He pushed Grog ahead of him, and the others fell into step behind.

"This is marvelous," the pastor crowed as they walked. "Now that he's back, we can travel to all the cities and gather the faithful. They'll have to believe."

"They'd believe anyway," Shadrach muttered. "Don't need this piece of crap." The pastor didn't hear his oldest son's words, instead continuing to chatter about his plans to use Grog as a church sideshow attraction.

The group turned a corner. The pastor's station wagon sat at the curb.

"Meshach, unlock the back door," Shadrach said.

"You have the keys."

Shadrach growled, and reached in his pocket with his free hand. And his grip on Grog's hair loosened just enough.

Grog jerked free and started running. He fled down the cracked side-walks. Buildings flashed by in his peripheral vision. Behind him, he heard angry shouts and pounding feet. He had no idea where he was going. It didn't matter. He dashed into an alley, dodging piles of trash and dented cans. Ahead of him, the alley was closed off with a tall chain link gate. Grog flung himself at it. "Up up up up," he chanted under his breath. The pur-suing footsteps were coming closer, driving him to climb faster. The top seemed so far away, but suddenly he was there, throwing one leg over, and then the other. He let himself fall to the ground on the opposite side.

Shadrach slammed into the gate. Grog jumped back, but the gate held. He shook the gate again, as if his anger would be enough to pop the pad-lock loose. Grog eased away, then turned to run down the alley.

"Keep running, Gordy," Shadrach yelled, his voice echoing off the walls. "You can't hide forever."

Grog ran until the only sound he heard was the slamming of his heart against his ribs. He stopped and bent over, leaning on his knees to catch his breath. It would be dark soon, time to find shelter for the night. Old build-ings stood silent and empty on either side of the street. A few people hur-ried on their way, not paying any attention to Grog panting on the sidewalk. On the corner opposite stood an old church. The door swung in the breeze. Either no one used it at all anymore, or someone inside didn't care who joined them. He shuddered at the thought of being inside a church again. It was shelter, though, and no one was gathered within to sing and scream. One night, he promised himself, and then he'd move on.

He climbed the steps, whispering an old counting rhyme Gordon had known as a child, and pushed on the unlatched door. It swung in, revealing an empty foyer. Old bulletins blew across the floor, catching on the leg of a bench next to the sanctuary entry. There'd been carpet once. Someone had pulled it up, leaving the marks of carpet glue and exposed nail heads on the unfinished wood. Ahead was the empty sanctuary, with a shadowed altar.

He walked as quietly as he could down the aisle. The pews were empty, but here and there he saw evidence of people. A forgotten purse spilled on the floor, shredded neckties tossed aside. Even a few empty plastic food containers, dried out enough to be free of the smell of rot. Whoever had worshiped here no longer came in.

Ahead of him, up two steps on a raised dais, stood the altar. Every church had one. He'd never feared them as a child. Not until the pastor had used the altar for something painful and terrifying. He shivered, remembering. "Cutting and blood, cutting and blood," he murmured, turning away. To the left rose a narrow staircase, leading up. No going up, Grog thought. Up leads to the sky. Angels live in the sky. There'd be no comfort there.

He walked back into the foyer, but before he reached the door, he heard the rumbling of an engine outside. Dodging away from the partially open door, Grog licked his thumb, rubbed clean a spot on the glass of a window, and peered outside.

The station wagon rolled slowly along the street, its headlights lit. Meshach and Abednego hung their heads out of the passenger-side windows. Grog took a breath and held it. Keep moving, he thought. Nothing to see here.

The car slowed to a stop in front of the church, and Abednego disappeared inside the car. They were too far away to hear clearly, but it seemed that an argument was taking place. A moment later, the car rolled on, Abednego resuming his lookout spot with a frown on his face.

Grog let out the air he'd been holding. They weren't coming into the church. That made the church a good place to hide, at least for the night. But he didn't feel right sleeping in the sanctuary, and the foyer was too open.

In the wall on the right stood a slender door. A closet? Grog pulled at the knob, and the door creaked open, revealing a dark stairway leading down. He smiled. Down was better. No angels in the basement.

He slipped into the shadows, pulling the door closed behind him, and took the stairs slowly, testing each step with his heel before shifting his weight to the next. Sometimes steps groaned, and sometimes they split under foot. Best to go easy.

The further he went, the darker the space around him became. Grog didn't mind the dark so much. Unless demons showed up—but he didn't smell their carrion stink. Nothing but dust and old wax.

The next step wasn't a step at all. It was cold, and hard, like concrete. He'd reached the bottom. He sat down on the next-to-last step, leaned back and dug in his jeans pocket for a cigarette lighter. He'd found it on the floor of last night's house. Scuffed and half-empty, but the yellow plastic glittered if he held it up to a light, and turned the whole world gold if he stared through it. He flicked the wheel, and a bright flame sprung into existence.

He stood up in a wide open room, the light playing off wispy cobwebs that waved and sighed in the corners of the ceiling. To his right was a wooden votive stand, filled with dusty red candles. Grog's lighter was beginning to flicker, so he leaned over and lit a candle, letting his lighter go dark. The candle looked lonely, burning all by itself. Grog removed it from its holder and touched its flame to all the others that would catch. The room filled with light.

On the floor, bluish-gray lines formed a circular pattern. Not just a pattern, but a maze. It filled the floor, looping, turning back on itself, and eventually leading to a perfect spot at the center of the circle. Grog couldn't stop staring. He'd never seen anything so intriguing. Returning his candle to its holder, he reached out a finger, tracing the whirls and turns of the labyrinth in the air. It reminded him of the mazes he'd solved on restaurant menus as a child, following the paper paths with brightly colored crayons. Whorls of disturbed dust, shining in the candlelight, spun past his hand. A wrinkled sign on the wall caught his eye, and he looked away from the fascinating maze to read the faded words.

Prayer Labyrinth

Grog frowned. Prayer brought the angels, and the angels hurt people. Why would anyone want to pray?

Feel free to walk the labyrinth at your own pace. If you come upon another walker in your path, quietly step around that person and continue. Let your thoughts rise to the Lord, that He may lead you to peace and understanding.

Peace? Grog stepped closer and touched the word with one finger, stroking the letters on the crackling paper. He hadn't known peace in a long time, and suddenly he wanted it. Maybe that was the trick. If he walked all the way to the middle of the labyrinth, he would reach God the Father. It made perfect sense. The blood flowed and madness raged because God didn't know. God would punish all the bad preachers and call all the angels back to Heaven. And Grog wouldn't have to hide any more.

Music played behind his eyes, different from the Angel's terrifying song, full of trumpets and anger. This tune sent him twirling across the floor, laughing at the sparkling dust that rose under his dancing feet. Lifting on his tiptoes at the edge of the painted lines, he bent his knees and hopped off the floor. He landed awkwardly, and nearly tipped over into the midst of the pattern. Panic gripped him at the thought of stepping into the maze from the wrong spot. He righted himself at the last second, and scurried back to the stairs, panting.

The music didn't stop. Gentle and soft, it filled his thoughts with memories of kindness and warmth. The quilt he'd snuggled under as a boy. Hugs and Pokemon stickers and loving voices. The smell of baking pies. Mama, before she'd gone crazy and clawed her eyes into bloody holes. All the things that didn't exist any longer were contained in the song and it was beautiful.

The maze opened before him, a simple break in the pattern right where the stairs faced. The light from the candles coalesced until it became a beam, pointing at the break. The beginning, he thought. I have to begin at the beginning.

The music swelled as Grog stood. He walked to the opening. His heart beat hard enough for him to feel it, and he marveled for an instant at the miracle of it. He hummed along with the strange song playing in his head, and took a step, planting his foot carefully in the exact center of the path. Another step, and another. The light from the candles flickered. Grog tried placing the heel of one foot against the toes of the other, until he reached the first turn and was forced to take a wider step. Nothing happened because of it. He didn't want to reach the center too soon, though. It probably took time to attract God's attention. Besides, he had all night.

"Bread of the world, with jelly and butter, wine of the world, spilled on my head," he sang, tiptoeing along the path. It was a hymn he'd known as a child, but he wasn't sure of the words any more. No matter. They went well with the music around him, and he liked singing.

He reached the turn and raised up on the ball of his foot to spin into the next leg of his walk. The center teased him, the way he seemed to come closer and then turn and discover himself on the outer edges of the path. He could jump over all the painted lines, walk straight into the spot in the middle. It wouldn't be right, though he didn't know why not.

Tilting his toes upward as far as he could, he walked on his heels for a few feet, until his calves threatened to cramp. "By froom the turds of blife are shtoken," he sang, entertaining himself with mixing up the words of the old familiar song, "And pin voose pleath . . .'"

A vision swept over his consciousness, blotting out the dusty basement. His mother, in their kitchen, baking cookies. Before she succumbed to madness. Before the Angel came. He drew in a breath of the rich baking smell. Snickerdoodles. Mama turned to him, a baking sheet in her hands. "We have to let them cool a bit, sweetheart," she said. "You don't want to burn your mouth."

Grog's voice caught in his throat. He wanted to tell her how much he missed her, how much he loved her. She smiled at him as if he'd spoken aloud.

"I love you, too, my precious boy," she said, sliding the oven mitts off her hands. "None of this was your fault." She closed the distance between them and wrapped her arms around him. The way she used to, so long ago. "The Angel doesn't mean you harm," she murmured into his hair.

Grog's eyes widened. She'd been gone before the Angel came. How could she know?

"It came to smite the pastor, and found him hurting you, an innocent. It tried to give you power, so that you could protect yourself, but it didn't understand your frailty." She leaned back from him, and cupped his cheek with one hand. "You're doing the right thing. Keep walking, and when you reach the center, you'll understand."

"Mama," he choked out in a harsh whisper. "Stay with me."

She released him, with a smile. "I have to take the cookies out of the oven before they burn. Don't they smell good?"

Grog blinked away the tears that filled his eyes, and the vision faded. Once again he was alone, in the shadowed basement of the abandoned church. He wiped his eyes with his sleeve. Mama wanted him to walk. He would walk.

~

He couldn't tell how long he'd stood still. The candles burned as brightly as when he'd first lit them, but the path wound on, around and back again, out and in. He'd lost his taste for singing hymns, preferring to listen to the music that echoed in his mind. It no longer exhorted him to dance.

His chest ached and his breathing was labored, as if he climbed a mountain, but he continued. What else could he do?

He reached a turn and pushed himself forward. And with that step, he found himself in Pastor Daniel's church. Blood stained his shirt, from where he'd tried to keep Mama from blinding herself. He'd come to the church, looking for people who hadn't lost their minds, people who might help him find his mother before anything worse happened to her. Pastor Daniel held a Bible and wore a smile.

"Welcome, son. You're safe with us."

Grog shook his head. "I'm not. You're going to hurt me. I remember . . ."

The pastor stepped forward, reaching out to clasp Grog's shoulder. "No one will hurt you here. Come in and join the flock."

People started appearing in the pews—a family here, a couple there, one pew of no one but children. All of them stared at him with frightened eyes. All of them had survived the madness, same as him.

"My mother—" Grog began, but the pastor interrupted him.

"We are your family now," he said. "I'm sorry to tell you, but your mother was a terrible sinner. Otherwise she'd be here with you now. The madness only struck the worst evildoers. Says so right in here," he said, raising his Bible high. His voice rose, too, as if he was talking to the whole room. "In the last days, the innocent will be saved and the evil will fall." He waved at the altar. "Let us bring you into the true faith, the only faith."

A woman sitting alone near the front stood. "Don't believe him," she said. Blood stained her teeth.

Two of the children nodded. Both of them had ragged cuts on their necks. "Run away while you can."

One by one, everyone in the church got to their feet, all telling Grog not to listen, not to stay. He knew their faces. These were all the people who'd sung hymns to cover his cries of pain. But now they were all wounded, bleeding, and they were telling him to run. Had they known then? Why hadn't they helped him before?

The pastor still gripped Grog's shoulder, and his smile remained bright. He tilted his head. "They didn't tell you because they feared being my target themselves. It's the way people behave. They're sorry, but they'd prefer you suffer instead of them."

His face changed suddenly, melting into a vision of blinding light. His voice deepened, strengthened into the voice of something inhuman. A voice that had once driven him to flee, bleeding, into the night. A voice only he had been able to hear. "I gave you a gift. Use it."

Once again, the vision disappeared, leaving Grog blinking in the half-darkness. What gift? Had he meant the softening? That hadn't come from the pastor—it only happened after he escaped the wild rampage in the church. But it hadn't been the pastor's face or voice. It was the Angel's. Had the Angel intended to help him? The gift . . . Had he somehow been blessed by the Angel with the gift?

The music that had been his constant companion since he began his walk swelled, surrounded him, and suddenly he recognized it. It was the Angel's song, the trumpets and grandeur that drove others wild. For the first time, the music felt like a safe space, a refuge.

"Gordon!"

Pastor Daniel stood on the outer edge of the labyrinth. Shadrach was next to him, holding a flashlight in one hand and a pistol in the other. He reminded Grog of a teenager who wanted to trick-or-treat but couldn't risk the social danger of wearing a costume, so he grabbed a revolver and hoped it would be enough. "This time, right between the eyes," Grog murmured. "Pilgrim."

"Best come on out of there, kid," Shadrach said. "I'm aiming for your leg, but it's awful dark down here. I'd hate to hit something you can't live without."

"I'm not in the middle yet."

"Fuck a duck," Shadrach growled. "I hate dealing with next-level crazy. Get out here."

"Son, come with us," the pastor said, smiling. Grog remembered how safe Gordon felt the first time he saw the pastor smile. But then he'd kept smiling while he cut Gordon, and the smile turned into danger. Grog turned away from them. He was near the center now. Something waited for him in the center. Just a few more steps and he'd be . . . free? Safe? He wasn't even sure what he'd find.

Between the pastor calling and the music in his head, Grog almost missed the sudden click of a hammer being drawn back. Would it hurt much to be shot? Was it like a knife slicing butter, smooth and painless? Or should he expect a ripping, tearing shock through his body? Shadrach raised the gun and aimed it, grinning.

Before he could pull the trigger, the pastor grabbed his arm, yanking his elbow down. The gun fired, the bullet striking the concrete block wall and sending chips flying through the air. Grog ducked, but unlike in all the cartoons he'd ever seen, the bullet didn't seem inclined to ricochet around the room. He was almost disappointed.

Shadrach and the pastor struggled for the gun, yelling at each other. Grog turned away again. As long as they were fighting, they weren't paying attention to him. This was his chance to keep walking, to reach the center and find what he knew must be there.

He followed the path down a long curve, turning ever inward. For the first time since before losing his mother, he had a purpose. The goal, vague though it was, calmed the storm in his mind, quieted the nonsense thoughts and focused him. He found that he enjoyed the peace. He wondered if it would stay.

Another shot rang out, and he risked another look. The pastor held

Shadrach's gun. Shadrach leaned against the wall, holding his hand against his throat. His eyes widened, and he opened his mouth, but no sound emerged. His hand fell. Gouts of blood pulsed from the wound on his neck, and he slid down the wall to the floor. Pastor Daniel tossed the gun aside and turned his attention to Grog once more.

"Gordon, son, come with me now. Nothing to worry about."

Grog's stomach twisted. In his mind's eye, he saw the pastor dripping with blood, red all over except for his shining white teeth. A monster, created by the madness. And the monster was determined to take Grog away with it.

He took another step, and stumbled over his own feet. Fear swept through him, a rushing cold that numbed his toes and fingers. The center, he had to reach the center before the monster ate his soul. The music swelled again, but this time, the voice he'd run from joined in the song. Grog didn't understand what it said, but it took away the paralyzing fear. He straightened, and continued on his path.

The pastor shouted, his words muffled as if he stood behind a velvet curtain. Grog understood well enough. They were the same words he'd always shouted. Words about sin and Hell, warnings about the suffering all of his congregation had brought down on the world by turning their backs on the church. He'd seemed so confident in those words once upon a time. Now, with the Angel singing into Grog's ear, the pastor's words sounded like the rantings of an angry toddler. Blame and fear. And none of it directed at himself.

"You're walking into Satan's trap, boy! This idolatrous maze is designed to confuse the weak. If Jesus wanted us to walk in circles, he'd have curled all the roads around each other!" The pastor paced around the edges of the labyrinth, his face red. Spittle flew from his mouth as he shouted. "This ain't the right way to God, and you know it! Get your ass over here so we can leave this tainted place."

Grog stared at him. How had he ever given in to the ugliness this man claimed was holy? No wonder the Host had punished people with blood and insanity. "I have to finish walking." He turned away. The center was close now, and he knew that everything he needed was there. Step by step, he moved forward. Step by step, the confusion and terror fell away. The wounds that never stopped aching began to ease. Just a few more steps.

"We can save them all, Gordon!" Pastor Daniel screamed from the darkness. "You come with me, and we'll visit everyone we can find, show them how to shed their evil. They'll feed us and give us money. We'll be rich, you and I."

"Money?" Grog asked, not looking away from his path. He remembered money. Gordon had used money to buy things he wanted. Things that no longer mattered. "You want to use me to get money?"

"It's the least of what they owe us, boy," he said. "All the sinners, all their evil, they caused this. Even my own boy over there, he was a sinner, too. You and me, we're God's chosen. We deserve to be put on a pedestal.

We're like angels our own selves. You know I'm right."

"My mother was a sinner?" Grog asked. Six steps. Five. Four.

"Especially your mother," the pastor said.

Three steps. Two. One.

He walked into the center. On the floor under his feet, he gazed at a flower, six petals surrounding a perfectly round circle. Like a daisy. His mother loved daisies. She hadn't meant to hurt herself, and she'd run away to keep from hurting him. The Angel sang to him, and at last he understood the words. The confusion he'd lived with for so long lifted, and his mind was, for the first time, clear. He turned toward the pastor, and held out a hand toward him.

"Come to me."

"What?"

Grog waved his hand over the labyrinth. "Walk to me and I'll leave with you."

"Fine." The pastor started to cross over the path, but Grog shook his head.

"You have to walk it the way I did. From beginning to end."

"I don't have time for this foolishness," Pastor Daniel said. Grog didn't respond. He didn't have to. The pastor would figure it out well enough on his own.

After a moment of silence, the pastor sighed, and walked to the opening.

At first, he almost ran around the turns and lengths of the pattern. He slowed down after a few minutes, his breathing heavy. From time to time, he jumped, looking behind him as if something followed. Grog stood in the center, watching him. Was he seeing visions, the way the Angel had shown them to Grog? Perhaps his sins lay too deeply within him to allow redemption. None of Grog's business, either way.

The pastor began to weep, and fell to one knee. He cried out, his words garbled with emotion, but Grog said nothing. He tore at his shirt, popping the buttons in his haste. Symbols matching those on Grog's skin were appearing on the pastor's chest. Blood ran from each new cut, and the pastor moaned and shrieked. He rose and stumbled forward, falling away from the path and rolling into the center. He lay on the floor, bleeding on the daisy.

"Son." His mother's voice again, gentle and kind. "Use your gift. Take this man's life. He destroyed your innocence and sought to use you for personal gain. His life is forfeit."

"You're not my mother," Grog said.

She appeared before him, in the same dress as before. But this time he knew. This was the Angel.

"Reach inside his chest, and take his heart in your hand. It will be quick."

"Murder is a sin."

"This isn't murder," the being who was not his mother said. "It is justice."

Grog gazed at the broken man lying below him. Pastor Daniel shivered, tormented by visions of the cruelty he'd inflicted on so many. "Forgive me. Forgive me. Forgive me," he mumbled. Tears streamed down his face, and he didn't seem to see Grog at all. He stared into the distance, begging for forgiveness that would never come.

Grog glanced again at Shadrach. In the shadows, he couldn't tell if the young man still breathed. His own father had murdered him. How many other deaths were the fault of the pastor? Grog leaned over and pressed his hand against the pastor's chest. The heart thudded, and for a moment Grog considered. It would be so easy to soften his aspect, slide his fingers between the bones of the old man's ribs, and stop that heart. So easy. He sighed. "I'm not a judge. His life isn't mine to take."

"As you choose." Light surrounded the Angel. It no longer wore the face of his mother, and the light was almost too bright to bear. His eyes watered under the onslaught, and he blinked to clear them. When he looked again, the Angel was gone. The church basement was swathed in shadow. In the flickering light of the candles, the labyrinth looked like mere painted lines on the floor. Something had changed. *He* had changed.

For an instant, the pastor focused on him, and raised a trembling hand. "I'm sorry, Gordon."

The Angel had given him a gift, but he would learn to use it for something other than vengeance. He would begin by finding the pastor's other sons, and sending them in to help their father. Grog wouldn't have bothered, but what Grog wanted didn't matter anymore. "Yes," he said, "I'm Gordon."

Set in Stone
6 PA / 2018 AD

Faith Hunter

Holy Amethyst reared back in the cockpit of her wheels, her eagle face forward, beak raised in screaming challenge. Her hands gripped the arms of her chair, talons scoring deep runnels in the gold. Her mate, Zadkiel, was taken. She saw it as it happened, a vision strong and true.

She felt the Darkness as it slithered across his wings, burning, scorching deep. Zadkiel screamed in agony. The Aqua Dragon and his minion, Forcas, swept forward, leathery wings beating the air, throwing dark lightning, dark energy so dense it covered the seraph scent like a flood. Her vision of Zadkiel, her awareness of him was . . . gone. Never since they mated had he been so far from her that she couldn't sense him. The space in her mind that he had occupied was an empty chasm.

She whirled to the throne of the Most High and screeched a prayer. The Light of the throne, the holy Shekinah, the cloud of glory, rested on its sapphire base, pulsing with power, with incredible might, hanging above the singing throng. She knew the Most High felt Zadkiel's pain. She knew He could help him. Yet He let her mate suffer.

She screeched in agony, howling above the song of the gathered seraphs. The other three cherubs stared at her across the holy Shekinah. Their singing fell silent. Below them, the throng that sang to the glory of the Most High fell silent. Disquiet filled the holy square. A hush seeped through the smoke of the holiness.

Amethyst screamed again. "Help him," she prayed. "Assist him," she begged. "Save him!" she demanded. The Light did nothing—did not even seem to hear her—as the Most High had not listened to their pleas in long years.

Amethyst powered up her wheels, the rings speeding into smooth rotation, one rolling east to west, another north to south, and the others from Heaven to Earth in oscillating harmony. "Holy Amethyst, no! Wait," Holy Citrine screamed. With a final screech, Amethyst powered her wheels away from the throne—away from the Host—away from the Light of the Most High.

With a roar of power, she dropped through the golden streets, scattering seraphs, and pointed the nose of the ship down, aiming for the River of Time. Calculating the descent and the angle of impact, she hit the River and cut through the glowing water. And out the other side, into the atmosphere of Earth with a boom of displaced air.

The scent of battle whipped by her, smoke and blood and death. She rotated, bringing her lion face to the fore. Sniffing. It had been long and long since she'd scented battle, not since the battle when Michael and his lieutenants, and the wheels to which they were bound, fought the Red Dragon and defeated him.

She pointed the wheels at the Earth, at the mountain that appeared just below. This close, she could sense Zadkiel once again. And she could smell humans—human blood. She blasted the rock with light, exploding granite away, revealing a chamber of a hellhole. She dove the wheels down, into it, screaming her mate's name, burning the spawn of the hellhole to vapor.

The rock closed over her as she bored deeper, dust flying. From a tunnel a dragon appeared, wings spread, the Aqua Dragon, his body scaled and glistening with dark energies. And he cast a sparkling net of Dark power over her. A trap.

Instantly, she reversed the wheels and strained against the energy net. Below her, she felt the shift of power. A human had offered his life for Zadkiel; had poured his own life-blood over the demon iron that trapped her mate. And Zadkiel was free!

Amethyst called to him. But the energy net caught the energies of the summons and bounced them back to her. Zadkiel and his seraphs flew from the hellhole, alive and free. Sending power to the wheels, Amethyst tried to draw on the might of the Most High, but it was as if she had been cut off from the Heavens. The net: a weapon of great darkness or a judgment against her?

The dragon laughed and threw himself at her, landing on the deck of her wheels. "You are mine, now," he said. "And you will mate with me. And your power and your wheels will be mine. And I will sit on the throne of the Most High." He reached out a hand and brushed her many breasts.

Amethyst screamed as the feathers and flesh beneath his fingers blistered and smoked. But her shriek was a ploy, and her hands shifted the keys of the cockpit chair. In a single instant, the wheels rotated upside down and reversed. The dragon was tossed against the floor of the rock chamber. The wheels opened up with the light, the purple lasers blasting an outlet. An incantation of protection was contained in a single *word*, and Amethyst spoke it as the wheels shot for the surface of the mountain. The navcone tore through the energy net the dragon had cast around them.

The wheels hit the atmosphere and exploded with the power of protection. But in that instant, the net dragged over the cockpit chair and snared Amethyst. Pain erupted through her. She was jerked from the chair, down into the chamber, hard against the dragon's chest. The wheels pulsed once, and they were gone.

The dragon wrapped his net tight around her, anger vibrating through him. "Your mate is free, but you are mine. And soon, your ophanim—your wheels—will be mine as well. Your energy is mine. Your *essence* is mine. With you I will create new life." His claws raked her through the energy mesh. "Call the wheels back. Now!"

Amethyst reached for Zadkiel—reached for the wheels—reached for the Most High. No one and nothing answered. She was a prisoner of the Darkness.

Wind Blown
14 PA / 2026 AD

Faith Hunter

Pearl stared out over the waves, the wind lifting the hem of her homespun cotton dress. Her eyes were closed against the bright sun, her hands fisted tightly, arms angled at her sides for balance. The pearls for which she was named were strung in disordered rows—round ones, rice-shaped, and the baroque pearls she loved so, the nacre shaped like smooth nails, small knives, and the teeth of predators. Some said they were ugly, but Pearl thought them all beautiful and wild, as untamed as the sea.

There were hundreds of pearls, each knotted with twine, intermingled with sharks' teeth, sea-smoothed glass, dried starfish and seahorses. There were skate egg sacks, black and crusted, sand dollars, and smooth drift-wood, shells of every kind, all tied and draped around her. Her amulets glistened with the power she had drawn in, the pearls so full they seemed to dance with might, with the stolen power of the sea, the teeth and glass and dried sea creatures shining with energy, like tiny suns.

Heated sand clung to her ankles, the thunder of the surf carried through to her bones. The salt air twisted her hair into riotous waves and curls, sun-bleached, sandy highlights that contrasted with her café-au-lait skin and dark green eyes, eyes that carried a hint of storm. She sighed into the wind, face turned to the sky. Her power and the wind lifted her hair in coiling ringlets and danced along her flesh, almost painfully.

The pull of the surf swept through her, waves churning and beating against the sandy ocean floor. A shark swam, far out in the waves, searching for meat and blood, hungry. A pod of mammals, perhaps small whales, though she couldn't tell for certain, swam closer in, feeding, playing, throwing themselves into the air in abandon, only to fall back to the waves with huge splashes that seemed to echo their joy. Their very lives were a sea-dance, mating as they pleased, skin brushing skin, wet and silken and raspy-coarse. Unlike her, they were never alone. She dove through the water with them, singing her incantation, *Sea, storm, waves, and tides, carry me, carry me . . .*

She was one of the treacherous ones, born eight months after the first plague. A neomage. A being not human, although born of a human mother who had survived all three plagues while pregnant. Scientists postulated that the genetic mutation that shaped her, and the others like her, had been caused by the viruses that had killed off six billion humans. She was a mutant who could twist the leftover energies of creation. But she was the only one she had ever heard of who could draw it from the sea, for salt-water blunted the power of all other mages. Or so they said—she had never met another mage. Pearl, at fourteen, was truly and utterly alone. Alone with this new power, this incredible might.

She had been drawing power, wild, dangerous power, for two weeks now, ever since her parents had thrust her out of their house, faces etched deep with fear. She was hungry, thirsty, sunburned. She hadn't slept. Yet she was getting stronger, because now she was no longer hiding what she was. Now she was free to experiment with the wild power of the energy particles that called to her, energy that she could see with a blink that opened mage sight and turned the world into an energy sink.

I see you.

Pearl opened her eyes, startled.

I see you. Female, Near the shore. Can you see me? the foreign voice asked. Odd; he had an accent in his thoughts . . . French? Pearl had heard a Frenchman speak once . . . *Can you hear me?*

Pearl turned away from the beach, seeking with her eyes, sniffing deeply. Searching. And she found the mind. It was male. It—he—was neomage, like her. Power swirled around him like a wind storm, like a small hurricane.

Air mage, he said, mind-to-mind. *But my power is less controlled near the ocean.*

Why? She thought back. *Can't you do* this? And she showed him how to twist the energy particles so they were protected from, and empowered by, the salt in the air and the water. She watched as his mind tried to follow the energy pattern of a riptide out into the ocean; she slid her mind around his, as if in an embrace, and shifted him closer as he reached out, struggling to hold the might of the sea. And she felt his helpless failure as he lost control of it.

But the strength of his mind was the strength of the wind, ceaseless and warm. And his thoughts were like the width of the sky, trying anything, all things, seeing the world as she never had. She turned in his mental embrace and smiled at him, knowing his mind, his heart. He held her as if she were a priceless pearl, a pearl of great price. There was a sheepish innocence in his thoughts. *I can't hold the sea,* he whispered. *But I can show you the wind.* He turned them into the sky, a dance like the waves in the ocean, but higher, freer. She heard the incantation of his passage. *Flight and storm and battle wind, carry me afar . . .*

But below the freedom, beneath the fierce independence, Pearl could hear an echo of loneliness in his mind. Could sense the fear there. The dis-grace. He pulled away in a whirlwind of shame, but not before she saw the image of the storm that destroyed his family's house. An angry wind, out of control, powered by the fury of a young boy's rage. And the vision of the beam that had fallen on his little sister. Anna. She had died. He had run, just ahead of the villagers who threw stones. *I didn't mean for it to happen. I'm only now learning how to control the wind. How to control myself.*

I destroyed the village's fishing boat, she thought at him, showing him the small craft caught on a shoal, holed through. When his thoughts made of it a small thing, she thought at him, *If they can't fix it, they'll go hungry this winter. Death is death. And because of it, they hate us—with reason.*

There is no one to teach us, he thought. *The Most High should have sent us teachers.*

The Most High? Does He even know that we are*? That we exist?*

Where are you? he asked, his mind darting fast from thought to thought. He showed her where he stood, inland. And he carried her back toward the sea, the wind of their passage held firm by her mind now as the salt tried to weaken his incantation.

He saw her, standing on the shore, sunburned, dirty, her pearls catching the sun, glistening. *You are close.* His thoughts sped, like a heated breeze. *You are beautiful. I can walk to you. Tonight. I'll be there by tonight.*

She opened her eyes, staring into the sky. And she laughed. "I'll catch some shrimp or crabs and a fish or two," she said aloud.

I'll start a fire as soon as I arrive. We can eat together. And sleep warm.

And Pearl knew she was no longer alone.

TNT
23 PA / 2035 AD

Faith Hunter

Junior knew the town was still there, buried beneath the snow and ice. His dad said the town was there, so it was there. Charles Crawford Senior had been hunting with his own father, high on the mountainside, when the seraphs' judgment had doomed the town. Together they had watched the entire town die in minutes. The old man, Junior's grandpa, had gone crazy with rage when the seraphs killed them all, and had raced down the mountain, firing his shotgun into the sky. He'd died of the plague too.

Charles Senior had turned his back on civilization and joined with the few survivors on the far side of the mountain to eke out a life by living off the land. Later he'd taken up trading, traveling through the growing ice age to scattered settlements, exchanging a surplus of this from one community for an excess of that in another. That was the name of his business—This-N-That—TNT. Clever, Junior thought. Senior had met his wife that way—trading. And now Junior was going to start a new phase of the family business, back at the site of the town where his grandparents lay buried.

A lot of people thought the plague was still active, that if you touched the bones of the past, you'd be infected and tainted with the deadly disease of the judgment. Junior figured that was hogwash.

Some other people, mostly the new spiritual "orthodox," thought that the towns that had been judged were no longer there, just vanished under the power of the seraphic judgment. Junior thought that was hogwash too. The seraphs had done a lot of crazy things, but making things vaporize into nothingness wasn't one of them, no matter what the new religious police were saying.

And it wasn't evil to uncover what nature and the perpetual winter had hidden—so long as the new Elders didn't find out. And Junior had covered his tracks well.

He stood beside the rock promontory his dad had described. From here he should be able to see an outcropping of tumbled red brick down below, less than a mile to the north. But the road leading down didn't look the way his father had described it. There had been an avalanche at some point in the last few decades, and the tree stumps, broken boulders, and huge ice chunks had buried what was left of the old road. And it was covered by the last stubborn drifts that remained when the rest of the winter snow had melted off the southern face of the mountains. Because no one had been here since the judgment, there wasn't a path even a sure-footed mule could navigate. Junior had to make one.

He tethered his two mules and his workhorse at the promontory near a bale of hay he'd brought. They'd be okay until tomorrow, and if he didn't make it back, they would find their way back home. The big Friesian was smart and strong, and no tether would hold him for long.

Then Junior shouldered two picks, a good, Pre-Ap shovel, and his pack of supplies and started down the mountain.

Junior reached the ice-covered rubble pile in just under six hours. The red brick had once been a drugstore and Charles Senior said it was full of useful stuff they could trade. The ice was only a few inches thick in most places, and he easily chipped through it. And the first thing he saw was bones. Scattered everywhere, bones, scarred and broken. Human bones. It looked as if they had been gnawed on by spawn of Darkness.

He almost ran—until he saw the tread of a tire. The rubber was in pretty good shape. So was the rim. A cobbler could make a lot of boots from the tire. A good blacksmith could work a rim into any number of things. And where you find one tire, you sometimes find a bunch.

Money. That's what he was seeing among the bones. Money. Charles Crawford Junior didn't run.

Two weeks later, a very changed Junior and his now-skinny horse-stock made their way back to New Hope Township. They were loaded down with Pre-Ap treasure: steel sewing needles, six pairs of scissors, four electronic stethoscopes that still worked, crutches, four wheels and tires, and jewelry taken from among the dead. This-N-That had a new niche market—mining the houses and businesses of the dead. And more importantly, Junior knew where to find more. And it was going to make the whole family rich.

Epena's Epiphany
34 PA / 2048 AD

Lou J Berger

The siren went off just before noon, shrieking into a blue sky and rolling across Moloka'i's western plain, scaring the silverbill birds nesting in the scattered *kiawe* trees.

Epena Kawai glanced up, brushing her hair out of her eyes. She held the knife poised against a peeled taro root, ready to cut it into chunks. Had that been three blasts or four? Three blasts meant the stone fish ponds on the coast were in danger. Four meant the nearby elementary school, the one her little cousin attended.

The siren sounded again, a long warning tone, then four short ones. The knife clattered to the counter.

Akamu.

She jammed her feet into slippers, and ran down the dirt road toward the school, a mile away. She'd walked him there just hours earlier.

She'd enjoyed his six-year-old excitement at discovering the world all over again, as he did each day on their walk to school. His sharp eyes had spotted red *'apapane* birds drinking nectar from the crimson blossoms of the *'ōhi'a* trees. Then, later, he laughed at the angry, waddling gait of a hissing *nēnē* as it passed him. He chattered constantly, leaping from one topic to another, pointing at oddly shaped clouds, the orange trumpets on a lantana bush, and this morning the latest addition to her *kakau uhi*, her collection of tattoos.

What's that *honu* mean?" He squatted in the dirt, brown legs splayed, squinting at the green turtle newly inked on her lower left leg.

She'd turned her foot to better show it. "It means good luck and long life."

"I want one," Akamu had said, his lower lip thrust out. "I want a long life, too!"

Her breath grew ragged as Epena ran toward the school. Smoke curled from the clustered buildings, but there was no sign of 'Ana'ana, the Dark seraph who ruled the islands. He'd destroyed and moved on, like he always did.

When she saw the splintered remains of the kindergarten, she stopped, feeling her knees go weak. Emergency workers pulled injured children from beneath the building's collapsed roof.

The uninjured students gathered in a small crowd, chaperoned by teachers.

Epena ran to one of them. The woman's face was pale and haggard. A stray tendril of raven hair hung from an otherwise severe bun.

"Akamu?" Epena gasped, searching her face. The teacher only stared back at her, wide-eyed.

Epena turned to the small group of children. "Akamu," she pleaded, "has anybody seen him?"

One little girl, dirty, with a torn dress, pulled a thumb from her mouth and pointed to the ruined kindergarten building.

Epena sprinted to the wreckage. An EMT grabbed her arm. "Sorry, miss. It's not safe."

"My cousin is in there," she snapped, yanking her arm free. Stretchers lay on the ground behind a low wall. White sheets shrouded three tiny, still forms.

She fell to her knees, her strength draining away. Her shaking finger pointed at the stretchers. "Is he . . ."

The EMT glanced to where she pointed. "What was he wearing?"

"I don't remember." He'd squatted in the dirt road, pointing at her *kakau* designs. What had he worn? "White shorts and an aqua shirt, big collar."

The EMT glanced over at the stretchers again and shook his head. "He's not there. He must still be inside, or on the way to the hospital."

The roof rested at a steep angle. It was hard to imagine anybody had survived.

But then another emergency worker came from behind the building, and Epena gasped. Akamu walked beside him, looking like a clay figurine, coated in chalky dust. Blood stained his white shorts, and he held his left arm tucked against his chest, inside his shirt. Tears had carved runnels through the dust on his face. When he saw Epena, he ran to her.

Still on her knees, she opened her arms and absorbed the impact of his little body.

"Epena, it was horrible," he yelled. "'Ana'ana came and threatened us! He wanted to know who'd been hiding from him! We didn't know and he broke the school!" He glanced over his shoulder at the wreckage.

Epena stood and walked Akamu to a crowd of kids gathered around the school nurse, who was focused on applying bandages to minor cuts and bruises.

When Akamu's turn came, the nurse ran expert hands over his tiny frame, paying particular attention to his left elbow.

"He has a dislocated elbow. Nothing major." The nurse pushed a thumb into the bend of his elbow, looked the boy in the eye and smiled. "Take a deep breath, Akamu, and when I push on your arm, yell as loud as you can."

Akamu inhaled deeply, wincing in anticipation. The nurse turned his wrist until Akamu's palm faced his shoulder. He paused, looking Akamu in the eye. "Ready?"

Akamu's eyes grew big and he bit his lip. "Okay."

With his thumb still in the crook of Akamu's elbow, the nurse pushed Akamu's wrist toward the boy's shoulder with a swift, decisive motion. When Akamu's palm struck his own shoulder, he yelled, but not so loud that Epena missed a muffled *click*.

"Hey," said Akamu, testing his arm's range of motion. "That's better!"

The nurse smiled, ruffled his dusty hair, and turned to Epena. "He'll be fine. Some aspirin tonight, maybe, and an early bedtime." He glanced at the ruined building. "You might as well take him home; no more school for awhile."

"Thank you. I wish I could stay and help."

The nurse shook his head. "He was one of the lucky ones. Go on, get him out of here."

Epena and Akamu walked along the dirt road toward home.

That night, Epena sat outside with her aunts and her grandmother, a roaring fire fighting back the evening chill, and told them about the school and the tiny forms under white sheets.

The stunned women silently stared into the crackling flames.

"Tutu," Epena said, her brow furrowed. "Why does 'Ana'ana hate us so much?"

The aunties glanced at one another with guilty expressions. Her grandmother's eyes were like black cinders, peering into her soul.

"Aunties," said Tutu with a hint of iron. "Leave us. It is time I spoke with Epena about her mother."

Epena's eyes widened. Discussing her mother's death had been avoided as if it were *kapu*. The aunties gathered their things and walked to the house.

Tutu stared into the fire. "I noticed you had more work done on your *uhi*. You added a *honu* to your left leg?"

"Yes. For long life."

Tutu's face wrinkled mischievously. "And is that lazy boy designing your patterns?"

Epena shook her head. "No, Tutu. I design them. And his name is Kanoa, not 'lazy boy'. He's studying to be an engineer, but he's also the best on the island with the *kakau* stick. He lets me use my ink."

"*Your* ink?"

"I find the cruelest chunks of *'a'a* lava, and I grind them into a fine powder. Kanoa mixes the powder with seawater and taps the patterns into my skin."

Tutu's voice fell to a whisper. "*Wahine*, why do you use powdered lava?"

Epena clenched her teeth. Memories of girls at school calling her *mud-girl* and *orphan* came flooding back. "My name means mud, right?"

Tutu's voice snapped. "Your father's name means stone, not mud, and your mother gave you a boy's name out of love for him. *Kawai*, our family name, means water, and honors the ocean that surrounds us on all sides. You are a mixture of both, but stone and water doesn't make mud."

Epena stared into the fire, her jaw set. "I'm a mud-girl named after a boy, and my parents are dead."

They sat in silence for a bit, and a *pueo* owl glided by, flying close to the fire before wheeling away.

"Do you know how they died?" Tutu's voice floated on the darkness like gossamer.

"You told me they died in an accident."

"No, it isn't true. You are very late in embracing your *kuleana*, your life path, like your aunties did when they were younger than you are now. You work around this house like an old woman, when you should be attending college or working a real job. For you to finally grow up, it's time you learned what really happened."

Epena frowned. "It wasn't an accident?"

Tutu's face grew stony. "'Ana'ana came to the islands when I was still a young woman. He was evil. He hungered for all the power he could acquire, even if that power was in the frail bodies of two teenagers—your parents."

"What power did they have?"

"They were both neomages. They could draw energy from stone. It didn't seem like much; when they were young, I remember them playing games where they used to make sparks leap from lava rocks to their fingertips."

Tutu's expression softened.

"Our families were close and the two of them grew up together. Eventually you were born. On a day when I was away shopping, 'Ana'ana visited your mother, disguising himself as your father. Your father heard them talking and tried to attack the dragon. 'Ana'ana killed him."

Epena stared, but Tutu wouldn't look in her direction. She kept speaking, unshed tears reflecting firelight.

"I returned from my shopping to see your mother standing over your father's broken body. She snatched up a chunk of *'a'a* from the ground and dragged it across her bare belly, drawing blood. She held the stone to the cut, which caused her to glow for a moment, and then hurled a bolt of energy at the dragon."

Her grandmother took a shuddering breath, but continued. "More energy flowed into her from beneath the ground, and I watched your mother die, burning from the inside out as the lava's fire overwhelmed her. I still hear her screams in my nightmares."

"And the dragon? What happened to him?"

"'Ana'ana limped away, burned. He's been angry ever since, and has sworn to root out and destroy any other mages he finds."

Ice water poured into Epena's veins as she remembered walking along the shoreline after dropping Akamu at school that morning. She touched her scraped knee, where she'd fallen against the cruel lava rocks and felt harsh vibrations coming from the stone.

She stood. "Tutu, thank you for sharing this with me. I have much to think about."

Tears finally flowed down her grandmother's lined cheeks. "Epena, my sweet child, I only wish I had told you sooner."

Epena bent and gently wiped her grandmother's face. "Tutu, I love you. You told me now." She kissed her grandmother. "I have to go."

"At this time of night? Where are you going?"

"I need time to think."

Epena ran into the night, away from the fire and toward the shore. Toward Kanoa.

Kanoa's light still burned, so she knocked and turned the knob. The tattoo parlor's interior was brightly lit, and paper *kakau* patterns were scattered across all the walls. A little bell over the door tinkled as she stepped inside.

"Hey, Epena. What brings you out this late?" Kanoa pushed aside the book he was reading, stood, and hugged her. He let his arms linger around her bare shoulders just a few moments longer than she was comfortable with. She liked him enough, but he sometimes got a little too fresh. She pulled back and shook her head, grimacing.

"'Ana'ana attacked the school today."

"He did?" Kanoa asked, his brow furrowed. "Is Akamu okay?"

"He hurt his arm, but the school nurse fixed it."

"Oh, Epena."

Epena sat down on the closest table. "I think it was my fault."

"What? How could that be? That dragon is evil and does whatever he wants. You had nothing to do with it."

Epena shook her head. "My Tutu told me tonight that my mother could draw energy from *'a'a*. She burned 'Ana'ana with it, but the energy she'd pulled from the lava built up inside her and consumed her in fire."

Kanoa turned pale and sat down.

"After I left Akamu at school this morning, I went down to the shoreline for a little walk. I tripped on some *'a'a* and cut my leg." She pointed to a scrape on her knee.

"So?"

"What if I'm a mage like she was?"

"Why would you think that?"

"When I cut myself, I think the dragon sensed it somehow, sensed my mother's power in me, and came looking for me. Maybe he destroyed the school out of frustration."

"It's a coincidence," Kanoa muttered, color returning to his face.

Epena shrugged. "I'm not so sure. I've always hated walking barefoot across rock. The stone vibrates beneath my feet, tickling me. I hate it. Which is why I wear slippers all the time."

Kanoa thought that over for a moment, then glanced at his electrical engineering textbook and pursed his lips.

"What?"

"You said she died from the energy she pulled from the *'a'a?*"

"Yes."

"What if your mother took in too much for her body to hold? What if her body overloaded because there was no way for the extra energy to get out?"

"I don't understand."

Kanoa tapped the textbook with a finger. "Maybe the energy flows like electricity, and with no circuit, the energy had no outlet, nowhere to go, so it overheated and blew out."

She frowned. "But she was standing on the ground. Wouldn't that complete a circuit?"

He shrugged, then brushed hair out of his eyes. "I don't know. Maybe with electricity, but I don't know about this . . . stone energy."

Epena thought of something else. "Kanoa, I've been using powdered *'a'a* to make my *kakau* ink. Do you think the stone in my *kakau uhi* protects me?"

Kanoa scratched his head.

"If the energy acts like electricity," she continued, "how should I change my *kakau* so I don't burn up like my mother?"

A half-smile quirked his lips. "You'd need to add a ground wire to your design. We'd need to connect your existing patterns together to make one big one, and then extend your leg *kakaus* down to the soles of your feet. Then you'd have to stand barefoot on *'a'a* to fully ground you."

Epena's mind raced. "Kanoa, I want you to do it. I want you to give me a ground wire of *'a'a* powder. I need to stop 'Ana'ana."

Kanoa laughed. "*You* wanna stop the dragon?"

She gritted her teeth. "If someone doesn't do something, he'll continue to attack us—forever." A vision of the still, tiny, sheet-covered bodies at the school flashed into her mind. "I can't let that happen."

"Epena, that dragon will kill you." Kanoa's eyes grew mournful.

"I don't have a choice."

He looked at a clock high on the wall. "Well, it's almost midnight. I don't have enough ink, anyway. You'll have to make more. If I agree to do it, which I'm not happy about, when would you want to start? Tomorrow?"

"Tonight. I need to start right now. Please?"

Kanoa thought for a few moments, his brow furrowed. Finally, his shoulders slumped. "Well, okay. But I need more ink. I don't have enough for what you need."

She kissed his cheek quickly, then moved to the door. "Thank you, Kanoa. I'll get more now."

Grabbing a burlap sack and hurrying before he could change his mind, she left the shop.

Outside, the moon spilled silver light across the landscape, making it easy for Epena to find her way to a nearby lava field. Chunks of 'a'a lay about, varying in size from pebbles to house-sized boulders. She filled her sack with several fist-sized pieces, then stopped.

Before she went ahead with her plan, maybe she should test it first.

She bent and picked up a small bit of lava and pressed it against her left arm's *kakau*, but not quite hard enough to break skin.

The tracings of powdered rock glowed beneath her skin, absorbing energy from the stone in her hand. At the same time, a faint throbbing nibbled at her. She removed the stone and the sensation faded.

So it was true. Her ink glowed when it drew energy from rock. But was it enough to summon a dragon?

She pushed the sharp rock against her arm again, gritted her teeth against the pulsing and dragged the stone's edge across her arm. The sharp edge bit through her skin and into the etched stone-powder pattern under the surface.

Her entire arm lit up with a flash of bright light, startling her, and she dropped the rock. In a sudden panic, she turned and ran from the lava field, toward a cluster of nearby buildings, a strong sense of imminent danger goading her. Her slippers slapped against her soles, and she didn't stop until she stood beneath an overhang, gasping and looking at the sky.

Then she saw him.

A dark shape rose into the moonlight and hurtled toward her. She bit her lower lip as 'Ana'ana moved to where she had stood moments earlier. She tore a strip of fabric from the hem of her skirt and wrapped it once, twice, thrice around her arm, stanching the blood and covering her left arm's *kakau*, blocking the weak light it still threw off. She crouched, hoping to remain hidden, but his head swiveled in her direction, his eyes blazing.

She mentally kicked herself for not having waited until she'd connected her *kakau* before experimenting.

Too quickly for her to follow, suddenly 'Ana'ana was in front of her, hovering, a sulfurous reek wafting from his body. Although his form was human, black, feathered wings sprouted from his shoulder blades. His face had a rugged beauty in the moonlight that washed across his naked form, even the tuft of black feathers near his genitalia. He hovered lazily, stirring the warm night air around them with each beat of his powerful wings.

She shivered anyway.

"Have you seen anyone in the lava field?" His voice rumbled.

"No."

'Ana'ana sniffed, then pointed to the strip of cloth around her arm. "You have been injured. How did this happen?"

Epena trembled, knowing she could not survive if he chose to attack her, at least not at that moment. "I cut myself with a knife, making *poi*."

The dragon didn't seem convinced and hovered, glaring.

"If it helps," she said, "I saw a flash of light moving across the water near Lana'i." She pointed a trembling finger at the dark hump of an island across the moonlit water.

The dragon smiled. "You'd better not be lying to me, human." He flew away slowly, in the general direction of Lana'i.

Epena let out a long, slow sigh of relief, then unwrapped her arm, which had stopped glowing. The bleeding had stopped as well, but her heart pounded like a rabbit's. She walked to where she'd dropped the burlap sack of 'a'a, picked it up, and then scurried back to Kanoa's shop, glancing furtively at the sky, hoping the dragon wouldn't return.

Epena dropped the sack on the workbench.

"I'm going to need more than that," Kanoa said, glancing at the sack with dismay.

"It will be enough. Are you ready?"

Kanoa shrugged and tucked his hair behind his ears. "I guess."

"Then I'll make more ink while you work." Epena grabbed a bottle of seawater and a hammer. Wielding the hammer like an expert, she pounded the 'a'a inside the sack.

There was no way she was going to tell Kanoa about her encounter with the dragon. But, thinking about it, she hammered harder and harder.

"Epena?" Kanoa's voice sounded strained.

She looked at him. He held his *kakau* stick in one hand, the almost-empty bottle of 'a'a ink in the other. "I need to start connecting your arm sleeves to your back design."

"Oh, sure." Epena put the hammer down and grabbed the hem of her shirt. She hesitated for a moment, then pulled it over her head. She wore nothing underneath.

Kanoa drew an involuntary breath.

"Let's focus on our work," she said, a hint of steel in her voice.

"Okay," said Kanoa, his voice strangled.

She picked up the hammer and continued pounding the sack as the first tentative bites of the *kakau* stick stung her back. She winced, but worked with determination, smashing the pebbles into ever smaller bits while Kanoa timed his *kakau* taps between her hammer blows.

It was going to be a long night.

Kanoa held up a mirror to show her his finished handiwork and how he'd inscribed thick, black lines down each leg to wrap under the soles of her feet. Epena clucked approvingly and put her shirt back on. She tried to walk, grimacing as her tender feet touched the grass mats Kanoa had scattered across the concrete floor. Pain lanced up her legs and she stumbled.

"I'm sorry," Kanoa said, and rushed to help her into a chair. "I had to make the bands under your feet extra wide and dark. You couldn't afford to have too little stone powder there. And to get through the thick skin of your soles—"

"Good thinking," she said, trying to keep her voice normal. "Can we bandage them?"

"Sure thing." He collected thick gauze bandages and tape, then knelt at her feet and bandaged, reverently, first one foot and then the other. "There. Try that out."

She walked across the floor with hesitation at first, then with more confidence. The gauze cushioned her feet, but they still hurt. A lot. "Thank you, Kanoa. You did a magnificent job."

He shrugged as if it were no big deal, but his eyes were bloodshot. "Be careful if you go after that dragon."

She slipped her toes into her slippers, placed a hand on Kanoa's arm and kissed his cheek.

"Thanks for staying up and helping me with all this."

A red flush suffused Kanoa's neck. "Go on, get out of here," he growled, his voice soft.

Epena stepped outside and squinted into the morning light. She couldn't remember having been so tired before. As she walked home, she thought of her mother, burned alive from within. Of her father's lifeless body, inert on the floor. Of 'Ana'ana standing over him. Her fists clenched at the thought of those three children dead on their stretchers.

It could so easily have been Akamu's still form beneath those sheets. Her rage intensified.

It took her forty minutes of mincing footsteps to reach home. She kicked off her slippers and went straight to bed, falling into a deep sleep.

When she awoke, Akamu stood over her.

"What are you doing?" she asked, sitting up and rubbing sleep from her eyes.

"Tutu wants to speak with you." Akamu's soft voice was oddly subdued.

Epena reached out and drew him into an embrace, murmuring into his hair. "Are you okay, *keiki*?" He was as precious to her as if he was her own child.

His thin frame shuddered. "'Ana'ana killed my friends. He'll come kill me, too, I know it. I'm scared of him."

Akamu leaned away from her and dragged a grubby fist across his nose. "Do I have to go to school tomorrow?"

Epena shook her head. "No, not until it's rebuilt. You'll stay home until then. Is that okay?"

Akamu nodded and wandered out of the room.

Epena stood, wincing at the dull pain in her feet. She removed the bandages and studied the bottom of each foot, pleased that the redness had diminished. Replacing the bandages with new ones, she limped to the living room, searching for Tutu, and finally found her in the kitchen, wrapping cleaned fish in a *lawalu* of broad leaves, in preparation for steaming.

"Good morning, Tutu," she said, noting the dim light outside.

"Ha," snorted her grandmother, a kindly smile crinkling the corners of her eyes. "You think it's morning? You slept all day. It's almost night."

Tutu put a wrapped fish on the counter with delicate grace. "I worried when you ran off that you were upset with me for having told you about your parents. I wasn't sure you would come back home." Her voice was barely a whisper.

"Oh, Tutu," Epena wrapped her arms around her grandmother, who patted her with moist hands.

"It's okay, *wahine.* You had a lot to understand, and it was time to clear the air. The lies had gone on long enough."

"I have some more questions, if you feel like talking." Epena unwound her arms and picked up a plate of sliced pineapple, then hobbled over to the kitchen table. "Would that be okay?"

Tutu picked up a dish towel and wiped her hands, then joined Epena at the table. "What do you want to know?"

"When my mother attacked 'Ana'ana, how did she do it? I know that she drew energy from *'a'a,* but how did she make it work against him?"

Tutu's face fell. "I have no idea. I'm not a mage, and I'm still unsure how your mother became one. All I know is that when she cut herself with that rock, she glowed and lava fire cooked her alive."

Epena frowned. "When she attacked the dragon, how did she move her hands?"

Tutu held her fist close to her chest, then thrust it away from her body, palm out, splaying her fingers in one motion. "Like pushing away a boy who's gotten too fresh. But fire leapt from her open palm and struck 'Ana'ana."

"What did it look like?"

Tutu picked a bit of pineapple from Epena's plate and bit into it. "It was so fast, and I was in shock from your father's murder." She chewed, eyes looking into the distant past, but she didn't say more.

Epena stood and looked down at the gray halo of her grandmother's hair.

"Tutu, I have to leave. I need to go and stop the dragon from hurting anybody ever again."

Tutu leapt to her feet and clutched Epena to her bosom. "No, child, don't you dare face that evil creature! I cannot allow it! I lost my baby girl to him; I can't lose you too!"

Akamu appeared at the kitchen doorway and stared at them.

"Tutu," Epena pleaded. "I must try. I can't sit by and do nothing." She pried herself from her grandmother's grip, ruffled Akamu's hair. "Besides," she said, as she stepped onto the front porch, "I may have some built-in protection."

Akamu followed her. "Epena?" His voice quavered.

She turned to him, her heart fluttering.

His eyes were big and round. Then a snarl crossed his youthful features. "Kill that nasty dragon and come tell me the story, okay?"

Her eyes stung. "I'll do my best. Take care of Tutu."

Akamu ran to her and crushed her in a little boy's fierce hug. He looked up at her and whispered, "Go get him!"

She stepped off the porch in quick strides, ignoring the sharp stabs of pain radiating up her legs as she moved into the blood-red sunset.

A short distance down Pohakuloa Road, an unmarked dirt trail led her toward the coast. After three miles of steady limping, she heard the ocean pounding on the shore just ahead. She left the trail and stumbled onto the dark sand of a sheltered beach, scattered with massive outcrops of black 'a'a.

In the soft sand she paused, steeling herself for what she was about to endure, then kicked off her slippers and peeled off her bandages.

Immediately, a thin tingling buzzed underfoot as her feet sank into the sand at the water's edge. Small pebbles throbbed against her tender soles.

Overhead, a faint blue haze was all that remained of the day's light, and some of the brighter stars twinkled.

With a clenched jaw, she climbed onto a large, broken chunk of 'a'a, four feet high and flat-topped. The vibration in her sore feet increased as she stood on the jagged surface, energy sputtering from the hardened lava into her soles. It was both painful and ticklish, and she desperately wanted to leap off the rock and put her slippers back on.

She spotted a black thorn of 'a'a jutting from a natural cross formation, fashioned from sharp lava crystals. Taking a deep breath, she lifted her right foot and stomped down, heel first, on the stone spike, praying that her faith wasn't misguided.

Pain shot up her leg, at first from the piercing wound but then from sudden heat. The *kakau* on her right leg illuminated, bathing the rock and sand in golden light, glowing like light bulb filaments beneath her skin, from her foot all the way up her body.

Epena reeled and almost fell off the rock. She closed her eyes to overcome sudden vertigo. Overwhelming dread tickled her consciousness, then became stronger, as if she sensed an approaching evil.

She opened her eyes to see 'Ana'ana swoop from the north in human form, screaming in rage. She ducked as he rushed overhead, the trailing tips of his wings brushing her.

He flipped in midair and hurtled toward her. She recalled what her Tutu had said, and thrust her arm forward, splaying her fingers.

Nothing happened.

He slammed into her, knocking her from the rock, onto the sand. Once her feet left the 'a'a, the light drained from her designs and the beach around them plunged back into darkness.

Epena sat up, spitting sand, and scrambled to the rock, climbing it like a lizard, finding hand- and toe-holds in the narrow crevices.

'Ana'ana stood on the sand, watching her in confusion, his hands held limp at his sides. "You are the one I saw under the moonlight. It was *you* I sensed . . ." His voice held a note of wonder. "How did you hide your true nature from me last night? What manner of mage *are* you?"

'Ana'ana grew very still. He shifted to dragon form, losing his feathered wings and turning into a large lizard. He took slow, measured steps, closing the distance between them. A long tongue flicked out, tasting the air.

With a burst of speed, Epena got atop the rock, away from the dragon's probing tongue. She found the spike and lowered her lacerated foot back onto the sharp protrusion, grinding her teeth against the agony. Her tattoos lit up again, and her skin burned anew. A powerful vibration thrummed up her leg.

"I have no idea!" The voice bursting from Epena's throat wasn't quite her own—hoarse, angry. Her parents dead, the three children at the school —all gone because of this monster. She squared her shoulders, rage boiling within her. "I'm just a mud-girl. And you killed my parents."

The dragon froze, then shifted back to human form. "Your parents?" He stepped into the circle of light cast by her *kakau*, though his expression remained hidden in shadows. "Ah, of course. You would have only been a child back then. I remember now. She showed promise, your mother did. I offered her more power than any human deserves and her man . . ." 'Ana'ana stopped talking as a sly smile spread across his face. "I see clearly, now. That was your father, was it not?"

Epena glared.

'Ana'ana chuckled. "Oh, that's rich. He challenged me and I cut him down with the slightest flick of my wrist. Just as I shall do with his child." He flew at her, shifting in mid-air, razor-sharp talons extended.

Her eyes flew wide. Child.

Akamu.

"No!" The rage gathering inside her boiled over. Cold fire raced up her right leg, drawn from deep inside the *'a'a*. Sprang from her outstretched palm. Struck the dragon squarely in the chest. Inundating him in brilliant flames.

'Ana'ana flew backward like a struck baseball. He hit the beach and slid, dark sand bursting up into the air in a glittering fan.

Epena squinted at the dragon's motionless form.

Was he dead?

The dark mound of dragon-flesh stirred. 'Ana'ana gathered himself and stood, then flew at her, too fast for her to react. He struck, and everything went black.

Epena came to her senses wracked in pain. She looked around, woozy. She was still on the beach. Her left arm was bloodied and numb.

'Ana'ana.

She could feel him, could sense him nearby. She crawled back to the rock and peered over it. The moon had just crested the horizon, and threw a pearly light across the shoreline, silvering the waves rolling in. The dragon paced back and forth between her and the ocean, muttering to himself.

Epena struggled to think. Every inch of her body ached. His power was too great. She could very well die on this beach.

He must already think she was dead. It's why he hadn't finished her off.

The dragon turned, pacing back toward the water, and Epena scrambled up, whimpering. She stumbled forward onto the 'a'a, the designs glowing faintly as the almost-dried blood on the bottom of her feet touched the rock.

Kanoa's *kakau* worked, but only partly. The first time she'd tried to attack the dragon, nothing had happened. What was different the second time? The glow of the *kakau* hadn't changed. Her motions had been the same.

She couldn't face the dragon again until she knew. But she *had* to destroy him, for her family, for Akamu.

Akamu.

When she'd thought of her little cousin before, fire had burst from her palm, injuring the dragon. It had taken emotion to draw the energy from the stone. Feelings. Like hatred. Fear. Anger.

She bit her lip and ground her right heel down on the rock. As before, the right side of her body lit with a brilliance that drowned out the moon's pale light.

'Ana'ana spun in surprise. He moved to the edge of the rock, assuming human form and putting his hands on his hips. "Why aren't you dead yet?"

Epena flexed her fingers, feeling them tingle with building energy.

The dragon stared, waiting to see what she would do. Epena thrust out her hand, punching him in the chest with another bolt of energy. It sent him stumbling backward. From the darkness outside of her projected circle of light, he laughed.

"This is the best you can do? You have spirit, I'll give you that. You should stop fighting and join me. You'll be the first queen these islands have had for centuries. Without my help, you're nothing. Without my support, you're just—what did you say you were? Ah, yes—a mud-girl."

When Epena didn't answer, the dragon took a step into the pool of golden light that surrounded her. His eyes flashed red. "Join me, or die."

Epena knew she didn't have the raw power to defeat 'Ana'ana. But she *couldn't* accept his offer. These were her last moments on Earth. She felt an overwhelming sadness at the thought of not seeing Akamu again, at the anguish her death would cause Tutu, at never knowing what it might be like to kiss Kanoa, her shy tattoo artist and engineer.

Engineer.

His words came flooding back. *What if your mother took in too much for her body to hold? What if her body overloaded because there was no way for the extra energy to get out?*

The energy stored in free chunks of lava rock was weak, drained away over millennia, disconnected from the Earth's core. She needed connected rock, still in contact with the island's roots and buoyed by the molten lava of the mantle, touching the core's primal energy.

Epena leapt off the rock and ran through the sand, toward a large ribbon of hardened lava flow right on the water's edge. As soon as she hopped up on it, her feet throbbed with a strong energy she'd never experienced before. This was exactly what she needed: untapped, raw power.

She turned and grinned at the dragon, then stomped her right foot down hard. Her heel caught a shard of *'a'a* just right. It punctured the hard callus of her heel and buried itself deep into her flesh, cutting through the layer of powdered lava embedded under her skin. A momentary flash of pain was washed away by the fresh energy coursing into her.

Then she lifted her left foot and stomped it down onto a mass of dark, stony thorns jutting up from the lava.

Her awareness exploded outward. Although she still stood on the beach, facing an attacking dragon, she was, at that same moment, beside her grandmother, feeling her dread and fear. Her mind expanded to swallow the entire island, from the birds that flew above it to the *kiawe* bushes scattered across its slopes, to the island's foundations, to pulsations of power throbbing deep within the dark, basaltic heart of the entire island chain.

She grabbed that pulse and wrapped herself within it, folding it around her like a warm blanket.

The dragon snarled and she casually hurled a fireball in his direction.

He caught it with his wings and absorbed it, grinning maniacally. "You dare to attack me, still?"

She threw another fireball, and then another. Each one impacted the dragon's body with a bright flash, but was then absorbed.

He shifted into lizard form and hunched, malevolently, on the beach. Every fireball she threw, he snapped from midair with powerful jaws, swallowing the energy.

Was he growing bigger?

Her focus shifted as she relaxed, opening herself up even more to the river of power flowing up through the rock she stood upon.

She threw another fireball, and then a bigger one. The dragon absorbed them all, growing in size and ferocity.

"You are merely hastening your own demise," the dragon boomed, his ragged voice echoing off the rocks around them. "Keep feeding me, though, if you wish. I will end your life quickly once I tire of this exercise."

Epena reached deep inside herself, found the last remaining traces of fear and caution, and wiped them away, relaxing to the torrent that raged through her.

Light, brighter than the sun, burst from her *kakau uhi*.

She thrust her hand at the dragon and light boiled forth in a continuous column, directly into his gaping maw. He gulped and swallowed in panic, trying to keep up with the sudden onrush. He swelled like a balloon, and Epena saw fear in the dragon's eyes.

Too late, he clamped his mouth shut, swung his muzzle away, and tried to avoid the lashing energies erupting from Epena's open palm.

'Ana'ana took flight in a desperate escape attempt, but Epena tracked his movement with her palm, burning him out of the air, crisping his wings and sending his charred body plummeting, fire consuming his body until it was an unrecognizable, blackened mass.

Then she turned her attention back to the wonders uncovered by her expanded awareness.

Shimmering curtains of visible energy undulated around Moloka'i, reaching deep into the planet's core, and she could not only see them, she could *feel* them, like a blood-warm pool of electrified water. She immersed herself in them, feeling power like she'd never felt before. The kind of power that would enable her to do things. Great things. She could even—

The *honu* design on her leg blew out, shredding her calf muscle in a gout of flame. Epena collapsed back into her physical body, smoke curling from the cauterized gash. She screamed into the sudden darkness and rolled off the *'a'a* rock onto the soft sand, passing out mere meters away from the burned, shriveled corpse of 'Ana'ana.

Akamu ran ahead, chattering and pointing out the *'apanane* birds drinking their nectar. "Epena, come look! Hurry! They'll fly away!"

Epena grimaced, then hobbled faster, leaning heavily on her cane. "Akamu, I'm not as fast as I was a month ago."

Akamu turned worried eyes in her direction and ran back. He squatted in the dirt and pointed to the ugly scar on her left calf. "That was where you had the turtle?"

"Yes."

"Wasn't he supposed to give you long life?"

Epena smiled. "Yes, Akamu. You'll notice that I'm still alive, so it worked."

Akamu pushed out his lower lip and frowned. "Well, that nasty *honu* tried to kill you." He spun around and ran down the road again, spotted a *nēnē* and yelled, then chased it in hot pursuit. The gray goose honked angrily and flapped its wings as it ran.

Epena laughed, and followed her cousin down the road, limping slowly in the warm sunlight.

The Price of Power
36 PA / 2048 AD

Ken Schrader

"College Station, Texas," the ancient sign read, "Population: 106,000."

Not anymore, I thought.

Gary Stockton, the leader of our deadmining expedition, stood beside me in much the same way as a mountain would. At six foot seven, he towered over me by nearly two feet.

"What do you think, Elise?" His voice was deep and sounded like he was grinding rocks to sand with his throat. With a neck like his, he probably could have.

Great chunks of pavement jutted from the earth in all directions like a mouthful of broken teeth. There was no way the wagons would get through the wreckage.

I shrugged, already tired and irritable. Moon mages don't get along well with the sun and it hits me harder than most. With the rising sun, my eyesight was already going downhill and I was feeling the tingling chill of my power evaporating. By noon, both would be all but gone, as would my ability to draw power from the power sink at the Enclave. I'd be on my own with only the power I'd stored in my amulets.

Behind us, two set of boots clomped. "Maybe there's another road we can take," Derek said.

Javier spat. "Not without backtracking."

Derek and Javier Rocha were Gary's partners. They claimed to be twins, but Derek was taller and Javi was thicker. Both had skin the color of old leather. Javi's hair was dark. Derek's was currently an aggressive shade of blue that he kept hidden under a battered hat; he'd lost a bet to Javi before we set out. The three of us made up our night-time security.

Gary took a deep breath and let it out slowly. He looked over his shoulder. "Sandra? The map please?"

Sandra Warfield, our quartermaster, climbed down from her bench. She wore tan coveralls that shushed as she walked to the rear of her wagon. She reached inside and produced the map, spreading it out across the tailgate.

Gary pointed to a thick line marked with the number 6. "If we wanted to try another road into the city, we'd have to go back to here—half a day lost."

"What about the smaller roads?" I bent low, squinting, and traced my finger on the map. Our destination was Easterwood Airport. "They're probably still there."

Gary rubbed his chin. "Okay." He straightened and stretched, scowling at the broken road. "Let's move, people. We're spending daylight."

The way was rougher than I thought it would be, but I was right about the smaller roads. They were clear, for the most part, though overgrown, cracked, and narrow.

Around noon, Mack's voice drifted back to me over the creaks and rattles of his wagon.

"We're here, Elise."

Mack was our medic and he'd taken a shine to me not long after we'd met. He never spoke about his last name or the burn scar he kept hidden under a dirty, blue bandanna, and I never asked, so we got along fine.

We forded a shallow creek, and followed a service road that had regressed to little more than a wagon-wide gap in the trees. We soon rode out onto a wide expanse of flat land and I felt concrete under Celeste's hooves —a runway. The land around was eerily silent—no birds, no insects. I hadn't heard an animal other than the horses for more than a day.

Great chunks of the Easterwood terminal had collapsed, and as we rode past, I saw the scars of fire damage. We settled in a small hangar that had held up better than the rest of the airport. The rusty sheet metal had holes in it, and the hangar doors had fallen down, but it would give us walls and a roof we could shelter under.

Derek and Javi couldn't wait to explore the nearby college campus and took off shortly after we'd set up camp. Gary and Mack at least waited until after lunch before leaving.

Mack borrowed Celeste, promising that he'd take good care of her, and I settled into a chair by the campfire, stuffed on cold sausage and cheese. I didn't mind staying behind. I'd pulled the third watch, so I'd been up since well before dawn. Full and tired, I fell asleep in the shade.

By the time Celeste clopped back into camp, the Moon had already begun Her trip across the sky. My eyesight was back to normal and the tension I'd been carrying before sunset, the fear that my eyes wouldn't return to normal when the sun went down, was gone.

Mack led Celeste into the hangar, took off her saddle, and cleaned her hooves. I walked over and she whickered in greeting.

"Find anything interesting?" I said as I gave Celeste some feed and brushed her coat.

He glanced at his pack. "Bandages and a few odds and ends." He straightened. "Gary's got some locations he wants to go back to. Good salvage."

I took my time with the brush, whispering silly stuff to Celeste, as I settled her down for the night. The skin of my hands glowed against Celeste's darker hair and I activated my *Glamour* amulet. Tonight—a night shy of the full Moon—I'd be glowing nearly bright enough to read by if I didn't damp it down. The full Moon was a powerful time for me and my skin shivered to be out underneath Her light.

By the time I was finished with Celeste, the smell of beans and bacon filled the air.

The cookfire crackled just outside the hangar. I poured myself a cup of hot water and dropped a mesh tea ball filled with loose leaves in to steep. I slid my chair into a patch of moonlight and sighed.

Gary reached into a pocket and pulled out a walkie-talkie. "Javi," he said into the transmitter, "you and Derek are about to miss another exhilarating round of beans-n-bacon."

Sandra scowled at Gary, and I snorted.

"Don't listen to him, Sandra," Mack said. "You've elevated beans-n-bacon into an art form."

"Thank you, Mack." Sandra turned to Gary, pointing a spoon at him. "You hear that? An art form. I should be charging you . . ." She trailed off.

I followed her gaze to Gary, who was staring at the silent device in his hand.

He glanced at us. "Javier, Derek, respond."

The fire popped, sending sparks into the sky.

"Derek, Javi, come in."

Silence.

"Why don't they . . ." Sandra stopped.

Gary glanced at me. There were any number of things that might keep either of them from replying. Dead batteries. Damaged gear. Accidents happened. The only things I could think of that would prevent both of them from responding involved the words "collapse" or "trapped" or were armed with claws and teeth and burned to death in sunlight.

"Can you track them?"

I thought about it. "If I had something of theirs, like hair or fingernails, I might be able to. Otherwise, no."

"Blood and blades!" Gary stood. "We should go look for them."

"We only know the direction they took when they left," Mack said. "They could have gone anywhere after that."

Gary scowled, and dropped back into his chair.

"We can't leave them out there," Sandra said.

"We won't," Gary said. "But we can't track them in the dark either." He raised the walkie-talkie again. "Javi? Derek? Please respond."

Nothing.

He let out an explosive breath. "We keep the fire up all night. We watch in shifts in case they come back." He raked a hand through his hair. "And we go after them at first light."

By midnight, I was the only one awake. I tossed another log on the fire, grabbed my telescope bag, and walked into the night. At a clear, dark spot away from camp, I sat on the concrete with my legs crossed and unrolled a square of thin, brown leather in front of me. The wind whispered past, carrying the scent of wildflowers and wood smoke. I arranged my amulets on the leather, aimed the telescope at the Moon, and looked through the eyepiece.

For an instant, I saw Her in crystal clarity and my breath caught. She was beautiful. My skin prickled and I reached for Her. She entered me in a rush and I gasped.

The blue-white of Her light seared through my eyes and every hair stood on end. Power flowed through me like a river, cool and inexorable, threatening to carry me away with it. Part of me wanted to go, to lose myself in Her and drift away.

I shuddered, fighting for control. Her presence filled me and I exhaled, long and slow, a pleasant warmth building deep inside me. One by one, I filled my amulets, starting with my prime. The moonstone warmed against my chest as she charged and I spent extra time caring for her, checking for surface scratches and cracks in the stone. I ran my thumb across her rounded edges a final time then tucked her back inside my shirt.

When my amulets were charged, I drank in Her power. She tingled across my skin like the caress of a lover. My toes curled and my body trembled, overcome with sensation. I didn't want to stop, even when I knew I should. I was full of her, but She was so close. I could handle it—I knew I could. She felt so good, one last pull couldn't—

I tore my eyes away from the eyepiece and slumped onto the concrete. Heart pounding, I shivered from my core as the feeling subsided, leaving me breathless. I rolled onto my back, panting.

"That was close," I whispered. A lingering flash of pleasure shuddered through me and I closed my eyes.

Metal grated on stone in the darkness and I snapped my eyes open. I drew my kukri knives and stood, looking out into the night.

In the distance, a figure shuffled toward me.

"Javi!"

I sheathed my knives and hesitated. I didn't want anything to happen to my telescope. If it fell and broke . . .

Hating myself, I took a minute to properly stow my telescope in its bag and then raced for the hangar.

"Mack!" I shouted, setting the bag with the rest of my gear. "It's Javi!"

I led Gary and Mack at a run back into the darkness. When we found him, Javier bled from dozens of cuts and bites and I wrapped a *Healing* amulet around his wrist as Gary and Mack carried him back to camp.

"Set him there." I pointed to a patch of hangar floor and went to my gear. I'd need a *Charmed Circle* for a proper healing. Celeste whickered nervously at the scent of blood, but I couldn't spare more than a quick word of reassurance. I pulled a lump of chalk from my bag.

I ran back to Javi and drew a wide circle with the two of us inside of it.

"Derek," Javi moaned. He tried to raise his head.

"We'll find him," I said, easing him back. Javi's forehead was warm, and gritty with sweat and dried blood. "You rest."

"No." He shook his head, his voice strained. "Derek . . ." he trailed off. The timbre of his voice changed. *"He fought, Elise."*

I turned, looking at his face with mage sight. An opaque mask clung to his face and head. A chill ran through me. He had some kind of conjure on him.

"He fought, but, in the end, he told me what I wanted to know of you."

I swallowed. "Who are you?"

"Call me Anette."

"What do you want?"

"You."

Javier grabbed my wrist with one hand and his other arm shot toward me. I grabbed his wrist, stopping him.

Gary lurched forward.

"Don't break the circle! I've got him," I said.

Javi held a black stone pinched between his fingers and he tried to force it at me. In my mage sight, the stone lay in the center of a seething black cloud. Flashes of red, like lightning, traced over its surface.

Outside the hangar, devil-spawn howled. Sandra cursed and a gun fired.

"Elise?" Gary asked, urgently.

"Go!" I said through clenched teeth. Gary drew a claymore that was at least as tall as I was and ran to the wagons. Scowling, Mack followed him. More gunshots ripped through the night.

"Don't worry, Elise," the voice coming out of Javi's mouth said. *"It'll all be over soon."*

"Fight her, Javi." I panted. He was stronger than me, and pushed the stone closer. "She's *in* your head. Fight!"

"He has been, sister. He struggles even now."

Gary bellowed and the gunfire increased. I had to get out there.

I twisted my wrist and jerked against his thumb, freeing my arm. Desperate, I reached for the circle.

My fingers touched the line and I cast a conjure, sending power through the chalk line. The *Charmed Circle* flared to life, sealing Javi and me off from the outside world, cutting the connection between Anette and Javi. He collapsed and the stone hit the concrete with a soft click.

Panting and trembling, I stripped off Javi's boots. I pulled the laces out and tied his hands and feet. I scooped the stone up into a boot and got as far away from him as I could before I dropped the *Circle*.

He didn't move.

I stepped over the chalk line and raised the *Charmed Circle* again. I set the boot down, drew a quick circle around it, and conjured another ward. I drew my kukris. The curved blades felt reassuring in my hands as I raced outside.

Gary, Mack, and Sandra were surrounded by dead and dying spawn. Sandra favored her left leg and leaned on Mack. Gary was decapitating fallen spawn. Black blood spattered the concrete as he moved. When he saw me, Mack slung one of Sandra's arms over his shoulder and helped her toward the hangar.

"Javi?" Mack asked.

"What about Javi?" Sandra left bloody footprints behind her.

"Bound and contained." I took up Sandra's other arm. "He was possessed."

"Possessed by what?" Gary looked at Javi, laying where I'd left him. He bent down toward the boot. "What's—"

"Leave that!" My voice cracked through the hangar and Gary straightened. "I don't know what it is, but she sure wanted me to touch it."

We got Sandra settled in a chair and propped her leg up. Something had taken a bite out of her. I gave her a *Healing* amulet, then turned to Javi. He still needed help.

"Who did this?" Mack asked.

"She calls herself Anette. She's a mage." I looked at Mack. "Ready?"

At Mack's nod, I dropped the protective circle. Javi lay limp, but he was still breathing. Gary and Mack got him into Mack's wagon and Mack went to work on him, cleaning and bandaging his wounds.

I filled a tin cup with water, dropped the second *Circle*, and picked up Javi's boot. Sitting next to the fire, I poured the stone from the boot into the cup. Part of me expected the water to hiss and boil, but the stone dropped in with a quiet plink and sank to the bottom of the cup. When I looked at the stone with mage sight, the cloud was gone. I took the stone, water, and cup well outside of camp and buried them.

I came back and found Mack bent over Sandra. The smell of coffee drifted to me from a pot near the fire.

"How's Javi?" I asked.

Mack dabbed at Sandra's leg and she hissed. "He'll be out for a while. With those spawn bites, it's a miracle he wasn't poisoned." He taped a bandage around Sandra's leg. When he straightened up, I handed both of them coffee.

"This Anette is a mage?" Mack asked.

"Like you?" Gary said from the hangar door.

"I don't know." I shook my head. "Not like me." I stared into the fire. "She knows everything Javi knew."

"What about Derek?" Sandra asked.

I exhaled. "She needed Javi to get close to me." I glanced at Mack. "She must've countered the poison." I paused, turning back to Sandra. "She'd have no use for Derek."

Sandra closed her eyes. "The Lord rest his soul."

I stood. "Anette knows where we are, so we need to move." I went to the wagon and got out the map while the others gathered around.

I pointed to an unmarked spot a couple of miles from the airport. "The college had an observatory. Might be it's still there." I glanced up. "I'd been planning to check it out on my own, but from what I've read, there's room for the horses and it's defensible."

Instead of splitting up watches for the remainder of the night, I let everyone else sleep.

Guilt gnawed at me and I would have almost welcomed a second attack. I'd've been glad for the opportunity to hit something, to distract myself from my failure to protect the others.

I'd failed. Derek was dead and an evil mage had used Javi to try and get to me. What was Anette doing out here? And what did she want?

When the sun rose, Gary grumbled about not being called to watch, but Sandra looked better for the sleep. Mack nodded his appreciation to me as we struck camp. He let me tie Celeste to his wagon so I could sleep in the wagon back as we moved. I drifted off to the feeling of my power evaporating.

The observatory complex was a ruin. Even day-blind, I could see that. A wheeled chain-link gate once guarded the entrance, but it had long ago collapsed to the street. To the right was a large silo, a building attached to it. Ahead, on the left, were two smaller silos. Taking Mack with me, I checked them out.

A tree had fallen into one of the silos, caving it in. The other had a ten-foot-wide hole in its wall, and had a small meadow taking root where dirt had worked its way inside. Both contained ruined telescopes.

Beyond the silos was an open-air observation platform floored with wooden planks. Sixteen concrete posts were spaced evenly across the deck. I stepped onto the platform. The wood was old and sagged under my feet. I wasn't more than a foot off the ground, but seraphs only knew what was beneath me. My mind conjured up images of rusty nails and enormous wasp nests and I repressed a shudder. My steps made tiny creaking sounds as I walked to the nearest post. A telescope had been mounted here and its remains lay on the deck. Seeing the cracked barrel and the broken glass gleaming in the sun was heartbreaking.

"Elise!"

I jumped. Sandra leaned out from a doorway, face grim. "It's Javi."

Stomach sinking, I followed Mack toward the building. When the sounds of struggling reached us, we ran inside.

Our gear was strewn everywhere. Gary had Javier's arms wrapped behind his back, fighting to keep him still. The three of us wrestled Javi into a chair and tied him down.

"Elise," Javi purred, *"you never told me you liked it rough."*

"I'm going to get you out of this, Javi," I said.

"You're assuming that he wants to be free of me. Taking control was so much easier this time." A soft laugh bubbled up his throat. *"I'm only going to make this offer once, sister: Come to me and I'll let your friends leave this place with their lives."*

I scowled. "Even Derek?"

Javi shrugged.

I leaned down, my head only a few inches from Javi's. "Leave him alone."

He sucked a breath between his teeth. *"Wrong answer."* He turned his head and I grabbed his chin, forcing him to look at me.

"An observatory." Javi's smile widened until a burst of laughter ripped out of him. The insane sound bounced around the room like a ball bearing in a tin can. *"Clever. Especially after what happened to your little toy there."*

I jerked my head away in a panic, following Javier's glance to our scattered gear, to my telescope bag. Crushed.

"I have such use for you," Javi said and I snapped my eyes back to him. His expression changed. *"They're going to die, Elise,"* he snarled. *"All of them. And when I've broken you, the last thought you'll have is that this was all your fault."*

I looked away again.

"Are you paying attention, Moon mage?"

I stood, trembling. I wanted to punch him. No, not him, Anette. I pulled the chalk from my pocket and drew a circle around him.

"That won't keep me out forever."

I bent to touch the circle, looking him in the eye. "Good-bye, Anette."

The *Charmed Circle* flared to life and my friend went limp. I made sure he stayed down with a *Sleep* conjure.

Anette would come for us as soon as the sun went down. Without my telescope, it would take much longer to recharge myself—time we didn't have. I headed for the last silo.

The room was maybe thirty feet across, and the telescope took up most of it. It was mounted on a thick, metal shaft sunk into the cement floor. Long-dead computer equipment surrounded it. I stepped forward, crunching glass underfoot, and climbed the steps leading up, getting close.

The telescope had several holes in it and a crack ran almost the length of the barrel.

"Stars and feathers." I rested my head against the barrel. All of them were useless.

I exhaled, turning to go. Something caught my eye and I looked through one of the holes. An idea hit me and I ran to get Gary.

The Moon rose. The sky was clear. A breeze rustled through the trees, bringing the smell of warm grass and earth to me. It was quiet and as I sat on the observation platform, I had an unobstructed view of the sky in every direction. I felt Her on my skin. I took a deep breath and closed my eyes. Exhaling slowly, I reached for Her.

She wrapped me in Her cool embrace. I laughed softly, drinking Her in like pure water after weeks in the desert. The flow was gentle and slow— and frustrating. I couldn't draw what I needed as fast as I needed it. A flash of anger ripped through me and I nearly lost touch with Her. It had been a long time since I'd been forced to recharge unaided and Anette was already on her way. I forced myself to relax, to open myself fully to Her, and absorbed the power as She was willing to give it.

When I had enough to work with, I touched a conjure-less amulet and focused on its structure. I layered protective conjures within the stone. When activated, it would shield Javi's mind. Anette wouldn't be able to possess him.

"Do you think it'll work?"

I jumped, startled out of my near-trance. Sandra stood at the edge of the platform. At first, I thought she was asking about the charm, but she was looking at the array of mirrors we'd hastily erected. Gary and Mack had salvaged every mirror they could find, including from our personal gear, and Sandra had fashioned mounts for them.

The mirrors were arranged in a crescent at one end of the platform. Each was aligned to face the Moon at different points of Her journey across the night sky, and to reflect Her light at a large mirror at the opposite end of the platform. That mirror would catch the light, concentrate it, and send the beam of reflected Moonlight along a single path. If I stood anywhere along that path, it should give me a boost during the fight. And at midnight all of the mirrors would have Her at least partially in their frames, all would be reflecting Her, and the beam's strength would peak.

"It will." I hoped.

We went inside. Gary had lit two lanterns, filling the interior with a wan light. He frowned, drawing a whetstone along the blade of his sword.

Mack nodded at me and went back to repacking his medical kit, a brace of pistols and a longsword close to hand.

Sandra limped to her gear and sat. She tied her long, brown hair back with a leather strip—better for fighting. A machete lay next to a shotgun on her bedroll. She reached over them to pick up a pistol and check it for the third time since the sun had started setting.

I looped the amulet around Javi's neck and he groaned in his sleep like he'd just set down a heavy burden.

"That will keep Anette from reaching Javi again." I looked at my friends. "It's safe to untie him." I glanced over my shoulder. "I need to get back out there and charge some more."

"What can we do?" Mack asked.

"Take care of Javi." I said, walking toward the door. "I'll be back in a little while."

A curious expression came over Mack's face, and he started to rise from his bedroll. "Elise?"

I slipped through the metal door and activated a *Locking* conjure. A second later, the handle rattled. "Elise!" Mack roared. "Let us out of here. Now!"

Something hit the door and it shook in its frame. I backed away.

Sandra's voice drifted through the metal "What are you doing?"

"Keeping you safe. Something I couldn't do for Derek."

"Elise!"

I left the silo.

A gibbering screech sliced through the night. Another. They were coming.

I rose from where I sat, lotus style, at the center of the platform. I drew my kukris, and walked to the gap in the fence.

Spawn flowed over the ground like an oil spill. One of the largest skittered on top of a rusted-out car. It roared and charged at me.

"Adonai Yir'eh!" I shouted, activating an amulet. The world blurred for an instant, fracturing into possibilities as the *Precognition* conjure spread over my sight. Potential actions the spawn might take appeared simultaneously, with the most imminent retaining clarity and the others fading to near-transparency. A grin spread across my face as I charged the Darkness.

We came together in mid-air, my kukris driving into the darkun's eyes. I rolled over its back, ripping my blades free, and landed in a crouch, facing the oncoming horde. Behind me, the corpse of the monster came to a tumbling, skidding stop before it reached the fence.

For a second, the charge broke. I stared at them, the blood of one of their champions dripped from my blades, the droplets hissing as they hit the earth.

"I will fear no evil," I said.

Howls exploded from the spawn and they swarmed forward.

They came at me by the dozens and I met them, my body bathed in the fullness of Her light, my limbs singing with Her strength, and I cut them down like grass.

It wasn't enough.

Teeth snapped all around me. Claws ripped and slashed. I took heads and limbs with every turn, carving a ring of death.

They kept coming. There were so many that my precognitive battle sense was nearly overwhelmed. I triggered a *Strength* amulet, then lopped the head off a spawn and kicked it in the chest, sending it into the three behind. There were too many of them and I was no battle mage. But I had to keep my friends safe. Stepping back, my boot caught on chain-link. I lost my balance and fell backward.

Spawn surged forward, but I turned the fall into a roll and came up on my feet. A wide double-swing of my kukris claimed more of them and bought me a precious second. I leaped into the air, flipping backward, and dropped a one-use amulet—one I'd bought before the trip and had saved for a special occasion—into the mass of spawn below me.

Lightning tore through the ranks of spawn, frying the ones in front and blasting the lines behind. It spread through the metal of the fence. As far as twenty feet away on either side, spawn spasmed violently, then burst into flames.

I landed, coughing, and still they came. They flowed over the fence, stepping on the smoldering corpses of their brethren to get to me.

A *Blinding Flash* sent spawn reeling. Then I sent a *Madness* conjure into them. Blind spawn howled and tore into the first thing they touched, until a great mass of them were ripping each other apart.

I took advantage of the confusion and maneuvered myself back into the thin beam of reflected Moonlight coming from my mirrors. I pulled in as much power as I could, but I was like a drowning woman breaking the surface to gasp for air before being dragged under again.

And they came at me. Panting, I waded into them. I didn't know how long I'd been fighting, but my strength-boosting amulet was spent. I fought to stay in the path of the Moonbeam.

Where was Anette? I glanced at the building and paid for it with a long gash down my arm. I growled and cut the spawn into three pieces.

I lost more ground.

I sensed the Moon as She made her way across the sky. She was close. Her power grew stronger as the spawn forced me back along the beam, closer to the platform. Suddenly, the trickle of power thinned and cut out altogether. I glanced at the mirrors and then upward as an enormous cloud skated across the Moon.

"No," I whispered.

Claws raked across my middle. Desperate anger flowed through me and I sliced the filth's arm off at the shoulder.

I bled from hundreds of tiny slashes and dozens of larger ones. Exhaustion and spawn venom burned in my limbs, making them tremble. Even if they'd been fully charged, my *Healing* amulets wouldn't have been able to keep up with this much damage. I was probably going to die here, but if I was going out, I'd make them remember me in legend.

"They shall fear thee as long as the Moon endures!" I yelled as I stepped into the press of spawn, blades whirling. The quicker ones fell back, those that weren't as fast simply fell. Changing direction, I sliced apart the thinning spawn to my sides. Retreating, I faced the horde.

"Be strong in the Lord and in the strength of His might!" I shouted into their faces even as they drove me back.

A pinpoint of cool power struck me in the back and I drew it in. It widened into a steady flow, and then a flood. The cloud was passing. I laughed into a spawn's face even as I drew back from a mouthful of finger-length teeth. I stuck my blades into that face and wrenched them free.

I fed Her to my hungry amulets and the trembling in my limbs vanished. In an instant, my amulets were full and Her light kept pouring into me.

I swept my gaze to the thickest concentration of spawn and sent a blast of concentrated Moonlight into the mass of spawn. Moonlight, bright as the sun at high noon, flooded the area. The spawn caught in the conjure shrieked, their skin smoldering, smoking, and burning away.

Even as the ashes of the first began to fall, my energy was already being restored. It was glorious. Her light sang through me, filling me completely. We'd never been so close. Her presence was a gentle but irresistible pressure against my back, urging me onward.

I raised my hand, triggering the conjure stored in a silver ring on my little finger. "And He created the Moon to rule the night!" A beam of Her cold power, as thick as my wrist, lanced into them. Where it touched, limbs, heads, entire bodies, froze solid, then shattered.

Spawn clawed past each other to get away from me. I refilled my ring, ready to hurl Her light at them again.

The Moon had been progressing across the sky, and now, at midnight, She aligned perfectly with the mirrors that up until now had been channeling only a fraction of Her light.

Her full might drilled into me and my body bowed. I screamed as white light filled my vision, light so cold it burned. I couldn't see. I couldn't hear. She filled me completely, every sense, every pore. I was full—I could hold no more, and still She flowed into me.

Searing cold light burst from my eyes, spearing into the night. It exploded from my mouth. I couldn't release Her power fast enough. My ring exploded. Silver shrapnel ripped into me, white-hot pricks of agony in my hand and arm that quickly went cold and numb.

A hideous impact in my chest took me off my feet. I flew, tumbling, until my body hit the center mirror and shattered it. The weakened mounting arms dug into my side before they gave and the whole thing snapped off the concrete post. I hit the platform and bounced, trailing glass and debris, until I rolled to a stop in the grass on the other side. A stone the size of my splayed fingers bounced to a stop nearby.

Everything hurt. I blinked my eyes, trying to clear my vision, and stood, wincing at the pain.

"Nice to meet you, Elise."

My head snapped up. Anette stood between the fence and the platform, surrounded by spawn. She wore a black coat that hung down to her knees. Faded jeans were tucked into heavy boots. Her hair was long and black and streaked with crimson. What skin I could see was flawless. Her eyes were hazel, maybe a little sunken, like she was tired.

She looked . . . pretty, like a lost piece of something beautiful there in the filth, her hands in the pockets of her coat.

A ridiculous flash of self-consciousness washed over me, and I was acutely aware of my dirty, mouse-brown hair and sweaty, bloody clothes.

"That was a nice trick with the mirrors." She said. "Can't have you doing that again."

Mage quick, she flung her arms out wide.

"No!" I shouted. Tiny stones flew from her outstretched hands and hit my mirrors. The sound of breaking glass filled the night. Moonlight glittered off the pieces as they tumbled to the wooden planks.

"Are you sure you don't want to reconsider my offer?" Anette asked.

I faced her, panting. "Well, you know how it is. If I spend all my time with you, the other lunatics in my life get jealous."

She chuckled. "Nice."

I'd dropped my kukris on the platform when Anette's stone knocked me off. I flung power to them and drew them to me. One settled into my right hand, but the other hit my left and fell to the ground. I stared at my left hand in disbelief.

I was missing two fingers.

"Ooo," Anette said, her voice low and mocking. "I'll bet that hurt."

I flexed my remaining fingers. My *Healing* amulets were keeping me moving, were blocking the pain. I bent down and grabbed the knife. My grip was all wrong—I could barely hold onto it. I activated the recharged *Strength* amulet, so I'd at least be able to hold the kukri firmly.

Anette glanced over her shoulder at the remaining spawn. "Take her." She looked back at me and smiled. "Alive."

As one, the spawn let out a hissing roar and swarmed forward, attacking with a renewed ferocity now that their master had arrived.

Nails scrabbled on the wooden planks and I fought through a kaleidoscope of teeth and claws. I couldn't avoid them all. Spawn venom burned me, but I drove them back, blades whirling around me like a silver shield.

I caught a precognitive flash out of the corner of my eye as a rock streaked toward me. I twisted partway out of its path, using the force of the impact to spin around, into a defensive stance.

"You've been keeping secrets, Elise." Anette bent and picked up a rock the size of my head. She bounced it in her palm as if it weighed no more than a pebble. "Javi hasn't seen half of the wonderful little tricks you're showing me today. He'll be so jealous." She smiled. "Personally, I'd thought that your kind was too touchy-feely for a real fight. This is a pleasant surprise."

I was already in motion when Anette thrust the rock in my direction. It exploded, sending hundreds of deadly shards at me. They ripped into the spawn I used as a shield, even as I dove to the side, rolling to keep my momentum going.

I came to my feet and kicked out. My boot sent a spawn tumbling as I drove my kukri into the throat of another.

Stinging black blood splashed over my hand. I swept into a whirlwind, forcing the closest darkuns away. Battle sense clamored another warning and I ducked as a rock shot past me.

Desperation fueled my movements. I couldn't fight both Anette and her army.

I flashed a look at her. She stood watching, her eyes wild. She'd backed away from the combat. If I could finish her, the spawn would be leaderless. They might scatter.

I threw everything into a series of sweeping, almost wild, attacks, driving the spawn back. The approach cleared, I ran to the edge of the platform and leaped with every ounce of strength I had.

Anette smiled and my heart sank.

She'd seen it coming. As I reached her, she stepped backward and opened a hole in the rock.

I flicked my left hand out, hurling a kukri at her and dropped into the hole.

Darkness surrounded me as I hit bottom. I bounced off a wall and jumped just as the hole began to close.

The rock solidified around the toe of my boot and caught me just as I emerged from the hole. My leg was wrenched painfully and I crashed to the ground.

Anette slipped twin axes from under her coat and ran forward. Standing, I ripped my boot free of the rock and parried her first attack. She drove me back, our blades ringing.

Grace and fury, she was fast, and she had two blades to my one. I couldn't keep up. And she was a better fighter; her kick caught me in the middle. I tumbled into the waiting arms of spawn.

Claws scrabbled at me, drawing more blood. I twisted, slicing through the spawn. It only bought me a second. I lashed out with a beam of cold, freezing the creatures nearest to me. I screamed my defiance at the rest, as they shattered their fellows and came at me.

The door to the building next to us flew off its hinges, slamming into a group of spawn. Gary's voice rang through the night like an angry rockslide. "Blessed be the Lord, my rock, who trains my hands for war!"

He charged into the spawn, his claymore flashing in the moonlight, carving a path in front of him. Sandra came behind him, her shotgun blasting to either side, preventing the spawn from closing behind him and swallowing him up.

Mack followed, his knives making short work of any spawn that Gary and Sandra missed. Behind him came Javier, a machete in his hand and my amulet around his neck. He focused on Anette and howled, cutting his way toward her.

Anette looked at me and our eyes locked. Frustration boiled under the hazel surface of her eyes.

"As long as the Moon endures!" I shouted.

She scowled and raised her hand, but I was already rushing her.

The ground exploded behind me, throwing dirt and deadly sharp spikes of rock into the pursuing spawn.

I called my blade to me and began a spinning attack.

Anette met my blades with her axes and the impact rang out. The shock sent a wave of agony up from my maimed hand, but I kept hold of my knife. We glared at each other, our eyes only inches apart.

"This ends tonight," I said.

A wicked smile flowed across her features. "Sister, we're just getting started."

She shoved me. I knew it was coming, but she was as implacable as a boulder rolling downhill and I stumbled back several steps.

Anette stalked forward, then threw herself back to avoid a blast from Sandra's shotgun.

"Damn you!" Anette raced forward, plucked the weapon from Sandra's hands, and turned the gun on her.

Before Anette could pull the trigger, Javi rose up behind her and slashed down with his machete. The blade struck her coat in the shoulder and threw the mage forward. The shotgun clattered to the ground and Anette rolled to her feet. Her coat wasn't even scuffed.

"Oh, it's dear Javier!" Anette exclaimed. "I'm sorry, but I didn't see you before."

Javi didn't speak. He closed the distance between them and swung again.

Anette caught the machete on her axe. As she twisted it aside, she stepped forward and drove her knee into Javier's groin, lifting him off the ground. Javi groaned and crumpled in front of her.

"We had so much fun, Javi. I'm going to miss you." Anette raised her axe and then swung it down.

Clanging into my blade.

Anette looked in surprise at me crouched below her as the kukri held in my weaker hand slipped underneath her spelled coat. She twisted away, but not before the blade caught and tore . . . something. She screamed.

Anette's blood sizzled on my blade, mingling with spawn blood. She backed away, looking at the dwindling number of spawn that fought against my friends. Something like frustrated hurt crossed her face, then she ran, mage-quick, into the forest. I turned to help my friends.

"Go!" Gary sliced the arm off a spawn. He spun and took another in the head. "End this!"

I turned and raced after Anette.

Drawing on the Moon to boost my speed, I chased Anette. We raced past the airport and into the university campus. She flowed over the broken concrete and shattered stone like it was flat ground. She pulled away from me. I switched to mage sight to track her by her energies and came to a staggering halt.

Invisible to normal sight, in mage sight the area was covered in a dirty, gray fog. It billowed and rolled over me, blown by an unfelt wind, and now that I was sensitized to it, it left a bitter, metallic taste in my mouth. As I watched, patches of the fog turned a sick yellowish color, while others turned to that of blood and bruises. Some blackened as if burning.

All of it spiraled toward a darkness at the center of campus, making me think of a slow-motion tornado, or filthy water spiraling down a slaughter-house drain. It was obvious where Anette was headed.

I found her at the bottom of a crater in the middle of a cluster of res-idence halls. Broken windows stared at us like blind eyes and the buildings listed precariously.

She stood on top of an enormous crystal. It was six feet high and twice that around. At the center of the crystal was a roiling blackness. A wave of nauseating power dropped me to my knees.

Three skeletons were locked within the crystal, the long bones broken as if they had been shoved inside and made to fit a space too small for them. Some of the bones were from misshapen wings.

"Those are—" I staggered to my feet, unable to continue. I swallowed. "What is—"

"This," Anette said, "is my first step to freedom."

I stepped back, horrified. "You can't use that!"

She hopped to the ground. "It's easier than you think." She caressed the stone. "All you have to do is touch it."

My skin crawled. "Anette, get away from that." I shuddered. "Bright Moon above, please just get away."

"That's what I'm trying to do. Get away." She leaned her back against the crystal and I was sure that the blackness reacted to her presence. "Get away from all the damned struggle."

"That won't take you away from anything." I said. "Look at it. It's drawing things in."

"For now."

"Anette—"

She scowled at me. "When I control it, the stone will do as I command!"

My stomach churned. How could she bear to be so close to that thing?

"Anette, you can't control it." I stepped closer, my boots sending loose dirt into the crater. "It's not your freedom, it's a prison." As soon as the words left my mouth, I knew that they were true. I heard pleading voices in my head. Demanding voices. The skeletons weren't dead things. They were Fallen. And they wanted out.

"You're being used," I said. "They're not going to let you go."

"They will!" Anette took several steps toward me and I tensed, attempting to draw in Her power. It felt like breathing through a filthy sock. I coughed, nearly retching. The unnatural fog cut me off from the Moon.

"I will have the power to make them!" Anette pointed at me. "And you are going to help me."

An oily vice closed around my head and squeezed. I fell to my knees and clutched at my head, a cry ripping from my throat. I raised mental walls, and Anette swarmed around them, looking for a way in. *Stars and feathers,* the rancid taint of the Fallen clung to her.

I closed my eyes, panting through clenched teeth, a sour taste at the back of my throat. I couldn't keep her out. The Fallen were helping her ooze through, and once she was inside, she'd have me just as she'd had Javi.

Cold fingers pressed into my temples. Blood trickled from my nose. My eyes shot open.

Anette smiled down at me.

"I wanted this to be easy, sister." She caressed my face. "Remember that."

Trembling, I gritted my teeth. "I am not your sister."

With a single word I cast a simple conjure and Moonlight exploded in Anette's face. Reflexively her hands went to her eyes, and I staggered to my feet. Unsteady, I grabbed her and heaved her at the crystal with the last of my strength.

Blackness seethed within the crystal as Anette crashed into it. She tumbled to the dirt and lay still. Her blood smeared one of the facets. As I watched, the blood vanished.

Anette moaned and slowly pushed herself away from the crystal.

"It's over, Anette." I threaded my words with a trickle of persuasive power, hoping to nudge her thoughts away from a fight I couldn't win. "Your spawn are gone and I will see to it that the seraphs find out about this place."

"No!" Anette looked around wildly, then focused on me. "No. No. *No!*" I felt her draw power from the stone. "I won't let you."

The ground trembled. Loose stones tumbled into the crater. Anette stood with her head bowed and her fists clenched.

The trembling increased. Somewhere nearby, glass shattered. I backed away from the lip of the crater and nearly fell. I heard a tired groan from one of the nearby buildings.

Anette lifted her head and I flinched at the insane light in her eyes. She trembled with power.

The building behind her collapsed in a roar of concrete and glass. Dust billowed in a wave, engulfing Anette, the crystal, me. I coughed and spat as buildings crumbled on all sides, caught in the grip of Anette's earthquake.

I fled, stumbling away from the destruction. I don't know how long I ran, but I stopped when the dust and blackness thinned and I could feel moonlight on my skin.

I was spent. I had nothing left. I couldn't even send my mind out to see if Anette was still alive in the middle of the shattered campus.

I told myself I'd come back the next night and search.

I never did.

As I staggered into camp, the Moon had started below the horizon. It was still an hour before sunrise, but already my vision was growing blurry.

Gary, Sandra, and Mack were loading the wagons. When they saw me, they rushed over and eased me into a chair.

"Water," I croaked and someone pressed a cup into my hands.

Sandra caught her breath. "Your hand!"

Mack cursed as I rinsed out my mouth and then took a long swallow.

"Javi?" I asked, before he could say anything.

"Back of the wagon," Mack said. "Asleep. Elise—"

I shook my head and scrubbed the dust off my face. Haltingly, I told them what happened. I didn't mention the crystal. That was for the seraphs to deal with and I didn't want any of my friends getting within a mile of that thing. I'd report it when I got back to Enclave.

"Do you think she's still alive?" Gary asked, as he and Mack continued to load the wagons. They had decided to head back to Houston at sunup.

"I don't know." I got up to get more water and I tripped over something and nearly fell. My eyesight was never this bad this early, and it scared me.

"I'll get that." Sandra took the cup from my hands and I tried not to flinch. I hadn't seen her approach. The campfire was only a brighter patch in a field of blurry gray. I shivered.

"Elise?"

I jumped. "What?"

"Here." I turned in the direction of Sandra's voice. "I brought another—" She gasped and I heard the cup hit the gravel.

"Your eyes . . ."

I couldn't see Sandra, and as I felt the last of the Moon slip below the horizon the last of my vision bled away.

"*Power comes with a price,*" was something that my old mentor and friend Raylene told me back in Enclave. Anette paid for hers. Was I paying for mine?

". . . they're all white!"

Day One
38 PA / 2050 AD

Faith Hunter

Burkhold locked the bars on the windows while Sharia locked the doors and passed the keys out the mail slot to the waiting mule. Regina was a sterile half-human, half-mage; a longtime, trustworthy friend; the kind you could depend on when a mage-rut was scheduled.

The couple was now sealed in together, safe from sexual approach by other mages and unable to leave the small house to join the mating frenzy that would soon take place in the streets among the unmarried. Regina would be back in five days to unlock the door and set them free. Five days of bliss and love unlike any ever known by the poor humans.

He watched as Sharia moved across the living room and checked yet again that there was food and water enough to last them the full heat. Mages had been known to forget to eat or drink, almost dying of dehydration while caught up in mage-rut lust; having both ready to hand was wise. This would be their first rut since they'd come into their gifts, and Burkhold and his mate had been meticulous in their preparations. All their amulets were locked up in a trunk in the hall, and Regina had the key; there would be no unauthorized release of creation energy by one of them while caught up in the heat. Their weapons had been left at the dojo, under lock and key; there was no way for them to hurt each other—Burkhold smiled: except by wild and raucous sex.

As if sensing the train of his thoughts, Sharia looked up and met his eyes. Warmth and excitement filled her face. And a bit of fear. "We'll be fine, Sweetheart," he said, understanding. "No one ever died from mage heat."

"No. But they did have to sit in healing baths for a month after," she said wryly.

Burkhold dropped a kiss on her forehead and checked the position of the pillows on the floor, careful to cover the hard wood. Rugs, pillows, and mattresses would protect their skin from damage should the rut take them away from the bedroom. He looked back over his shoulder at the bower they had prepared. The bed was made up with sage green silk and emerald green pillows. A comforter was folded at the foot and emerald mosquito netting fell from the ceiling in a drape. *Illumination* amulets—minor ones with little useable creation energy in them—were scattered about the room, ready to be activated.

Outside, the sound of revelry was rising. Fireworks exploded against the Enclave dome overhead. Boisterous music blasted down the street from the house shared by five unmated mage men. They had been drinking hard all day, and had advertised a party, a mage-heat orgy. It had attracted several dozen unmated mages, mules, and humans. They were dancing and drinking, and several of the mages had already tossed aside their clothes. One mage woman was standing on the street corner, dancing; the men watching applauded. It had been five years since the last flyover, and the populace was eager.

In all that time, no mage children had been born. For a mage female to ovulate, seraphs had to fly directly over the Enclave and hover close to the dome, wings beating. Such proximity would fuel both ovulation in the females and almost unbearable sexual heat in all mages. In the seraphs as well, but they were not allowed—by the Most High—to participate in the mage heat they stimulated. Instead they would hover until they could bear it no more, then they would fly back to the nearest Realm of Light, to be tended by seraphs until their own heat dissipated.

In eight months, the litters of little mages and bigger mules would be born to the Enclave and be taken, squalling, to where mules trained for crèche duty would care for them, bringing them back to mage mothers as needed for mother's milk and energy feedings. Hopefully Sharia and Burkhold wouldn't have a litter after their first rut. They, along with twenty other mated couples, were testing a new birth control method. If it worked, female mages who wanted to could avoid the twice-a-decade childbearing. Mage population numbers around the globe were comfortably high, and the Enclave councils wanted to avoid future overpopulation.

Burkhold felt a tingle in his fingertips and looked at his hands. Warmth shot through his blood, electric and arousing. The music in the streets fell silent, cut off in mid-note. A heated silence filled the air, expectant and eager. "They're early," he said. But Sharia was looking out the tall, barred window at the scene in the street. His blood heating, he joined her.

He could feel the pressure building in Sharia's belly as her body responded to the presence of seraphs, her ovaries swelling, her breasts growing tender. Desire like molten gold filled his veins, and he growled with his own need. He *wanted*. *Angel tears*, he wanted.

From the window, they heard shrieks. Their hearts pounded, breath heaved. Excitement and power rose in them, intensified, gathered strength. Power leapt between them, fueling their shared release.

The rut of mage heat had begun. And there were four days more to come.

MONSTER
38-51 PA / 2050-2063 AD

Spike Y Jones

38 PA

"You know, Dam, the way you handle that sword, I think it's right; you're gonna end up a Steel mage. It's almost like that sword's a part of you, or you're a part of it."

"And what . . . would you . . . know about . . . sword play . . . Ike?" the dark-skinned boy replied, his words in rhythm with his feints, thrusts, and advances.

"Not much," the skinny redhead said, reclining on the levee, "but I know about prophecy. And yours says you'll be made of steel."

"Which means . . . you don't . . . know pro . . . phecy . . . either . . . spawn-for-brains."

"He's right . . . Ike," huffed the third, older, boy, as he retreated, his muscular parries barely blocking the younger boy's fluid attacks. "Kibed . . . the Moon mage in my cohort . . . he says . . . prophecy is never straight-forward . . . If the meaning . . . is obvious . . . then the meaning . . . is wrong."

Damocles launched a killing blow at Mosiah's neck, followed by another at his groin, and then a third at his heart, all before the older boy could react even to the first.

"Hey! You weren't supposed to speed it!"

"I got tired of waiting for you to make a move, Mo," Damocles said, breaking into a cool-down kata to ease his muscles out of full-combat mode.

"The Moonies make that *'Look at me, I'm so mysterious'* stuff up. Without it what've they got? *'You are feeling sleepy, very sleepy.'*" They all laughed, and Damocles and Mosiah flopped down on the grass beside Icarus. "I mean, my prophecy was clear: *'Heat—'*"

"Oh, we know your prophecy. *'Heat of the Sun warms every heart, but wax wings that flyyyyyy tooooooo hiiiiigh melt',*" Damocles and Mosiah sing-songed in something approaching unison.

"Which is why you don't see me flying too high, working up a sweat swinging steel or memorizing workings, when I can just lay back and soak up my sunlight, keeping myself tanned and toned for the tesses."

"The only way a priestess is gonna fall for you is if she trips over you on her way to me."

"I think the both of you children are years away from having to worry about priestesses. You'll be lucky to have hit puberty by the *next* overflight, and it may be another one before even a heat-crazed female'll be willing to bed you."

"Not much longer for me," Ike said, stroking the scattering of dark hairs on his upper lip that he referred to as a moustache.

"Yeah. Right. You keep thinking that. But low-flying Icarus might have a point, Dam. I mean, *'He shall be as strong as steel, but with a legacy more enduring',* does sound like the prophecy for a Steel mage."

"Or for a River or Air mage who just happens to enjoy working out," Damocles countered.

"Well, you better hope you end up a Metal mage, or else that chain you've been wearing around your neck for a decade is gonna be a lousy prime amulet," Icarus pointed out.

"They're coming."

Damocles and Mosiah sprang up, and even Icarus got slowly to his feet and searched the sky in the direction Damocles stared.

"I don't see anything."

"Me neither."

"They're coming," Damocles insisted. "I can feel them."

Suddenly all noise from the city—the distant mix of music, people shouting, the explosion of conjures and fireworks the boys had been ignoring—stopped.

"They're here," Damocles whispered, absentmindedly swinging his sword in a complicated slow-motion pattern, as much a dance as a battle exercise, just as two tiny figures appeared in the air above the city's protective dome, seraphs hovering in midair, their presence awakening uncontrollable mage heat in every mature neomage.

The two neomages were only eleven years old, born just before the Enclave was established, so the overflight wouldn't affect them. Mosiah was seventeen, but as a human he was, of course, immune to mage heat. So the three had felt safe sneaking to a thicket springing up amid the ruins just outside of the Enclave, preferring to avoid both the adult revels in the streets of the French Quarter and the indignity of being locked up with the other children in the confines of human-run safe houses within the city.

There probably would have been some opportunities for Mosiah in the city; the party atmosphere infected many female humans even without heat. But an offer to spar with Damocles wasn't something to be passed up. Despite his youth, Damocles was probably the most skillful neomage savage blade user in New Orleans. There were adult mules who could best him, but mostly because they had muscle mass on him and the ability to channel creation energy into their efforts. Once Damocles grew into his oversized sword and came into his magical gift, those advantages would probably be canceled as well. Mosiah learned more in his tutoring sessions with the

younger boy than the mage learned from the older, supposedly more experienced, human.

Still, the rut would last for five days. They'd probably end up sneaking
back into the city before it was over, if the food they'd brought ran out or if
they got bored, and Mosiah could leave his neomage companions behind
for some other company.

"D-D-Dam? Guys? I don't feel so good."

Mosiah and Damocles spun around to see Icarus glowing, light leaking
out of his eyes and heat pulsing from his skin.

"It's the seraphs!" Mosiah exclaimed. "It's your gift comin' in! It happens sometimes if you're just starting puberty. I heard about it after the last
flight."

"It hurts! It *hurts!*"

"Your amulet, Ike. Use your prime to control the energy. You can put
the light into it."

Icarus clasped his hands around the crystal prism hanging from a thong
around his neck. "It's not working. I can't feel anything in the amulet."

The waves of heat grew more intense and Icarus' clothing began to
smolder. Flames appeared at his fingertips, and when he tried to shake
them out, the flames fell to his feet, lighting the grass on fire.

"Hellhole! He's not a Light mage. Ike's a Fire mage! Dam, what can we
do?"

"I don't know! Everyone in the Enclave's rutting by now. Maybe an
amulet—a *Control Power* conjure."

"Where?"

"In the school. They've got plenty of them in the school."

"But they'd be locked."

"I can't hold it! I have to let it out!"

A flash of light, a blast of heat, and an explosive concussion wave
knocked Damocles and Mosiah to the ground. Icarus still stood, but trees,
bushes, and grass in all directions around him burned. He turned in a slow
circle, staring wide-eyed at the destruction that surrounded him.

"Ike, you gotta calm down!" Mosiah yelled at Icarus, as the human
levered himself off the ground. Then, more quietly, "Do the rhyme, Ike.
Stone and fire, water . . ."

"*. . . water and air, blood and kin prevail.*" Icarus' voice quavered, but years
of repetition had drilled the words into him, as they were supposed to.
"*Wings and shield, dagger and sword, blood and kin prevail. Stone and fire, water . . .*"

"'Wings and shield. Wings and—' Seraphs." Damocles calmly stood up.
"It's happening because of the seraphs."

"Yeah, but so what, Dam?"

"They caused it, Mo; they can fix it. Ike, don't worry; I'm getting help,"
and then Damocles ran a short distance along the levee, out of range of the
flames. Lifting his sword to the sky, he pointed in the direction of the
seraphs and called out, his voice ringing above the fire in a way no ten-year-
old's had a right to: "You! Seraph! You did this! Come down here and

help!"

Seconds ticked by and nothing happened. "Maybe they didn't hear you . . . which would be good."

Then one of the winged warriors turned in the air and swooped toward the three boys at the edge of the city.

The seraph came to a hovering halt yards above them. He wore no armor and carried no weapons. His robes and wings were purest white, his hair golden, and the light that shone from him the yellow of the Sun. His voice thundered, "Who calls the Hand of Purification? Who summons the Seraph of Chastity? Who would *command* Taharial of the High Host?"

Mosiah fell to the ground, averting his eyes and praying fervently. Damocles, though, stood his ground. "I called. My friend," he said, pointing unnecessarily at Icarus with his sword, "his gift was awakened by your presence. He can't control it. You gotta help him."

Taharial turned stiffly in the air to observe Icarus, the boy's skin having taken on a reddish glow. The seraph then turned back to face Damocles.

"There is nothing I can do for him, young mage. His condition cannot be ameliorated." The seraph turned his face skyward and his wings began to flap harder.

"No! There must be something you can do," Damocles pointed his sword at Taharial again, the pink quartz crystal in the pommel glinting in the light shining from the seraph. "Do it!"

"Hey, guys, I dunno—*wings and shield*—I think I'm getting the hang of this." The glow from Icarus's skin changed from dull red to orange.

"Again you command me, mage, with a sword and wild magic in your hand."

". . . *dagger and sword*—it doesn't hurt anymore. It actually feels, I dunno—*blood and kin prevail*—I feel strong, full of power." From bright orange to yellow-white. "I can control it—*stone and fire*—"

Flames exploded from the Fire mage's eyes, his hands, his skin, rushing hungrily outward to engulf Damocles, Mosiah, the Louisiana countryside—and were extinguished as they struck a dome of energy that sprang up around Icarus at a gesture from the seraph. The flames pouring uncontrollably from the pre-teen's body grew in heat and intensity, and with a blinding flash of light and a roar of sound Icarus disappeared from sight.

The seraph's voice penetrated the ringing in the neomage's ears. "But commanding a thing to happen is not always enough. There are some things beyond the power of even the seraphim."

Mosiah struggled to his feet, tears streaming down his face. Damocles slowly turned from the fire-blasted circle that marked the extent of the seraph's now-dissipated energy dome and faced the seraph, still hovering in the air. The neomage began to speak, but the seraph cut him off.

"You are a rock in my River of Time. We will meet again, mortal with the will of steel." And Taharial rose into the sky, arrowing out of sight to the northwest.

51 PA

The mixed band had spent days steaming north on the Mississippi from New Orleans, and then, when the drifting ice on the river was too dangerous for their boat, days riding along the river bank to the outskirts of St. Louis. The horses and mules had all died in the fighting toward the city's center, where the Darkness had its lair—horses, mules, and two of Damocles' band. The first was a neomage named Spirit, half a decade older than Damocles, an Air mage who was a child during the Mage Wars and who'd now been experiencing real combat for the first—and last—time. After Spirit was trampled into the ground and partially eaten by a herd of man-eating cattle, the mage's human champard, Jeff Mackintosh, had only lasted another few hours before breaking away and diving headlong into the fangs of a hundred-headed snake, severing dozens of heads before succumbing to the venom of the scores that remained.

They built a cairn of broken concrete over Mackintosh's remains, passed around the group's collection of *Healing* amulets, and ate their last meal before plunging into the ice tunnels.

"I've been running it over and over," said the only human left in the group, "and I don't understand why you didn't call mage in dire, Dam. We were certainly in mortal danger."

"There wasn't enough time, Mo. It all happened too quickly. And anyways, the snake thing wasn't threatening *me*. There wasn't neomage blood involved, so the seraphs wouldn't have answered."

"But you were still bleeding from the razor-sparrows. All of 'em come from Tera . . . the Monster-Maker, so it should all be one big event."

"I don't think it works that way. You're a human; you wouldn't understand."

"Yeah, I've lived twenty-three years in a neomage Enclave, a dozen of them as your best friend, the last two as the champard of one of the best warriors and mages the world has ever known, and I somehow managed not to learn a single thing about the way the important things work. Thanks a lot, Dam."

"There is no need for us to bicker, Mosiah. We are all equally sworn to Damocles and to this mission."

"But it's not just this mission, Phin. He never calls mage in dire. Not for Jeff, not for Spirit, not for Deborah, not for—"

"That's enough, Mo. I said it wouldn't have worked."

"And we have more important things to consider. Phineas and I were talking." Cleopatra and her brother were Damocles' two remaining half-breed champards. "Everything we've fought so far have been mindless animals and spawn. They didn't have the feel of deliberate attacks—more like random encounters, or at best preset patrols. But what if the Monster-Maker has observers scattered on the approaches to his lair, or if we missed one of the spawn and it returned to its master to report our location? We have to assume that we've lost the element of surprise. The Fallen will be waiting for us. The odds against us have increased."

"Are you saying you want to back out, Cleo?"

"No, Damocles. We always knew this was likely a suicide mission. But it's not too late for us to make a tactical retreat. If there's no chance of success, then there's no reason to throw our lives away."

"Retreat, regroup, reinforce, reassess, and return," added her brother.

"If we go back now, he'll have more time to breed more monsters and we'll be stuck in this same spot having this same conversation a month or a year from now. And how many more people will he kill or worse in the meantime? How many more towns will be wiped out by his mutated . . . things? No. We go forward now, before *he* can reinforce."

Damocles looked from face to face around their fireless encampment, catching the eyes of each of his champards in turn and holding their gaze until each of them nodded acceptance.

"And don't worry; I've got some tricks up my sleeve still."

The matter settled, the reduced band gathered their equipment and marched in single file into the mouth of the ice tunnel that had once been a street leading into downtown St. Louis.

They couldn't be certain that Phineas and Cleopatra's fears of early detection were unfounded, so they had to be prepared for ambush while hoping that they still had surprise on their side and working to maintain that edge. An amulet Spirit had created provided a dense, sound-deadening mist to conceal their movements, and by choosing the least-frequented tunnels, they hoped to get as close to the Dark Power's lair as possible before their location was pinpointed and they'd have to fight for every foot of progress. Damocles couldn't risk using mage sight, a mind skim, or a conjure to scan for the fallen seraph within the maze; the neomage would have to pump a lot of personal energy into the scan to cover such a large target area, which would open him up to detection by the Dark power—assuming the power hadn't veiled himself from detection, which was just as likely.

A map an artist named Skylark had drawn for them back in New Orleans was of limited use; things had changed since she'd lived here before the abandonment of the city. The Arch Skylark had told them would be visible for miles as they'd approached had apparently succumbed to the glacier. The streets had once formed a regular grid, but now most were blocked by ice, and the tunnels were as likely to meander through the lower floors of buildings as to follow the grid.

The group had discussed with Skylark the most symbolically important places for Teratos to build his lair, and they'd marked those on the map. Though the Arch was gone, the other landmarks might still exist. Without the map, they'd have to use dead reckoning, lesser landmarks, and passive senses to laboriously find their way to them.

Stores, offices, warehouses, and apartment buildings had been converted into stables, breeding grounds, laboratories, and refrigerated meat lockers. The raucous sounds and rank smells emanating from them gave the band ample warning to steer clear of contact with any number of creatures.

The group couldn't find the open-air stadium Skylark had marked, and assumed it had been buried in snow and ice early in the city's decline. They found city hall, but judging from the smell, it was now an over-crowded dormitory for spawn servants of the Monster-Maker; not the sort of place their master would choose to live in. Three failures, leaving only one major site on the map.

West of where the Arch should have stood, they came to an ice-enclosed sloping ramp that matched the description of their last guess. The passage opened into what had once been a domed football stadium, now converted into a winter palace. Scattered sunlight from translucent ice-covered holes in the icicle-festooned roof haphazardly lit the space. Tiers of seats, mostly hidden by feet of snow and ice, surrounded a vast central floor, unevenly covered by masses of ice and drifts of snow. Damocles and his champards had emerged among the seats at one end of the arena, while near the other end of the floor stood a soaring multi-level platform of debris frozen into place by yet more ice. A beam of light from the roof illuminated sparkling ice sculptures on the dais and another was centered on the stadium's opposite end, at the tunnel mouth Damocles had just come out of, coincidentally enough.

Something felt odd to the neomage, but before he could identify it a voice rang out.

"Welcome to the frozen heart of my St. Louis, Damocles, Metal mage, litter of six, of the line of battle mages Cynthia and Wilson, and your little friends with their own tiresome names and pedigrees." The voice was easily heard across the intervening space, sounding like stone and iron being scraped against each other. Ice creaked as parts of the ice sculpture began to move. A giant ice serpent eased its body away from its position wrapped around the base of the dais and began to spiral up the platform. As it rounded a corner, instead of a snake head, a larger-than-life man's torso, arms, and head made up the front of the serpent's body. The enormous creature had snow-white skin and icy-blue hair and scales.

"You knew we were coming. Why didn't you stop us?" Without strain, Damocles' powerful voice carried as far as the serpent's.

"It amused me." He laughed—a frightening, inhuman noise—and their attention was drawn to his face. While its human body was without apparent flaw, the former seraph's face looked like it had been broken and molded only imperfectly back into shape.

"Laugh while you can, Monster-Maker." The mortals walked down the steps to the playing field and began to close the distance to their enemy, taking positions in a well-practiced battle formation. "We're here to end your reign of terror."

"You? Four mortals armed with pointy sticks? I had expected your military to launch an airstrike against me. Against you I needn't even fight back." Teratos turned his back on them, slithering upward to the top of the platform.

"Some sticks are pointier than others, Monster-Maker." With that, Damocles pulled a large, battered leather gauntlet from a pocket and pulled it over his small hand. He then drew an iron dagger, one his champards had never seen him use before, out of a concealed sheath.

Brandishing it before him, the neomage loudly proclaimed, *"And the great dragon was cast out, that old serpent called Tamiel. And I heard a loud voice saying 'Now is come salvation and strength, and the kingdom of God the Victorious'."* Then he reached into the pocket and pulled out a blood-stained cloth.

"Spirit's scarf," Mosiah nodded his head, "and Jeff's glove."

Damocles wrapped the scarf around the crossguard of the dagger, *"And they overcame him by the blood of his victims, and by the word of their testimony."*

Teratos paused in his crawling. "You left off the rest of that verse, little mortal. *'And they loved not their lives unto the death.'* Very telling omission. It tells me that you're afraid to die, that you don't have in you what is necessary to defeat what is in me."

Energy began to pour from Damocles into the dagger, *"And I saw an angel come down from heaven . . ."*

"'I saw an angel'? You have no angel, little mortal. From where I sit, you have very little at all."

". . . and he laid hold on the dragon, that old serpent which is Tamiel, and cast him into the bottomless pit," electricity crackled along the knife blade, *"that he should plague the nations no more."*

"And a second time you try to use a name against me, thinking it's a name of special power. The Most High has denied me that name. It has no power over me . . . especially not coming from your mouth."

The serpent-seraph waved a hand in dismissal, and the electrical sparks dancing on the iron dagger winked out. Damocles stood stunned for a moment, seeing his coup so neatly negated.

"You play a dangerous game, mortal—to pick and choose from His precious words, taking one out of context, skipping over another, adding a word of your own—for two can play at that game. I give you another verse from that book, mage. *'And I saw a great white throne',"* he spread his arms to indicate the ice chair on which he now sat, made exceptionally wide to accommodate his coils *"'and him that sat on it, from whose face the peoples of the earth and the seraphs of the heavens fled away, and there was no place for them.'* You seek to cast me into a bottomless pit, but don't the Scriptures promise, *'And the Beast shall ascend out of the bottomless pit, for He has given their kingdoms unto the Beast'?'*

Without warning Cleopatra yelped and was gone, held in the talons of an enormous, silent, multi-legged snowy owl, flying toward the fallen seraph. Her arms pinned, Cleopatra jack-knifed her lower body up and grabbed the owl's head with her legs. A savage twist pulled the owl's head to the side, and the bird's flight path changed accordingly. Sprinting at inhuman speed, Phineas ran ahead of the owl, stopped, whirled about, and flung two throwing knives into its eyes. Mortally wounded, the dying bird released Cleopatra, who dropped in a battle crouch beside her brother, almost as if the siblings had practiced the maneuver in advance.

"I now have a name of my own," the fallen seraph thundered, "a name that proclaims me to be a creator of things as much as He." Instantly, monstrous creatures of all types rushed forward from tunnels spaced around the stadium at multiple levels, the nearest attacking Damocles and the others, with those further away took up defensive positions between them and Teratos.

Dropping the dagger and human-sized glove, Damocles drew his pink-quartz-pommeled longsword, touched one of the rings on his free hand to the flat of the blade, and muttered a few words. Suddenly the edges of the blade blurred, as if they were rapidly vibrating. He pointed the sword in the direction of Phineas, Cleopatra, and Mosiah, and their blades took up the vibration. He yelled "*Vibro-blade!*", warning his champards of the incantation, because even a minor nick from the blades could now slice off their own limbs.

The mortals began advancing through the maze of ice pillars toward their enemy, hacking their way through endless waves of giant spider-legged house cats, swarms of saber-toothed squirrels, and more of the carnivorous cattle. And always one of the four had to face backward, fighting the dragon-roaches and yapping squid-tentacled dogs that followed in their wake.

And whenever the fight was the most intense, Teratos's voice boomed over the din, insulting his opponents, lovingly describing his abominations as they tried to get past the invaders's flashing blades and magically-toughened armor. Advance a few feet and a giant porcupine blocked their path, firing armor-piercing explosive quills at them. "An early effort and a bit of a cliché, but the demon iron tips make it interesting, don't you agree?" Dispose of the porcupine, and flying stingrays attacked. Then brilliantly colored poison-dart sheep. And always more of the cows: different sizes, different colors, with horns or without, but always more.

At times Damocles or one of his champards tried to taunt the Fallen. "You're awfully proud of your creativity," Mosiah shouted, "but it seems like every second thing you throw at us is a cow. Not all that impressive, Misfit-Maker."

"The Most High had an unfortunate obsession with beetles." The fallen seraph shrugged his enormous shoulders. "I work with the raw material that's made available to me."

Unfortunately, they couldn't keep up the patter, forced to devote all their attention and energy to pushing forward. The monotonous sounds of battle were broken only by barked instructions—"On your left!", "Covering you!", "High!"—and the Monster-Maker's commentary and derisive laughter.

The encounters soon blurred together: exploding turtles, giant mosquitoes, constrictor rabbits, battering rams, bat-cats. Occasionally a handful of spawn would leap from behind a knot of cattle or drop from the girders above, but without the weight of numbers, they were easily dealt with.

"It's odd, isn't it, to find so few devil-spawn?" Cleopatra asked nobody in particular, while she methodically swung her shortsword and battleax, killing and then beheading the spawn she faced. "I mean, every other hell-hole they come at you in the hundreds."

"And the things he does throw at us make no sense." Mosiah added. "Why bother with the stupid bat-cats and the cows? Just hit us all at once with his biggest and meanest."

"*He* is his biggest and meanest," Phineas said, his words punctuated by the tiny explosive noises made by the glowing snails he crushed beneath his steel-reinforced boots. "He is a seraph—fallen, but a seraph. If his goal was to defeat us rapidly and certainly, then surely he could do it with his own muscle or magic."

"Okay, then why the menagerie merry-go-round?" Mosiah asked, using his greatsword as a spear to penetrate the tough hide of a lumbering mega-gator.

Phineas thought for a few moments before answering. "The Fallen succumbed to the entire array of sins. Some to lust, others to rage or greed. This Monster-Maker must have fallen victim to jealousy and pride."

"These are his favorite creations. He's showing off," his sister finished.

"And he is confident that he will be able to overwhelm us when he tires of the slaughter."

"Oh how right you are, half-breed," Teratos interrupted, having heard their discussion despite the distance and the din of battle, "I will crush you in my coils, sterile mule, fry the mage with bolts from the sky—"

"You can't frighten us, Abomination!" Damocles broke his silence. "We have the strength of righteousness in us. I vow that we will defeat you and release the people you've enslaved from their bondage."

"'Free the people'? I think you'll find that especially difficult. Oh, you'll see a few of them about—or parts of them, I should say. Humans aren't very useful to me: weak bodies and even weaker minds that go quite insane at the slightest transformation. I can use bits and pieces of them for this or that," he said, scratching behind the ears of what they now realized was a tail-wagging, dog-headed man crouched at the side of his throne, "but mostly they're feed."

"'Bits and pieces—'" Mosiah vomited on the icy floor next to the corpse of the half-bull, half-human he'd just gutted.

The fighting continued. Alerted by a buzzing noise as they banked in for the kill, Phineas planted his twin swords in a snowbank and whipped the M4 carbine off his back. Firing single-shot, he methodically killed bee after buzz-bomb bee, their explosive energies dissipating harmlessly in the air, reloading and continuing like a machine while his sister protected him from threats at ground level. After the bees were dealt with, Phineas whipped the carbine around to fire a string of rounds across the stadium at Teratos, but all of them ricocheted from a magical *Shield* the fallen had erected.

But even when their attention was ground-focused, keeping their footing on the blood-slicked ice wasn't easy, and occasionally one of the four would crush an egg or mushroom, releasing a cloud of noxious fumes or choking spores. *Shield* amulets pushed the toxins aside, as well as providing protection from attacks, but the *Shields* were immobile and their supply was limited.

Hours after the battle began, exhausted and still only half-way across the stadium floor, Damocles called a break. Choosing an ice-free area, the neomage took a small sack from his backpack, and poured salt from it to trace a circle a few yards across. Then Phineas, Cleopatra, and Mosiah hurried in from their protective positions at its rim, and he activated a *Charmed Circle* amulet, the shimmering ward springing up along the salt line. Then, using another amulet, he opened a *Shield* with the same perimeter. If Phineas was right about the Monster-Maker merely toying with them, then the fallen seraph would probably have allowed them to rest and regain their strength unmolested, but the neomage couldn't afford to take chances.

While the others ate and tended to their battered bodies and equipment, Damocles settled down onto the concrete to recharge his prime and the assortment of *Healing, Shield, Boost, Counter-Conjure, Vibro-Blade,* and other amulets they'd burned through. He didn't have time to perform a complicated ritual, so he cleared his mind of all external stimuli and opened it fully to his prime amulet; he'd recharge that through his *Link* to the creation energy power sink underneath the New Orleans Enclave, use that energy to charge the other amulets, and then top-off his prime once more.

But nothing happened. The *Link* conjure in his prime was intact, but somehow he couldn't find the power sink. With increasing desperation he tried two more times, before realizing what had been bothering him at a subconscious level for some time: His *Link* to the power sink, to the Enclave, had been severed since they'd emerged into the stadium. They were cut off as if they'd gone deep into an underground hellhole.

Damocles was shaken, but didn't want to let his champards see it. He shifted his position to put himself in contact with some steel reinforcing rods sticking out of the cracked concrete and drew energy from that exposure-limited source. It was enough to partially recharge his prime and some of the most important amulets, but unless they stopped frequently to do this again, eventually they'd be down to only their personal strength. And if need be, the mage could draw creation energy from his champards to power his conjures—if he could force himself to do it.

The mage passed out the recharged amulets and then ordered the group to move out again. His champards grumbled, but quickly quieted down— there wasn't any way to restore their strength to full. During the weeks coming north from New Orleans, there'd been enough members of Damocles's assault force to permit rotating positions so that they could take turns in a protected middle spot after a tiring shift on point, in rear guard, or on night watch. He had no extra troops now, and fatigue preyed on them as hungrily as the Monster-Maker's beasts.

Even momentary pauses in the fight provided little relief. More than once during a lull they were startled by the threatening sound of unseen rattle-rats; the few times they did spot the little creatures, the rats scurried away from too close an approach without a fight. But even such non-threats proved tiring as the group reacted to the sound, then relaxed, and then had to force themselves back into ambush-ready battle status. And real ambushes were frequent.

At one point, a crippling wave of nausea overcame all four of them at the same time, just before the two-pronged attack of a mixed pack of Texas longhorn dire wolves and normal-sized winged wolves. Despite their discomfort, they managed to dispatch the wolves—some of which seemed to be suffering from the nausea themselves—but the waves of sickness didn't abate. The *Counter-Conjure* amulet Damocles triggered had no effect, and when Phineas cast his better-than-human senses about for an unseen menace, the best he could do was determine that something invisible was flying somewhere above them. "Shotgun spread!" Damocles ordered, and Cleopatra fired a handful of shots into the air. Unsurprisingly, the blasts didn't hit anything, but once the fast-moving clouds of pellets were in the air, Damocles cast a *Ferro-kinesis* conjure and steered the pellets in a searching pattern back and forth across the enclosed space. It took only a few passes before one tiny pellet hit something, and then all the pellets veered toward that spot, tearing a suddenly-visible giant bat apart as it ceased its ultrasonic screams and fell dead to the ground. And just as abruptly, the illness that had afflicted Damocles and his champards ceased.

An immeasurable time later, a swarm of hand-sized grasshoppers came at the invaders from all sides. Apparently the cold made them sluggish, and moving at mage speed Damocles, Cleopatra, and Phineas easily killed all their attackers before any got close enough to employ their wicked-looking mandibles. Even at mere human speed Mosiah mostly held his own, but a few managed to bite holes through his armor before he could kill them. Suddenly a barracougar pounced on Mosiah from atop a pinnacle of ice. Slapping a hand to a conjure amulet hidden in a brass buckle, Damocles shattered exposed steel and aluminum fittings protruding from the ice, creating bursts of metal fléchettes that sliced into the big cat, but not before it bit through Mosiah's weakened armor, tearing a chunk out of his shoulder and rendering his left arm useless.

Although the human was in the worst condition, by this time they were all seriously wounded, and the *Healing* amulets were long drained. The conditions were fulfilled; the situation was dire.

Waving Phineas and Cleopatra into defensive positions around them, Damocles called out: "Mage in battle, mage in dire, seraphs, come with holy fire."

There was no way to predict when the mage-in-dire call would be answered. It would depend on how close the nearest seraphs were, if the seraphs were listening, if they had other—

With a crash the ice covering three of the holes in the roof shattered, and a trio of seraphs burst into the stadium. Two had black hair that streamed backward to blend with their black wings, their dark armor reflecting silvery glints as they moved. These two sized up the situation and immediately darted toward Teratos, their long, straight swords held out before them.

The third descended to land a little ways in front of the mortals, clearing a space among the monsters with a burst of elemental wind. He wore golden armor that almost matched his hair.

"Yes," Cleopatra exclaimed, fervor brightening her tired eyes. "With three seraphs we outnumber him!"

"Alas," the third seraph sighed. "The fallen one was a higher order than us when he enjoyed the communion of the High Host."

"'A higher order'?" she asked, devoting most of her flagging energy to the almost-mechanical slaughter of a new wave of mutated animals.

As the Ravens crossed the intervening space, a howling headwind rose up, slowing their advance. Flocks of blue-white seagulls circled over the seraphs at almost roof height and rained icicles onto them. As the ice hit the Ravens's bodies and wings, it spread out, creating a coating that resisted their efforts to shake it off. More icicles fell and the coat of ice got thicker, heavier, stiffer, slowing the Ravens' progress against the wind. Eventually, unbelievably, the ice covered the seraphs from head to toe and wingtip to wingtip, and they plummeted downward.

"These *minor* seraphs merely carry out His will," Teratos smirked. "*I* reflected His perfection back at Him every moment of *time*."

Phineas looked at Taharial quizzically. "That was the meaning of his name," the seraph responded quietly, "when he had his name."

"But now I alone create, while He is nowhere to be seen!"

The ice-bound Ravens crashed to the stadium's concrete floor, the impact fracturing their icy straitjackets. As they shucked off the remnants of the ice, the seraphs were set upon by a pack of silent coyotes. Not stopping to deal with the canines, they returned to the sky, dragging with them a number of coyotes that had fixed their lamprey jaws on parts of the seraphs's bodies not covered by armor, where their seraphic energies shone through. The coyotes began sucking creation energy like blood from the Ravens, who, without stopping to discuss a plan, paused in flight and blasted each other with the concentrated power of the Sun, reducing the creatures to ash while leaving the seraphs untouched. Freed, they resumed their flight toward Teratos.

Damocles had hung back when the seraph came down to face them—when *this* seraph came down to face them—pointedly fixing his attention on the battle in the sky and on the struggles immediately at hand. But now Damocles stepped forward to face the seraph who'd answered his summons. "Taharial. You've come again."

"You are remembered, mage of steel, as I once promised."

"Well, at least this time there's something you *can* do. Heal us."

"I am yours to command," and with a gesture golden light streamed from the seraph and healed and reinvigorated the mortals.

"Right. Now it's our turn. Taharial, you stay with us, give us cover from the air and take out whatever you can at range."

As Taharial took to the air, the voice of the seraph's former comrade boomed across the stadium. "You follow his commands, brother? You rise to attack me? What is mage that thou are mindful of him?"

"Do you feel no compulsion in his presence, Corruptor?" Taharial asked, receiving only a puzzled look from the fallen seraph. "No. No, I see that you do not."

"You debase yourself, Hand of Purification. What does Scripture have to say about us? *Thou was perfect in thy ways from the day that thou wast created. Thine heart was lifted up because of thy beauty.'* But what does Scripture say about the creation of mortals? *'And the Lord God formed man of the dust of the earth'.* As for the *accidents*," he looked sidelong at the neomage and mules, "where is the Scriptural blessing for them? They aren't created in His image. They're not *creations* at all, for on the seventh day did not He cease from His creating?"

The accusation hit Damocles hard. There did seem to be one reference in the Scriptures to mages: "Suffer not a witch to live."

Damocles silently glared at the fallen seraph, but his companions weren't cowed.

"What do the Scriptures say?" Phineas bellowed. *"Be afraid, for he beareth not the sword in vain!"* as he charged forward.

Not to be outdone, Cleopatra let loose her war cry, *"Thus shall the Lord do to all your enemies against whom ye fight!"*, punctuating it by felling a snake-headed ox with a single swipe of her ax.

The newly healed Mosiah joined in with, *"Woe be unto you for perverting the ways of the Lord!"* The animals they fought paid no attention, but those weren't the ears the war cries were intended for.

The excitement of the moment quickly gave way, though, to the grim slog of death, and only occasionally in the battle did *"Be afraid!"*, *"Woe!"*, and *"Thus shall the Lord do!"* ring out again.

The Ravens eventually won through to Teratos, diving at him from either side, swords forward. The fallen seraph reared up, extending the blue-white wings that had been hidden behind his back. With a shimmer of light Teratos manifested dark demon iron armor, shield, and a sword half again as long as those carried by the Ravens. Springing into the air, the winged serpent whipped his coils around one of the Ravens, momentarily immobilizing him, while his over-sized human upper body engaged the second in sword-and-shield combat. The seraph steel of the Raven's armor and weapon was stronger than the demon iron of Teratos's manifestations, and each ringing blow was accompanied by the sizzle of the weaker iron being ablated away, but the Fallen's devices held his opponent off long enough for him to marshal gale-force winds that blasted the Raven across the stadium.

The other Raven was too strong to crush, but a bluish pallor spread across his armor and skin from where his body touched the serpent's scales. Inch by inch the Raven succumbed to creeping paralysis, and once he was entirely incapacitated, Teratos loosed his serpent coils, dropping the seraph crashing to the ground—again. By which time the other Raven had recovered and begun fighting his way across the sky back to Teratos. The jumbled terrain prevented the ground-bound fighters from seeing the missing Raven until, a few minutes after he fell, he again rocketed into the air, slicing his way through a cloud of winged rattlesnakes to get to their exemplar.

Watching the Ravens' repeated defeats in glimpses between attacks on the ground, Mosiah asked Taharial, "Why only three seraphs? That's not many to take on a major Dark power."

"It is foretold: Alongside the omega, three will suffice."

"What's an omega?" the human asked, but Taharial either didn't hear him or refused to answer.

"I wouldn't put much faith in prophecies, dust-of-the-earth," Teratos thundered. "Unless you want to consider my victory inevitable. Scripture says: *'Great beasts came up. The first was like a lion, and had eagle's wings. And behold another beast, and they said thus unto it "Arise, devour much flesh." And lo another, like a leopard, which had upon the back of it four wings of a fowl, and dominion was given to it. And behold a fourth beast, and it had great iron teeth, it devoured and brake in pieces, and stamped the residue with the feet of it.'* All these and more I have created, and you are hardly the Ancient of Days to cast me from my throne." If Taharial responded, they didn't hear it over the fallen seraph's laughter.

Even with three seraphs fighting in the air, the fighting continued on much as before. The seraphic aid the invaders received was countered by a more serious effort on the part of Teratos, who now hurled more dangerous creatures and his own personal energies at Damocles, his champards, and the three seraphs. When electric eagles screeched overhead, releasing deadly blue-white lightning bolts from their beaks, the electricity changed direction in midair, attracted to Taharial's upraised sword. The seraph gathered up the energy and hurled it at Teratos, but it couldn't penetrate the Fallen's *Shield*.

More than once the attackers got tantalizingly close to Teratos; close enough to throw hand grenades and mage metal knives and to fire close-range rifle bullets that, unfortunately, bounced off his *Shield* just as the long-range attacks had. But then they'd be dragged back by the grasping tongues of titanic frogs or pushed back by oversized armored bull-dozers.

Bursting out of a dark tornado that had temporarily held him, Taharial himself taunted the fallen seraph. "You only delay the inevitable, Corruptor. We will win through to you. As it is written, *'Over My faithful servants thou hast no power'.'*"

"*Faithful*, my brother? There is not a mortal born without sin. And where there is sin, *'I shall come upon them from before them and from behind them and from their right hands and from their left hands, and Thou wilt not find most of them faithful unto Thee'.*" And as if to punctuate his point, acid-dripping centi-cattle attacked from all sides on the ground, while Teratos directed concussive thunderclaps at the flying seraphs from his perch on his ice throne.

The Monster-Maker's supply of mutated creatures seemed endless, his own personal power effectively limitless, and the battle almost hopeless.

"We can't fight him with swords or guns, Taharial, and we're wasting time trying to fight him with words." Damocles interrupted. "I need power!"

"It would not be wise, mage-lord."

"I don't care about wise, Taharial. I can destroy them now, but I need more power. Get down here and give me the power!"

Taharial alighted on the concrete a few yards from the neomage and turned his face upward, silently calling the Ravens down from their aerial fight. Rage distorted their angelic faces, but they took their positions on the ground, forming a triangle with Damocles at the apex, the Ravens facing stiffly inward. Taharial, standing in the middle of the formation, spoke to those outside of it: "Mage champards, you must protect your mastrend from the onslaught of Darkness on all sides while we work. He must not be disturbed."

Dropping his combat stance, Damocles stood straight and still facing the oncoming demon horde, one hand clutching the prime amulet on its chain around his neck, the other holding his sword's tip pointed at the serpent perched above his sea of minions. Creation energy poured from the Ravens, fierce beams of brilliant sky-blue and blinding sun-yellow streaked with the other colors of the rainbow blazing from their hearts, striking Taharial's outstretched wings and being absorbed by them. The Seraph of Chastity took the energy, calmed it, and fed it in a steady silver-wrapped stream into the prime-amulet chain around the battle mage's neck.

Ravens radiated the powers of Air and Sun, but like all seraphs they had within them energy from every element. At first Damocles cast conjures he knew well, using the Ravens' minor stores of Metal creation energy to sharpen and strengthen his own Metal mage attacks: spears of sharpened steel girders, coils of writhing copper wires, and crumpled wreckage cannonballs he hurled against Teratos. But as he gained confidence, he drew on their other energies to deal with threats to himself and his band.

Teratos raised a flock of foul pigeons that rained burning droppings from the sky, but Damocles pulled Air from the wings of the Ravens and battered the birds against the far corners of the stadium roof.

A cloud of acid gnats descended around Damocles's head, but he pulled Sunlight from the faces of the Ravens and vaporized the tiny monsters.

Cleopatra called out from her position behind and to the side of him, and glancing away from the fight before him, the battle mage saw his champard fall under a gout of acid spat by a phalanx of towering garden slugs. Damocles drew the water elements from the Ravens, throwing clouds of stinging Sea salt onto the sensitive skin of the slugs, and using a localized rain of clean River water to wash the caustic sputum off the half-breed. Then energy from the elements of Earth and Stone to heal Cleopatra and his other champards and give them the endurance and strength to continue fighting their defensive battle.

When the ground beneath the neomage's feet trembled and cracked and great stone-chewing worms burst forth, Damocles drew more Earth and Stone magic from the Ravens and collapsed their underground burrows, crushing the worms' vulnerable bodies under tons of dirt and concrete.

He used Air to blast galloping scorpi-horses with lightning. And still more Stone energy to pin honking multi-colored geese to the ground under their many-times-multiplied weight before they could even reveal what threat they posed to the attackers.

With the power of the seraphs he utterly devastated the ranks of the Monster-Maker's monsters. Even stampeding cattle were calmed and then lulled into sleep with a touch of Moon power.

Damocles hadn't scored any direct hits against Teratos, but neither had the fallen seraph been able to prevent the attackers from advancing. Their progress was punishingly slow, but it was also inexorable.

Phineas began to shout, but his words were cut off. Spinning to face his friend, Damocles was momentarily shocked to look *through* one of the now-translucent Ravens, and even more stunned to see only the body of his warrior champard on the trampled ground, dismembered, the ends of his limbs smoldering, his head rolled a short distance away. Gigantic crabs advanced on Damocles and the seraphs, sparks flying from the demon iron-lined edges of their claws. The battle mage disintegrated the demon iron with a seraph-enhanced Metal conjure and then turned back to Teratos.

Cleopatra and Mosiah repositioned themselves to try cover the gap left by Phineas's death, but even assuming that Damocles would handle all threats within his field of vision, the task was too much for only two of them. "Dam, if you're gonna do something," Mosiah yelled back over his shoulder, "you'd better do it soon. We don't stand a snowball's chance."

"A snowball's—" A suspicion had been growing at the back of Damocles's mind for some time. He opened himself wide and examined Teratos with the powerful full-senses scan he'd developed. He saw the aura around the fallen seraph, and deeper he saw the braided filaments of creation energy that made up its otherworldly nature: Earth, Air, Water, Stone, Metal, Light, all the magical elements—all the elements but one.

Damocles knew no Fire conjures—nobody did, really. A simple cantrip to start or put out a campfire, sure, but nothing like what he'd need now. He'd have to improvise, take the basic fire spell, power it with elemental Fire from the Ravens. Creation energy flowed into him from the Ravens through Taharial—Fire energy he was never meant to touch. Damocles doubled over in pain. It had to be released before it consumed him, but unlike the other power he'd drawn from the seraphs, this energy resisted his attempts to channel it through his prime amulet. It burst forth uncontrolled, like fireworks shooting randomly at monstrosities to the left, one of his champards to the right, and ineffectually into the sky.

He had to bind it into a form. Without an appropriate conjure, he returned to Scripture—"Uh, *The Lord went before them by day in a pillar of smoke and by night in a pillar of fire!'*," and a writhing serpentine torrent of flame sprang forth from the point of Damocles's sword, while the crystal in the pommel began to glow from within, pulsing in time with his heartbeat. The flame didn't seem to want to lance directly at Teratos, but Damocles experimentally shifted it around and found that aiming it at a point on the roof of the arena above the fallen seraph's throne brought a pillar of fire pouring downward onto the icy demon.

With a scream of pain, Teratos tried snaking to the side, but Damocles easily followed his movements with the pillar from above. The fallen seraph raised shields of ice, snow, rain, and freezing fog, but the fire punched through them, raising new screams as the flames renewed their consuming thaw. Damocles echoed his enemy's screams, the pain he'd felt at first when the Fire entered his body turning into burgeoning strength, his cries turning into cheers of exultation. "We have him! *I* have him! Nothing's going to stop me! His fate is mine, and *I condemn him*—"

A thunderous explosion threw Cleopatra, Mosiah, and every mortal monstrosity unconscious to the ground, and blasted the battered remains of the roof away in all directions. Twisted steel girders and hundredweight boulders of ice fell onto the bodies below, crushing many animals, but miraculously missing the two champards.

When Cleopatra and Mosiah awoke uncounted minutes or hours later, they saw Taharial, armor- and weapon-less, wearing robes of unblemished white, standing within the triangle formed by three scars scorched into the concrete beneath his feet. A fourth circle of blasted rock still smoked at the far end of the arena. The seraph offered no words of consolation or explanation or excoriation to the mortals. They would have to wrestle on their own with what they saw, heard, and felt that day, and then decide how they would tell the story to the people of New Orleans, now and in coming generations, on their return home.

After a moment's consideration of the omega mage's ashes already scattering on the wind, his remaining champards picked up his sword, remarkably unscathed by the energies that had rushed through it. Reverently, they carried it away. And through it all Taharial silently wept.

Wheels in Motion
52 PA / 2064 AD

Faith Hunter

Daria bent over the fire, feeding green branches to the flames, a sort of living sacrifice to the night. Power grew in the fire and she absorbed the released energy. Using the life stored in the branches was only one step away from becoming a death mage, but, unlike a neophyte, Daria had control over her power lust. She would not steal the life-force of another mage or a human, or rape the life from the flora and fauna on the face of the Earth.

Beside her was Evelyn, a Moon mage. They sat so that Daria's right shoulder brushed Evelyn's left. Daria faced north; Evelyn faced the rising Moon in the east. The moon mage lifted her face to the Moon, drawing in power, transferring it to the boulder buried beneath the ground a scant ten paces from them.

To Daria's left, facing west, was Woodrift, a River mage. A stream gurgled nearby, swollen by melting winter snow. He had stood in the icy water for hours, filling himself with energy and creating a power sink in the ground water below them. Even Daria could feel the hum of energy he had gathered, whispering in the earth, counterpoint to and energizing her own life-force gift.

Beside Evelyn and Woodrift, facing south, his back to Daria, sat a first generation kylen, Emilel, whose gift was rare—the gift of Fire. He was Daria's son, one of her first-born. Emilel had borrowed a sigil from an angel of punishment, and, though he was fully grown and full of the energies of the High Host, he could be in their presence for four hours before they all gave in to mage heat. If it was discovered that he had taken the sigil, he would be severely punished, perhaps denied access to the Earth until the end of time. But he was willing to risk it to set into play the incantation that would save his father, the watcher Barak, who had been captured by the Darkness.

The incantation should be finished by then, the genetics of the two unwilling ones merged, drawing them together. With Fire gift, drawing on the seraphic energies of the newly created Realm of Light, they could create an incantation of unimaginable power. And as long as they didn't slip into the use of Scripture to empower the conjure, the Most High might never notice. Might not. They all risked their lives on that hope.

In the distance, an owl called, a lonely hooting sound followed by abbreviated hoots as it sought the presence of its mate. Taking that as an omen, Daria lifted her arms, her dark skin glistening in the light of the fire, her curly hair reflecting the flames.

"I seek the sound of lovers, heavy beneath the moon," she said of Evelyn's gift, threading her power through the Moon mage's, gathering it up into her own.

"I seek the echo of passion, bright as flaming wings," she said of Emilel's element, accepting as he gave over his gift to her use.

"I seek the timbre of ardor, essential as the water of life." She pulled Woodrift's hoarded power into her, feeling the energies rise up through the ground like a mist.

"I seek the song of devotion, heartbeat of the earth." Daria wove the massed power together, into a skein of energies, a tapestry of a working.

She repeated the chant, over and over, as they all sank into the working, merging the powers of creation energy into one purpose, one function.

With a small part of her consciousness, she sought out the watcher, knowing he was waiting for her, eager; knowing he had just been tortured yet again, and that his blood flowed; knowing that he resisted the blandishments of the Dark for her, for the power of their love, and for their children, the kylen.

Barak, his mind so clouded with pain it was like a ruptured dam, spilling out, destroying all in its path. But the spirit hand she held out offered respite, and he looked up from the pallet of his shorn wings, from the floor of the barred cave that kept him prisoner. Mentally, he took the hand and sighed as the massed power of the elemental ring eased his pain. "Tell me," he said softly.

"Can we not simply lift you," she murmured, "and take you from this cell?"

"The rock walls are woven with Darkness," he said. "It would render me nigh unto death, a husk until the end of time."

"Then know this," she whispered. "In two generations there will be born a litter of mages capable of merging with a seraph, mind to mind, without mage heat, without danger of censure from the Most High and the High Council of the Seraphim. I will send one to you—trade one for you, if need be—but send one close, so that you might sense him, know him, and merge with him. The weapon you create together will surely bring you to the notice of the Most High."

"And our hopes will be fulfilled," he said. "Souls for the neomages, redemption for the watchers."

"And permission for our union," she pressed.

Barak folded his mind against hers, a purr of love and need sparking and sparkling through her. "Always that, my love, in this world and in the one to follow. Soul to soul, mind to mind, spirit to spirit. Forever."

Daria pulled her thoughts from him, easing away, retreating like mist from sunlight. This time, she saw the energy mesh that rested just below the surface of the cell walls, like a sieve that would disrupt the life-force of any who sought to pass through. She had been lucky not to be trapped by it, burned by it, and mentally she shuddered at the thought of what so much Dark energy would have done to the circle of power.

Returning to the tapestry they were weaving, she considered the genealogy of the candidates. And she chose two who seemed most likely to produce an omega mage, a mage who could force her will upon the High Host—and perhaps upon the Most High as well. Dangerous. Dangerous indeed. And a sin worthy of a horrible death, or, worse, a never-ending half-life of eternal pain. A sin that Evelyn and Woodrift had no idea they were contributing to. Deception, thy name is Daria.

Bait
53 PA / 2065 AD

Faith Hunter

Achmed bowed his head. "All glory be to the one creator god, Allah, and to His holy ones." His chains rattled softly, the demon iron burning his wrists, in spite of his affinity with metals. The scent of gangrene was only faint at the moment, but if help was long in coming he would lose the use of his hands.

Deliala laughed softly. "Not exactly a traditional response, Achmed. There is no need to feel hurt or shame at being bested by a succubus. You are, after all, only human."

He closed his eyes against the allure of her voice. "Allah refines me in the fires of Hell. Allah seeks to teach me strength and great use of creation energy. Allah is one and Mohammed is His prophet."

"Allah has abandoned you," she said tartly, "to me, to do with as I will. You are familiar with the ancient story of Job, as told in the tales of the sons of Judah, your enemies."

Allah has not abandoned me. He has not. He shivered as Deliala trailed her fingers across his naked chest. Her nails raked, drawing blood close to the surface of his skin, welts that ached in the cold air of the hellhole. Achmed knew that to engage in discourse was foolish, perhaps even deadly, but to stay silent left him with only the scent of her to focus on. And his need of her was growing. He had been chosen for the role of bait because he was strong in the Prophet. He was the least likely of all his Enclave companions to give in to temptation, the one most likely to resist, allowing then others to carry the battle into the deeps before they were discovered. Yet he wanted this woman who was neither human nor mage. He wanted this image of physical perfection, though he knew she was immoral, iniquitous, a sister to the Darkness who slept in the deepest chamber of the cave.

He licked his lips, tasting her on his mouth where she had kissed him with an unholy kiss. Desperate, he whispered, "My people and the people of Judah are enemies no longer. The seraphs have willed it so."

"Enemies forever," she spat. He heard the spittle land and the soft sizzle of acid on the dust at his feet. "The infidels and the false seraphs have brought you only pain and loss of life. I—*my master* can give you victory over them all."

"Allah is great. Before Him there is no other."

The stone to which he was chained vibrated, a faint tremor. Deliala tilted her head, as if she too felt the quake and was puzzled by the sensation. But Achmed knew what it was, and triumph shot through his veins like lightning. It was the sound of rescue. It was the sound of battle. Finally, at long last, they had come.

In the distance, he heard the clang of clean steel on demon iron—a scream of pain. With a sudden hard crunch of his jaw, he broke through the false tooth, revealing to his tongue the nugget of pure gold hidden beneath. With the power of his mind, he activated the amulet and felt the surge of creation energy that in an instant replenished his body's vigor.

With one hand, Deliala reached for her knife. The other grew talons. But it was too late. Power wrapped around and threaded through Achmed. "Death to the infidel," he screamed. He completed the incantation. Fierce glee roared through him. "Whoever seeks power should know that *all* power belongs to Allah!" he shouted, reciting from the Koran. Fire blasted from his bound hands, leaping out to engulf the succubus.

A whirlwind of flame roared to the stone ceiling of his prison chamber. The demon iron shackles crackled and cracked and fell at his feet. For the first time in untold hours Achmed was free; the succubus mere ashes at his feet. Naked, he rooted in the corner for his robes. He would not shame his god by appearing clothed only in his sin. Dressed, he wiped his mouth free of the kiss of evil. And he raced into the hallway, shouting his battle cry, "Praise be to Allah!"

Karida met him in the darkened hall, her body glowing bright with mage attributes. Her tribal Bedouin mage-warrior tattoos glistened with gold and copper, the precious metal dust having been thrust beneath her skin with both needle and incantation. Hilt first, she tossed his sword high into the air, followed by his kris-knife, and he caught both, whirling into the walking horse stance of savage blade as the first of the spawn scampered into the tunnel.

"Allahu akbar," she crooned, the words the opening to her favorite battle incantation, "Allah is able to do all things." From her tattoos burst fire and light. Left-handed, she threw a vial of oil into the flame. The scent of rosemary and myrrh filled the long narrow space. Spawn crisped into dust.

Ashes and Dust
57 PA / 2069 AD

Diana Pharaoh Francis

1.

Mistral smelled the daywalker long before he saw him. He was overdue for his so-called schooling, and he'd been expecting someone. A messenger of his slavemaster: a dragon chained but not helpless. Never helpless.

Mistral's stomach tightened with dread memories. His lips peeled from his teeth in a silent snarl. Anger, frustration, fear. No point in running. Trees crowded the excuse for a road, making it impossible to turn around. Not that he would run. He'd not leave his mules to be torn apart.

Not much time. He pulled the team to a halt. He'd been leading them up the steep grade to Tarrytown, the last stop for trading before heading for the hellhole. The tires on his brightly painted caravan were mostly bald. He hoped to replace them in town.

The mules protested, tossing their heads and snorting, eyes rolling white. They could smell the Darkness closing in. Mistral spoke softly to them, reaching out to stroke their necks and scratch behind their ears. Gradually they lowered their heads. Ben rubbed his head up and down Mistral's shoulder, rubbing at the itch beneath his halter. Buck thrust his nose against the man's chest, demanding a treat. The pair's bridles hung loose around their necks. Mistral tended to lead the team, rather than drive them. The caravan was already heavy enough and the hardy beasts had pulled it many miles this season.

Once they calmed, Mistral dropped the ropes. "You two stay here."

He'd long ago taught them to ground-tie and trusted they'd not run off without a good reason. The coming daywalker provided a better than good reason, though creatures of Darkness were no strangers to them. Darkness clung to Mistral like a shadow. His master kept a close watch on him wherever he went. Mistral would not be allowed to slip his leash.

He rolled his shoulders, the memories of unending pain shooting fire down his nerves. His entire existence was pain. Day and night punished him for living. Only the twilight of morning and dusk and the gray of overcast days granted him any ease at all.

Mistral strode back to the caravan, reaching up under the seat to touch the wooden amulet he'd placed there. It throbbed with ready power. He activated it. Magic rolled outward from the spell inlaid in the wood, pulsing through and around him and the mules. The two shifted uneasily, but remained where they were. It wasn't the first time he'd used the protective amulet. Hopefully it wouldn't be the last.

He returned to the front of the mules. Picking up their leads, he clicked to them. "Let's go now, boys. Not far now."

Ben and Buck started up the track again, the protective ring of magic Mistral had activated moving with them. It was a strong working, and one he kept charged at all times. Easy enough, since his element was everywhere. Life itself. Or the potential.

The product of a Dark mage mating with a captured seraph, Mistral was unlike any other creature in the world. Half neomage, his other half captured seraph, he was a creature of neither Light nor Darkness, but of the space between. He clung to that knowledge. Neither side had claimed him, nor would anyone else. He might be a slave, but he'd never be one of them.

He drew his power from the air, from the fertility of the ground, from water, even stone. When he drew down hard, he not only killed everything around him, he sterilized it forever. He made a habit of sipping his way through the world, stealing nibbles of life here and there where the taking did little harm.

Mistral smiled. He could suck evil dry just as fast as anything else, whether the evil came from the Most High, the Darkness trapped underground, or the daywalker that hunted him now. Which was why his dragon master had him watched and made him return at the end of every season to remind him who he served. And to breed with whatever creatures his master splayed in front of him.

So far Mistral had proved sterile, for which he was eternally grateful. Not that he gave thanks to the Most High, or the Most Low, for that matter.

They'd not gone much farther up the rutted road—perhaps a mile— when Ebet emerged from the shadow of a tree. He moved into the center of the road to face Mistral, his movements flickering fast. The daywalker was inhumanly beautiful, with black hair that hung to his waist and a lithe, muscular body. They were all of a kind—black hair, slender, piercing eyes, and Michelangelo faces. And evil.

"You are late for your lessoning," Ebet said, his voice sweet as a clarinet. "The master grows anxious."

"The roads washed out south of the delta. I was trapped on the wrong side." The floods and delay were not news. Nor did they make the delay forgivable.

Ebet dipped his chin, a slow, vicious smile curving his mouth. "I am to remind you to hurry." He lifted his hand and held it out. Dangling from his fingers was a collar.

Mistral blanched despite himself.

Ebet saw and his smiled widened into a dimpled grin, revealing his too-long canine teeth. The only outward mark of what he was, aside from the red flickering in the depths of his eyes. "I asked the master to let me bring it to you myself. And to make sure you put it on. Come now. It's time."

Mistral's hands clenched tight on the lead ropes. Refusal to put it on would invite worse punishment.

Uncurling his fingers from the ropes, Mistral let them go. A word anchored them to the dirt. The mules might bolt with what happened next. They were safer here. From Ebet and from himself. The protective ward should last until the punishment was done. He hoped.

Mistral went back to the driver's seat. There he removed his cloak and hat. His shirt was next. He removed his belt pouch and knives next, and finally his boots and socks. His master's punishments tended to wreck good clothing. He'd only just broken in these boots. He didn't remove the wide silver cuffs that circled his wrists. They anchored the spells hiding his true nature. Nor did he remove the collection of amulets he wore on the chain belt around his waist.

He turned and walked out of the protective circle. The bright light of morning sent lashes of agony over his exposed skin as he approached Ebet.

"Kneel," the daywalker ordered. Eagerness danced in his eyes.

It took all Mistral had to lower himself.

The collar was made of hide, though of no animal that walked above ground. Copper threads picked out words that Mistral did not understand. The buckle was gold etched with arcane symbols. The daywalker put the collar around Mistral's neck, drawing it tight enough to make breathing a struggle.

Ebet grinned. His pale fingers lingered a moment on the collar and he spoke a string of nonsense. Words of power taught to him by the master, Mistral knew. Words now only spoken among the Most High's minions and the Fallen. Ebet likely had no idea what they meant.

That was his last coherent thought.

The master knew the art of pain—how to make it unbearable while tethering his victim to consciousness, how to loop time so that the torture spanned a year or ten while only a moment passed in this plane.

No words could describe Mistral's suffering. He was slowly torn apart and put back together. Again and again. His skin was peeled away and his muscles were unstrung from his bones. His wings were broken into matchsticks and then uprooted from his back. Massive black talons skewered him. He should have died, but he did not. Nor did he cry out or beg, though he knew the master wished for it. Eventually the agony would give him no choice, but he'd keep his screams bottled up for as long as he could.

All the while he heard the guttural scrape of his master's voice inside his head. *You are* mine. *Never forget, puny worm. It's almost time for you to become what you were born to be—a sword in my hand to fell the Most High and all his minions, to take back the world above and bend it to my rule. These chains will not hold me much longer.* The dragon's voice resounded through Mistral's skull, echoing and crashing until he thought he might shatter.

He woke flat on the ground, his body drenched in sweat. The lash of the light seemed almost sweet after his master's torment. Mistral rolled onto his back, ignoring the rocks beneath him. The glamour hiding his wings was more than a mere illusion—it made them invisible to others, certainly, but it also made them insubstantial so that he could wear clothing and sit in a chair. Right now he wanted nothing more than to remove the spell and shake out his feathers. He wanted to fling himself into the sky and feel the powerful sweep as he rose on the winds. It was always like that after his master came for him. He dreaded that one day the dragon would rip them away forever. He didn't know if he could survive it.

Ebet stood over Mistral, nudging him hard in the ribs with his foot. "Was it good, golden boy?" he asked, voice thick with spite.

Mistral sat up. "It was tolerable," he said, his smile doing nothing to hide the rage roiling in his gut.

The daywalker's beautiful face twisted. "Why you?" he spat. "*I* would have taken your gifts and been eternally grateful. But you shit on them and the master who gave them to you."

Mistral laughed, a hash sound. "Gifts? They are shackles, as you know well all too well." He touched the collar around his neck.

Ebet sneered. "You need them. The Light has too much power over you. Your seraph blood makes you weak."

Fury roared in Mistral. He clenched handfuls of dust, his throat working. "Neither Dark nor Light will ever make me bow," he declared. "I'm no filthy cur to be trained and used. Not like you, who grovels in ecstasy at the dragon's feet."

Ebet's hand flicked out in a blur, gripping Mistral's throat. Pointed nails pierced deep into Mistral's flesh. Five runnels of blood ran down his neck and bare chest. "One day the master will decide that you aren't worth the bother anymore. When that day comes, I *will* be there to help him destroy you." He gave Mistral a hard shake, then flung him down onto the road again.

Mistral's gray eyes flattened, hatred spiraling through him. "I don't think so."

He grasped Ebet's foot in a vise-grip and drew hard on the creation energy around him. Power struck him like an avalanche. He gasped. In an instant he was drunk, swollen with power and craving more. He dragged harder, a druggie searching for a better high. Energy electrified his body. His blood pounded and pulsed with unconstrained rapture. What couldn't he do? The whole world was his for the taking, and neither the dragon nor the Most High could stop him.

The bray of the mules broke through his fog of euphoria and thrust a spike of ice through his chest. Recoiling, he made himself release the flow of power. He panted, his ribs bellowing. His body buzzed with stolen creation energy even as disgust rolled through him. He'd given into the greed and arrogance of his blood heritage. If he wanted to kill Ebet, he should have done so with a knife. Drawing deep of creation energy— For a moment he thought he'd vomit.

Mistral clenched his jaw. What was done was done. He swallowed, forcing down the bile and shaking shook away his gray vision. He twisted to look at the mules. Relief crashed through him. The protection circle had kept them safe.

He drew a breath and looked at Ebet's leg, still clutched in his hand. It was white-gray now, as was the rest of the daywalker. Dead lips pulled back in a snarl and his eyes stared wide. The ground beneath them both was powdery and white. The trees on either side of the road had blanched as well, the leaves stiff, the branches spreading above the road like finger bones. No bird would nest in them, no insect would burrow into their trunks, no flame would eat the wood.

The damage wasn't so bad. Only about a twenty foot radius of sterility.

Buck snorted and pawed the ground. Mistral took the hint and clambered to his feet. He hoisted Ebet over his shoulder and strode into the trees. He deposited the daywalker's body in a nearby ravine. Hopefully by the time someone found the body, Mistral would be long gone and they'd not connect it to him.

He found himself growing strangely dizzy as he returned to the road. By the time he reached his caravan, his heart raced and cramps forked through his chest. The wounds on his neck continued to bleed. He fumbled at the collar to remove it, tossing it on the floorboards. Flipping up the padded driver's bench he fished out an old shirt and tied it around his neck to stanch the bleeding.

By the time he'd drawn his clothing back on, cold sweat turned his skin clammy and his hands trembled with palsy. His head throbbed and his mouth tasted of metal. What was wrong with him? But the answer came to him on the heels of the question. Ebet had poisoned him. Nothing else made sense. He touched his fingers to the wounds on his neck.

Mistral snarled and activated his *Healing* amulet. It was minor, meant for bone healing or small cuts. The one thing he couldn't make for himself was a decent *Healing* amulet. He'd hoped to buy a good one on this journey, but hadn't found any at the markets. He needed to get to Tarrytown before he passed out. He doubted their doctor could help him, but at least the mules would be safe.

2.

Tarrytown nestled in a flat-bottomed basin in the green coastal foothills, only a few steep forested miles from where Mistral had killed Ebet. The journey should have taken a quarter of a day. As it was, more than half had passed by the time the caravan crested the valley's rim.

Sheep and cashmere goats pocked the green swath of the valley floor, mixed with a few horses and cows. The economy relied on yarns and weaving. The stone and brick buildings of the town sat square in the center, giving residents a long view of approaching visitors. Cottages and barns dotted the rest of the valley.

Mistral drove down the long road, his caravan rumbling over the wood bridge. A river ran swiftly below. He hunched on the driver's bench, the reins looped around his wrists, his body drooping drunkenly. His feet were anvils, his fingers sausages.

He was hardly aware when the mules pulled to a stop outside Harvey's general store across the road from the mill. Boots thumped on the wooden sidewalk.

"Who is it?" a man asked.

"Looks like that tinker's caravan. Woods, right? Mistral Woods?" a woman answered.

Mistral thought her recognized her voice. Older, certainly, with a fierce note of no-nonsense determination. He fought to open his eyes, but they were crusted and far too heavy. Weight rocked the caravan as someone stepped up on the foot ladder.

"What's the matter with him? No, don't touch him! He's sick. What if he's got the plague?"

"If he has, then it's already too late for us," the woman said acerbically. Hands tugged at the make-shift bandage around Mistral's throat. "Anyway, he's probably not sick. Looks like he's been attacked. Help me get him down and call the doc."

"Doc's gone out to the Loomis place," the first man said, closer now.

"Take him back out to the edge of the valley," another man said. "Don't want his kind of trouble here."

"What kind of trouble would that be?" the woman asked. "Afraid he'll bleed on you? If we don't help him, he's sure to die." A cool hand pressed against Mistral's forehead. "He's on fire."

"See there? He's sick with more than just a wound," the first man said.

"Now you've gone and done it, Nara," the second man said. "You could be infected. You both have to be quarantined 'til the doc gives the okay."

"Feathers and locusts," Nara swore. "Charles Flanders, your soul is shriveled as a raisin. You'd better go to kirk right now and pray for more charity."

"Ain't about charity and you know it, Nara," came Flanders' reply. "The man might be carrying plague and if he is, then it's either from the Darkness or he's crossed a seraph. Either way, Tarrytown don't need him waltzing it into our houses and bringing down the High Host's anger on us."

He pronounced Tarrytown as Tarton.

"So you'd let him die?"

"If it be the Most High's plan."

"Well, *I* sure as feathers don't plan to die," Nara said. "And I'm not going to let him either. The good book has something to say about letting others suffer and I mean to obey. Anyway, what if the Most High sent him to us for help and we don't bother? What if helping him *is* the plan?"

Mistral's muzzy mind struggled to keep up with the back and forth. He remembered Nara March now. She was in her fifties, lean and muscular, abrupt, sharp as nails. She always got the better side of a bargain.

"Best take him to your place, then," Charles Flanders said. "Mind that you don't show yourself again in town until the doc clears you. And Nara, if you and yours do die, have the decency to keep your bodies in the house so it's easier to burn out the disease."

Others chuckled and murmured agreement. Nara muttered under her breath epithets that would have caused the kirk elders to burn her at the stake.

"All right, then," she said, dropping back down to the ground. "Let's go."

Mistral heard her click to the mules. The caravan jolted as they started off.

Mistral did not remember arriving at Nara's croft or anything after. Nightmares plagued him. The loathsome face of his dragon master. An enormous eye. Wormy tentacles tipped in razor mouths. A dripping, lipless maw.

The dream dragon raked Mistral with putrefied claws. The beast's ulcerated tongue licked Mistral's neck where the punishment collar had wrapped it. Acid ate deep into his flesh, bubbling and dissolving.

When he thought he must break, must lose himself in the pain and foul Darkness, the dragon spoke, the entire world rumbling with his anger. *If you will not come to me, I will come to you.*

At the end, he heard an explosive noise like a bomb. Like the world cracked in half. It send a shuddering chill through Mistral's gut, loosening his bowels.

The dragon had been working magic in secret and snapped his shackles.

Hell was on its way.

3.

Mistral woke and bounded to his feet, moving at mage speed. He spun around, gaze sweeping his surroundings. A bed, a small window, a dresser, a plank door, a fireplace. Woven rag rugs scattered across the floor. Light edged the curtains. He drew in scents and sounds. Nara and three other humans. Two human heartbeats sounded in the house, and a dozen smaller ones. Dogs or cats, rats or mice. He pushed his senses farther, feeling the hum and spark of life, sorting the bugs and grass and birds out and picking up two humans, sheep, hogs, horses, Buck and Ben, along with an assortment of smaller beasts.

His muscles contracted as he caught a faint hint of . . . something. Had Darkness arrived already? As he stood there, the ground shook, rattling the windows, the pictures on the walls, and the lamps and candlesticks set around the room.

His heart thundered. *Flee!*

He made it to the door, hand on the handle, before reason rejected instinct. He could run. He could maybe even escape for a while. Buck and Ben couldn't. Neither could Nara, who'd taken him in and nursed him. He owed. Out in the far west fringes, you didn't take charity lightly. What was given was usually hard given. Too hard, if it meant he left her and her family to the bloodlust of the dragon and his Darkness. And the mules . . . they trusted him, depended on him. He'd never let them down yet.

If he were a true kylen or a true creature of Darkness, he wouldn't care. But he did, and he clung to that, because it meant he hadn't yet fallen to the blandishments of either side. Not that what they offered promised anything but pain and endless horror.

Mistral released the door and turned away. If he fled, he'd lose all he cared about. He'd lose what honor he could claim and open his soul to the evil of the Dark and the Light. He would become the monster they both wanted him to be. He'd be damned if he'd let that happen.

His mouth twisted. Damned indeed. But if he was going to Hell, or whatever the afterlife had in store, he wasn't going there alone.

Mistral had been stripped to his underwear and he stank. His hair was stiff with dried sweat. A bandage circled his wounds. He pulled it down and checked the damage with his fingertips. The gouges from Ebet's nails had scabbed over. His muscles ached and his legs felt watery, but the poison seemed to have passed from his system.

His clothing sat, clean and folded, on top of the dresser. His chain amulet belt lay on top. He examined them, touching each. They remained charged, except for the *Healing* amulet. He'd exhausted it before ever reaching Tarrytown.

Mistral dressed, clipping on the belt and tying down his knife sheaths. His hat, coat, and boots were nowhere to be seen. Scowling, he headed for the door.

He found himself in a narrow hallway with several doors opening off to the sides. He looked in them. Three bedrooms and a bathroom. He eyed the shower, but stopped only long enough to empty his bladder and scrub his face and hands. The soap smelled of lavender and lemon.

Stairs at the end of the hallway led down into a broad room. On one side was the kitchen and dining area, on the other was a sitting space surrounding a massive fireplace. Mistral paused halfway down. A young boy with red hair sat at the table. Nara chopped vegetables on the slate-covered island. She had a hatchet face with thick iron-gray hair she wore in a braid to her waist. Muscles wrapped her arms in cords. She moved with quick, electric energy. She glanced up.

"Hungry?"

Mistral's stomach growled loudly. "Appears so," he said.

"Stop hovering and grab a seat, then," Nara said, pointing to the table.

While he did as told, she scooped a bowl of soup from a pot on the stove and set it before him, bringing a half a loaf of bread and a crock of butter.

"There's plenty," she said and went back to chopping vegetables.

Silence descended. The boy watched him eat until Nara reminded him of his chores, and then he got up, washed his dishes, and disappeared through the mudroom.

"How long have I been here?"

"Two days, give or take," Nara replied. "Something attacked you."

He nodded, aware of the question pretending to be a statement. What was out there? Was it dangerous to the town?

He surprised himself when he answered with the truth. "A daywalker."

The woman froze, knife raised. "Come again?"

"A daywalker attacked me." Mistral set his spoon down. He watched Nara digest his revelation.

"Seraph's blood. Why was it here?"

He should have said he didn't know. But then he shouldn't have told her about Ebet it all. "He came to see me."

Nara's narrowed. "Why?"

She should have been panicking or dialing up the elders.

The corners of Mistral's mouth quirked in a humorless smile. "Jealousy, I'm afraid. An ugly sin."

"Maybe you should just explain," Nara said, facing him.

Mistral could smell the fear she didn't let him see. Her heart raced. If he dropped into mage sight, he would see the colors of her aura whirling with agitation.

"Ebet's leash was shorter than mine and he had fewer freedoms, so he was jealous. Less was expected of him."

Nara glowered. "If you think you've explained anything, let me be clear. You haven't. You have managed to tell me you were associated with a day-walker, enough to know his name and have him be jealous of you. In most books that puts you on the wrong side of the Light."

The fact that she hadn't tried throwing her knife at him or sprung for the phone was a minor miracle. Mistral didn't know Nara well. He didn't know anybody well, despite the fact that he'd been coming through Tarry-town for years, since he was given permission to travel and learn human ways so he could blend into their society. The dragon wanted to recruit humans to his side in his war against the High Host.

His lips parted and then he hesitated. He'd started down the road to defiance, but he could still turn back. Once he told her, changing his mind would mean killing her and her family, and maybe the rest of the town. If he did that . . . the seraphs would come. They'd want to know what was responsible for that kind of death. That would make the dragon happy. Mistral would be forced to surrender or kill the seraphs. Killing them didn't bother him—he had no love for his winged brethren—but doing so would make the dragon happy, and that was the last thing Mistral wanted to do. Neither did he want to kill the people of Tarrytown. Perhaps he *had* gone too far to stop.

He rubbed a hand over his face. "I am not human," he said at last, his decision made.

Nara flinched back a step. "What are you?"

"I'm—" He hesitated. Technically he was kylen, but he'd never accept that name. A snarl twisted his lips. He would not let the Dark or the Light claim him. With an effort, he focused on Nara again. "Would you like to see?" He'd never willingly showed himself to another person.

Mistral didn't wait for the answer. Something inside him *wanted* to be seen by more than just the dragon and his demon kin, wanted to be seen as himself, not Dark, not Light. He rose and stepped back from the table, dragging his shirt over his head and dropping it on the floor. He pressed his palms together fingertips to wrist so that he could touch the two silver bracelets and deactivate them.

The glamour hiding his wings fell away and he released the spell suppressing the glow of his skin. Nara gasped as he stretched his wings wide. He glanced at them. Cobalt along the lesser coverts, they darkened to iridescent black along the primaries and secondaries. The nervure was dark red, the color of old blood. His skin glowed like moonlight on troubled water, flickering and moving.

"You're—" Nara broke off, frowning. She took a few steps forward and stopped, her brows knitting together. "You're *not* a seraph," she said. "Are you kylen?"

"I am the child of a seraph," he said unwillingly. And then, after a moment— "And Dark mage."

Her eyes widened and her jaw knotted. Fear thickened around her. "And you're friends with a daywalker."

Mistral shook his head. "Not friends. Ebet *did* poison me . . . before I killed him. But I have a Dark master who claims possession of me." His lips twisted. "No more. He is coming. I plan to kill him, but you need to leave. All of you. The entire town. Take everything with you. Our battle will destroy everything. You won't be able to return."

Nara goggled at him a moment, then fury swept her features. "The devil we will! This is our home."

"Stay and you'll die." An observation, not a threat.

She strode over to him, her finger poking hard into his chest as she met his gray gaze. "Take your fight somewhere else and leave us out of it."

He looked down at her hand and then gently wrapped it in his own. "My master is coming here. Did you not feel the earthquake a short time ago? Whether I remain here or not, he will destroy this place. He will enjoy it."

Nara blanched. "Earthquake? Oh mother of demons," she whispered. "Spawn?"

He nodded. "Those too. But my master is a dragon—one of the Fallen."

Her face went white as milk. "The seraphs . . ." she said in a choking whisper.

Mistral's lip curled. "And if you do summon them? Will they protect you? Or will Azrael visit more death and destruction on you?" He shook his head. "The wings of the seraphs are drenched in the blood of humanity."

Nara stared at him. "Blasphemy," she whispered.

"Truth," he countered, his voice gravel.

Taut silence filled the air between them. Mistral waited. Nara's forehead furrowed, her eyes narrowing. He reached out with a mind-skim. Her thoughts ricocheted and crashed into one another, shattering and reforming into other shapes. What surprised him was how she discarded everything beyond survival. She didn't care what Mistral was, only that he was here and he was a weapon against the Dark. Nor did she want to call the seraphs. Like any sane being, she feared them. They were capricious and held little love for humans. Tarrytown would become a battlefield and the residents nothing more than cannon fodder.

He closed his mind off. Nara gathered herself. Strength and determination wrapped around her like steel. Her chin lifted.

"You brought the dragon to us. How will you stop it?"

"I will kill him."

"A dragon. Just like that." She snapped her fingers. "By yourself. Can you really do it or is that just an empty boast?"

"I can. I will." He need only make the beast drop his protective conjures. Mistral would then suck dry his creation energy. Simple as breathing, though the dragon would not make it easy. Mistral wasn't worried. In the end, one of them would be dead and he would be free. He hoped he'd be the one left standing, but at the moment, he didn't really care how he escaped the dragon's clutches, so long as he was free.

"Killing him will kill everything else in the valley at the very least. I am—" He paused, letting go of her hand, his arms dropping to his sides. "I am a living nuclear bomb."

Her lips pinched together and she shook her head. "There has to be another way. When this dragon of yours arrive?"

"A day, maybe two. There *is* no other way."

She crossed her arms again, her chin jutting. "You'd damned well better find one. I know I speak for the whole town. We're not losing everything we have, everything we've built. This mess is your fault. You figure it out."

Mistral blinked at her. She'd accepted everything he'd said, hardly batting an eye. She should hate him. Knowing he was tainted with Darkness—ruled by a dragon—she ought to be running for the hills.

"You don't understand—"

"And I don't care!" she snapped. "You fix this, whatever it takes."

"But—"

"Whatever it takes!" She prodded him in the chest again. "No excuses." She turned and reached for the phone. "I'm calling a town meeting in two hours at the kirk." She eyed him. "I expect you to be there."

Mistral watched her dial. He'd expected vitriol and repulsion. No one liked neomages, and most blindly hated them. But this—

He hardly knew what to make of her. In his whole life, the thing he was was all that mattered. It made him a pawn and a weapon and a target. But Nara expected more. She expected him to have . . . compassion. Honor. *Morals.* To help those in trouble as she'd helped him. To take responsibility for the people he'd endangered.

Lost in thought, he didn't notice her put the phone down.

"What can I do?" She asked him.

And just like that, she put her trust in him. Not in the seraphs or prayers, but him. It was a gift greater than she could ever imagine. Emotion rose in him, thick, hot, and unforgiving. He would not, *could not*, fail that trust.

4.

By dusk two and a half days later, Tarrytown was as prepared as Mistral knew how to make it. The townspeople had not accepted him as Nara had, but once they'd decided he was their best hope, they bent themselves to his orders.

All of them crowded inside the granary with all the arms they possessed, some toting rifles and shotguns. Mistral closed the protective circle he'd established around them. He'd already drawn a similar one around the valley to protect the animals.

"Why don't you just suck up demon lives and use that against them?" Nara had asked over breakfast after he'd explained his power to her.

"Doesn't work that way. I can't pick and choose what I draw from. Even the dirt will die."

Jason, her eldest son, picked apart a slice of bread. "What if you fly up in the air? Wouldn't that cut down the amount of damage on the ground?"

Mistral shook his head. "The dragon will wait for me underground where he is strongest."

"What I'm wondering is why you didn't kill that bastard before you lured it here?" Robert asked, not bothering to hide his hate. He was Nara's younger son. His wife had died and he'd returned home with his son.

Mistral looked around the table. "I wasn't ready then."

"And now you are?" Doubt dripped from the words.

He looked at each of them. "Now I am."

The earthquakes jolted through almost non-stop now as the dragon and his horde tunneled toward Tarrytown. Mistral stood on an outcropping on the south side of the valley, outside the protective circle. He had little faith that it would hold long against the tide of devil-spawn, but he hoped it would give him time enough to find the dragon. He eyed the darkening sky, then reached his senses out. Evil pulsed close.

He touched the pommels of his two swords, one on each hip. He had a variety of knives stashed around his body and a bandolier of six across his chest. A couple dozen throwing stars filled three pouches on his belt and another on his bandolier. He'd activated his *Shield* amulet. They'd keep the beast of Darkness at bay.

The ground lurched and shuddered violently. Grinding filled the night, an avalanche of sound. From a distance, he heard a cracking like the mountains sundering. It echoed through the valley and vibrated through his chest. His heart skipped and jumped, then settled back into its rhythm. Mistral took a breath, anticipation spinning through him.

His lips pulled back in a fierce grin as a river of demonkind gushed from a massive hole in the escarpment just below the shoulder of a nearby peak. He launched himself into the air, drawing both his swords, though in truth they were hardly necessary. He didn't need weapons to kill. Thousands of demons of every shape and size crawled and leaped down the slope to the edge of his protective circle.

Time to go to war.

Mistral folded his wings and plummeted, landing in the middle of a ravenous horde of spawn. His swords whirled as he chopped and slashed, while at the same time drawing in life energy to feed his conjures and amulets. He entered the unrelenting blackness of the hellhole. He needed no light to see—a perk of being born of the Dark.

Soon he felt drunk from the influx of power. His head spun and he staggered over the husks of spawn, his blood frothing. He kept the draw of energy steady, but tried not to push it out into the land. He only needed to kill enough to clear the passage through to where the dragon waited.

Something bounced off his *Shield* near his head and knocked him sideways. He tripped and crashed to his knees. More struck. Boulders the size of tires and larger. They landed in front of him and to the sides. They were thrown by rock trolls, who were able to sink into stone at will. Perfect soldiers for an underground battle.

Mistral blasted the boulders apart and broke into a run, ducking and spinning to avoid the missiles. The barrage continued. He stumbled and staggered over the bodies of the spawn littering the floor. He couldn't seem to overtake the trolls before they disappeared into the walls of the cave.

They continued to torment him until he was driven into a wall of boulders, each the size of his wagon. A grinding sound behind him made him spin around. The cave behind him had collapsed. He was alone. The message was clear: no escape.

Mistral went to work tunneling through the mass of fallen rock in front of him. Not wanting to waste energy, he made holes just large enough to crawl through. He no longer had an easy supply of demons to draw on and he didn't want to kill any more of the world than he had to.

The rockfall was broader and deeper than he expected—maybe fifty feet. The dragon wanted him to exhaust him before they met in battle.

At last he reached the end. Just beyond, a steep, smooth slope led deeper underground, but the passage was too small to spread his wings and float down. Mistral drew one of his swords again and began sidestepping down. He slipped and skidded, but managed to keep his feet.

A wave of fire hit him before he found the bottom of the shaft. It boiled and churned around him. His *Shield* kept out the heat and the smoke, but did nothing to give him oxygen. In moments he began to cough and soon his lungs were aching with need. He pulled at the flames, but fire offered little creation energy. Mistral's feet slipped out from under him and he landed hard on his side. He tumbled down the rock face into the heart of the inferno.

He slammed into the bottom, rolling to break his fall. Lunging to his feet, he whirled in a circle, trying to get his bearing. He couldn't see beyond the flames and he was nearly out of air. A gesture sent a smothering wave outward and the flames fell. More burned beyond, eating what air the passage had to offer.

The dragon was taunting him. Mistral snarled and staggered forward. Before long he found himself panting. Spots danced across his vision. He clenched his teeth. He would *not* go down so easily. He pushed outward, gathering raw energy from the stone. He thrust it upward, blowing a shaft through a hundred feet of rock and soil. Dirt and pebbles rained down on him. He reversed the magic and created a whirling twist in the atmosphere above, pulling air into the tunnel and driving it forward into the fire. The flames vanished like blown birthday candles. Mistral let the magic unwind. The wind broke apart and gusts blew in every direction as they sought escape. After a few minutes, the air calmed.

Sweat matted Mistral's hair to his forehead and tremors ran through his body. He'd never channeled such power before. He didn't know his limit, but clearly his body had begun to reach it. Exactly what the dragon wanted.

He continued on. The tunnel floor was mostly flat, now. He walked another mile or two with no further attacks, going deeper into darkness with every step. He knew he was close when he began to smell the gut-twisting stench of carrion mixed with sulfur and rotted fish carcasses.

The passage twisted twice and then emptied into a massive cavern. A quarter the size of Tarrytown, it appeared to have been carved in preparation for this confrontation. Except for Mistral and the waiting dragon, it was empty.

Ouza.

The dragon's true name rolled through Mistral's mind like thunder, quaking through his flesh and making his bones ache marrow deep. He'd never dared think it before, unwilling to call attention to himself. Now he silently sounded the word in angry defiance. He struggled to keep erect, even as his mind twisted off its axis and vertigo overwhelmed him.

The dragon hulked halfway to the ceiling. Supposedly the Most High had turned the bodies of the Fallen into reflections of their inner ugliness. Ouza's body was jointed like a scorpion's and covered with bony yellow plates that clicked and snapped when he moved. From his sides sprang a multitude of spidery legs, each arcing high over his back and ending in three massive barbs. Wire hairs pricked from his legs, throat and belly. His thin, whiplike tail was as long as his body. His pale white belly and neck were pocked with great oozing sores.

His head was the worst of all. A bulbous pink eye sat in the middle of a frill of pink tentacles, each ending in a razor-toothed maw. Bloody pus wept down, crusting the dragon's throat and chest in a scabrous cowl. An opening below and behind the eye was covered by puckered black skin, opening only to speak and eat. Thick green strings of acid drool dangled from the center sphincter.

Finding his equilibrium, Mistral reached out to draw life-giving creation energy from the dragon. As expected, he met a wall of magic. Ouza laughed, a choked bubbling sound echoed by chittering from the tentacles.

"Did you really think I'd make it so easy for you?" He asked, his cavernous voice edged in a high-pitched whine that made Mistral's ears ache. "You are *mine*. My slave, my tool, my weapon. It is time you learned what that means."

Magic lashed Mistral. It battered his *Shield*, stabbing and pecking like a thousand steel beaks. Sweat beaded on his skin as he poured energy into the *Shield*. He knew he'd have to drop it and lay himself open for whatever torture the dragon dished out. It was the only way. But he couldn't make it look easy.

He gathered creation energy, pulling it in from all around him. The rocks of the cave turned a dead gray, all the minerals that might have provided life in a future eon emptied of fecundity. He shook with the torrent of power passing through his body, his head spinning and gray swirling at the edges of his vision. Behind his own *Shield*, Ouza remained impervious.

Time to end this.

Mistral thrust power into the dead rocks beneath his master, blasting them to powder. The nightmare creature heaved and caught himself before he plummeted into the newly formed pit. Mistral didn't even consider using Scripture against the beast. Just the idea of uttering the words of the Most High made him want to burn his tongue out at the roots. This was a battle for his soul—if he even had one—and he wouldn't dip his wings in the filth of the Dark or the Light to win it. He would be his own man, make his own destiny.

The dragon's magic continued to pound. Mistral flung bolts of power at the beast, loosening boulders above. The massive rocks tumbled off the monster's back like wadded paper.

Slowly Mistral let his *Shield* spell thin and his attacks grow weaker and more wild. It was not like he actually had to fake his exhaustion. He dropped to his knees, fear sluicing through him. What came next—it would be worse than anything he'd ever suffered before. Beyond imagining. His entire being cringed and fought against surrendering to that hell. But it was the only way, he told himself. The only way to win; the only way to freedom.

At last he let his protective magic go completely. Exhaustion laced his muscles and he shook like an aspen leaf.

"Come get me, you freak of nature," he demanded hoarsely. "Or are you afraid I might win?"

Magic swept him up and smashed him against the cavern ceiling, pinning him there. He made himself laugh, despite the searing pain of broken ribs.

He'd be willing to bet all of them had broken. It wasn't even the tip of the iceberg of what the dragon had in store for him.

"No wonder the Most High banished you. You are a coward. You lost the First War, you lost the Last War, and now you hide underground in the dark like a cockroach, terrified of the Light, terrified a seraph will step on you and crush you," Mistral taunted.

The dragon screamed fury and flung Mistral to the ground, then snatched him up in his claws, holding the man close to his great eye, shaking him, his talons puncturing Mistral's flesh and one of his wings.

"Did you really think you could ever escape me? I *own* you. I made you. Bone of my bone, flesh of my flesh," he said, then laughed at his mockery of Genesis, the sound twisting Mistral's entrails into knots.

"Before you were born you were shackled to me. I chained your father and filled your mother to give you life. You will serve me until the end of time."

Mistral inwardly recoiled. Did Ouza speak the truth. But no. No. It was not true. A captured seraph was his father and his mother was a whore of the Dark. The dragon was merely a farmer of evil. Even so, Mistral's making did not fate him to serving the Dark or the Light. He thought of Nara. *Fix this*, she'd said. Because she trusted him to do the right thing, the moral thing, and the Light and the Dark be damned.

"You are a puny fungus, do you understand? You are *nothing*. Merely livestock. I have lost many things in my existence, but I am still far greater than you will ever imagine."

Flecks of acid drool flicked over Mistral, melting through his clothing and skin.

"You will kneel to me. You will grovel and you will beg for my mercy. I will give you none. Do you understand, worm?" The dragon shook him again.

Mistral didn't answer. Couldn't have if he wanted to. His head spun from crashing against the wall and the shaking the dragon had given him. He scraped together what wits he had left and drew hard, gathering energy, releasing all restraints on his hunger. In that moment he did not care what he might kill, so long as Ouza died as well. In his arrogance and anger, the dragon had let his protective wall drop in order to grab Mistral, exposing himself. It was the opening Mistral had bet his life and soul on.

Power flooded him, greater than anything he'd ever known before. His spirit caught fire, burning with white energy as hot as the sun, as cold as empty space. For a moment, he touched something vast and alien. It looked at him—through him. He felt himself measured, marked, and then the thing turned away and Mistral fell down and down and down and back into himself.

He lay on the ground, shuddering and convulsing. Weight pinned his legs and his left arm. Blood ran from the hand-sized holes made by the dragon's talons and puddled beneath him. His heart fluttered madly. He glowed with the creation energy he'd consumed. He was dying. Even so, he didn't care. Bliss wrapped him.

Mistral tipped his head to see what was left of his former master. Ouza's body was gone. Sucked dry of life, his husk hadn't enough strength to hold the dead weight. It had plummeted into the pit and all that remained were broken off legs, like logs. One of these and a set of claws held Mistral trapped.

"I win," he whispered, then chuckled. It quickly turned to a cough that squeezed his blood faster from his wounds.

Shadows drifted across his sight. He could hear death's footsteps. And then what? Would he meet the dragon in the Hell of Scripture? Or would his spirit fly across the stars? Or more likely, there would be nothing at all.

He closed his eyes. Nothingness would be welcome enough. He'd made his stand on his own terms and he'd broken his own shackles. That was everything.

He drifted, the flow of his blood slowing as his heart stuttered.

Mage in battle, mage in dire . . .

The words whispered through the cavern, repeating and echoing until it sounded like it came from a thousand throats. They netted Mistral, wrapping his brain in steel cobwebs. What did they want? He could not, *would* not, speak those words. Would not bow to the seraphs, anymore than he would the Dark. He was free now, belonging only to himself. And the mules. Inwardly he smiled. Ben and Buck would not appreciate being forgotten. He didn't have to worry about them. Nara would take good care of the pair when he was gone.

The whispers went silent. Mistral felt the world pause, as if it had taken a breath.

. . . holy fire.

And then he was alight. The influx of creation energy from the dragon was nothing compared to this. Like he was bathed in joy and washed clean of Darkness. A vastness filled him like the breath of the universe. His spirit sang on an invisible wind made of dreams and wonder. He burned and died. He broke into ash, and then was born again, his bones shining silver, his veins gold ribbons weaving through flesh made of the dust of ages.

5.

He woke to bright sun on a promontory high above Tarrytown. The sun warmed him with gentle rays. Mistral examined himself in wonder. His skin glowed like moonlight on ruffled water, but he felt no pain from the light. He ran his fingers over his chest and ribs. He had no wounds, no scars, as if his skin was brand new. He felt strong. He spread his wings. They, too, were healed, and . . . the edges of every feather shone silver, as did every nervure. How was it possible?

He remembered. The whispers. The chant, leaving out the calling of the seraphs and summoning something else instead. Something vast and more powerful than anything he'd ever imagined. Something that could have crushed him, but instead healed him. Remade him.

Holy fire.

Slowly Mistral folded to his knees, unable to hold himself up as realization came to him. He wanted to deny it. To refuse the possibility. But it wasn't just a possibility. It was the only explanation.

The Most High had come to him, touched him, healed him, remade him.

Why?

Mistral's heart clenched, anger and resentment coiling through him. Was he now to become a slave to the Light?

Never.

Reason asserted itself. If that were the case, he'd be surrounded by seraphs.

Still, everything he knew of the Most High said the being was angry, selfish, capricious, and unjust. So why? What did the so-called God want of him?

Then again, what did it matter? He'd been willing to suffer and die to be rid of his dragon master. He was more than willing to do the same for the Most High. All that mattered now was that he was free. Alive, whole, and free.

He sprang into the air, spreading his wings and riding the air currents. The hellhole gaped in the mountain, surrounded by a ring of white death. The destruction was smaller than he'd feared. He flew over the valley. Nothing had breached the protective circle he'd made around the emerald basin. There would still be spawn in the hills. They'd have to be hunted. And then—

And then?

For the first time in his life he had no place he *had* to go. He looked down at the roof of Nara's house. Ben and Buck waited for him. He'd been born anew. He could go anywhere. His life belonged to him.

He folded his wings and dropped out of the sky, eager to begin.

Storm Songs
63 PA / 2075 AD

Faith Hunter

The dome of New Orleans above them rippled with energy patterns, a coruscating wave that fractured into a rainbow magnified and brought to life. Protected within a triple circle, the cadre of mages—four Air, two River, and one Sea—worked to steer the hurricane in the Gulf north, where it would drop much-needed rain on the sun-parched land. The incantation was in two parts: The first part was to weaken the storm's winds; the second part was to move the high pressure cell blocking its passage out of the way. It was a high-level conjure that required both exacting precision and rigid control of enormous energies.

Richter watched the mages from the shelter of a dome of protection—a ward that would keep him safe should the conjure go horribly wrong, killing the mages. As the only Sea mage born in his generation to the Seattle Enclave he was too valuable to the priestess to be risked. But he needed to watch and learn how those of his rare and difficult-to-master gift worked with others of differing elemental talents.

In the middle of the square, in the heart of the New Orleans Enclave, the Sea mage master was sitting on a round mat of sea salt in the center of the other six mages, as if she were the center of a clock. A River mage sat behind her at 12, the other sat at 6, both mages close to the center, but not touching the salt mat, and enclosed by a circle of alternating river rock and freshwater oyster and mussel shells behind them. The four Air mages sat two and two outside the inner circles, facing inward. Behind them was the circle that contained their part of the conjure, an usual choice but one that the Air mages had insisted be used. It was composed of parrot feathers, the bold green and red placed each half over the next. And at the compass point for north was a seraph feather. The rare and amazing feather had been handed down from father to son for three generations, and was used only in the most delicate and important of conjures.

Richter, the young Sea mage, watched as his mentor, the venerable Oh Mai, opened her circle. She put her hands flat on the salt mat, fingers spread wide, and called on the power of the sea. "Water of life, water of death, rollers crest and fall. Water deep and salt marsh sea, mother of us all." Power gathered in the salt mat, soft aqua and roseate hues, and lifted slowly upward, not like a circle or dome, but like a sea mist, filling an invisible bowl. The glowing fog rose until the mist reached its zenith just over her head.

The River mages opened and stabilized their conjuring circle next, doming it only a bit above the sea circle. Once deployed, their circle was a murky construct that moved like water in a glass. The moment their water circle was in place, the air circle began to rise. The feathers comprising the physical boundary of the outer circle trembled and quivered, as if they were caught in the barest of breezes. It looped up, an irregular dome of energized fog. The nested conjuring circles were hemispheres, really, not passing through the floor, but caught in the boundaries of the feathers, salt, river rock, and shell. They didn't touch one another, which could have resulted in detonation, but arched over one another—air over fresh water over salt—just as a hurricane was wind driving rain over sea.

Oh Mai looked like a wizened mummy within the hazed energies. When she lifted her arms and began to stir the sea-mist around her, it formed a swirl, just like a hurricane. Oh Mai began to sing. "Water, sea, air and wind, rain and storm pay heed. Move and shift, trade winds guide. Release your bounty o'er land."

The words didn't rhyme, which Richter didn't like at all. Rhymes were much easier to memorize. But then, Oh Mai didn't need to memorize things. She had done them so often she just remembered them, perfect-like.

As old Oh Mai sang, the River mages whispered to the clouds of the hurricane. "Draw and seek and hold and drop, the tears of the world. Plagues and death and humans gone, the tears of the world." He knew they were making the clouds heavy with rain, while allowing only a bit of the moisture to fall to the earth, holding it to drop it over the cropland they had been paid to water.

And then the Air mages began a descant in a minor key, pushing at the high pressure that was stalled over the Mississippi Valley, obstructing the hurricane, insisting it move east and out over the ocean. "Hot and dry and entropy, and parched and empty air, break and move and slide to east, to ocean space and free."

Richter liked that one. He decided that when he cast his first conjure, it would be a complex rhyme and be sung in a minor key. He liked the haunting melody, the way it flowed over and through the River mages' whispers. He had only come into his gift a few months before. Oh Mai wouldn't let him conjure yet. Stubborn old woman.

He watched as she gripped her prime amulet, a worn, chipped, megalodon shark tooth as big as her hand and a million years old. Excitement shot through him. Now. Oh Mai was doing it *now*. The tooth sparkled, shooting flames like the petals of a flower as she pulled the gathered might of the Air and River mages to her.

Oh Mai . . . pushed. Richter felt it in his bones, a shifting of the world, a flowing of forces too long stymied. Ponderously, the high pressure began to slide out of the way. And the hurricane began to edge north, over land. Over crops that humans needed to live. Well, mages needed crops too, but mages had Earth mages to get things growing. Humans didn't.

Two hours later, the air circle thinned out and began to fall back into the feathers of the boundary. Then the water circle began to slump. Finally, the sea circle dropped away, absorbing into the salt mat. The hurricane was on its way. Younger acolytes would monitor the position of the storm overnight, calling in the more mature, fully exhausted mages should there be problems.

And they would be richly paid for the rain. Very richly.

Richter ran to help Oh Mai to her feet.

Defiance
76 PA / 2088 AD

Christina Stiles

"Again!" the drill sergeant yelled. The six tired kids ran through the obstacle course for the seventh time, alternately jumping through tires, scrambling under a metal bed of strung barbed-wire with fake rifles held in their arms, crawling up and over a ten-foot-tall wall with the aid of a rope, and then climbing the stairs to the tower to zip-line down over the river and run to the finish line—all while wearing fifteen-pound packs, running through snow, and wearing heavy winter gear in below zero-degree weather. The youngest stumbled more than once, but older squad members grabbed arms and helped them make it through. No man—kid—left behind.

The tow-headed twins, Davey and Colin, collapsed at the end of the course, unable to move further. But Alaska, the only girl in the group, and the three teenaged boys, Ezekiel, Harper, and Jeremiah, had been doing this for years; they were barely winded. Within a few months, ten-year-old Davey and Colin would start holding up better to the exercises.

Behind Alaska's squad other teams of six were running the same course. Nearby, an elite team of mules was on the hardest course, which included jumping ten-foot-wide pits, climbing a sixty-foot wall without a rope, and combating "hostiles" just past the river—with the occasional firing of live rounds above their heads.

As Alaska bent over to gather her breath, she glanced toward the elite group. They were smiling and roughhousing with one another, while the baddest of the badasses, Jeep and Hog, were singing to the rhythm of the gunfire. Although Mule Team 1, as they called themselves, were captives just like her team, they enjoyed testing their strength and endurance. Their kind were often bred for war, and this all-mule squad would be readiest of all when it came to battle.

Above the gunfire and song, the sound of a vehicle engine alerted her. Her bad day had just gotten worse. It was Sergeant Suarez, the mocha-skinned, dark-haired man who'd stolen Alaska from the real Army base years before—she wasn't sure how many years, but she guessed at least seven or eight. Here, they called him Colonel Suarez, though. He owned this base and everyone on it.

He was sitting in a Pre-Ap green Humvee just beyond the rappelling tower, wearing a thick green coat and a fur-lined hood. He lowered his protective green face mask and stared at her; he liked staring at her—probably because he knew she hated it. Then he smiled and winked at her. A chill ran down Alaska's spine as her mind was flooded with images of the soldiers Suarez had slaughtered to clear his way to her. The worst was the officer who'd tried to shield her with his own body. He'd been a friend of Alaska's mother, and had taken Alaska in when her mother died. Only to end up with his brains spattered over Alaska—a head shot, because a shot to his body might've gone through him and damaged Suarez's prize.

The images were familiar, painful, and when she first came to this god-forsaken camp—and for years afterward—they brought her to uncon-trollable tears. But she refused to cry anymore. She wasn't a little child now. She was hardened. Few things brought her to tears now. She couldn't even remember the name of the officer who died for her. He wasn't a part of her life anymore.

She returned Suarez's stare, crossing her arms and refusing to turn away. Defiant. If the so-called Colonel shot her, too, then so what? What did she have to lose? Dying would be better than training to fight for the asshole. Just who was he plotting to kill with an army of children, anyway?

One of the soldiers walked to the Humvee. Still maintaining eye contact with Alaska, Suarez handed the man a note—spoken conversations around the "specials" might be overheard, after all. His orders received, the soldier worked his way to the other side of the training field. Suarez didn't imme-diately leave but continued looking at Alaska.

While she had him in sight, she opened her mind to his surface thoughts, something she'd only recently found she could do. She fully ex-pected resistance against entering his mind, but his thoughts flowed freely into her. Feelings of lust and desire and need washed over her. At the forefront was an image of Alaska, naked, struggling unsuccessfully beneath him. Her face burned when she realized what he wanted from her. Her eyes grew wide, and he smiled at her. Fear suddenly struck her. *Did he know Alaska was reading him?*

The image flickered. Now, Suarez slung a small dark-haired girl over his shoulder. Alaska couldn't see the girl's face, but Suarez broadcasted satis-faction, eagerness, but strangely not lust this time. She caught a clear thought: "This will be fun to watch." Then his mind filled with vile images of something monstrous hovering over the girl and attempting to—"

Alaska gritted her teeth, and started to advance on the animal posing as a man in the truck.

Zeke, a broad-shouldered mule in her crew, pulled her elbow, stopping her progress. "Don't rile him, Alaska. We don't need trouble with the Colonel. He'll see to it that it's taken out on everyone but you. You know that, right?"

"Yes, I know, Zeke," she whispered, remembering the whipping Zeke, Jeremiah, and Harper had received when she'd last been "uncooperative." It had taken the scrawny Jeremiah a week to recover, while the mules bounced back in a day. She would risk her own life and health, but not theirs.

That was her weakness. And Suarez knew it. Sometimes she longed to escape, run away to . . . wherever . . . but she knew the others would be tortured to reveal her whereabouts, even if they had no knowledge of her plans. She couldn't do that to them.

"I know. But you don't know what he—"

Harper, the shorter mule interrupted. "Leave us out of your personal war."

Jeremiah appeared beside her other elbow and pulled his face mask down, his breath misting in the cold. She looked up into his thin face and at the long, puckered scar running along his left cheek, a scar he'd never explained. His returned stare was serious, and he shook his hooded head. "No, Alaska."

"Okay, I'll behave today. But one day, Jeremiah, I *will* kill him."

"Jeremiah," Alaska said to the lanky teen on the other side of the metal table, "I got something from Suarez's mind earlier."

"Shhh. Hold your voice down." Jeremiah's eyes furtively scanned the yellow-painted room where Suarez's men kept watch. "Please don't bring them over here, Ala. I'd like to eat my lunch in peace."

"You really want to savor this?" she said, looking down at her plastic tray at something that passed for meat.

"Ala, I don't want to have to run any punishment laps, thank you."

"Don't worry about them. I think Jeep can keep them busy." Alaska looked over at the bullish, almost-black-skinned mule with the braids at the next table. The half-breed girl's muscular upper arms were thicker than Alaska's thighs. "Hey, Jeep," Alaska drawled, "I hear Hog's been eyeing you in a special way, if you know what I mean."

The fifteen-year-old Jeep looked up at Alaska, and when the human winked at her, she nodded her understanding.

Jeep stood up suddenly and smashed her sea-green tray against the fake-wood tabletop. The clanging noise echoed through the room, silencing the few conversations. The guards turned in her direction. "Keep your stinkin' eyes to yourself, Hog. You ain't allowed to look at me like that!" she yelled at a boy sitting across from her, a blond mule at least a year her junior who was almost as strong, and certainly as bull-headed. "You keep those crazy eyes on your food!"

He stood, a toothy smile cracking his face. "Oh, yeah, Jeep? I like lookin' at you. You're damn pretty, and I'll look at you anytime I want. Nothin' you can do about it, *girl.*" He stretched out a hand and jabbed a finger at her chest.

Jeep looked down at the finger, and slowly brought her eyes back up to meet his. Her fist shot out, punching Hog square in the nose. The pain would have taken down a grown human, but Hog just squinted his eyes and let out a grunt. "You'll pay for that, Jeep!" He bolted over the table. They crashed into the table behind them, sending food, trays, and other kids flying.

"That flirting should give us a little peace," Alaska said, as the guards rushed to the fight.

"Damn, but you are crazy, Ala," he said. "Fine. Tell me what you saw."

"I saw him carrying a dark-haired girl. She was bound in rope. He was thinking very . . . unpleasant things about her." Alaska didn't add that he'd been thinking about her, too. "You haven't seen a girl brought in, have you?"

"No. Besides, she'd end up in your barracks."

"Right . . . if they took her to the barracks."

"Maybe he was fantasizing. Maybe the girl doesn't exist, and you're worrying about nothing, Ala."

"I know what I saw, Jeremiah."

"Yeah, Ala, but have you spent enough time in the Colonel's head to know what it means?"

"I don't—"

"You told me yourself that you only started doin' this a couple weeks ago. And this has got to be the first time you tried it on him, right?"

"Well, yeah, but—"

"So maybe his fantasies are so strong that they feel like reality. He's a sick man, so he has sick fantasies."

"I guess . . . maybe you're right."

"And maybe *you're* right, Ala. There's just no way to be sure."

Jeremiah started to give Alaska a hug, but suddenly snatched his hands back into his lap, beneath the table. Alaska caught a fleeting glimpse of bandages she'd mistaken for gloves before.

"What happened to your hands, Jeremiah?" Alaska asked.

"It's nothing. Don't worry about it."

She probed his sense-memories. She could feel a burning, searing sensation. "Seraph stones! What did they *do* to you?"

When he turned away from her, Alaska leaned in and said, "Please tell me what happened." She tried to make her words as soothing as possible to convince him it was safe to talk. She was often good at soothing others. She eased the thought into the forefront of her mind that he *would* talk.

"Ala, stop it. I can feel you in my head. I don't want to talk about it."

"But we're friends...best friends, Jeremiah. You don't have to hide anything from me. I'm here for you. Tell me, please."

He sighed, and then leaned forward to speak directly into her ear. "*They* didn't do this to me. I did. Or the flame did, actually."

"I'm not following you."

"See, Ala, there's this . . . ball of fire. It's been visiting my cell. It's friendly—well, most of the time. It just got a little too excited while we were playing last night. That's when it toasted my hands. Accidentally."

"A ball of fire? You were playing with a ball of fire?"

"Yes. It came to me one night a few weeks back. I was in my dorm room, just hating this place and wishing I could get out. I was crying to myself and I even sent up a prayer, like I remember doing in kirk. And a bit later, I see this little light appear on the ceiling, kinda like a targeting laser, but it was orange not red, and it flickered. It floated down toward me, and got bigger and bigger. I absolutely *freaked!* I rolled out of my cot, and hit the floor. The thing zipped around to where I was on the floor, like it was checking me over. And . . . it had bright sparks in front, like eyes on a face."

"Eyes? A floating dot with eyes? That's really crazy, Jeremiah."

The table between them scraped across the tile floor, shoved by a guard as Jeep punched him in the gut. Then Jeep turned her attention to the one choking Hog with a baton. Hog struggled to get hold of the man's arms, but the guard—a mule himself—pressed the weapon against Hog harder. Hog's eyes were starting to bulge from his head. Jeep snapped one-two punches to the mule-guard's face, knocking him backward. Hog fell and began coughing. Knowing that they'd receive a share of collective punishment even if they stayed out of the fracas, the smaller mules from Mule Team 1 jumped the large mule-guard from behind, dragging him down to the floor. Might as well have some fun before the inevitable pain.

"Let's go over there," Alaska nodded toward the far side of the room.

When they were safely away from the brawl, Jeremiah looked into her eyes. "I know it sounds unbelievable. I do. And that's why I didn't bring it up before. But it *really* has been visiting me. And it's like a kid. It just wants to play."

When Alaska didn't say anything, he continued. "I'm *not* crazy, Ala. I'm not. I promise you. It's real."

"Like the tied-up girl that's just in my head?"

The two stared at each other. Then Jeremiah sighed. "You've never lied to me before, Ala."

"And you've never lied to me." Alaska paused to duck a thrown plate. "Okay, I believe you. I just don't understand how such a thing could be. But I've seen some very odd things, so I'm sure it's *possible*. Why would it come here, though? What is it?"

"I don't know, Ala. Maybe I brought it here. Maybe *I* have a special ability."

A sound distracted Alaska. Jeep had picked up one of the human guards, who was now fervently blowing a whistle. As easily as tossing a ball, she sent him soaring over two tables, into a serving station, and crumpling onto the ground. The cafeteria doors banged open and several other guards burst in. Guns leveled, they shouted for everyone to get on the ground.

"Looks like the party is over," Alaska said to Jeremiah from her position on the floor, hands on the back of her head.

"Yep. Joy," he dragged out.

Hog hadn't dropped to the floor. Instead, he sent a different guard soaring toward the new arrivals. Reflexively, one of the newcomers fired a handful of shots. Most of the bullets flew wild, but one grazed Hog. He grunted his displeasure as a red stain bloomed on his grey shirt.

"On. The. Floor!" a different guard yelled. "Nothing bad will happen to you, if you surrender now."

"I think the Colonel would be mighty mad if anything happened to us," Hog said. "But I'm surrendering. See me gettin' down on the ground with my hands behind my head? I'll go quietly, Boss Man."

"I knew you couldn't take me," Jeep said, as she lay down, facing Hog.

He winked. "Ah, sweetness, you know I like your love licks. We'll certainly continue this another time. Maybe next time we'll be alone."

After the cafeteria fight, the guards put everyone in lockdown for two days without food. The guards whipped Hog and Jeep before putting them in solitary confinement. Alaska hated that her friends had suffered just to provide a distraction.

On the second evening, Alaska heard voices through the barred window in her door, an argument between one mule guard and his superior.

"Mules will be mules." one of the sergeants said.

"Keeping them locked up will just make them want to fight more."

"Not my call," the sergeant replied. "Tell it to the Colonel!"

"Bet your seraph-sucked stones we want to fight!" Alaska muttered to no one, her back against the wall of her dark room, not caring that she'd cursed. The Most High paid little attention to worms like her, she'd decided long ago. If He had, then He wouldn't've let these men drag kids like her away from their families.

Worse, why had God taken her mother away from her? And that officer at the Army facility who died for her? Had her parents offended God in some way? Maybe her father, Jason, had. Alaska didn't remember him, but she recalled Aunt Cora telling her mother numerous times not to cry over Jason, that he was a user and not good enough for her and her daughter. Alaska did know that her mother and Aunt Cora were good, God-fearing people, though. She just *knew* it. They hadn't deserved to die.

An image came to Alaska of her mother, her bright red hair—looking like Alaska imagined her own hair would if she were allowed to grow it long—lying on the snow, her dead blue eyes looking up at the sky, a hole ringed in red in the center of her chest. Then scenes of erupting chaos. People shouting. Guns firing. "Momma! Momma!" she'd screamed, shaking her shoulder. "Wake up, Momma!"

Then Aunt Cora came running toward them, crying out, "Cassie! Cassie! No! No! No! My Cassie!" She stopped beside her sister's body, bent over double sobbing. Bullets flying, pandemonium around them, she somehow regained her composure, and put out her arm to Alaska. "Come to me, Alaska! Come to me!" she cried. "We can't let them take you, Alaska, just like they took—" There was a loud crack, and Aunt Cora's head jerked backward. A hole appeared in her forehead and red rain fell down on Alaska. Cora fell over. Her body pushed the child into her mother's breast. The girl huddled between the two women, protected.

She and her mother had been walking home from kirk before the horror struck. They were all happy and celebrating the Most High.

Then they were all dead.

Strange that she could still hear it. Women yelling out for their husbands, sons, daughters. High-pitched howls of despair. Alone in her room, the sound of a woman screaming grew louder and louder. Alaska couldn't get it out of her head. So loud!

It sounded so close now. So close, as if it was coming from the hallway. And then there were grunts and muffled noises and a man's voice.

"Mage in battle, mage—" a female voice started in a rush but was quickly cut off.

"I thought you bound her mouth, Caden! You can't let mages have their tongues! She'll spell us!"

"She's biting me!"

"Tape her mouth shut, Caden, and then grab her feet."

There were some rustling struggles, but they were quickly muted. "Ready, Gus."

"They should have gotten the mules to bring her back." He grunted. "She's a fighter, this one. Best be careful, though, or she'll break something."

"Little Miss, you need to calm down," said Caden, his voice almost gentle. "Stop thrashing, now. You'll break an arm or leg if you don't stop struggling with us."

There were a few more grunts, but eventually they stopped. "Now, that's better. Be nice, and we'll be nice, Little Miss."

"Drag her to that room there, Caden."

Alaska scrambled to the window. The corridor was dark, but that wasn't an issue for her. Her night vision had steadily improved over the last year, a gift she had kept from her instructors. She saw two guards, humans, hauling a light-skinned, dark-haired girl to the empty room across from hers. There were few girls in the complex, and they were kept away from the boys on the other side of the dorm. They'd called this one a mage. They were so rare outside of their Enclaves that Alaska had only heard rumors about them. Now Suarez's men—no, Suarez—had one. The girl. This was the girl in his thoughts, the one he wanted to watch when—

"Get away from the door, nosey," the skeevy guard with the stringy hair yelled at Alaska. "This pretty little thing is gonna keep a Dark one company," he continued. "You want to join her? We can arrange that," he cackled. "Of course, I might want to try you out first." Gus backed into the doorway of the empty room, as his partner, Caden, she guessed, followed with the small girl's feet. She wasn't big enough to need two to carry. These guys were wimps.

"Mind your business, Little Miss," Caden said to her as he passed by the window. He was several years older than Gus, and a head taller. She'd never seen either of them before. "Get back to your bed, now. Nothing for you to see here."

She didn't back away. Defiant. If they wanted her in bed, they'd have to come inside and tuck her in. She almost wished they'd try.

Gus turned on the room's light. "They're prepping C Building for her and her new boyfriend," he laughed.

"We'll have to come back to move her again at some point, but until the Darkness gets here, she's to stay locked up." Caden said. "You tell the others not to mess with her *at all!* She's the most dangerous of our prisoners. And now that she knows she's going to be breeding with a demon, she'll be even more problematic."

"Ugh! Just think of the ugly babies she'll be making from here on out."

After a few more minutes, the men exited the room and locked the door. As he passed Alaska's window, Gus let out one last "Go back to bed," but he didn't stop. They headed up the hall, and she heard the door to the outside open and close.

Alaska pressed her head against the bars. Suarez was going to make that girl—that mage—*breed* with a Dark power. A wave of nausea struck her empty stomach, and something changed in her. Like a wave rolling back, her attitude to the camp just . . . changed. No more, she thought. No more.

The muffled sounds of the girl sobbing echoed down the hallway. They'd left her gagged in the room. "Hey, don't worry over there," Alaska whispered. "I'm not going to let him do that to you!"

She paced the room, banged her fists against the wall. There had to be a way to free the girl.

"Bones and stones," she muttered, as she plopped herself on her cot to await the dawn.

The guards roused them before sunrise. They told the kids to gear up for the outdoors, and when they were ready, marched them single file into the assembly hall. There they were given hard, tasteless dried food bars, but after two days without food, anything was a feast. The mules were given six each to sustain their high metabolism. The humans got two. Alaska pushed one of hers into Jeep's hands as the broad girl walked by.

"No need to do that," Jeep whispered. "It's all good. I'm still your girl."

"Please take it. I am so very sorry."

"No worries. They whipped like little boys," she winked, "so it was nothin'."

Alaska continued to press the food on the mule.

"If it'll make you feel better, girl, sure thing. I *am* a bit hungry."

"Line up in your squads!" one of the guards ordered, and the child soldiers shuffled into position, munching the food bars as they stood. "Attention!" he yelled when they were all against the wall.

Their right hands snapped to their heads in salute as Colonel Suarez sauntered in front of them, a long drill cane held under his arm. He didn't return their salute, so they were forced to hold it.

He was dressed in his green day uniform, no winter gear. A very large, very dark mule, wide and standing about seven feet tall, followed two paces behind him. The two checked each soldier with a critical eye as they walked by. Alaska guessed Suarez was in a good mood for a change: He didn't use the cane on any of them—he didn't even stop to irritate her.

"You've got a new drill sergeant today," he said, turning to face them, twirling the cane with an air of menace. "His name is Sergeant Hawkes," he pointed the stick toward the sergeant. "It's his first day here, so make him feel welcome and obey his every command."

He glared at the kids, waiting to see if any of them would dare to even smirk.

"Since you all seem to have energy to spare to play with your food, Sergeant Hawkes here will help you burn off that excess energy with some outdoor exercise. Isn't that right, Sergeant Hawkes?"

"I'll absolutely strip every last ounce of that energy and more from them, Colonel," said the mule.

"Those who fail to obey the sergeant will become food for the compound's forthcoming illustrious guest, who may, in fact, arrive tonight. Those who don't want to serve our master in his army will be *served* to the master. Understood?"

No one spoke, though a few gulped reflexively. They all remained against the wall, holding their salute for their despised Colonel.

"Good." Suarez turned to Hawkes. "They're all yours, Sergeant Hawkes. I want to hear all about their exciting day when I return in the morning."

"Yes, Colonel."

Suarez finally returned the salute, letting them rest their hands. "Play time is over, soldiers," and then turned and strode out of the room.

They all released a held breath and relaxed a bit.

It didn't last long.

Sergeant Hawkes stood tall and bellowed, "Head to the practice fields, you pieces of shit. I don't care how hard you think you've trained before, you'll be working twice as hard today. And no one . . . *no one* . . . better fall out. You *will not* have the energy to fight in the cafeteria when I'm done with you!"

No one argued. No one dared.

Before Jeremiah could pull on his gloves, Alaska saw that he wasn't wearing bandages. She grabbed his hands, scanning them front and back. From wrists to his unusually long index fingers—a trait they shared—his hands were now smooth: no burns, no scars. She looked at him quizzically as they marched.

He shrugged. "Last night I had a dream that they'd healed. When the nurse checked them this morning, they had."

"No talking. Move!" Hawkes yelled.

When they left the warmth of the assembly hall, the cold air hit their faces, forcing them to pull their face masks up and down to take bites. They ate. They marched, double time. No one talked.

In the field, they broke into their groups. "Mule Team 1, you are supposedly the best. But you are also the most undisciplined, I hear," Sergeant

Hawkes said. "We will work on that. If I have to beat each one of you down personally, I will. You *will* learn discipline. The rest of you watch."

Hawkes blew a whistle, signaling the group to start the obstacle course. Hog and Jeep led the way. The mules took off howling, rushing into the snow, through the tires, over the high wall, jumped a pit, hurdled over low walls, and swung across the iced-covered river. At various points along the course squads of human soldiers made futile attempts to stop them, but the mules raced past, barely even slowing. Mule Team 1 completed the course in minutes. They made it look all easy.

While the others were cheering Mule Team 1, Alaska sidled up to Jeremiah and whispered in his ear. "Keep looking forward. Act natural. Don't react. I've got something important to tell you. That girl I told you about. The nonexistent fantasy girl. They have her. They captured a neomage girl and brought her to the girls' block last night."

She saw Jeremiah stiffen, but he kept looking forward, feigning interest in Mule Team 1's exploits.

"They want to breed her with their master, the one Suarez said was coming. It's bad enough that we have to fight for this thing, but having babies with it? We've *got* to get her out of here."

"What can we do about it? We're only kids."

"Kids with powers."

"But they've brought in more mules to keep us in line. Plus, some of the kids *want* to be in Suarez's army."

"I know who we can trust. I can sense the ones who've already given over their hearts to Darkness. Harper's one of theirs, unfortunately, and Zeke is leaning that way, as well, so say nothing to them." She paused. "Did your fiery friend return during lockdown?"

"Yeah. I called it and it came to me."

"Any chance it could help us?"

"Maybe."

Hawkes yelled to the young mules, "Back Here! Run it again." When the last member of Mule Team 1 arrived back at the start of the course, Sergeant Hawkes threw a quick punch to the boy's gut and then swept a leg behind the mule, knocking him down.

He then turned to the nearest adult soldiers: "They need some opposition this time. Mules, replace the humans. Use whatever force necessary to bring them down. I don't want them dead, but hurting is good. Our young friends have lessons to learn, and you will be their teachers." The five adult mules grinned.

To the others, Hawkes ordered, "You heard the Colonel: Play time is over. Get the other teams running. Move it. Move it!"

The rest of the day was spent on the course. Hawkes continued to beat the slackers in each group, and he grew more brutal as the day progressed. Harper took the brunt of Hawkes's beatings in Alaska's squad, although she did take a jarring kick in the flank after the final run; fortunately, the massive mule held back some on the humans.

When the exhausted child soldiers were finally marched back to the dorms after dusk, they had to pause as a line of vehicles started coming through the gates. There were four Humvees, a flatbed truck with a large container on it, and four more Humvees. As the truck passed, Alaska felt her knees buckle as a wave of fear rolled over her.

"The Darkness, Jeremiah," she whispered. "It's here. There's no time to waste. We've got to do something *now!*"

Jeremiah turned to her. "Get to the girls' quarters and free the mage." His face was stern, serious. "Let Jeep know the shit is about to hit."

"What are you going to do?"

"I'm going to call a friend and see how well some things burn around here. Then I'm gonna make a lot of noise out by the vehicles' gas tanks. I sure could use some backup from Hog, if he can get a weapon."

Alaska grabbed his hand. "Stay safe," she said, looking him in the eyes. "I need you." Jeremiah nodded in return.

As the convoy headed toward the building the guards had been preparing for the master's arrival, a mule in the lead Humvee motioned for Sergeant Hawkes and his crew to follow them. Hawkes yelled to the remaining guards, "Get the soldiers indoors, feed them, and keep them quiet. Our master is here, and they *will* behave." Then he and his men departed.

"Food!" Mule Team 1 yelled, as they took off running toward the cafeteria, jostling each other to be first in line. Alaska and Jeremiah split up, him hanging back while she double-timed it to stay close to the mules.

In the cafeteria food line, Alaska whispered at Jeep's back, "Suarez's men captured a neomage. They intend to breed her with his master—make some sort of half-Dark monsters. We've got to get her out of here. Get weapons off the guards. Guns too. Send Hog out back to help Jeremiah."

"Holy hellhole," Jeep muttered, and nodded her assent.

After eating half her meal, Alaska got up and shuffled to the guard blocking the doorway. He straightened from a slouch, his hand drifting to his baton. She held up her hands in surrender. As she spoke to him, she *pushed* with her mind against his. *You will believe me. You will do as I ask.* "Sir, would you take me to my dorm? I'm not feeling so good." She grimaced, and rubbed her stomach. *You will believe. You will believe.* She thought it helped that she really was hurting.

He was silent and motionless. "Uh, okay," he finally said, stepping aside to let her lead the way out of the cafeteria building and over to the girls' dormitory. When they arrived in the dorm, Alaska preceded him down the dark hallway to the door to the imprisoned neomage's room. She tried to transmit soothing calm through the barred window to the girl, but she couldn't tell if it had any effect.

Turning to the guard, Alaska said, "Open this one, please. I'll hold your baton for you while you do it."

"Yes, hold this," he said, handing her the weapon while he searched for the right key and then unlocked the door.

"Thank you. By the way, you're looking a little sleepy," Alaska said to him, sending some element of her own fatigue into his mind. "I think we should have you lie down in another room." She pointed to an empty cell. "Let's unlock that one, too, so you can rest." After he did so, she said, "Give me the keys—oh and your coat and gloves. You won't need them on while you're sleeping."

"Yes, so tired," he yawned. "Gotta get some sleep," he said, handing her the keys while he shrugged out of his coat. He yawned deeply again, shuffled through the door, and fell onto the cot. Within seconds, the sound of his snoring filled the corridor. Alaska shut the door and locked it.

Then she rushed into the neomage's cell. The girl was tied to the bed, a gag in her mouth. Alaska removed the gag; the girl took a gasping breath. "Keep quiet," Alaska shushed. "Your sperm donor has arrived, and we need to get you out of here before this becomes your wedding night." Alaska released the girl's bindings, and then helped her sit up. "Can you walk?"

"I think so," the girl rasped.

"Better yet, can you run?"

"They told me what they were going to do to me. I don't want to meet that . . . thing! I'll run myself to death first."

Alaska took off her coat and gloves, handing them to the girl. Although the girl appeared to be a teenager, she was very thin and short for her age. "Put these on. I know they're too big, but the guard's clothes are even bigger." Alaska put on the guard's gear.

They started walking down the corridor. "That door leads to the vehicles. We wait for a loud boom, and then we run out the door. Hopefully, my friends will keep the guards occupied. Good?"

"Yes," the dark-haired girl said, placing her arm on Alaska's as they settled in the doorway. "I'm Marta. I'm very grateful you were here to help me."

"Alaska. And we aren't away yet," Alaska replied to the smaller girl.

An explosion rocked the complex, and something banged against the side of the building. Smaller explosions followed, and they heard yelling, and then gunfire, and . . . singing.

"That's our cue." Alaska half-pulled Marta through the exterior door, which sounded an alarm. The buzzing noise was lost in the cacophony outside. Several vehicles were on fire, and guards were rushing about, weapons in hand. Some moved to fight the fires, while others, the elite mules, raced toward the center of the conflagration to where Jeremiah stood in the midst of the flames belting out a strange song about bullfrogs and joy, a Pre-Ap song he'd told Alaska that his grandmother used to sing to him.

The enemy mules stood confounded. Then more shots rang out. One of Suarez's mules fell, bullets hitting him in the chest and neck. Hog was on a rooftop, taking aim at another. Alaska and Marta crept through the shadows, away from the burning and noise. Jeep met them around the corner of the building, and the three stopped to watch as an odd apparition appeared in the battle.

A ball of flickering orange flame separated itself from the burning vehicles and flew at the soldiers. It expanded, formed hands, and leaned over a group of them, looking like an attacking bear. Then a slim flame jutted out of its headlike feature and slid along the face of one like a tongue. The guard reflexively screamed when the flame-tongue swelled to cover his face, a scream that was cut short by the fire entering his mouth and plunging inside. The mule's body exploded from within, and the flame ball reformed itself, bouncing up and down in what could almost be mistaken for excitement. Gleaming yellow spark-eyes appeared on the ball, and it turned in place looking for more fun, then darted off to somewhere out of Alaska's line of sight.

With a shout, Hog launched himself from the roof at a handful of soldiers who'd been quietly setting up a firing position lined up on Alaska, Jeep, and Marta's escape route. He speared the first man as if his rifle had held a bayonet, and then picked up another to use as a club against the others. All the while, Hog brayed and howled like a wild animal—like a bunch of wild animals—which attracted other soldiers armed with bigger weapons than mere billy clubs and rifles.

In the other direction, more screams. More gunfire. More singing.

Thinking him an easy target, a squad cornered Jeremiah. Transparent orange fire sprung up around him an instant before Suarez's soldiers fired at him. The bullets hit the shimmering screen and fell harmlessly to the ground.

"Yes!" Jeremiah shouted, dancing behind the protective screen. "Can't shoot me, you son-of-a-darkun' scum!"

"Get out of there, Jeremiah!" Alaska yelled to him. "Come on!"

He turned his back on her and resumed his oddball song, seemingly oblivious to the troops coming from all directions.

"Don't be stupid! Come on!"

"We've got to go, Ala! You know he's not comin' with us. He and Hog are settin' us free. Don't waste their sacrifice."

Jeep was right. Tears filled Alaska's eyes as she took the semi-automatic weapon the mule handed her. She and the mage set off at a run toward the training grounds, Jeep bringing up the rear.

Years of familiarity allowed Alaska to navigate easily across the training fields in the dark. When they got to the edge of the forest on the far side, Jeep took point, scouting a path through the shadows and trees. Alaska looked back and saw Colin carrying his twin over his shoulder. Colin had multiple wounds. Davey's head was drenched in blood. Still, Alaska could see by his aura that he was still alive.

Alaska turned to follow Jeep, but the neomage dropped her hand and faced back toward the open field. "Don't stop now, Marta. We gotta get deep into the woods."

"Something's coming," the mage said.

As Alaska looked behind them, she saw Sergeant Hawkes emerge from a building on the far side of the training fields. He saw them, growled, and moved with superhuman speed toward them, his muscular arms pumping up and down, his face a mask of rage. When he caught them, they would all be dead.

"Jeep! Jeep!" she screamed. "I need help here!" Alaska said to the mule who'd already reached the woods. Alaska turned and fired the handgun at the approaching soldier the way they'd trained her: two quick shots, reacquire target, two quick shots. Blood stained Hawkes's tight green T-shirt, but he kept running, taking evasive action but still closing fast.

"Holy hellhole," Jeep yelled from behind Alaska, bursting out of the woods seconds later, and making straight for the incoming tank of a man. "Hawkes, you hurt my friends, and I will rip out your eyes and feed them to your intestines! Pick on somebody your own size."

Jeep raced into her field of fire and Alaska couldn't shoot at Hawkes anymore. The two mules struck each other mere yards away from Alaska and the mage, Jeep diving headfirst into his chest. The move didn't faze the bigger mule. He grabbed her legs and, with a twist, had her hanging upside down as he continued relentlessly advancing on the others. Taking advantage of her position, Jeep dug her fingers into the man's bullet wounds and began twisting and tearing. Hawkes laughed.

Jeep's attack did have one effect, though: He turned his attention toward the young mule. He didn't notice when Colin passed Alaska racing into enter the safety of woods.

"You said you were going to do what with my eyes, little girl?" the massive mule growled.

"You heard me, you piece of shit. When I'm done with you, you're going to be a pile of bile. You won't be fit for dogs to eat." She connected with a punch to his groin. He flinched, but didn't double-over like a human male would have. Then he lifted her as high as he could, releasing one hand to grab her securely around the throat. He squeezed.

Alaska could already hear Jeep gasping, trying to say something—probably trying to threaten her strangler. Jeep should've been able to break his grip with some flashy mule move, but she didn't. She just hung there, dying. Sacrificing her life . . . as a distraction.

And then, all of a sudden Hawkes was choking. It was nothing Jeep was doing. Or Alaska.

Keeping his hold on Jeep's ankle and neck, he turned to glare bulging eyes at Marta, the Air mage at Alaska's side. The girl stood still, shivering in the cold. Sweat broke out on forehead, and she looked like she was going to faint. Another sacrifice. Another distraction.

And Alaska wasn't going to waste it.

She eased back into the woods, and once out of the sergeant's sight, rushed a short distance to the side, to emerge in Hawkes's blind spot. Sneaking up behind the mule, she got as close as she dared and aimed the weapon directly at the back of his head, careful not to risk Jeep. "Help me now, oh Lord. You owe me," she said, squeezing the trigger twice. Two swift bullets into the man's skull. Hawkes stood motionless in front of her, no longer struggling with Jeep. Without waiting to see if he still lived, she fired another two rounds into his head.

Pieces of skull bone, blood, and brains spattered her, as a fist-sized hole formed three inches above the back of his neck. His body toppled forward, onto Jeep. Alaska heard a terrible snap beneath him, and Jeep screamed in pain. Alaska dropped the gun and scrambled to move the big mule from atop her. She couldn't budge him.

"I got it. I got it," Jeep said, her voice muffled. Slowly she edged her way out from beneath him, using her legs and one arm. Her left arm dragged limp at her side. Jeep started to lever herself up, but an explosion jerked her attention to a point in the distance. "Holy hellhole," she whispered.

Along the access road leading away from the main compound, they could see vehicles driving away, including the flatbed carrying the Darkness. Behind the vehicles ran Jeremiah, the orange flame he'd befriended hovering above him. Soldiers in the turrets of the Humvees and perched atop the container on the truck fired rifles and RPGs at him, but the flame extended itself into a shield in front of him, deflecting the bullets and letting the grenades explode harmlessly inches away from his face.

The vehicles picked up speed, starting to pull away from the "human," but Jeremiah raised his arms and the flame flowed onto them. Balls of fire formed in his hands, and he threw them at the escaping vehicles. The fireballs streaked through the air, unerringly striking soldiers, who fell from their vehicles engulfed in flames, screaming. One burning soldier fell back inside his Humvee. The vehicle swerved and crashed into the vehicle behind it, forming a burning barricade stopping the flatbed truck.

Jeremiah advanced on his target, launching fireball after fireball at the container on the flatbed. At first, the fire seemed to have no effect on the metal container, but then, with a load groan, a hole ripped through the door of the container from the inside. A scaly, dark arm emerged, and a bolt of black lightning lanced out at Jeremiah. The orange flame extended itself into a shield around the human, but more lightning bolts arced from the Darkness to strike from all sides. The dark energy danced around Jeremiah's flame-ringed body, and in seconds the flame was overwhelmed. Lightning flashed through a gap in the flames, and with a massive "pop," Jeremiah exploded.

"No!" Alaska yelled, as her best friend flew apart, burning limbs soaring away from the detonation point. Tears flooded her eyes as grief crushed her to her knees, but unable to tear her gaze away from the scene, Alaska watched the fiery fragments that had been Jeremiah reverse course, coalescing into an orange ball of fire that rose into the sky. In the midst of it, they could see an image of Jeremiah's face entwined in the flames. The image rotated and the fire-Jeremiah seemed to see them. He looked oddly happy as the image slowly broke up into licks of flame that winked out one by one. Alaska tried to reach out her mind to his, but she felt nothing, not a ghost of a memory.

"We can toast marshmallows in his honor later, Ala. Now we move."

Alaska allowed Jeep to pull her toward the forest. "You and the girl follow the trail Colin and Davey blazed for us. I'll take the rear."

"Wait. I can help us." Marta raised her arms and the wind picked up, ripping the snow and ice away to hide their footprints and their scent, tossing obstacle course equipment about to complicate pursuit, whipping snow horizontally to hide them from normal sight and infrared sensors. Then she collapsed onto the snow.

"I got her," Jeep said. She handed Alaska her rifle, and lifted Marta over her good shoulder. "*You* take the rear, Ala. Keep checkin' behind us."

When dawn broke they were still plodding through the snow. They kept their heads down and kept moving, their fear of recapture barely holding their exhaustion at bay. Before noon fatigue won.

"Halt," Alaska called, her voice raspy, and softer than she'd expected. She was thirsty. She was tired. She was *cold*. "I need . . ."

She collapsed against the frozen bark of a tree. Her whole body hurt.

Colin found a tree and placed his brother down beside it. Davey had been drifting in and out of consciousness for hours—mostly out. Without medical care that none of them could give, Alaska knew he wouldn't make it.

Jeep eased the mage from her right shoulder and put Marta on her feet. Her left arm still hung useless. The neomage huddled beside Alaska. Only Jeep remained standing. She took back the rifle and faced outward, senses alert for pursuers.

"I'll keep watch in this direction," Alaska said. Jeep only smiled as Alaska quickly drifted into a troubled sleep.

Shooting and explosions sounded all around her—the attack on her hometown. On the ground lay her sweet mother, her lifeless blue eyes staring into nothingness. Aunt Cora lay nearby, her dead hand still outstretched to Alaska. And the Army officer—he shouldn't be here, and yet it felt somehow natural that he was. Alaska stood looking at her lost family...lost herself, unsure of what to do.

The people moved around her but there was only silence.

Then a man bent in front of her, lifted her chin with one hand, while the other held her arm. He was beardless and looked kind. His hair was long and dark . . . and he had wings . . . beautiful wings of interweaving purple and red . . . wings like the seraphs in the kirk paintings.

"Are you hurt, little one?" he'd asked. His voice was deep, musical.

"I want my Momma," she'd cried, and he pulled her to his chest and held her close, rocking her while she wailed into his neck.

"This pain will pass, little one. It will strengthen you. You will have the strength to lead the weak to safety, to banish those who would do humans and mages harm, to help the deserving overcome what your world suffers, and to kill those who cause the suffering, whether they claim to be of the Light or the Darkness. That is, if you choose to use your pain."

He kissed her forehead and said, "Know that I will always be watching you."

Then Jeep was saying something, but Alaska couldn't quite understand what it was. It was getting louder, though.

"Wake up, Ala. Wake up!"

She jerked awake. "What is it?" she said, her hands searching the ground for the handgun. "Are they here? Have they followed us?"

"I woke you because you were goin' on in your sleep. You were distressin' Marta," Jeep said, and she needs her rest."

Alaska felt her face, and there was moisture freezing there. "Was I . . . crying?"

"Yeah. It was weird. I never seen you cry before. It's unnervin'."

"Sorry. I was having a dream from the Before Times"—what they called their lives before Suarez—"a dream I haven't had for years."

"I'm cold and hungry," Marta said from the ball she was rolled up in, her head barely peeking out of the coat she wore.

"Davey's hurt bad," Colin chimed in. "Jeep's arm is swollen to three times its size. We need help."

A pang of guilt struck and Alaska sighed. "I'm afraid I didn't have much of a plan when I said we should save Marta. There wasn't time to prepare. We have one rifle, a handgun, no extra ammunition, no food, no clothing, blankets . . ."

"Don't feel bad for us," Jeep said. "We volunteered." Colin chuckled. "We have our lives. We have *us*," said Jeep. "The rest is details."

"She's right," a deep male voice came from a few yards ahead.

Jeep shifted the rifle muzzle at the newcomer. His hands were held up, empty of weapons—the only thing that prevented Jeep from shooting immediately. He was tall wearing a heavy coat. The features beneath his hood looked Native American.

"How did you sneak up on me?" Jeep demanded.

"I'm no threat to you, young ones," he said, not moving. The rifle didn't move either. "I've come to bring you the details. Here is food and other supplies," he said, his boot-toe nudging a heavy-looking sack on the ground.

"Who are you?" she asked.

"I'm, Noah, servant of the watcher Rama, once called Ramiel, before he sinned and fell from the Most High. My master had been the "angel of hope and interpreter of visions. He sent me to help Alaska Stanhope and her friends get out of here."

"I'm not Alaska Stanhope. My last name is Jonas."

"Jonas is your mother's name. You are also the daughter of Jason Stanhope."

"Fine. The father who abandoned me was named Stanhope. Big deal."

"Your cousin Jeremiah is . . . was . . . son of Sharon Anne Stanhope."

"Jeremiah was a long-lost cousin that I didn't know about? Is that it? Is Jeremiah the only one or do I have other cousins? Aunts? Uncles? Brothers and sisters?" her voice getting louder, angrier with each question.

Noah just shook his head. "I don't know. Your father's still alive, so it's possible. I *do* know that you're descendants of the Mole Man."

Alaska stood up, her face a mask of confusion. "Mole Man? Now I'm a descendant of the Mole Man? Like in the stories?"

"Enough about mole people," Jeep interrupted. "You said someone's watching us?"

"Rama, has been watching over you, Alaska Stanhope, since he first encountered you in the mountains."

"Watching over me? A *seraph* watching over me?"

Noah hesitated before answering. "Not—yes. Effectively, yes."

She thought of the winged being in her dream, the flames, the screams. Tears welled up in her eyes, rolling down to freeze to her cheeks. "If that's true, he's done a *terrible* job."

"You were where you needed to be, Alaska, as was Jeremiah."

"He let me be imprisoned? I needed that? I was just a little girl. And what about the other kids? All of us kids! Jeremiah!" she yelled.

"Lashon, was Rama's servant flame, sent to Jeremiah when he was most needed. He helped you escape. I've been sent to start you on your next journey."

"I'm not going anywhere with you."

"Yes. I was told you'd be stubborn."

"A strange man accosts me in the woods and tells me he's here to save us, and I'm expected to just go with him? I'm not letting you take me from one prison to the next."

Suddenly Colin was standing to the left of Alaska, brandishing a butcher's cleaver menacingly, his glare grim. Jeep stood on Alaska's right with the gun.

"I am here to help you, not imprison you," Noah said. "But have it your way. These supplies are yours. Five miles from here I have a truck that can take you to a town where they won't ask questions—or further, if you'd prefer."

Alaska turned to Marta and Colin, "I think maybe you should go with him. He can get you to safety and help Davey. I need to go back. Suarez wasn't there last night, but he'll be coming when he gets word of what happened. I want to make sure he pays for what he did to us."

Noah sniffed the smoke-filled air. "You and your friends have destroyed his camp—though I know he has others. You've killed several of his trainers and troops. But more importantly, you've taken away some of his best —alive. He won't sleep comfortably until every last one of you is dead. You can barely stand, and his men will be ready for you. You've done plenty for your first day of independence, Alaska Stanhope, don't you think?"

When Alaska didn't reply, Noah shrugged and started walking west. As he wove through the trees, he began singing Jeremiah's frog song.

The group watched him go, and then turned their eyes to Alaska. Half a minute passed in silence.

Marta broke the silence. "I trust you. I go where you go."

"What the mage said," Jeep added.

"We're in," Colin said, rifling through the supplies for food, and brandishing a package of crackers triumphantly above his head. He threw his brother over his shoulder and tossed the crackers to the neomage with his free arm.

"Holy hellhole," Alaska said, stealing Jeep's favorite term. "This isn't over, Jeep. Suarez *will* die at my hands."

"Agreed, Ala."

"Absolutely," chimed in Marta.

Alaska looked over her motley group and sighed. She could still hear the man singing in the distance. As she headed down the path he took, she couldn't help but join him, singing the frog song.

The Stars Were Right
84 PA / 2096 AD

Spike Y Jones

"Okay, everybody, look smart: thirty-five minutes to launch."

"Thirty-five minutes to nothing," muttered someone from behind his back.

"*Who* said that? Who was it?" Jay Kelly's face was already red from recent days of exposure to the Florida sun, and the rising blood turned it almost purple.

After a few awkward silent moments, a man stepped forward. Kelly didn't recognize him, but there'd been a lot of new people—replacement people—hired in the days immediately leading up to the launch.

"I said it. Because it's stupid. It's not a launch. The fly boys're just *putting* it there for you."

"*Fly*—? That's it. Talking back to the launch director? Fired. Jeopardizing brand integrity? Fired. Dragon-loving blasphemy—*in the presence of the High Host no less*? Fired!"

At the mention of the seraphim some of the other crew members glanced around nervously, but there was still only one seraph present, Ar-R'ad, Driver of the Clouds, and he was safely distant, apparently talking comfortably with the technicians making final checks on the refurbished satellite.

The now-unemployed gaffer left with only a rude gesture at Director Kelly, who turned to yelling at the rest of TV crew. "This is the biggest thing that ever happened to SNN. Launching our own branded satellite will put SNN on the map—on *every* map. Everything has to be perfect, so just follow the script. Now someone test the smoke generator again; how many times do I have to tell you that everything has to be just right?"

"Thirty minutes to launch. Going live in five, four, three, two . . ."

"It's 11:30 a.m. here at Cape Canaveral, Florida. Welcome to this special broadcast of the launch of the SNN Satellite News Network satellite. I'm Matthew Thomas."

"And I'm Mary McGowan."

"We're live in our special window-on-the-launch studio here at the New Kennedy Space Center, where in a few short minutes a septad of seraphs will launch the SNN satellite into orbit, to make SNN the only news network to have its own dedicated satellite in orbit. And, Mary, I believe you have a special guest . . ."

"Very special, Matthew. As we watch live the final countdown to the twelve noon launch, I'd like to bring in Administration of the ArchSeraph Envoy Eustace Madder, who was instrumental in securing the aid of the seraphim for the launch of SNN's dedicated worldwide broadcast satellite. Ambassador Madder, welcome to the broadcast."

"Thank you, Miss McGowan."

"Feel free to call me Mary. Can you tell our viewers a bit about your communications with the Herald Ar-Ra'd? Is he really as approachable as some have said? And have you met other seraphs? Is Ar-R'ad different in any respects from those other emissaries?"

"Well, Miss McGowan, we must be careful not to engage in gossip. But I'd be happy to provide education to your viewers about this emissary of the Most High. When . . ."

"Dragon's balls! I thought I told you to get the godforsaken smoke machine working. This is all about visuals. If we get this right, our viewers will feel like they're right here beside us. It'll be as big as sliced bread."

"What's sliced br . . ."

"Shut up. But if you spawn-brained idiots screw this up . . ."

"T-minus five minutes and holding. T-minus five minutes and . . ."

"As you just heard Mission Control say over the loudspeakers, we're still in a launch delay here at the New Kennedy Space Center. We've called our technical expert, retired Air Force pilot Colonel Richard Wainwright, into the studio to explain the technical issues that have delayed the launch of SNN's satellite, and to talk about some of the dangers that make this launch anything but routine. Colonel Wainwright, welcome back."

"Thank you. Glad to be here."

"So, what is Mission Control saying about the delay?"

"Actually, not a lot, Matthew. The countdown schedule has room built into it for any number of minor checks and corrections, so we have to assume that if they've actually put the launch on hold, it must be something mission-critical, something that could doom the satellite if it weren't corrected before launch. There's no primary propulsion system in the satellite . . ."

"No rocket."

"Exactly. No rocket. But there are attitude jets—small steering rockets, used to keep the satellite in proper position once in orbit. If something went wrong with them, then the satellite could find itself in space but unable to function properly. Then there are the folding solar panels on the side of the craft. If they don't unfold, or unfold incorrectly . . ."

~

"Get that spawn-screwing truck out of the shot!"

"But, Director Kelly, the technicians need to recharge the onboard batteries and . . ."

"I don't care what they say they have to do; that's their job. But they are *not* parking their truck in front of the network logo. Now you get that thing out of my shot or I'll call on Azazel and his demon hordes to move the truck and then move every last one of you to whatever hole in the ground he fell into at the end of the War."

"It's 11:59 here in Central Florida—one minute from the scheduled time of the launch of the SNN satellite, but we're still in launch delay mode. The technicians tell us that they can't predict how long the hold will last, but there's no likelihood of the launch being scrubbed. While we wait for the techs to give the go-ahead, we'll take a break for some messages from our sponsors."

"The following commercials are approved for all audiences by the Department of Information."

"Smoother, faster acceleration? Check. Increase, longer-lasting el-power? Check. Redesigned, sleeker lines? Check. The new 2097 El-Ektra is the first . . ."

"We inter—uh—there you see the seraphs—uh—okay, as they speed out of the shot, let's go back to a moment ago, when the septad of seraphs suddenly showed up and took their positions around the satellite in preparation for launch. There you see the six Aluf seraphs arranging themselves in a triangular pattern around the launch stack, while Ar-Ra'd, apparently the leader of this mission, presumably because of his associations with—uh—the clouds, is standing apart from them at one corner of the triangle. Uh—it looks like they bow their heads in prayer for just a moment, and then, they raise their arms, spread their wings, and the seven of them, and the satellite, accelerate into the sky."

"While we wait for Mary McGowan and AAS Envoy Madder, Colonel Wainwright, what can you tell us . . ."

"The countdown clock was on hold. What Dark-bound idiot gave the go-ahead order to the seraphs? Who cost us a live shot I'd been setting up for two months? Whose ass do I have to personally kick straight into the nearest hellhole?"

Most of the humans standing between Jay Kelly and the newly-returned-from-space Ar-Ra'd drifted out of the approaching launch director's way. At the sound of Kelly's blasphemy, a kirk elder quietly signaled to a knot of AAS warriors, calling them from their station in the shade. Oblivious, Kelly stomped toward the seraph.

"You weren't supposed to go up until everything was just right. There was a launch delay in place. Didn't you see the countdown clock was stopped? Of all the stupid—the launch was delayed until we got things right. Why on Earth did you have to blow the goddamned shot by . . ."

Ar-Ra'd's movements were almost too swift for the eye to follow, as a golden sword appeared in his hand, he swung it at Jay Kelly's head, and at the moment of contact a burst of light as bright as the sun blinded all the mortals in the area. Calmly, the seraph spoke, addressing the elder and warriors as if they'd addressed him: "We were asked to return the machine to its proper place among the stars when the arrangements were in order." As their eyesight cleared, the mortals could see that Ar-Ra'd's hands were once again empty—as was the pile of clothing lying on the tarmac, wisps of smoke still rising from the shoes. "We do not understand all your . . . technology, but we understand the heavens. The stars were right."

Alone
94 PA / 2106 AD

Faith Hunter

I had been in Enclave. Sitting at a sidewalk café on the corner outside of the priestess's home with my twin sister, Rose, reading aloud a poem written by a Pre-Ap poet named Henry David Thoreau. The language was formal and wandering, with images so intense it seemed to uplift me to some higher plane. I was reading a line about the full moon when my gift fell.

Hammered me.

All the mages and all the *voices*.

All of them.

In my mind.

The cacophony, the wild blast of need and outrage and want and love and lust and *power*. The voices in my head. The voices of every mage in Enclave. Desires, hatreds, petty angers. So little kindness. So little love.

Puberty and my gift descended like a seraph in battle armor, brutalizing me, sending me screaming, falling to the street. Moaning. Gasping. My mind invaded by voices shouting, demanding.

And then Lolo's voice, soothing, a bitter tea at my lips. And then nothing.

When I woke, it was in an odd little bed that was rocking beneath me. The flannel sheets were rough compared to the mage-touched sheets I slept under in the priestess's house. The clothes I was wearing were cotton, my socks knitted wool. Human-made clothes. Around my neck was a leather thong, the opal disc pendant lying on my chest. My mage attributes didn't glow and I intuited a connection to the opal: I assumed it blanked them, making me look human, dull and ugly, keeping my secret from the human world.

There were handrails on the side of the bed. I levered myself over them and down to the floor to find myself in a private cabin of a sleeper car on a train. Outside of Enclave. Alone.

Six hours after waking, I was still here. *Alone*. I hated that word: *Alone*. And bored, with nothing to do but stare out at the world beyond the frosted glass as it rocketed by. For *days* more according to the porter, a tall, broad man with one blue eye and one brown eye. He also had the scar of a kirk brand on his face, but from the way the light diffused slightly around his cheek, I could tell he wore some sort of glamour. The branding was probably a response to the odd quirk of genetics that had given him mismatched eyes. Humans were afraid of anything different. Brandings were designed to be visible, as lessons to those who saw them. Facial scars could be horrible, and if the porter's was still partially visible through the glamour, it must be worse underneath. The glamour could have been worked to completely hide it, but humans probably would have considered that a sin worthy of more punishment.

I was curious, but I didn't ask. That would have been rude. And foolish. So I just tipped him well when he brought me meals and answered my few questions about our destination and the length of the trip and when and where on the train I could eat.

His name was Taft. And he didn't ask questions, which I appreciated.

He withdrew as I stared out the window into the falling night, eating the excellent grilled cheese, spinach, mushroom, and tomato sandwich and drinking the tea—black tea with real cream. Not thinking. Not feeling. Just staring out at my new, frozen world, so different from the New Orleans Enclave, with its damp heat and the smell of coffee and gumbo and beignets on the air. And the feel of creation energy dancing along my skin.

Beyond the ice-rimmed windows of the train were mountains and evergreens and the stark branches of leafless trees. Snow and ice covered everything. Everywhere. Except the vertical walls of rock the train passed between. The stone was cracked, split, splintered, and coated with an ice glaze, but so full of power that it called to me, called to my mage gift, the desire to work the energy stored in the stone heart of the world.

Beyond the windows of the train car was this unfamiliar place, this impossible scenery. The scent of ice on the ground, snow in the air, the stink of the steel rails and wheels, steel-against-steel, all assaulted my Stone mage nostrils with each breath. Yet even here, so far from Enclave, the distance growing with each moment, there was the presence of mage magics. The engine was powered by mage might, bartered and paid for. The rails kept free of ice, also by mage power. Despite the cold outside, the window didn't have ice covering it, except for a little frost in one corner. I touched the glass and felt the tingle of magic there too. The glass had been treated with a warming spell; the magics in the corner had begun to wear thin and would have to be recharged.

Mages were everywhere. We were nowhere. Humans used our magic but hated us for making it, for having access to it when they didn't. Humans were vile. And if I slipped up, they'd kill me.

The stories we'd been told in Enclave of what humans did to unlicensed witchy women had been vivid and intense. Remembering them now left my mouth dry, my heart pounding, my breath coming too fast. My reflection in the window changed as my skin began to glimmer, to glow, shining through the working of the amulet. In my panic, I'd released my neomage attributes, my eyes mirrored in the glass with the gray-blue of labradorite, my flesh like pearls. Even my red hair glowed scarlet. And the scars on my legs were pure white, evidence of my damaged body and a childhood marred by danger and Darkness.

I stared at myself, terrified. If the wrong person saw me like this . . .

But I had been trained since the crèche to control my powers and myself. The simple mantra taught to every neomage child forced its way up through my panic. "Stone and fire, water and air, blood and kin prevail," I whispered. "Wings and shield, dagger and sword, blood and kin prevail."

I said the phrases over and over, breathing deeply with each repetition, each breath fogging a round spot on the window only to have the conjure evaporate it away. I kept it up until I was calm, until my fears weren't somehow overriding the opal *Glamour* amulet's pre-programmed conjure.

The mage glow faded to human-ugly. Tears blurred my reflection, making it waver. My *Glamour* amulet was a comforting warmth in my fist, my true nature protected once again.

As my body calmed, my hunger returned. I finished my sandwich and the tea and then drank several bottles of Mason's Pure Godly Deep Well Water. Most local streams, lakes and wells were perfectly safe to drink from since the Apocalypse had eliminated diseases, overpopulation, and industrial pollution. But well-to-do humans still preferred expensive brand name water imported from trusted purified sources. And a neomage in hiding could piggyback on that affectation. We needed to know where our water came from, since some waters interfered with our elements. Well water was safest for me, and Lolo had probably ensured that the train was well stocked with Mason's.

And once again the window drew me. I turned off the light, crawled close on the small couch, and studied the new world beyond. And for the very first time, in the dark, I began to experiment with my Stone-gift. All by myself. Because I was *alone*. I would have no teachers. Never would, ever again. I knew that—despite Lolo's promise that she'd find a way for me to return.

But I still had the lessons I'd been taught in school. They would help. They could steer me.

Remembering the lesson of *sight*, I let my eyes fall out of focus. Within minutes, I figured out how to use mage sight. It wasn't nearly as hard to achieve as I'd feared, but it was a lot harder to hold onto. Mage sight was disorienting, made worse by a vague motion sickness from the movement of the train car. But when I could hold onto it, I was able to see the foulness of allergens, of ice and metal and trees and even air currents, bright but sickly.

Beneath my clothes, my prime amulet was glowing softly, automatically protecting me from the effect of the allergens, the elements that I couldn't use. But when we passed rock, I could see the might of stone, the granite glowing a warm and perfect blue/pink/lavender of might. The rock called to me. I hoped that wherever I was going I'd have access to stone. To the heart of the world.

A handful of pre-conjured amulets were in my pockets. I wasn't sure what they did, but I had days to figure them out. They would need to be charged when I got . . . wherever I was going. To the mountain "city" where Lolo had decided to send me. *Alone.*

Alone with my worthless, dangerous, extra gift. A gift that allowed me to read the minds of mages. Any mage, all mages I was close to. *Forced* me to read their minds. Though the train car was warm, I shivered remembering the horrible things mages thought.

Tired, I turned on the lamp and slid into the bed that Taft had made for me when he brought my dinner. The sheets were cold, and I pulled the heavy coverlet up. I withdrew the letter I'd tucked into my shirt, unfolded the single sheet. The note was dangerous to have, and I'd read and reread it so many times already that I almost had it memorized anyway, but I hadn't been able to destroy it. Not yet. It was written in Lolo's crabbed penmanship and with her Cajun phrasings.

> *Thorn.*
>
> *When you wake, you be far from other mages, as safe as I might manage. You should still have you memory, but if not, know this. When you gift descend, you develop a condition I am calling mind-openness, allowing you entrée to all other mages' mind. It was more clamor than anyone could handle, especially a mage so young and inexperience. Thus, I have you on a train, sending you away to safety, for now.*
>
> *I sending you to a human man named Lem in Mineral City. No one there has ever seen a mage. They won't know what to look for. They won't expect one to arrive via train. You weapons case is in luggage with you chest. It will arrive with you, never fear, along with other necessities. In the sleeper compartment is enough to get you to Mineral City, including amulets and a* Book of Workings. *You recharge the stone and keep you mage attributes muted. The simple spells you need to survive be easy to follow in* Book of Workings. *If you have question, answer in the* Book.
>
> *Tell no one what you are. Not even Lem.*
>
> *Know that I begin search for a cure for you mind-openness. Practice you savage chi and savage blade. You and Rose will be battle mages, together, a weapon against Darkness.*
>
> *Learn how to use and control you Stone-gift.*
>
> *I send supplies.*
> *Lolo*
> *P.S: destroy this note*

What Lolo hadn't said was that I was now *rogue.* From the bitter taste in my mouth and the carpet fibers on my clothes when I woke up, I figured out that I had been drugged, smuggled out, and sent away. A mage away from Enclave, without a visa, without ID. Without protection. If discovered, humans would have the right to rape me, torture me, and kill me.

If there was a sin in being out of Enclave, it wasn't mine, as all children are innocent, but that wouldn't stop humans if they learned what I was. Humans were inherently bitter and violent. Everyone knew that.

Yet Lolo was sending me to a human. What kind of man was Lem? Was he a better human than others of his kind? How did Lolo know him? Or of him? Not that it mattered.

I was in so much danger that I should have been immobilized by fear. But I had survived being trapped in a nest of devil-spawn. I had the scars to prove it. I could survive this too. If I was careful.

I refolded the letter and hid it away again. Tears threatened, tickling beneath my lids. Missing Lolo. Missing Rose. *Alone.*

"Stone and fire, water and air, blood and kin prevail," I whispered again. "Wings and shield, dagger and sword, blood and kin prevail."

The train rocked me, soothing in its own way. I slept at long last, clutching the opal amulet.

Morning broke and Taft woke me with a three-tap knock. I pulled the coverlet over me against the cold and for the modesty that the human would expect me to feel. He took my breakfast order, and fired up the water heater in my shower alcove. I had no idea if I would be able to use the shower. If the water the train had taken on at the last stop was collected rain water or river water, water that had been in recent contact with air, I might be in trouble. Everything about living with humans was going to be difficult.

I was in luck. When I tested the water with a fingertip, the shower water didn't drain all my energy on contact.

Refreshed, I put my red hair—human drab—up in a big messy bun and dressed in clean human clothes in somber greens and blues instead of the vibrant shades I was used to. It was no secret to the world that mages had flamboyant style, whereas humans were chaste and dull and unimaginative. I made my own bed. I knew it was Taft's job, but I figured he would be busy with all the old humans who had boarded at the dawn stop in Opelika, Alabama, a day outside of Atlanta. There must have been twenty, all self-important humans, all traveling in the sleeper cars.

I could tell Taft was harried when breakfast was late. As he opened the door, I could hear a human woman demanding, "More towels, more wash clothes, and hot tea. And hurry up about it, you genetic abnormality."

Her words made me angry. She was insulting the man who was waiting on her, which seemed foolish, cruel, and unnecessary. If it had been me, I'd have cooked something slimy into her eggs and given her salt instead of sugar for her tea. But then, I'd been called impulsive all my life.

I leaned until I could see out the door, beyond Taft's bulk as he maneuvered my food tray inside the small space, and took in the blonde, blue-eyed woman. She had diamonds on her fingers and wrists and around her neck, and she was tall and lean, with perfect skin and that look that only money can buy—"money" meaning expensive amulets full of glamour that hid the imperfections. In her case, she was glamoured all over, from her hair, eyes, skin, and waist, to her elegant ankles. In reality, the woman likely looked totally different.

I wondered who she was faking for, but then the middle-aged man behind her said, "It's all right, dear. He'll get to us."

"He'll get to us *now*," she snapped, "or I'll see his other cheek branded too."

Taft paled.

"It's okay," I said to Taft, my voice soft. "Go help her. I'm fine."

"Thank you, Miss," he said, and he was gone.

The moment I was alone, I sat down on the couch so I wouldn't make the motion sickness worse, and calmed myself down. It took a while. By the time I turned to the food, it was stone cold. So was the tea. And with the glamoured woman giving Taft so much trouble, I'd never call for fresh.

Instead, I pulled out my amulets, looking for one that might contain a pre-programmed conjure to reheat the food, the sort of convenience that would be commonplace in Enclave. The stones were brilliant in mage sight, glowing red, blue, emerald, and purple-black. They were mesmerizing. I could stare at them all day. But they were obviously more than pretty. The crystalline microstructure of the stones contained power. Each amulet's structure was different and told an experienced mage what the amulet did. To me they weren't as obvious.

One of the simplest, a small carved soapstone cat-paw, looked like it should store and release heat. Most amulets require a spoken word or a physical gesture to activate, and I had no idea what sign or word would work. After several attempts, I placed the cat-paw on a small bit of egg and said the word, "Warm."

The soapstone glowed red and then orange . . . and burned the egg to a crisp. "I need to learn control first," I informed the scorched egg as I waved away charred-egg smoke. "Then I need to learn how to recharge you pretty little amulets. You'll make my life much easier in Mineral City. And yes, Lolo, I am talking to the stones you sent me."

More carefully, I heated the rest of breakfast and the cup of tea, and enjoyed the meal immensely.

I traveled alone in my private cabin all day, curled up on the couch with blankets, reading the *Book Of Workings*, and trying different conjures with the amulets—simple ones that didn't require a mage circle. The Book itself didn't really contain detailed, spelled-out, step-by-step conjures as much as discussions of them, hints, and other nonhelpfulness.

Through trial and error, I learned how to spark a flame with the handy-dandy cooking amulet, and how to use the black and clear agate healing stone. It looked roughly like a frog and, if I was still in Enclave, I'd take the agate to the stone-working class and get them to show me how to carve and polish it to enhance the froggy shape. Still, it was cute.

The white onyx fish likely held a sphere of protection or battle shield.

The clear quartz was used for illumination in the dark, like a flashlight or torch.

There was a pink quartz rose I had shaped and polished myself in class. Now just holding it filled me with a sense of calm and peace. I tucked it into my chest pocket.

I'd need a necklace for them all, like other Stone mages wore. But that would be foolish because then humans might discover what I was. I'd have to hide it beneath my clothes somehow.

I fingered a large cabochon of picture jasper, the lines of minerals looking like a scene as viewed from a Pre-Ap airplane—roads across a hilly desert landscape. In one corner was a greenish diffusion that looked like a desert oasis. It was beautiful and felt warm in my hand. I wasn't very good at it yet, but I focused my mage sight on it. It lit up as if I'd pointed a lantern at it, the light fracturing through the green minerals. It was a disruptor charm, but I had no idea what it was intended to disrupt, which would make it dangerous to test. What if it disrupted the train and the cars flew off the tracks? But Lolo had given it to me, so I assumed it would reveal itself to me eventually.

Then there were two amulets I couldn't figure out at all.

One, an onyx Arctic seal, seemed to be empty of energy, but it had a pathway to . . . somewhere inside of it.

And the last amulet was carved out of wood, which meant it had most likely come from Lolo herself. The microstructures of the wood were alien to me; I couldn't read them to tell me what the amulet did. But it had to be something special.

After lunch, I went through the carry-on luggage Lolo had packed for me. Her gifts didn't include salt mined from below ground, the only salt a Stone mage could use in workings. And the wood floor of the train car would have made a working circle impossible anyway. She didn't provide any personal items from my past except my comb, brush, toothbrush, and a silk-stitched needlepoint in shades of beige and brown framed in painted wood. The needlepoint had hung above my bed for all fourteen years of my life, stitched with the prophecy given by Lolo when my twin and I were born: *A Rose by any Other Name will still draw Blood.* Birth prophecies were usually obscure. Mine had been interpreted to say that the rose and the thorn worked together to draw blood—that Rose and I, together, would be warriors unlike any other. Meaningless now that Rose and I were separated.

The only other thing of real interest was a small jewelry box, black velvet with a hinged lid. I opened it to find a tiny chip of teal and aqua stone, zoisite. Crammed inside the lid was a folded scrap of paper—a note in Lolo's crabbed hand: *"This here a one-time charm. Use once, then it nothing but a rock. You in danger with a conjure, you drop stone in water—any kind—and it activate. It stop all conjures except them in contact with you body. Use with care."* Lolo was canny. Some said she had second sight. More than useful, this charm was important.

She'd also packed three books for me, though I wasn't particularly interested in reading. Two were Pre-Ap fantasy novels, and one was a mystery set in the Last War. *Boring*. I stared out the window instead. But by mid-afternoon I was bored beyond belief—almost bored enough to try to read a book—and wandered down the train to the dining car for tea. The car was only sparsely occupied, so I had my own table. Taft, moving quickly and economically despite his large frame, took my order and left me to the book I'd carried in, one of the novels. But I left the covers closed, sipping tea and staring out the window, surreptitiously watching the half-dozen humans in the car. Humans were not complete unknowns in Enclave, but I had never spent much time with them, as there were none living in the priestess's home where I grew up. I saw how often the well-dressed, upper-class humans used magic. They wore it as cosmetics, as charisma enhancers, as luck inducers. Some of them fairly glowed with applied creation energy.

When the dining car emptied, I left too and returned to my cabin.

After dinner, late on that full first day of consciousness, the opal *Glamour* amulet that hid my mage attributes stopped working. It was sudden and shocking, and I instantly began to glow. At first I tried what had worked before, reciting the "Stone and fire, water and air" mantra over and over again, but it had no effect.

When I finally gave up on that, I turned mage sight onto the opal disc. The *Glamour* amulet had run out of power.

For a continuous conjure, my prime amulet should have picked up the duties of the working, automatically recharging the *Glamour* amulet. That's how things worked for other neomages. But it hadn't.

I pulled out the *Book of Workings* again. Things in the *Book* weren't arranged in any obvious way, but after some false starts and cross-referencing I found my problem in a section on puberty. Since my gift had opened, my prime was no longer fully attuned to me. All I needed to do was to reset my prime to adult specifications through the Ceremony of Attainment, the ceremony all mages went through when their gift fell upon them.

That brought me down hard. That clearly would not be happening while on the train. I'd need blood and massive amounts of stone. Stone like the huge, broken cliffs and mountains we passed. I'd need to get off the train for that. "Seraph bones," I muttered, cursing. I wondered when that would occur to Lolo and what she would do about it.

I went through the book again and found that there was no Ceremony of Attainment in the *Book of Workings*. "Of course there isn't. The one thing I need most I don't have access to."

Desperate, I paged back and forth through the *Book of Workings*, and found an entry that taught me how to recharge my amulet stones from an elemental source when they ran out of power. In an addendum, someone had written how pre-conjured amulets could be recharged from primes in an emergency. Which this was.

I had no idea if the method would work with my poorly attuned prime, but the recharge conjure seemed simple enough: Just press the empty stone against my prime and place both in contact with my body, then push power into the empty, assuming I could figure out how to do that. I didn't even need a circle to contain the energies, as they would be in constant contact with my body. It sounded easy.

But it didn't feel easy to me. It felt terrifying. What if the poorly attuned prime ruined the amulet? And itself? I'd heard of such things happening and the mage having to be given a brand new prime amulet. "Yeah, that door's shut too now."

I pulled the blanket up higher, reheated my tea, and tried to figure out what to do. Back before Enclaves had been created as safe havens in which to test our gifts, before the *Book Of Workings* had been compiled through decades of trial and error, neomages developing new conjures had been known to disintegrate, to burn to death, to explode. And that was before mages had prime amulets. Maybe the primes helped to prevent that. Maybe not having a fully functional prime would leave me open to all that danger.

Mages were supposed to have help in their first, most important year of settling into their gifts, of finding a niche in Enclave. I would be going it alone. I didn't know what I'd do if my prime ran out of power before I got to my destination, but for now, I could try to transfer some creation energy from my not-quite-perfect-prime to the pre-conjured disguise amulet.

I double-checked the lock on the outer door, opened the small door to the minuscule bathroom so I could see myself in the mirror, and pulled my tunic top up, exposing my belly. I pressed the stones together above my navel, on bare skin. Not because there was anything in the entry in the *Book* that specified contact with bare skin or the navel, but I knew that some older mages wore their primes inside their clothes on long chains, so it seemed to make sense.

Moments later my mage attributes flickered off, then on, and then off again. And they stayed that way. Mage sight showed the prime holding steady and the opal fully charged. It was a beautiful stone, but not so valuable that it would look out of place adorning a teenaged girl.

Relieved, I washed my face and was about to change into my night clothes when I heard voices in the hallway, a woman's shrill voice shouting, "You stupid defect! Look what you did!"

I cracked open the door. The blonde woman was standing in the corridor in her night-robe, a luxury that mage sight confirmed was mage-touched, the velvet catching the lights, glowing as it flowed across her body, emphasizing breasts and hips, hiding belly and soft underarms. She was rich, like Midas rich. None of the other humans on board wore so much magery. Most wore none. Mage magics were expensive.

On the floor near the woman were trays with empty wine bottles, lipstick-smeared glasses, china plates and bowls, and silver utensils. Somebody had been having a party.

"You stained my dress!" the woman screeched, lifting a royal blue formal gown to the lights. Her voice climbed higher, "It's *ruined*."

"No, ma'am," Taft said, quietly, deferentially.

The woman stepped forward, her face inches from Taft. "What did you say?"

He hunched as if afraid, but his right foot slid backward, stabilizing his center of gravity; his right hand fisted behind his back, invisible to the blonde—all one motion. The reflexes of a man with plenty of martial arts training.

Then his fist opened, his muscles relaxed, and I wasn't sure what I had seen.

"I didn't stain your dress, ma'am. I was just taking it to be cleaned."

Her eyes went wide and she shook the dress at Taft. "I'll have your job and you branded again. I'll have you stripped naked and flogged in the streets."

"Please, ma'am. I didn't stain your dress. It was—"

"Are you calling me a liar?" Her voice dropped into a hiss that would have done a water moccasin proud. "You despicable, flawed, aberration. You *dare* to call *me* a liar, you malformed . . . *deviant*."

I pushed my door fully open and said, loudly, "Taft, thank you so much for the excellent dinner tonight! I appreciate . . ." I let my words fade away, paused, looked around wide-eyed, then asked, even more loudly, "Is this woman hitting you?" I stepped fully into the hallway. "Help! Help! There's a woman hitting the porter! Help!"

Doors opened all along the corridor.

I continued shouting. "She's drunk and I think she's beating Taft!"

"I am not drunk, you—"

The door behind her opened and her tirade abruptly cut off. The middle-aged man traveling with her said, "Koren, it's all right. Come back inside."

"It's not all right. Look what he did! You always say it fine, that it's all right when it isn't. That porter ruined my dress!"

"No, Koren," the man said. "You dropped whiskey sauce on it at dinner. I asked Taft if he'd try to get the stain out. He was taking it away to work on it."

Koren's face shifted from fury to embarrassment to calculation and back to fury. She glared at me, and I dropped my shoulders to make my already small frame look smaller and opened my eyes really wide to look younger. *Afraid.*

Koren turned to Taft and whispered, "You fix this dress or I'll see you lose your job."

"Yes, ma'am. I'm sorry, ma'am. Thank you, sir. I'll try to get the sauce out of the dress." Taft skittered down the hall, the dress in his hands.

I gave Koren my meanest look, "You're nasty. And spiteful. And cruel. And selfish. And now your boyfriend knows how mean you really are."

Koren turned and looked at her man friend. His eyes were downcast, embarrassed and humiliated for Koren's behavior. "Hope your beauty glamours don't fail. Then he'll know how you look physically too. He'll have the full picture of what you actually are." The man looked up quickly, taking in his mean-spirited girlfriend, his eyes narrowing. Maybe he'd finally figured out he'd been bamboozled. I shut the door.

I slept deeply, with a sense of malicious satisfaction and woke up just after dawn with the train slowing rapidly. I gripped the hand rails on the bed. Steel screeched on steel. The car shuddered, making my jaws clack together.

The jarring, quaking, deep vibration faded as the train came to a stop.

Nearby, I heard a loud crack. I leaped from the bed, threw on yesterday's human-ugly clothing, with the amulets still in the pockets. Barefooted, I rushed into the corridor along with most of the other occupants of the sleeper car. The woman, Koren, was standing there, dressed, her blonde hair up in a twist. Behind her the door stood open, her compartment revealed. Her traveling companion lay on the floor, head turned to the side, in a pool of blood. His chest was unmoving, his eyes open.

I heard voices shouting, "Get down! Get down on the floor!"

In an eye blink, I realized several things.

The man was dead.

Koren held a pistol. Pointed at Taft. Who was on one knee on the floor. Hands raised.

Koren was surrounded by masked men. All dressed in black. All with guns. Pointing at the people in the hallway and away from Koren. And they were the ones shouting.

Also, Taft was armed. The outline of his gun was visible beneath his clothes, at his back. Taft was far more than he seemed.

Last, I realized that the train was being robbed.

My fingers twitched for the sword I had been learning to use. But it was safely stowed in the baggage car. I had no weapon but my wits. I figured that meant I'd be dead in seconds.

My amulets warmed up. My prime and one in my pants pocket. The disruptor jasper. Was it for guns? Oh. *Wrath of angels.* Lolo and her second sight.

"You." Koren shifted her aim, pointing the gun at me. "You've been nothing but trouble."

I gripped the jasper and whispered, "Guns."

Koren pulled the trigger. Nothing happened. Not a thing. "*Yes,*" I muttered.

From the floor, Taft struck out in a long, loose, easy, and deceptively powerful kick. His foot hit Koren's arm. The gun flew. Bone broke with sharp *crack*. Taft rose from the floor, fast, in the lion stance. He spun in a complicated set of moves that incorporated parts of several advanced techniques. Hands and feet snapping out. In less than two heartbeats, the men wearing black were down, disabled, incapacitated, dead, or unconscious.

My mouth fell open. Taft knew savage chi. He was a half-breed. Half-human, half mage.

Taft stood and adjusted his white jacket. "You folks go on back in your cabins. Everything is under control here."

A man down the corridor gasped, "You're a . . . *mule*." The last word was filled with distaste, his face pulled down into harsh lines, as if he was disgusted to have been rescued by a half-breed.

Taft's disfigured face twisted, but before he could speak, I said, in my best little-girl voice, "And he saved our lives. Taft is a *hero*." I clasped my hands in front of my chest and stared at Taft with what I hoped looked like adoring eyes. I wasn't much of an actor, but the man who clearly hated half breeds went silent. "*Our* hero!" I added just in case the humans were stupid as well as racist.

Taft chuckled and raised an eyebrow at me in a look that the others couldn't see. He turned his attention to them. "Not a hero. Just a train marshal, a Hand of the Law doing his job, and unspeakably grateful to the Most High for a misfire." He shook his head in wonderment, completely missing my horrified expression. "Seraphic intervention. Surely an instance of seraphic intervention."

Taft was *police*. Taft was undercover. *Sweet seraph*. I was I trouble.

I swept the horror off my face and tried to restore the adoring expression I'd been wearing only moments before.

Koren was on the floor of the cabin amidst the bodies of the men in black, holding her arm, making a piteous mewling sound.

"Koren Steinwald," Taft said, his voice officious, "You are under arrest for the murder of Harold Meechum, and for attempted train robbery. You and your men will be kept in the mail car under the watchful eye of my partner, and remanded over to the proper authorities at our next stop. May the High Host have mercy on your soul, for the court system will not."

Turning back to me, he continued in his normal voice, "I've got it all under control. You're safe now. Go back into your room, little miss. I'll bring you breakfast soon."

I backed away and closed the door. Leaned against it. Tried to remember how to breathe.

Behind me, I could hear Koren curse as Taft handcuffed the prisoners, and then dragged them down the corridor to the next train car. The doors closed.

A Hand of the Law would arrest me. Torture me. Turn me over to the kirk. I was an unlicensed neomage who had just released a conjure in his presence. But maybe he hadn't noticed. *Misfire*, he'd said. Was I safe? I must be safe. He hadn't arrested me and dragged me away with Koren.

I fell on the bed and pulled the covers over me, shaking with cold and shock.

It took quite a while to get the train back up and running. And then more time at the next stop. It would put us a day late getting to Mineral City, but I didn't care how long the trip was. I would be spending the rest of the trip locked safe in my room, having my meals left on the other side of the door.

~

The days dragged on. I practiced with my amulets. Studied the *Book of Workings*. Got bored again and read one of the Pre-Ap books. It was about a place where dragons and humans were friends and worked together to try to save their world. A world where people could *ride* dragons to fight a menace in the sky. It sounded amazing and made me want to soar on a dragon. But no way were the dragons in my world going to work with anyone. No way were they going to allow a human to ride them. Humans and their souls were tasty treats to dragons in my world.

Four days passed. We were a little over thirty-six hours late so far, making the trip far longer than Lolo had expected. Four days as my opal *Glamour* amulet faded and died several times and had to be recharged from my prime. And then my prime began to fade. It needed to be attuned to my energies. It needed to be recharged. And for that all I needed was a long train stop at a depot near rock. Lots of rock.

We had been climbing into the Appalachians for days now, our forward progress hampered by the meandering route necessary for a train to rise in altitude. And the Appalachians were stone.

Most of our stops to take on water and supplies were near towns, and towns were usually built on at least marginally farmable land, the soil of centuries overlaid on the bedrock. The train sometimes stood still for an hour or more, and passengers would leave to shop in the stores near the depot. But even with the town built on soil, there would have to be ex-posed rock somewhere—the dirt could be thin in the mountains. Given time and rock, I'd be fine. I just needed to know when the next appropriate stop would be.

Summoning my courage, I dressed in long sleeves and thin gloves to cover my softly glimmering limbs, a kerchief over my hair. Lolo had packed human makeup, and I used some of that, inexpertly, on my face. I was surprised that Lolo even thought of makeup.

When Taft knocked on my door to deliver breakfast, I opened it wide and backed away.

"Are you okay, little miss?" he asked. "I know the robbery attempt was a terrifying thing for you. I promise you're safe now."

"Thank you. I do feel better. But I need to get out a bit. I want to buy a present for my adoptive father. Do we have a long stop soon?"

"We'll be pulling through Hendersonville at 10 a.m. and our layover there is close to four hours. We'll be shuffling the deck." At my blank look he said, "The cars have to be uncoupled and recoupled to a different kind of engine, one that's equipped with the proper devices to melt snow and ice as we climb the last leg. You can shop, eat a meal, even take a tour of the old ruins, if you want."

Hendersonville had been badly damaged in the Last War, and a tour might give me a chance to get close to stone. "I'd like that," I said. "Thank you."

"Any time, little miss." He backed away and closed my door. I had to wonder why Taft was still on the train; he had foiled the robbery. But maybe train marshals lived on trains.

Promptly at ten, I was standing at the vestibule at the end of the car, holding a large bag and dressed in heavy layers, a knitted hat, and thick gloves for the weather, which had gone from cold to glacial with the elevation change. My makeup-covered face was the only skin showing.

The moment the train stopped, I scrambled down onto the platform. Rushing into town, I found a shop, where I bought a candle, a pair of knife-pointed hair-cutting scissors, and a box of salt that had a healthy mine-salt glow. Then I found a rickshaw with a runner who was willing to take me to the ruins. He was a strange little creature, not much taller than I and stick-thin, with an accent I couldn't place.

As he trotted away from the town, I lied, "My great-great-grandparents' home is supposed to be over that way," I pointed in a random direction. "It's a brick house that was destroyed by a stone spear in a battle with Darkness. According to my grandmother, it's a little off the beaten path. Do you know any houses with stone like that?"

"Aralbet knows everything about these ruins, missy ma'am. Everything. I know of five such destroyed houses, but only one with a spear of stone through its heart. I can take you to it, lady."

We passed numerous boulders and rocky outcrops, but they'd all lain exposed to the elemental damage of ice, snow, and air—useless to me. But in less than an hour Aralbet had delivered me to what I wanted. The remains of a brick house were scattered around a single shaft of mountain heart stone. Luckily, the stone didn't glow with the remembered taint of Darkness and it had been partially protected from rain by the house's metal roof that was still partly in place. "This is it."

Aralbet stopped the rickshaw and I slid to the ground. "I'm going to walk around it, okay? And stop to pray. My grandmother lost her entire family here and I promised I'd light a candle and pray for them."

"Not until Aralbet sees if it's safe, missy ma'am." He pulled a short spike from the floor of the rickshaw beneath my feet. It was a flame-blackened and hardened stick with a makeshift iron point affixed to one end. He jogged around the house, stopping every now and then to poke the spike into holes. He wasn't very bright, but he had been working for tips for a long time, and he knew how to look important. He was also awfully sweet. Missy ma'am? Odd. "Okay, missy ma'am. You're safe to say your prayers. I'll stand here and guard you and wait."

"Thank you, Aralbet," I said, gravely. Satisfied that I might get away with my less-than-half-baked-plan, I walked around the house, and chose a spot where brick and stone met and Aralbet wouldn't be able to see me. I'd forgotten to bring a blanket, so I emptied my bag and sat on it. With the last sparks of the handy-dandy cooking charm, I lit the candle and set it as close to the north as I could figure. I poured a narrow salt ring around me. And I stabbed my left thumb with the scissors.

"*Fire and feathers*," I cursed and lowered my voice, "that hurt!" I smeared the welling blood on my nearly dead prime amulet, and then on the roof-shielded side of the upthrust stone. I leaned into the rock, head bowed as if I was praying. "Stone and fire, water and air, blood and kin prevail," I whispered. "Wings and shield, dagger and sword, blood and kin prevail." Beneath my fingers the prime hummed, the vibration high-pitched and fast. And it . . . sucked up my blood, pulling it into itself. Even the blood still dripping from my wound hovered in midair and then slapped wetly onto the amulet.

Light glowed. Energy, raw and intense, flooded from the stone spear into my prime amulet. Energy flowed from my prime to me, and back to the prime. The microstructures in the amulet shifted, realigned, reformed themselves. And all of a sudden I felt . . . whole.

The white onyx Arctic seal amulet that had been sitting dormant in my shirt pocket for the entire trip began to glow through the cloth. With mage sight I could see energy flowing into the seal from somewhere else, much more energy than even the stone spear had given me, energy waiting for me to tap it. Lolo had given me a lifeline: a preprogrammed link to an alternate CE source!

I wasn't sure exactly what I was doing, but with my prime amulet properly attuned I didn't have to know. I could just let creation energy flow from the *Link* amulet to my prime, and then into each of the pre-conjured charms. Relief left me breathless. My skin stopped glowing. My throat, which had been sore because my prime wasn't protecting me from elemental allergens, stopped hurting.

I sat back. I wasn't tired anymore, but I was hungry. Starving. I wanted peanut butter and jelly sandwiches. Muffins. Even tofu would be good about now.

I stood and scuffed the salt into the grass, knowing this much salt would kill even weeds, and feeling sorry for that. My Earth mage twin would have been furious. *Rose. Gone. Alone.* I forced tears away, snuffed the candle, and repacked the bag. I was alone. But I was surviving. That's what mattered.

Feeling better than I had since I left Enclave, I climbed back into the rickshaw and asked Aralbet to return me to the train depot.

I went to bed that night and slept well, knowing I could keep my secrets as long as I wasn't searched.

On the next day I sat in the dining car with the other passengers. I read the dragon book again and enjoyed it just as much the second time. And I went to sleep knowing that it would be my last night on the train.

As my thoughts drifted toward slumber, I felt warmth against my skin coming from the amulets I'd placed under my pillow in the bed with me. The wooden charm that I hadn't been able to identify was hot. It was activated now and I could feel a spell of forgetting. *Lolo.* What had Lolo wanted me to forget? *Seraph bones!*

Sleep took me.

When I woke, it was in an odd little bed that was rocking beneath me. The flannel sheets were rough compared to the mage-touched sheets I slept under in the priestess's house. The clothes I was wearing were cotton, my socks knitted wool. Human-made clothes.

Memory returned, of my gift descending. Of the bitter tea Lolo had forced down my throat. I had been smuggled out of Enclave and put on a train. And—where was I?

Around my neck was a leather thong, the opal disc pendant lying on my chest. My mage attributes didn't glow and I intuited a connection to the opal: I assumed it blanked them, making me look human, dull and ugly, keeping my secret from the human world.

There were hand rails on the side of the bed. I levered myself over them and down to the floor to find myself in a private cabin of a sleeper car on a train outside of Enclave. Alone.

But, oddly, it didn't seem as terrifying as I might have expected it to be.

I dressed in the unfamiliar clothing and then looked to see what Lolo had sent along with me. Not much.

There was a knock at the cabin door and a branded man with mismatched eyes asked what I wanted for breakfast. When he returned with my meal, he told me to pack and be ready to leave. "We'll be at Mineral City at the 3 p.m. stop. I'll be bringing the rest of your luggage here shortly."

"Thank you," I said. "I'll be ready." And I tipped him well. He looked as if life might be hard for him.

At 3:10 the train stopped, though I could still feel it moving in my muscles and nerves. I was sitting on my luggage. The porter knocked on my door and when I opened it, he said, "Little Miss, this is your stop."

Little Miss because I was only four feet tall and skinny. The porter thought I was a pre-teen human traveling to family. Rich family, hence the private compartment in the sleeper car.

He stacked my stuff on a cart and I followed him down the narrow corridor, through the crush of people, my eyes on his mop of hair high above everyone else. The porter was tall, which was handy.

Outside, the smells hit me: ice and water and snow and the smoke of wood fires. The scent of stone, which was amazing. There was no natural stone in Enclave—New Orleans was built on centuries of accumulated river silt. The only rock was carried in by traders for use by Stone mages like me. But here, the very ground oozed stone power!

"This way, Little Miss. Your grandmother said the man meeting you would be in the station and that I was to see you personally into his hands." I followed, feeling a hint of excitement. "Lemuel Hastings," the porter called out, his voice nearly as penetrating as a conductor's. "Lemuel Hastings! Got a passenger for you!"

"Thorn St. Croix?" a gravelly voice demanded. I turned, the anticipation quivering in my chest. He was a grizzled old human, maybe forty-five or even fifty years old, though I had little familiarity with old humans. The humans in Enclave all looked young, healthy, strong. This one was red-faced, his skin lined and browned, his head covered by a hat, his lanky body mostly hidden by layers. His eyes, brown as swamp water, landed on me. "A *girl?* What in saints' balls good is a girl?"

I felt as if I'd been hit with a mallet. All the air left my lungs. My excitement evaporated.

Hastings turned to the porter. "It was supposed to be a boy! Someone I could train up for my business, who'd get strong when I got old. Someone to take care of me." He leaned in, examining me, and the scent of the old man hit me. Pipe smoke and aftershave, something Lolo might mix, with sandalwood and sweet orange. And the scent of stone dust. I surprised myself by picking out the smell of raw hematite. There was reddish dust ground into his clothes.

The porter said, "Sir, I—"

I interrupted. "You've been working old bloodstone. You mine it yourself?"

Hastings stepped back. "What do you know about *old* bloodstone?"

"Not heliotrope. Reddish bloodstone. Hematite. Full of iron. It can be used in cosmetics and industry and traded to mages in the Enclaves."

"How would I mine it?" he barked.

"Very carefully," I said, smirking.

"How old are you?"

"Fourteen," I said.

The porter's mismatched eyes widened as he took in my small size.

"I haven't hit my growth spurt yet," I lied. I'd hit one. There might be another. Or not. Neomages are much smaller in stature than humans.

Hastings grunted, and dug in his pocket, pulling out a stone. "What's this?"

"Heliotrope," I said instantly. "What a rock-hound would call bloodstone in these days."

"And this?" He handed me another rock, coarse to the touch, vaguely pyramidal in shape. There was a crystal buried in the rough, but not enough of it exposed to tell for certain by color alone. The rough was grayish, with maybe a hint of faintest lavender.

I rubbed my thumb over the sliver of exposed crystal. The gem hummed at me, rich and nigh unto perfect. I squinted up at him. "You sure you want me to say this out loud? In public?" I left the last of the phrase silent. *Where someone might steal your find and jump your claim.*

The man snatched the rock from my hand and the cart handle from the porter's. He glared at the porter. "I'll take her. You tell the old witch we're even now."

I didn't know what that meant, but when Hastings whirled and left the station, I followed, until the porter put a restraining hand on my shoulder. "I'm through here every month. He mistreats you or . . ." He stopped and rubbed his chin. "He mistreats you *in any way*, you meet me here next month, same date, same time. I'll take you back to New Orleans."

That was odd, for a human to feel such interest in—maybe compassion for—a person he'd just met. "Thank you." I took his hand and shook it. "You're a good hu—person."

Before he could figure out that I'd nearly called him a human, I spun and followed Lemuel Hastings out the door and into the frigid air of Mineral City.

Mettilwynd
95-103 PA / 2107-2115 AD

Tamsin L. Silver

September 9, 95 Post-Ap / 2107 AD – Mumbai, India

Rocking slowly with the sway of the pirate ship, silent tears slid down Chopra's face as she closed the lifeless eyes of the girl whose head lay cradled in her lap. "*Shaanti dhoondhen*, my friend. I'm so sorry."

Chopra ran a hand over her own half-inch of recently shaved, dark brown hair, and looked up at her best friend, Miku; the Asian girl had been stripped to her undergarments, hands bound together with rope above her head, then attached to a hook in the ceiling.

"Is she . . ." Miku asked, hesitant to finish her sentence.

Chopra nodded. "Delphine is gone."

"Nooo . . ." Miku moaned, tears streaming down her face.

"What a waste," grumbled the large man Chopra'd heard referred to as Val. He stopped behind her, smelling of whiskey and pungent body odor. "She was the prettiest, too. Throw the blonde one overboard and weigh anchor. Jetrel is expecting our *special* cargo." Grabbing Chopra's arms from behind, Val hauled the Indi-girl to her feet and held her while another crewman took her friend's lifeless body away, her blonde hair hanging, her limbs limp.

"No!" Chopra screamed, trying to pull free of Val's big, rough hands as the double, complicated locks were undone on the only way in or out of the hold.

Sharing a knowing look with Chopra, Miku tugged at the ropes that bound her, yelling in protest as Delphine's body was carried out. Kicking her closest captor, Miku rammed her heel into his nose, spraying blood across the small room.

Pretending to faint, Chopra dropped, her body weight surprising Val into letting go. Freed, she somersaulted forward, using her neomage speed and strength to rise and run for freedom.

Outside the entrance, a man swung a sword to block Chopra's path, but she slid under it like a Pre-Ap baseball player sliding into home plate, before rolling up onto the balls of her bare feet and rushing down the hall.

"Run, Chopra!" Miku shouted.

The fastest and most agile of the three captives, if anyone could escape and fetch help it was Chopra. The pirates had confiscated her change-purse full of spelled coins, but the ones on her belt were still there. Plus, her prime amulet might still hold enough power to protect her from the salt-water below.

She barreled up a set of stairs, the smell of fish and spicy food from Mumbai's harbor slamming into her. Finding herself on the main deck, Chopra wove between the busy crewmen, her bare feet slapping the damp wood. Rushing up a second set of stairs to a higher deck, she dove between someone's legs as the *Persephone* began to pull out of the harbor, and leaped to the ship's rail.

Her only option was to jump and swim for help. Everyone knew who owned the *Persephone*. Though the Indian Ocean was ruled by many pirates, this ship and her captain, Katara, were famously feared.

The rail was no more than four inches wide, but Chopra confidently balanced on it. Judging distance for the dive into the water, she squatted for push-off when a scream pierced the air and her heart. Even though she knew better, Chopra turned to look. Standing at the door that lead to the lower decks was Miku, her blue eyes alight with fear as an Indi-woman with long, dark hair pressed a knife against her throat and walked her across the main deck. Val joined them, shoving the barrel of his gun against Miku's temple.

"Do it and she dies," said the Indi-woman.

Miku's voice sounded in Chopra's mind, *"Jump!"*

"You know I can't. Not now," Chopra mentally replied. If that gun fired, it wouldn't matter if she escaped.

The woman tilted her head slightly, eyes narrowing as they flicked from Chopra to Miku and back again. "Well well. Val, you *definitely* have some explaining to do."

Hearing her displeasure at her own crewman, Chopra wondered if the Indi-woman might be open to a bargain. "How do I know you won't kill us anyway? You have a reputation, Katara."

A smile crept over the captain's face. "Do I, little one? Even where you come from?"

Chopra sat, straddling the rail. "Yes, ma'am. So I'll ask, do you swear an oath on your ship that you'll keep us safe?"

Someone near Chopra whistled low at the challenge. To swear an oath on one's ship was something even the darkest of pirates took seriously.

"I'll swear, on one condition," Katara said, adding, "Liran?"

A slender man in glasses and short, curly brown hair, who moved with the ease of one who'd lived his whole life at sea, rushed to Katara's side. She whispered something in his ear, and with a nod, he maneuvered up to Chopra and sat on the rail. Leaning in, he whispered, "What is your ele-mental affinity?"

Chopra turned to stare into Liran's bi-colored eyes, one sea-green, one honey-brown. For a moment, she entertained the idea of playing dumb. But when Katara raised an eyebrow at her, Chopra knew that lying was point-less. "Yes, I would be willing to be your bladesmith. Bargain?"

Katara removed her knife from Miku's throat. "Yes, agreed."

Begrudgingly, Val holstered his gun and untied Miku's hands.

Chopra hopped down to the deck and ran to Miku, throwing her arms around the slender sixteen-year-old.

"You should've jumped," Miku whispered in Chopra's ear, the fierceness of her embrace belying her words. "We're dead anyway."

"Not necessarily."

Liran placed a blanket around Miku's shoulders, which she promptly used to cover her mostly naked body.

Katara pulled the captives apart and looked at Chopra. "What's your name, boy?"

"Chopra Adya Gulati," she said with pride and a pinch of snark.

Katara touched Chopra's half-inch of hair. "So, you're a girl."

"Don't let my straight frame and flat chest fool ya. I've got me some lady parts."

Katara lips pressed together, doing their best to conceal a grin her eyes couldn't hide. She turned her attention to the Asian girl. "And you?"

Chin high, Miku replied, "Miku Rin Bhatti-Sato."

Katara motioned to Liran. "Go with my boatswain. He'll get you settled. Behave, sleep well, and maybe I won't kill you in the morning." Without waiting for either to respond, she looked to Val. "Come with me, quartermaster. You have much to explain."

Chopra kept a protective arm across Miku's shoulders, pulling her in close as they followed the boatswain back into the belly of the massive ship, their future in the hands of the most feared pirate of the South Seas.

November 19, 95 Post-Ap – South China Sea

Days turned into weeks. Two months went by and the girls spent most of their time assisting crew members before doing their own chores, which included Chopra creating blades as promised. They fell onto their mats every night exhausted, sacrificing precious sleep to talk, the sound of water slapping against the hull of the wooden ship their only company.

Miku rolled over to look at Chopra. "Did you hear those crewmen at dinner talk about what they do to neomages?"

Chopra lay looking at the ceiling. "Katara and Liran will keep our secret and Val is dead, so try not to think about it."

Miku fingered her bird bone and feather bracelet. "She gave it back today, but I'm afraid to wear my prime amulet during the day. It's an obvious sign I'm a mage. I wish mine was like yours . . ."

Chopra rolled to face Miku. "You wish a watcher had experimented on you, leaving you unable to work spells that require your prime be placed away from you? Always carrying an easily detectable proof of your true nature?"

"Obviously not. That's not my point." When Chopra grunted, Miku added, "He did it to save your arm."

With a dramatic sigh, Chopra replied, "I know, it's just . . ." her voice drifted off.

"At least they allowed us to become mind-bound. This way we could use my prime when we work inside a circle together."

Chopra lifted her right arm to stare at the long scar there, the only clue to the metal prime amulet hidden beneath the flesh, used to heal her shattered bones years ago.

Miku traced the crescent scar from eyebrow to jaw on the right side of Chopra's face. "You mask your mage glow but not your scars. Why?"

"I might've only been eight, but I knew what I was doing when I tried to save your mother. I just wish I hadn't failed."

"You saved me," she said, taking Chopra's hand.

"That's why I wear them. They're my badge of honor. I may not have saved our Enclave's priestess, but I was able to save her daughter."

Miku smiled as a tear trickled down her face. "She'd be so mad at me right now for letting this happen."

Chopra wiped it away, gently easing an arm around Miku. "Shhh, don't think that way."

Miku rested her head on Chopra's shoulder. "You'll hide my prime amulet for me then?"

Chopra nodded. "Yes."

Miku gazed at her bracelet. "I'll feel naked without it, but it'll be here with me at night, and I'll have you." She paused and added, "Better together . . ."

"For you'll always be in my forever," Chopra replied with the other half of their saying, meaning it with all her heart.

"We should do it now, just to be safe," Miku suggested.

"As you wish."

They rose and worked together to cast a spell on the metal box Chopra had originally made to hide her amulets, giving it the power to boost the range of Miku's prime amulet. This would allow Miku to cast her own *Glamour* to hide her neomage attributes even when her prime wasn't with her, instead of relying on Chopra to disguise them both.

Sliding the box under a loose floorboard, Miku set her mat over it and they went to bed.

Chopra pulled Miku's head to rest on her shoulder. "Now sleep. We have the same horrible routine tomorrow."

November 20, 95 Post-Ap – Bandar, Malaysia

"Land ho!" someone shouted from the crow's nest on the mainmast.

Chopra and Miku rushed to the rail to stare at the city from the main deck.

"That, my little ship-rats, is the city of Bandar, Malaysia," the new quartermaster, Val's replacement, explained while wiping sweat from his bald head. "It's where Jetrel reigns. His men will pay us handsomely for you."

"What?" Chopra blurted.

"Well, maybe not you, with your boyish looks, but I know Jet has a soft spot for pretty Japanese girls."

"I'm only half-Japanese," Miku stammered.

Chopra took Miku's hand. "I won't let him take you without me."

"If Katara chooses to sell you, then you'll be sold. The sex-slave trade is very profitable."

They'd heard rumors about Jet and his business. But to have it validated *and* learn Katara was involved caused Chopra's stomach to flip.

"Chopra," Miku asked, her voice trembling, as the new quartermaster walked away, "What if she splits us up? What if—"

"Shh." She pulled Miku close and kissed her temple. "I go where you go. I'll do all I can to keep you safe, you have my word. Better together, remember?"

"Chopra! Miku!" Katara shouted from the quarterdeck before leaping down to land in front of them. "Come with me. Now!" Katara grabbed their hands and dragged them into the captain's cabin. "Stay here. Don't come out for anything!"

"But—" Chopra started.

"If Jet's men find mages on board, they'll take you, do you under—" Katara flushed. Sudden fear lit her eyes. "Son of a seraph, he's here! He's *never* here. Quick. Hide!" Katara slipped a few things into the rear pocket of Chopra's pants and opened a secret panel. "Get in now!" Katara shoved them into a narrow space. As the door closed, they heard the captain moan.

Unable to reach behind her in the painfully tight space, Chopra whispered. "What's going on? Can you reach my back pocket? I think she put—"

"Can't you feel it?" Miku said mentally, pressing her body into Chopra's.

She felt something, new, unknown. Chopra had no idea what the warmth in her center could be, but it was growing by the second, causing her heartrate to speed up. *"What is this?"*

"Mage heat . . . oh my . . . a seraph or kylen must be on board."

"Or a watcher," Chopra stated, understanding now what Katara had meant.

Looking up at the delicate face of her best friend, Chopra desperately wanted to touch it. Unable to move much, she took Miku's hands in hers. This amplified the heat she felt and when Miku leaned in and kissed Chopra ardently, she kissed back. Unsure of many things, the least of which how this made her feel, the fourteen-year-old let herself fall into the kiss as tongues entwined and quiet moans escaped lips.

Hearing voices, Chopra fought hard to listen, pulling away from Miku to catch her breath.

"Where are they, Katara? I can feel the heat of more than just you in this room. We had a deal, you and I."

"Never for mage children, Jet," Katara said, her voice strained.

"Tell me, or I'll tear this ship apart and when I find her, I'll kill her."

Without warning, the panel opened slightly. Chopra could see Katara through the crack as the captain gripped the cabin door like a lifeline, fighting the mage heat that threatened to consume her.

"It's okay. Come out. I won't harm you," Jetrel said. "You can call me Jet."

Unable to resist, Miku began to slide out.

Chopra grasped her hand tight. *"No, don't go!"*

"His power calls to me," she told Chopra. *"He'll not harm us. Come, he means well. I can tell."*

Chopra didn't feel that safety. She mentally pleaded, *"Stay with me!"*

Miku let go of Chopra and pulled free. Instantly, two spots of heat burned in Chopra's back pocket. She attempted to lunge for Miku, but was unable to move. She cried out, but her voice made no sound.

"No," Katara cried, as Miku exited the hiding space.

Chopra watched in fear as Miku dropped to her knees before Jet and reached for his belt.

The tall, handsome man, with dark hair and green eyes, calmly took her hands and knelt before her. "Not now, my Asian beauty. I'm spelled so as to resist your kind at the moment. But soon, don't you fret." Jet caressed Miku's face, causing her to moan. "Good girl, Katara. Now, where is the scarred Indi-girl with the lovely, waist-length hair?"

Chopra again tried to step forward, but still couldn't move.

"I'm sorry . . ." Katara said, her voice but a whisper.

Chopra felt a third, heated, stinging sensation in her back pocket as Katara opened the door to the hiding space completely.

". . . but Miku is all we have," Katara continued.

Jet stared into the small space, obviously unable to see Chopra at all. Standing, he handed Miku off to one of the men who'd come with him. "How is that possible?"

She now understood Katara had slipped amulets into her back pocket and tears ran down her face. The amulets kept Chopra silent, immobile, and invisible.

"As you can see, Miku is all that's left. The Indi-girl jumped ship when Val killed their blonde friend."

"No!" he shouted, backhanding Katara across the face, knocking her to the floor. "How could you let that happen? They are more powerful together! I needed them *both*."

Katara wiped blood from her lip. Standing, she gripped a table to steady her resolve as sweat glistened along her brow, evidence of her fight against the mage heat. "That's what you get for using Val to do your dirty work," she said through clenched teeth.

"And where *is* my good and faithful servant?"

Eyes full of hate, a slow smile crept over Katara's face. "I slashed his throat and tossed him in the ocean like chum!"

Jet grabbed Katara's chin, forcing her eyes to his. "You'll pay for that, for I'm not so easily disposed of, Katara. And neither is *Nakir*."

Use of the Black Angel's name chilled Chopra to the core, and likely

Katara as well, seeing as the captain's body visibly shook. Somehow Katara was still able to resist the watcher even though he touched her.

Jet stared Katara down. When he finally let go of her with a frustrated growl and stepped away, her suffering visibly eased. "How do you fight your heat for me? I can *smell* your need. I'd be more than happy to give you a litter of kylen—"

"Over my dead body," she growled as she sat behind the table.

"Tsk tsk, that's no way to answer your master. How do you—"

Leaning forward, she spat, "I despise you! That helps a lot."

Tossing his head back, a deep, mocking laugh escaped him. "Fascinating." He walked over to Miku, who reached for him. Placing his hand on her breast and his lips on hers, his passionless kiss swallowed her groan of pleasure.

Chopra fought the bonds that held her. Pulling on the power in her prime amulet, she moved an inch forward.

Katara's head whipped in surprise to glance at the space where Chopra stood, "No!" Quickly she refocused on Jet, adding, "Leave her be!"

Without looking away from Miku, he replied, "You know I'm going to investigate your story, Katara. If you're lying to me about the Indi-girl, I'll find out. Then I'll hunt her down and own her, just as I do you."

"Damn you to the eternal fires of Hell!" Katara said, shooting out of the chair, her venomous tone raising goose bumps on Chopra's flesh.

Jet laughed, but there was no humor in it, as he glared at Katara. "*You* have no power over me."

He again handed Miku off to one of his men and Chopra saw a hint of fear in his eyes. Maybe Katara's words *were* powerful enough if a seraph of the light was nearby and heard her. Chopra could only hope.

Without warning, Katara closed the door to the hiding space, the latch on the secret panel nestling into place without a sound. "I'll show you out."

"That won't be necessary," he said. "Have no fear, Katara, this Air mage will fetch a good enough price to save your hide, for now."

At these words, Chopra once again tried to break her bonds. Unable to, she fought to reach her back pocket in the tight space to remove the stones.

"You're a monster," Katara growled.

"And yet you take my money." A clinking thud could be heard—a change-purse hitting a table. "I know you stop at Mumbai often. If you see that girl again and you don't bring her to me, I'll have your head mounted at the palace as a decoration," he promised. "Let's go."

Chopra screamed without sound, fear squeezing her chest as she fought against the conjures, yet all she could do was listen in horror, the weight of unfulfilled promises settling onto her heart. Miku was alone and Chopra had failed to keep her safe.

Chopra awoke on the carpeted floor of a small, oddly shaped, low-ceilinged cabin she'd never seen before. Rolled sleeping mats were nestled in a corner with blankets and pillows that appeared to be moving. A black and white cat emerged from them, stretched, and gracefully maneuvered across the room to sit by the door moments before it opened.

Liran walked in and petted the cat. "Hey there, Sadie." He stood hunched over. "Please, come in and beware of the low ceiling."

Filing in behind him came fifteen women of different ages and ethnicities, smiling as they followed his instructions. One in particular, a red-headed woman, had to bend over a good amount to enter the room.

"It's late," Liran continued. "You're all tired. Select sleeping accoutrements and find a place on the floor to rest."

Katara came in last, barely ducking her head inside the room. "My name is Indira and I'm taking you where you'll finally be safe. Once we make it past the checkpoints, I'll return to answer all questions."

"Liar!" Chopra shouted, springing to her feet.

Liran blocked her path, clamping his hand on her shoulder. "Stay calm."

Feeling suddenly tranquil, Chopra stared at him in disbelief, "You too?"

Liran nodded once and removed his hand.

"My daughter," Katara explained to the group, motioning toward Chopra. "She's mad at me. Early teens, you know how that is. Excuse me a moment." She carefully maneuvered through the women as they grabbed mats and blankets. With an arm around Chopra's shoulders, Katara led her across the small room. "I'm sorry about Miku."

Chopra fought tears. "Liar."

Katara's eyes, the same golden brown as Chopra's, narrowed. "I didn't have time to get amulets on her. If you two had held onto one another, she might have been protected. I tried, Chopra. I really did."

"You're saying this is my fault?!" Chopra shouted.

Katara placed a hand over Chopra's mouth. "Shush! No. We'll revisit this later. Right now, I need to get these women to safety. I've helped build an underground railroad to free as many of Jet's sex-slaves as I can. Yelling at me could scare them. If they run, we'll get caught, probably killed. You'll never save Miku if you're dead."

Chopra stood speechless as Katara handed her off to Liran before stepping over to the rolled mats, grabbing one, and laying it out on the floor.

"Though many believe we hand women over to Jet and let that stand, we do not," Liran quietly explained. "By being in Jet's employ, we have free rein to sail where we please without anyone questioning why we are there or looking into our activities. Jet has more than just the *Persephone* buying and kidnapping his slaves. Indira and I are the only ones who also work against him. Do you understand?"

Chopra nodded, then shook her head.

"You will. Indira will train you. You'll see."

"Indira?" Chopra asked.

"Katara's real name. We're rogue mages doing our best to fight the Darkness. Thing is, that takes money and connections. This job creates both," Liran led Chopra to the mat Katara had set out. "Now stay put."

Chopra nodded and sat, too shocked to resist.

"It'll be all right," someone said.

Chopra turned to examine the Amazonian young woman with red hair and gray-blue eyes. "No, it will never be all right. Nothing is what I thought. I don't know what to believe anymore."

The tuxedo cat came over and the woman smiled, petting the feline. "I believe we all have a reason for being. I was meant for Indira to find me."

Chopra lay down. "She goes by Katara."

Laying down as well, the woman smiled as the cat curled up beside her. "Katara? Is that her 'captain name'?"

"I think so."

"I like it. A name says a lot about a person."

"Well, I'm Chopra. What does that tell you?"

The woman laughed. "You are stubborn but your energies are honor and loyalty."

"I don't *feel* honorable." Chopra paused, "What's *your* name?"

She sighed in disgust. "I don't know. My owner called me Frances. I *hate* that name. Actually, he referred to me as, 'Frances the mule' because I am a—"

Chopra shook her head and quickly touched the woman's arm to stop her from admitting she was a child of a mage and a human, properly known as a 'second unforeseen,' or a 'mule,' if one was crude. Once the woman nodded in understanding, Chopra said, "What should I call you?"

"Arcadia." She smiled. "We all have a purpose, and that name will fit mine."

"And what is your purpose?"

"I don't know," Arcadia admitted. "Only time will tell. But like you, *I* am meant for great things."

Chopra heard the anchor coming up and thought of her new purpose. "I hope you're right."

Eight Years Later: July 21, 103 Post-Ap – George Town, Penang

Katara stood on the quarterdeck of her new brigantine, also christened *Persephone*, as they docked in George Town, at the northeastern tip of the island. Staring out at the early evening hustle and bustle of Fort Cornwallis Market, a stone fortress built by the British, centuries previously, she saw little. Her mind was elsewhere.

"Have I ever mentioned how much I love this place?" Katara's quartermaster said, inhaling deeply and letting it out with a satisfied sigh. When Katara didn't respond, Arcadia continued, "I think it's the exotic spices in the air." With still no reply, she wrapped a green hijâb around her short, red hair. "Mostly I'm looking forward to a three-way with that royal guard and his goat."

Katara held the grin at bay for a second before it ticked at the corner of her mouth. She shook a finger at Arcadia. "You think I don't hear you, but

I do."

"Uh-huh. What did I say?"

Katara fastened a specially made abaya over her usual attire to hide her weapons, falling past her black leggings and knee-high leather boots. "Something about sex with a goat. And if you fly that way, hey, who am I to judge?"

"Nice try, but you're distracted. You need to stay focused."

Katara exhaled heavily, adjusting the hijâb that concealed her chin-length, dark hair. "What if she's not here, again? Or this is a trap? Or we're not prepared? Or—"

"Stop! She'll be here. The intel from Jassima is good and *this* plan is solid. We're ready."

Katara, a mere five foot three in her two-inch-heeled boots, looked up at Arcadia, still nearly a foot taller than her. "What do you mean, *this* plan?"

Before she could reply, Katara's boatswain and navigator—Liran's twenty-year-old son, Gamon—raced over. He came to a halt, shoved his black hair out of his dark, almond-shaped eyes, and said, "Gangplank is down, Captain."

Ignoring him, Arcadia rolled her eyes at Katara. "I *mean* our fly-by-the-seat-of-our-pants 'plan' in Ranong with Conrad. Who, I might add, is the reason the trip resulted in six dead, a destroyed bar, a duel to exit the country, and your nose being broken for the third time. Remember that?"

Katara pulled a map and key from her pocket and waved them at Arcadia. "Don't rag on poor dead Conrad *again*! He gave us these, didn't he?"

"Is that blood?" Gamon asked, pointing at spots on the paper map.

"Yes," the women replied in unison.

"Conrad, my contact in Ranong, gave us these, right before a blade went through his throat," Katara explained, "*Not* my blade."

"Ooh, I'm impressed," he said, winking at Arcadia.

"Shut it, Little Liran," Katara said, as Arcadia laughed. "Both of you can blow it out Jibreel's horn." Shoving the map and key into her pocket, she picked up her satchel, and headed down the gangplank, "Arcadia, grab your things and let's go. Gamon, purchase the supplies and return quickly. Do one last walk-through to verify *Persephone* is battle-ready."

"Aye, Captain."

"And get a haircut, for the love of Mika'il, or I'll cut it myself."

The half-Thai young man's face showed sincere fear as his hand rushed to touch his hair. "You wouldn't."

Arcadia slung the strap of her sword case around her body and shouldered her armor bag. "Trust me, she would. And you *really* don't want that."

Katara chuckled. "No, he really doesn't."

Entering Fort Cornwallis Market from the east, Katara caught sight of the xiangsheng players performing on a round stage at the center of the fortress. An amphitheater's stone risers spread like a fan from the performance space up to the north wall and were filled with market-goers as they ate and talked; some even watched the performers. Others wandered and shopped in the remaining space filled with tables and booths offering fish, fruits, vegetables, fish, grains, clothing, ship supplies, and more fish.

"Define irony," Katara said.

"A market for pirates, run by ex-pirates, in a fort originally built to keep pirates out of Penang," Arcadia proudly stated.

"At least someone listens to my history lessons," Katara said. "Early dinner?"

"Sweet seraph, please!"

They purchased food from one of the many vendors and sat on the risers to watch the show as they ate. They were just finishing their meal when a Malaysian woman approached.

"Ladies, might I interest you in some bunga rayas, our national flower?"

Katara looked up to find Jassima staring down at her. "Why yes. We'd love some."

Jassima carefully handed Katara a bouquet of red, five-petaled flowers. "Do not untie them until it's *necessary*."

Katara counted out a small stack of coins as Jassima covertly scanned the area for anyone watching them. Handing the money over, Katara said, "Is she here, the one they call Havâ?"

Jassima's lavender-blue eyes returned to her supposed customer. "Yes. Let me get your change." Putting her head down, she murmured, "No one's seen her in days. Not since Saval's supposedly psychic advisor told him a dark power was coming to take what he holds most dear."

"Keeping up the façade to hide his true sexual preference is dearer to him than Havâ," Katara pointed out.

"Yes, but she's part of that façade."

"Dragon bones," Arcadia muttered. "Has Saval canceled the event?"

Jassima squatted, handing Katara a change-bag. "He cannot. Tradition commands he must open the palace to all citizens for the Feast of Tithes day each month. Your pass into the event and tithe coins are in here."

Katara took the bag, a wicked grin on her face. "Thank you for the flowers. They will look lovely donated on the Wall of Royal Decree."

Jassima chuckled, and then walked away, yelling about flowers for sale.

Arcadia stood. "I'll get into my replica royal armor and activate my *Glamour*. See you in the throne room."

"Be careful."

"Aren't I always?" Arcadia grinned.

"No, you aren't," Katara muttered.

Arcadia headed west, toward the Royal Palace. Katara waited a few moments, then slowly followed her with a small satchel in one hand, a flower bomb in the other, and a silent prayer on her lips.

Employing a *Mindslip* spell so the guards would neglect a weapon-check for her, Katara entered the palace early in the evening. Untying her bunga rayas, she triggered the time-delayed spell, and inserted the stems into one of the many designated holes on the etched, marble Wall of Royal Decree. Following protocol, she bowed to the seven-foot-tall stone statue of Jet, proud of herself for not spitting on it, and followed the masses into the blue and white throne room.

The potent smoke of burning incense filled the chamber as the line inched toward Saval, Jet's human brother-in-law of one of his many wives, who sat in a golden chair on top of a two-level platform. He looked down his nose at the people gathered to pay their tithe, even those wearing traditional Muslim attire in honor of the monarch.

Approaching the platform, Katara worked a tiny weapon from the lining of her abaya. Concealing it between her fingers, she climbed the stairs to the level below Saval, and knelt before him. Reciting the Royal Creed for atonement, submission, and servitude, Katara ceremonially poured water over his well-manicured feet. She reached for a towel just as the Wall of Royal Decree exploded, rocking the palace.

Debris and flower petals flew everywhere. Screams erupted as citizens and guards ran in all directions. In the distraction, Katara stuck Saval's foot with a poison-tipped needle, so slim he didn't feel it, before dashing off like the rest. As Arcadia now appeared male, Katara only recognized the quartermaster by the slightest difference in the craftsmanship of her blue steel armor, and ran to her in feigned terror.

"Why, my lady, art thou scared of a little boom-boom?" Arcadia whispered in her ear.

Katara laughed. "Shut up and let's go."

Taking advantage of the mass panic to hide their exit, they raced down a hallway. Following the map Conrad had given them, they stopped at a pair of bolted doors.

Katara performed a mind skim of the room beyond. "This is it. She's here. But something's wrong." She slid a steel pick into the lock, using a hint of elemental power to glide the brass mechanism open, unlocking the door.

Entering the elegant sitting room decorated with colorful satins, artwork, and gemstones, Katara let out a low whistle. "Wow, this room's worth more than our whole ship."

"Don't take anything!"

"Too late," Katara said, sliding a handful of gems into her pocket. "Don't give me that look. We *are* pirates, ya know. We steal things."

Arcadia rolled her eyes.

Katara motioned toward a tapestry hanging on an inner wall. "According to Conrad, she'll be behind that."

Arcadia pulled back the heavy cloth to reveal a locked steel door radiating energy. Blocking Katara from it, she said, "It's spelled. Likely against mages."

"That must be why Conrad gave us this key," Katara said, handing it over.

Arcadia inserted and turned the key, drew her sword, and carefully toed the door open to find a pure white bedroom. Sheer white fabrics draped the canopy bed, billowing in the breeze from large windows. Sitting in a rocking chair was the beautiful woman the Malaysians called Havâ. She, too, was dressed in white, her long, ebony hair so glossy it appeared wet.

Katara rushed to stand before her, but Havâ didn't react.

"Is she alive?" Arcadia murmured.

Heart in her throat, Katara knelt in front of Havâ and carefully took her wrist, as the Asian woman stared past her at nothing. "She has a pulse, so maybe she's drugged or in some sort of trance. Either would explain why I couldn't contact her."

"I'm so sorry, Captain." Arcadia placed a hand on Katara's shoulder. "What's in this?" She tried to open a drawstring bag attached to Havâ's waist but was unable to. "Appears to be spelled closed."

"Leave it for now." Katara paused, hand on chin, finger tapping her lips in thought. "My concern is this white outfit. It'll be a bull's eye."

Arcadia made a quick search of the room for some color other than white, but found nothing they could use to hide Havâ's clothing.

"What about the colorful silks and satins in the other room?" Arcadia suggested.

"And do what? Roll her in them so she can suffocate? Or maybe use the drapes to make her a dress? This isn't the *Sound of Music*. We don't have that kind of time." Standing, Katara said, "Stones and blood, I didn't risk my life, yours, and our crew for nothing. Plan A won't work. Plan B definitely won't work . . ."

"So we go to Plan C."

Katara snarled. "We don't have a Plan C."

"I have an idea," Arcadia mused.

Katara pulled a white niqâb from her satchel. "Whatever it is, she'll need to wear this."

"You just happened to have one that matches her dress, so it appears genuine?" Arcadia asked, assisting the captain in fitting the headdress on Havâ.

"I brought three; one happens to be white. We got lucky."

"I don't think luck had anything to do with it."

"Don't start talking about 'one's purpose' and a 'higher plan.' Focus. What's your idea?"

"Closing time."

Supporting Havâ between them like a drunken friend after a night at the bar, Katara and Arcadia moved quickly down the hallway toward a side exit that had been marked on the map. Halfway there, medical personnel ran past, barking orders.

"Angel snot," Katara whispered. "That man just—"

"I heard, he demanded they fetch Havâ for medical assistance."

"Guess your poison worked on Saval after all."

"I hope it kills him," Katara said as they turned the corner.

The exit now in sight, they hurried down the hall and out the doors into the side courtyard without being seen.

"That wasn't so bad," Arcadia bragged—and an alarm sounded.

"You were saying?"

"Seraph bones!" Arcadia said, and scooped Havâ up in muscular arms. "Plan D! Run!"

They made it halfway across the Great Lawn between the palace and the fort before Saval's guards spotted Havâ's white gown and began pursuit.

Stopping in a stand of trees for cover, Katara panted, "The shortest route to *Persephone* is through the fort."

Arcadia agreed, and they picked up the pace again. Running through the arch of the west entrance, they found the fort deserted, save for a large gathering of Muslims kneeling on the stone risers, facing west toward Mecca in observation of the sunset prayer to Allah.

As Katara reached the empty amphitheater stage, sentries blocked the east exit. Turning, she saw the palace guards approaching the west entrance. "Wrath of angels!" Waving Arcadia to follow her, she sprang onto the stage. "Leave her up here."

"Over my dead body," Arcadia replied.

"I prefer not." Katara removed her satchel and the abaya, revealing her weapons and armor. Tossing the bag and cloak to the ground below, she left her niqâb in place to hide her face as the guards filed in through the west entrance, trapping them.

"Surrender the woman!"

Katara pulled a small, metal box from a pocket. "Set her down. We fight or we die."

"Then we fight," Arcadia said, laying Havâ center stage before drawing her broadsword.

"Drop your weapons!" yelled the guard leader.

"Stall them," Katara whispered to Arcadia before kneeling beside Havâ and placing a feather and bird-bone bracelet around the young woman's wrist.

"On whose authority?" Arcadia shouted in reply to the leader of the guard.

Katara kissed Havâ's forehead. "Better together, remember, Miku? You never stopped being in *my* forever. Come back to me; I need you."

"The authority of Saval, the royal representative of Jet, king of Malaysia."

Arcadia snorted a laugh. "Oh, him."

"You mock the king?"

"What she's implying, you buffoon," Katara said as she stood, pulling five amulets from the largest pocket inside her leather vest, "Is that we don't recognize his self-appointed authority."

Arcadia saluted Katara with her sword, a weapon forged from the same mage metal as her armor. "It's been an honor, Captain."

"We aren't dead yet. They'll come when called."

"Until then," she said.

"Until then," Katara replied, knowing Arcadia meant until they were assisted or met again in the afterlife her warrior champard believed in. Then, with a wink at the guard, Katara threw the larger amulet high into the air, where it exploded, a multi-colored flare.

"Take them!" shouted the leader of the guard.

A battle cry ripped from Arcadia as she leapt from the stage. Landing, she swung her blade and the leader's head flew into the guards behind him. The men and women praying on the risers leapt to their feet and sped for the west exit, some of them screaming.

Katara threw three *Elemental Blast* amulets, one after the other, over Arcadia's head into the larger group of palace guards. Explosions erupted like grenades, throwing guards, weapons, and earth in all directions, leaving only a quarter of the men still standing. Arcadia killed two more as Katara spun and tossed the last amulet at the sentries advancing from the east. The blast dropped five of them, the rest taking cover, while three guards from the west got past Arcadia and dashed for the stage.

Katara flipped the snaps on her wide leather belt, sliding two, seven-inch, mage metal dirks from their home, lying horizontal against her low back. Arms outstretched, she said, "I'll be right back, Miku. Don't go anywhere."

Dirks spinning, slicing, Katara took out one attacker and then another. Her blades whirled, dancing to a song of love and loss, yet filled with the discovery of life-purpose. These men had never fought a mage, especially one who'd trained for this day for the past eight years. They were many against one, yet they were outnumbered.

Katara slashed a soldier's arm to the bone as the blade of a different man slipped past her guard, piercing her above the belt. Crying out, she whipped her blade past him so fast, he was still smiling as his head fell from his body. Turning away from the arterial spray, Katara winced in pain as her stomach wound bled, darkening her green tunic.

Hearing a shout, Katara spun to see a huge man. With a head-butt, the man broke her nose, sending her flying backward, where she landed on her rear. "Nod da nose, again, damn id!"

He swung his sword down, a killing strike. She dove between his legs, flipped over, and kicked both steel-toed boots into his groin. The guard toppled. Katara dropped a dirk to yank a dagger from a thigh sheath and rammed it through his ear into his brain.

When no one else attacked immediately, Katara gathered her weapons, sheathed and secured them, then grabbed her nose and set it with a crunch.

Wiping away tears, she glanced toward Arcadia and saw beyond her that a number of the previously praying Muslims had stopped short of the western exit and had, with swords in hand, attacked the guards from behind. Standing up to join them, a sharp pain shot through Katara's abdomen, and she doubled over.

Gunfire filled the air and Katara reached for her pistol as the sentries at the east entrance fell. Katara's crew sped into the fort, trapping the remaining palace guards between the two forces until they were overcome and surrendered.

Arcadia, face aglow with the glory of battle, leaped back onto the stage. "Time to go, Captain."

Focusing energy from a *Healing* amulet to her nose and abdomen, Katara winced as she rose. "But who are all these people?"

A woman in a niqâb came forward. One look into her lavender-blue eyes, and Katara knew her. "Jassima, I don't understand," Katara whispered.

"You never ask anything for yourself from the network you built and use to save our daughters from slavery. When you told me of your need, I reached out. They answered the call."

"And the swords, you had those stashed up your..." Katara asked with a wink.

Jassima laughed. "Under our mats. We were just waiting for you."

"Captain?" Arcadia warned.

Katara hugged Jassima. "Thank you." Letting go of her, she added, "Tell them if they ever need anything, it's theirs. I owe them more than my life."

"You owe us nothing."

"Captain?" Arcadia demanded.

Katara ignored Arcadia a moment longer, placing a kiss on Jassima's cheek. "Bahut hî úukriyâ."

"Captain!"

"Yes, I *hear* you, Arcadia. We shall—" Turning, Katara found Miku standing. Their eyes locked.

Miku placed her palm on Katara's niqâb, against her cheek. "I know these eyes . . ."

Then it happened, like rain after a drought, Miku's mind touched Katara's, saying, *"Chopra, you came for me."*

Katara nodded, tears falling freely. *"Better together, always and forever."*

Miku threw her arms around Katara, who squeezed her back as an alarm sounded in the harbor.

"Captain, we—"

"I know." Katara let go of Miku, "Leave the niqâb on for now; safer that way." Taking Miku's hand, she nodded at Jassima, gathered her satchel and abaya, and sped for the east exit, adding mentally, *"I need you to refer to me as Katara."*

"Why?" Miku asked.

"Because I am her—the current one, that is. The four previous Kataras are retired, including Indira, the one who captured us and trained me. She's now in Israel with Liran at the Dead Sea. It's a long story. I'll explain it all once we're safely away."

Katara and Miku followed Arcadia, the crew behind them, down the stone steps to the docked ship. Black sails barely moving, the wooden body of the new *Persephone* gleamed in the rays of the setting sun, the *all* of her pulsing with creation energy.

Miku stopped as the gangplank lowered, her mage sight showing her the power that *Persephone* exuded. "This is not the same boat I remember."

Katara motioned her away-team to board. Quickly, they filed up the plank as Katara stayed put and explained. "No, Indira renamed that one and took it with her. This is a powerful replica built to my specifications 'under the hood,' so to speak. Metal now runs throughout *Persephone's* hull, reinforcing her. In her belly, there's even more as my power sink."

"Holy dragon bones! That's why she shimmers."

"Everyone is aboard, Captain!" Arcadia said.

A bullet zipped through the air, grazing Katara's jaw. "Spawn balls!" she cried out, drawing a gun and firing back. She dropped one attacker where he stood, but more shots rained down on them from the city wall, prompting her crew to return fire from behind the gunwales.

"Go up! Now!" Katara ordered.

Once Miku and Arcadia were safely aboard, Katara set a few spelled coins on the edge of the dock, between the approaching guards and her ship. Activating the conjure within them, she ran up gangplank as it rose, nestling into place with a thump. "Hold your fire and cast off!" she ordered. Yanking the niqâb off, she added, "Miku, go to my cabin. You'll be safer. I'm not sure how long the amulets to block bullets will last."

Gamon rappelled down from a spar, landing on the main deck. "We're clear, Captain. But we're dead in the water without a decent breeze."

"I can help," Miku said in Katara's mind, removing her niqâb as well.

Katara ignored her. "Good work, Gamon. Show Miku to the safe room, then meet me up at the helm."

"Yes, Captain." Gamon replied over the noise of the guard's gunfire, motioning Miku forward.

Miku didn't budge. Crossing her arms, she stared at Katara. *"Better together, remember?"*

Katara turned to Miku. "Don't start." Mentally adding, *"You'll out yourself as a mage to everyone and—"*

"I was wrong before. We can't live in fear."

Katara groaned, rubbing her face as the light breeze only inched them away from the dock. "How strong are you?"

"That year-round beautiful weather George Town has is because of me. It's fueled by a power sink I created in the harbor, consisting of bird's nests along the shore. With my returned prime," she held up her wrist to show the bird bone bracelet, "I have more than enough power to get us out of here."

"An hour ago you were catatonic."

"So I'm well rested."

"Dear Jibreel, I'm not going to win this, am I?" A short, strained laugh escaped Katara before she yelled out, "Arcadia!"

"Yes, Captain," the quartermaster said, loping over, her face now her own.

"Take Miku to the poop deck and keep her safe, you hear me?"

"Yes, Captain, but you should know," Arcadia said, pointing toward the exit. "Saval's ships are steamers. Once they get burning, we won't be able to outrun them."

Katara looked to Miku. "If you're going to out yourself, now would be a good time for it."

With a nod, Miku followed Arcadia to the highest deck at the rear of the ship while Katara and Gamon took their places below them on the quarterdeck.

Seeing Katara take the wheel, Miku reached out mentally. *"Hold on!"*

The former priestess' daughter raised her arms and wind filled the sails, jolting *Persephone* into motion. Katara steered them away from the dock, shooting a quick look at the poop deck. The belled sleeves of Miku's white dress spread wide in the wind, giving them the appearance of angel wings flapping beside her as raven hair whipped about a face full of serene determination. Heart full of pride in her friend's fearless power, Katara turned back around as the ship's speed increased, propelling them toward the steamers puffing black smoke, racing to block the narrow exit into open waters.

"They're gaining on us, Captain!" Gamon announced.

"Miku, we need more speed," she mentally told her.

"I can't make her go any faster! My power sink is limited, unlike an Enclave."

"Captain," Gamon continued when she didn't reply to him, "If we get past them in time, they're still in position to pursue."

If Miku could be brave enough to put her life and truth on the line, Katara could too. Better together.

"Gamon, hold her steady and be ready for more speed," Katara yelled, handing the wheel over to him.

Katara bounded up to the poop deck and stepped to Miku. "Are you willing to take this all the way? Is it worth your life to leave here? If it isn't, I need to know now."

Miku nodded. "It's worth it."

Katara nodded and looked to Arcadia. "We can't outrun the steamers as is. Prepare the crew for using Mettilwynd."

"Yes, Captain," Arcadia said, leaving them alone.

"Mettil . . ." Miku asked.

Katara took Miku's hand and they rushed to the quarterdeck while she explained. "That's the name I gave to a major modification under the ship—a hydrofoil system. And before you ask how, my boatswain is a genius."

A cocky half-grin filled Gamon's face. "I am! What are we talking about?"

"Operation Mettilwynd," Katara told him. "Now."

"Wind alone isn't fast enough to use the foils."

"I know," Katara said. "I'll operate her."

"Are you sure you want to do that in front of everyone, Captain?" he asked, knowing it would out her as a mage.

"We have no other choice." Miku's hand still in hers, Katara stepped in front of the wheel to stand between two aluminum flagpoles that began at shoulder height and ran down through the wood of the deck, into the heart of *Persephone*.

Speaking mentally, Katara said, *"Even with the foils in use we might not be able to outrun the steamers. If not, we'll need to do a joint casting, like when we were kids. But this one could kill us both."*

Miku's blue eyes darkened with a determination and strength she hadn't possessed the day she'd been taken away. *"If we don't escape, Jet and Nakir will make our fate worse than death."*

"All right then. You can access my power sink through me," Katara told her and grasped a pole in each hand, facing the bow of the ship.

Miku wrapped her arms around Katara's waist from behind. "I'm ready."

"Then here we go." Katara closed her eyes and reached down to the fully charged power sink, connecting it to the prime amulet inside her right arm. Sharing that energy with Miku, who filled the sails, Katara activated the hydrofoils below *Persephone*. The ship rose above the water's surface, the reinforced hull riding atop the waves on the metal blades, picking up more speed as resistance dropped.

Miku laughed, the sound joyous. "This is amazing!"

"Amazing or not, even with the foils, we've got steamers at four and eight o'clock aiming right for us." Gamon shouted over the whipping wind.

"Hold her steady, then," Katara told him. "We're about to try something that could very well get us—"

"Killed?" he asked, finishing her sentence.

"Yeah, that."

"Must be a day that ends in Y," he teased, then seriously added, "To the hilt, Captain!"

"To the hilt," she replied. *"Let's make her fly, Miku."*

"Like, actually fly?"

"Yes, with a joint casting."

Miku tightened her arms around Katara and laid her cheek against the exposed skin of her friend's shoulders, just below her neck. "I'm ready."

"Better together," Katara said.

"To the end," Miku replied.

Katara breathed in Miku's scent to ground herself as her childhood friend sent her creation energy into Katara's body to bind with hers. If rejected, they'd never outrun Saval's army. If accepted, the two energies would twist together like a double-helix of DNA, becoming one entity so powerful they'd have the leverage to escape. However, if not controlled, that level of energy could gain too much magical friction and possibly explode.

After only a moment's hesitation, Katara's energy acknowledged and accepted Miku's, the two winding together seamlessly.

"Whatever you're planning, do it fast! We're going to collide in the next thirty seconds, Captain!" Gamon announced.

Ignoring him, Katara focused on supporting both Miku and the hydro-foil with *Persephone's* power sink while Miku called on the ability of levitation.

Intense internal pressure rising, Katara cried out in agony. This heat spread to the flagpoles, singeing her hands as the core of her being felt as if it were roasting from the inside out. Spiral streams of energy spun so fast within them that both of their bodies began to glow like steel in a furnace, causing Katara to pant with pain.

"Twenty seconds until impact!" Gamon shouted.

"Almost there . . ." Miku said to Katara mentally.

"Mist, Gamon! Hide us from them just in case!"

"Aye, Captain!"

Eyes still closed, Katara felt the dampness of mist caress her skin, easing physical pain. But her fear for the life of her crew intensified. She had to keep them safe!

Detecting her friend's panic, Miku mentally sent Katara a picture from their past. It was Miku's perspective of the day Chopra had saved her life; an eight-year-old girl full of gallantry, strength, and fearlessness. The characteristics she still saw and felt in that same Indi-girl she trusted today.

"You are the reason I'm alive, Chopra. You're my strength, my equal, my rock to stand on, and my reason to push forward in this life. I blame you for nothing in our past or for this moment now. Let go of your fear. We are one, you and I. We can do this."

Tears sliding down Katara's face, she kept her prime amulet arm in contact with the metal pole and let go of the other. Taking Miku's hand, she gripped it tight, and with a single accepting breath of self-worth, forgiveness, and love, the double-helix bonded and the last bit of resistance dropped away. With the friction gone, the heat abated, and with the elegance of a kite swooping into the sky, *Persephone* soared upward and out of the water.

Katara opened her eyes and stared in awe as her ship rose high into the air, cutting through the black smoke of the steamers below as she flew over them, prompting the crew to erupt in shouts of amazement and joy.

"You did it!" Gamon said. "This is beautiful."

With the mist behind them, and the last of the pain gone, Katara watched the beauty of the setting sun below them. The sky, a bright magenta, faded into orange and yellow as they flew. Soon, with the sun down and no moon to brighten the Earth, the sky became as black as *Persephone's* sails, and the ship disappeared into the night.

Once sure of safety, Katara and Miku gentled *Persephone* back onto the water and discontinued the joint casting. Katara retracted the foils, and as a natural breeze picked up, Miku dropped her magical efforts—allowing the brigantine to naturally glide across smooth waters.

Free to sit and take stock of injuries, Katara immediately realized the glamour to hide her facial scars, cast in order to conceal her true identity, had ceased working. She must have drawn on its energy unconsciously. She'd deal with that later; there were more pressing problems.

"We should call the ship's doctor," Arcadia offered.

Katara quickly rebuffed her quartermaster. "No, I'm fine. Don't you dare go get him. He'll try to stick me with a needle again."

"So, how's your nose?" Arcadia taunted in reply.

Katara pointed at her quartermaster. "Don't start."

"You're bleeding from your ears, Captain," Gamon said. "You both are."

"Spawn balls," Miku blurted out as she wiped the blood away, causing everyone to turn and look at her in surprise. "What? Just because I look sweet and innocent doesn't mean I am."

Everyone on the quarterdeck laughed, even Arcadia, who Katara could tell was more than perturbed with her for trying such a conjure without warning her first.

"Here," Gamon said, handing Katara a flask. "I made a new batch while we were in Ranong."

Katara's nose wrinkled. "Does *this* one taste like horse manure?"

He laughed, "You exaggerate, Captain. It's not great, but it's a healing potion. Drink half and share."

Hesitantly, she took the flask, opened, and drank. With a shudder, she handed it to Miku. "Here," she choked out.

"Sounds promising," Miku muttered before finishing off the flask's contents, and handing it back to Gamon. "Thank you."

"See, it's not so bad," he said, encouraged by Miku's appreciation.

"Oh, no, it's horrible, I'm just more polite than she is," Miku explained.

"Isn't most everyone?" Arcadia pointed out.

"Funny, ha ha," Katara said. "Look, I get that you're mad, and I'm sorry there wasn't time to fly the idea by you, but—"

"Fly? Ha, punny," Gamon commented without thinking.

All three women stared him down and he stepped backward, "I'll just be over here at the wheel."

"Wise choice, Little Liran," Arcadia said.

An amused silence settled on them and Katara looked to her quartermaster. "You did great work today. If you didn't already own the best sword and armor I could make, I'd build them for you in honor of your sacrifice and a battle well-won." She paused, searching for words. "Know that I *always* hear what you say, Arcadia. You and your advice are invaluable to me. I am truly sorry to have scared you and made choices without making you aware. It won't happen again."

Arcadia stepped forward and knelt beside her captain. Grinning, she said, "Yes it will, but I appreciate the promise that you'll try."

Katara smiled at her champard.

"I'd not say no to a second sword or set of throwing knives, though. Just saying…"

Katara laughed. "Noted."

"But actually, I returned here to the quarterdeck for something other than to throttle you."

"Oh?" Katara prompted.

Standing, Arcadia said, "The crew are asking what course to set. We haven't burned the name *Persephone* since we never re-etched it into the wood after construction, so no one knows who killed Saval or kidnapped Havâ, but everyone thinks we should stay out of Malaysian waters for a while."

"I agree," Katara said, laying a hand on Miku's knee. "But didn't the crew see what we did?"

"See what specifically, Captain?" Gamon interjected before Arcadia could answer. "That you and Miku are powerful mages who just saved their lives? I think they all saw that, sir."

"Don't get smart with me, Sea mage, or I'll tell—"

"Oh, the crew figured that out ages ago," he said, grinning.

"I was going to say, 'tell your *Dad*'," Katara said, a mischievous grin on her face.

Gamon's eyes went wide. "That's just mean, Cap . . . You wouldn't really, right?"

Ignoring Gamon, Katara turned her attention back to Arcadia. "So they haven't demanded a vote to replace me?"

"No. Why would they?" Arcadia asked.

"Because accepting that they will encounter and work with neomages is what they each agreed to when hired. Not to work *for* a rogue mage. That's another matter altogether."

"To be honest," Gamon explained, "they've had their suspicions for a while. I mean, the strange construction of the new *Persephone*, all the secrecy over the years, and the hydrofoil system, too. Besides, if anyone has a problem with it, I'll toss them overboard myself."

All three women stared doubtfully at the slender young man.

Gamon cleared his throat. "I mean, I'll have *Arcadia* toss them overboard."

"Now you're talkin'," the warrior woman said.

Laughter bubbled up from Katara. "They're not a big crew, but they're an amazing one."

"So, once we stop in Sri Lanka to let your power sink charge, I suggest we rename the ship for a while, just in case. Question is, what to name her and where should we go to lay low?" Arcadia asked.

"The name is obvious," Gamon said, "Mettilwynd."

"Good call," Arcadia said.

Katara nodded. "Why not?"

Miku snickered. "You'd name this gorgeous ship after our band?"

"Band?" Arcadia prodded. "Oh, do tell!"

"Saint's balls . . ." Katara complained. "Fine. Okay. Back when we were young, we daydreamed of having a band. We were going to name it after our elemental affinities."

"But we couldn't use the *normal* spelling of metal and wind. Oh no, that was too boring for a certain someone," Miku teased.

"Who will remain nameless," Katara grumped.

Arcadia laughed, yet with a side-long glance from Katara, she pretended to cough it to a halt. "I'll get the crew prepared. Sri Lanka to . . ."

"Mumbai," Katara informed her.

"Why there?" Miku asked.

"To take you home," Katara explained. "I can't go back, but you can."

"Mumbai isn't my home anymore. I have no family there. *You* are my family and you're here."

Katara took Miku's hand. "Seraphs bless us, I missed you." Throwing her free arm around her, Katara pulled her friend close. "I love you so much."

"I always knew you'd come for me," Miku whispered in Katara's ear, tears gathering in her eyes. "That's why the break to my trance was my prime amulet. I knew you'd never lose it."

"I guarded it with my life."

Miku gently placed her hand along the crescent scar on Katara's face. "In doing so, you guarded me. Most of your life has revolved around mine. It's time you did something for yourself. When's the last time you went where you wanted?"

Arcadia smiled. "I like this woman. So, Captain?"

"If we had the funds . . ." Katara began.

Miku patted the pouch tied to her belt. "We might."

"Ah, yes, the bag we couldn't open," Arcadia said.

"It's spelled closed to all but me and Katara," Miku said, opening and holding it out for them to see the gold inside. "Will it help?"

"Fire and feathers!" Arcadia burst out, as Gamon whistled low.

"I'll take that as a yes."

"Glory and infamy, Miku!" Katara said.

"It's all mine, so now it's all *ours*. Where do we go?"

Katara looked at Arcadia, "Should we?"

"It'll be dangerous, but I say we do it."

"Um, where exactly, Captain?" Gamon asked.

Katara's eyes lit up. "The Red Sea to the Gulf of Aqaba. Dock at Port Eilat before heading overland to the Dead Sea. Indira always said if we wanted to truly make a difference . . ."

Gamon almost choked. "That means seeing my dad, which I'd rather not do, plus a journey past Africa with the glowing . . . things. No one goes to Africa, Captain. Not even mages."

"It's the best way to Israel, your father's homeland," Katara pointed out to Gamon. "Unless you'd rather we sail around *all* of Africa . . ."

"Noooo . . ." Gamon protested.

"Indira and Liran would be happy to see us," Arcadia said. "They could use our help mining salt from the Dead Sea and shipping it to neomages around the world."

"Yay, my father, so excited," Gamon grumbled.

Katara laid a hand on his shoulder. "If we want to hurt Jet, Nakir, and others like them—"

"And we do, so I'm in." Miku put her hand into the center of the group.

"You know I am," Katara said, placing her other hand on Miku's.

Arcadia put her hand on Katara's and turned toward Gamon. "You in, Little Liran?"

"As long as none of you ever calls me that again," he said. "Deal?"

Katara ruffled his hair to avoid answering his request. "Nice haircut."

"Cap?" he prompted.

Katara sighed. "Okay, okay. I promise to try."

"That's the best you're gonna get," Arcadia pointed out.

He slowly laid a hand on the pile. "Seraphs save me, I'm in."

"Oh man," Arcadia said. "The Darkness has a new enemy, and her name is *Mettihwynd*."

Sons

Faith Hunter

He reared back in his chair, his taloned toes clicking on the tile floor. The woman stared at him, her body scented with fear but her limbs loose and relaxed, her face composed, eyes seemingly serene. Her hair was a soft brown, neither reddish nor blonde, but rather nut-brown, like a pecan. At the thought, the taste of pecan flooded his mouth. Better—the taste of pecan pie, hot and rich and sweet from the oven, with whipped cream on top. He smiled at the thought.

The woman flinched, dragging his attention back to her. Baalfilel, son of Baal-Hadad the Storm Lord, let the smile widen, knowing that his fangs would terrify. She gathered herself, drawing up the strands of her dignity and courage. Her eyes narrowed in defiance.

Baalfilel wanted to laugh with delight, spreading his leathery wings. The red and orange that banded his body brightened with the energies of amusement. He had seldom met a human woman who could withstand a Fallen's true form, the shape of the dragon, without fear, without tears and mewling. For that he detested the lot of them. In curiosity, he opened one clawed hand, letting the candlelight glimmer on his razor-talons. She started. He smelled her bodily fluids shifting, altering. Her mouth went dry. But she stared at him, almost daring him.

He smiled, touching his lips with his tongue, delicately forked and black as soot. Her eyes followed it, but she didn't back away. This human female reminded him of Celvdia, his one love, his darling, the human for whom he gave up everything: paradise, his seraphic shape and form, the ability to transmogrify—and most important, gave up his innate right to be in the presence of the Most High. That right that had been part of his former nature, the right and ability to gather with the seraphs and sing beside the glassy sea.

Pain, like a lance-point of seraph steel, pierced him. Baalfilel closed his eyes. He had once thought that to lie with Celvdia was worth the loss of everything holy; to bear children with her was worth the loss of the River of Time. He had learned that nothing, not even the world's grandest passion, was worth banishment from Paradise. Not even Celvdia was worth what he had suffered.

When he opened his eyes, the woman still stood before him, trembling, the tiniest vibration of muscles and flesh. Much time had passed as he'd recalled the early times. Baalfilel sighed. He was getting too old to be dwelling on such ancient history.

He glanced at his second in command, the demon son he birthed off of Celvdia, his firstborn, Gilchamshriel. Most Fallen kept their children close by, safe from the predations of seraphs, mages, mules, and humans of the Light. Many of their children had been lost in the first hundred years of the Last War to warriors of the Light. With Paradise denied them, there was little else to fight for except their children, and the faint—ever fainter—hope of victory.

He brushed his hand through Gilchamshriel's aura. The tingle of energy was rich and dark, luscious as human flesh. His son leaned into him, drawing power from his sire, sating his own needs.

Gently his demon son leaned closer, merging their energies, a familiarity no other of his offspring would dare. "Let me have her, Father," he whispered. "Let me play."

"No, Son. Not tonight. You have other prey to taste."

Gilchamshriel sucked in energy, a hard, fast inhalation, as breath once filled his lungs. "Tonight?" he whispered, the woman forgotten. "You send me hunting?"

"Yes. Tonight, my child. But first, this woman." Baalfilel studied her. She had been standing for half a day as he considered her request. She was exhausted. She needed food and drink, and to refresh herself in the baths. But if he offered, she would shrink from that, having heard tales of his frolics.

She had come to him before dawn, begging the release of her son. The lad had been caught out after dark by his youngest son, captured, and brought here, to the deeps of his hellhole. The boy had been a comely lad, naive and delicate, his skin a perfect golden sheen.

Alas, he was no longer innocent and lovely to look upon. The child had been a plaything for two days for his demon sons Shagnarak and Ranc'arek. His screams had echoed down the long dark hallways. Now, if Baalfilel concentrated, he could hear mewling. Good. The boy was still alive.

"I will grant you your son," he said. The woman almost fainted, her legs growing weak as the blood rushed from her human brain in relief. "You will honor me for my benevolence by bringing me whatever I desire for the next moon. My first desire is you in my bed."

The woman fell to the ground. Her shock and fear were potent aphrodisiacs to Baalfilel. He felt heat pool in his groin. The dragon nodded to two Dark mages who stood watch against the wall. The men, Stone mages both, stepped close, the banded tattoos marking them as his coiling up from their feet and over their bodies. The pattern matched the pattern of his own coloration, coils of beauty that covered him from the claws of his feet to the scarlet crest on his head. They were powerful, these mages, their tattoos so instilled with his might and authority that they were like extensions of his own will. Few dragons had discovered ways to bind mages to them with such finesse. His skill was unsurpassed.

"Take our guest to the baths and prepare her for tonight. Take her son to the surface and release him."

"Your sons will object," one of the mages said, his voice expressionless.

Baalfilel nodded thoughtfully. They would indeed. His sons would kill the messengers, and he had no desire to create replacement Dark mages; it was profitable but tiresome work. And the woman interested him now. "Show them this." He removed a ring from his little finger. It was a demon iron setting in the shape of a queen dragon laying an egg. The stone of the ring was the egg, a fire opal in shades of stunning orange and flame. The first mage took the ring and the other lifted the human female. The three left, and he could hear the fast beating of her heart and her fearful exhalations. Tonight would be a thing of joy.

He turned to his son. "You hunt."

Gilchamshriel quivered, his noncorporeal energies swirling like thunderheads and lightning. He was beautiful, though not nearly as lovely now as his original physical form. His son had been worth everything; worth far more than the woman who had captivated him, lived only five hundred years, and died. "I hunt for you, Father, at your command and with your leave. Who do I hunt?"

"The humans who convey our dark product across the border have taken too much. A little pilfering is expected, but this time they have paid too little for what we gave. And the slaves were sickly. You are my vengeance. Go. Hunt. Destroy. And return with their ears."

The form that was his son rose from the floor and swirled, a dark cloud, a first-generation demon, a Darkness to be feared. The energies coalesced, thickened, and formed a shape, winged and taloned and banded with color; an image of his father—an honor to his sire. And his son was gone.

Requiem of the Sea
101 PA / 2113 AD

Melissa McArthur

My riding leathers were snug, stiff from disuse, and I shifted in the saddle as I made my way into the woods. Wicket neighed in response to my movement. "Sorry, Wicket. No more extra desserts for me, I guess," I said, as I patted his neck in apology.

I followed the tracks until they faded under the canopy of trees, hoping I'd find Betta—my best friend and littermate—and her horse, Wanderluck, before someone else did. I'd heard stories of mages who'd left the Enclaves and been found by humans, stories of pain and death and regret. If I could reach Betta before she reached the shoreline, I might be able to bring her home with little or no disciplinary action.

My face was frozen and my nose ran with the cold as we moved deeper into the forest. The little warmth that the morning sun afforded us vanished when we entered the cover of thick evergreen trees. I slowed Wicket to a walk and looked around, hoping for some sign of which way they'd gone. I thumbed one of the charms that hung around my neck, and warmth started to flood my body. Wicket snorted and shook his head, perhaps hoping it would extend to him as well.

I halted the large palomino and closed my eyes. The ground around me was cold, hidden from the sea and moon, drained of the energy I could use. "Seraph stones," I whispered. "I should have looked for you last night." I'd sensed something was wrong when Betta didn't come to dinner, but I'd convinced myself she was just in one of her moods. She'd taken to bouts of melancholy lately. I mentally kicked myself for not seeing the signs months back.

I took a deep breath to settle myself and extended my senses outward into the forest.

"Let's go, Wicket." I shook the reins and nudged the horse forward, headed into deeper woods and even deeper darkness. And with that darkness came danger.

Wicket slowed as the trees became denser and the undergrowth caught at his feet. I ducked under the low-hanging branches that crossed our path and patted the side of his neck, reassuring myself as much as him.

"Whoa, boy," I said, tugging gently on the reins. "Shhh . . ."

A drum beat in the distance, three distinct beats. And then silence.

"You heard that, right?" I asked. Wicket snorted in reply. "Right. Let's go."

Wicket and I headed in the direction of the drum, as best we could through the dense wood. Navigation wasn't a skill I'd practiced much; I'd never thought I'd need it. I expected to live my entire life safe in the protection of the Enclave. I'd expected that if I ever left—which I hoped I would someday so that I could see the seas in all their glory—I would be escorted and not really need to pay much attention to where we went, just absorb the sights along the way. I wished I'd paid more attention to the points on the compass and lines on the maps than to the bleached white shells that strung together to make my favorite bracelet.

The palomino reared. "Wicket, no!" I gasped, grabbed onto his mane and held tight until he had all four hooves on the ground again. "What are you doing, you beast?" Then I saw what had startled him. Wanderluck, just a glimpse through the trees.

"Whoa, boy," I said quietly as I slid off Wicket's back. My boots were silent on the frozen ground as I looped his reins around a tree branch. "Stay here," I whispered and kissed his nose.

I crept slowly through the younger pines to the small clearing where Wanderluck thrashed and bucked. Blood seeped from a gash on his shoulder and his eyes were wild. I pulled a small round charm out of the satchel at my hip. The wooden amulet was carved with a simple *Calming* conjure, and I ran my thumb across it, activating it. I held it out in front of me as I approached Wanderluck. He froze when he saw me and flattened his ears against his skull. *Well, that's not good,* I thought to myself. I whispered calming things, noises and coos, and crept close enough to tuck the amulet under his saddle pad.

He flicked his tail and shook his head as the magic took effect. I ran my hand down his neck and stepped closer to his face. He snorted out a sigh and looked at me. Fear showed in his eyes. "Where's Betta?"

He snorted and nudged me with his head. "Which way, Wanderluck? Show me." I took hold of his reins and let him lead me to the edge of the clearing.

"She wouldn't have gone through here. It's a mess of brambles and thorns! Where did she go, Wanderluck? Please show me." He nipped at my elbow and nudged me. "Hey! Cut that out." I straightened the stallion's stirrups and talked him through my plan. I wasn't sure if he could understand me, but it couldn't hurt.

When Wanderluck was ready, I climbed onto his back and settled myself into the saddle. Wicket neighed and stomped his hoof against the ground. "Give me a minute, Wicket!" The words were barely out of my mouth before Wanderluck bucked, throwing me off his back. I landed hard on the ground, breath knocked out of me, and rolled away from the spooked horse. "Seraph stones! What was that for?"

I got to my feet and dusted myself off. Wanderluck made a few laps around the clearing before dashing off the way I'd come, scraping himself on the pines as he burst through them and past Wicket. "Ugh! Betta, you should have trained that horse a little better!" My eyes prickled with the threat of hot tears. I went to Wicket and buried my face in his mane. He turned his head, nuzzling my hair. I sniffed and took a deep breath before untying his reins. So much for that plan.

"I'm walking from here. Can you find Wanderluck and make sure he gets back home?" I looked the horse in the eye and knew, somehow, that he understood. He nudged me with his head and turned so I could secure the reins. I smacked his rear and said, "Go on, boy. Be safe."

I returned to the clearing, the last place I knew Betta had been. I closed my eyes and opened my mind, scanning for her presence.

The world had changed when I opened my eyes again, the clearing now colored with the turquoise and gold of sunlight on the sea. She wasn't in the immediate area, so I fed creation energy from my prime amulet into the scan, broadening its reach. I let my mind roam the forest—through the trees, over the brambles and vines, deep into the wood. And there she was.

Caged.

She raged in the iron cage that held her, beating herself against the bars and clawing at her skin. I pushed deeper and gasped as my head split with pain, the image of a scarred face appearing, sniffing the air, recognizing the magic. It was as if lightning had struck my skull. I squeezed my eyes shut and fell to my knees, my forehead on the cold ground. Darkness. Betta had been captured by the Darkness.

"No . . ." I moaned as my vision cleared, the pain ebbing. "Betta, what have you done?"

I got to my feet, not knowing what to do, trying to get my bearings in this strange place. I took a deep breath, and my eyes widened as I caught the scent of salt on the air. Faint, but there. The sea was close. Somewhere. I reached out with my magics and tasted my first true taste of the sea. I could draw flavorless generic energy from the power sink under the Enclave whenever I wanted to, but the taste of true Sea energy was different . . . *intoxicating.*

I filled myself with it, and my amulets. I pulled a crystal vial out of my bag, wrapped my hands around it, and pushed some creation energy into the seawater inside. The water sparkled with the turquoise and gold of the energy, and tiny waves lapped at the side of the vial. It'd stay there until I needed it. I hoped I wouldn't need it. I tucked the vial into my leather vest instead of putting it back in my bag and turned to the forest.

The bramble-choked path that Wanderluck had shown me seemed to be the shortest route to Betta, and I felt a moment of guilt. Poor Wanderluck; he'd been right.

I hadn't brought anything to cut through the vines. I pulled a small knife out of my bag and flipped open the blade. Better than nothing.

I sawed at the vines that I couldn't step over or duck under and made slow progress down the path. Where did these things come from? I'm no expert on trees and shrubs, but these didn't seem like things that would grow around here, especially not in the winter in the middle of an ice age.

The path was well worn and seemed like it was traveled recently, but how could anyone have gotten past these vines? There were surely better ways to traverse the forest.

Rustling behind me grabbed my attention and I turned, blade outward.

I watched in open-mouthed horror as the vines I'd just cut through knit themselves back together, sprouted new tendrils that intertwined and grew thick. "What the bloody hell?" I backed away from those vines and took my knife to the ones still blocking my way—the way forward, that is.

Cut. Stomp. Saw. Toss.

I made my way forward, the vines moving and growing behind me. The faster I worked, the thicker the ones blocking my return path grew.

After a long, tiring time, the vines gave way to brambles, and the brambles gave way to evergreens. The warm light of a fire—small enough that I couldn't see it from a few feet back—caught my attention. I closed the knife and slid it into my bag. Moving as silently as possible, I approached the clearing where the fire burned. The drum beat I'd heard earlier came again, steady now, louder. I held my breath as I crept closer but froze when I heard a scream.

"Let me out! You monster! You can't keep me here!" Betta beat against the iron cage, pulled at her hair. She was naked and threw herself up against the iron bars with a grunt and whine. Ice blue magic floated around her like a mist but never drifted past the bars of the cage.

The warmth of the fire somehow reached me, warmed me from the inside out.

I moved back into the tree cover, but the warmth persisted, growing hotter in my belly. I moved around the clearing slightly and peered from behind another tree. I gasped. A kylen. I realized in that moment that the heat I felt wasn't from the fire. I was experiencing—for the first time—mage heat. My heart dropped, and I swallowed hard. Betta must've felt it, too. She wouldn't leave her clothes piled on the floor of a cage to freeze out here for any other reason.

I pressed my back to the tree and closed my eyes against the heat clouding my mind. I took a deep breath in and released it. I peered around the tree again, watching the kylen. His body was golden, tanned by the sun's rays, a stark contrast to the paleness of the Northwestern mages I'd known all my life. He faced away from me and Betta, toward the deeper forest and beyond, and grasped the bars of his own cage, struggling against the mage heat as much as Betta and I struggled. Broad shoulders tapered into a narrow waist cinched by a leather belt looped through his trousers. Muscles bunched as he fought against the bars. My fingers tingled with the desire to slide my hands over his flesh and touch the wings that lay furled against his back.

I was standing in the clearing before I'd even realized I'd stepped out from the tree line. A man hunkered down on the other side of the fire, a wizened figure clothed in tattered robes, a sprinkling of stringy silver hair sprouting from his scalp. *I've never seen a man this old before*, I thought as I opened my mage sight. I froze in horror when his head rose and he sniffed the air. I took one step back toward the cover of the trees, but it was too late. He turned and hissed, drawing the attention of both Betta and the kylen. I realized that he wasn't human.

"No, Piper. Run!" Betta cried.

He was old, but he was fast. In an instant he overtook me. His aura glowed dark to my mage sight, and I saw him for what he really was—a mule. His gnarled fingers encircled my throat and he held a wicked-looking blade to my side. "Another mage. What a treat." He smiled, revealing rotted teeth ground to points, and licked his lips, spittle trailing behind. "Two wombs for us to fill."

"Let go of me!" I shouted as the mule hauled me toward an empty cage beside Betta's—thankfully, the farthest away from the kylen. She reached out between the bars, the rough iron tearing her skin.

The mule purred at the sight of the blood trickling down her arm. I jerked harder, hoping he was distracted enough to loosen his grip. He wasn't. Instead, he pulled me closer to him and grasped my face in his pale hand. His long fingers dug into my skin as he turned my head, forcing me to look into his red eyes.

"Master will be pleased," he said, turning his head to the side. I choked at the putrid, hissing breath. He sniffed, pulling in air sharp through his teeth.

I fought, but he only held tighter. Trinkets jingled at his waist and bumped against me. I looked down at his belt and my eyes went wide. He shook me, hard, jarring my head and causing me to bite my tongue. I tasted the tang of blood and swallowed it back.

Pieces. Human? Mage? Bones. Tied to his waist.

I gagged and felt the bile rise in my throat. He threw me to the ground, and I landed hard on my hip. I winced and tried to scoot away, but he was too fast. He pulled open the cage, grabbed me under the arms, and threw me in. My head bounced off the bars and I crumbled in the corner. I looked over at Betta in the cage next to mine. She'd stopped thrashing against the bars and stared at me, almost as if she didn't believe I was here. I opened my mouth to speak, but no words came out.

"Piper?"

My name—carried on the wind from Betta's cage to mine—was the last thing I heard before the black blanket of unconsciousness fell over me.

"Piper, wake up. Please. Don't be dead. *Please* wake up."

A voice drifted through my dreams and I slowly became aware of how cold I was. I huddled tighter and the voice came again.

"Thank the seraphim. I thought you were dead for sure. Piper? Can you hear me?"

I opened my eyes just a crack and rolled over onto my back. Black iron bars rose around me and met in a circle in the direction of the sky. "I hear you," I said to the voice, still confused and distant. I pushed up on one elbow and looked around. Another cage sat near mine, a small blonde mage inside. Betta.

I sat up fast and the world shifted. I grasped my head and cried out. My hands came away sticky with blood. Then I remembered the mule, his trinkets, being thrown into the cage, the kylen . . .

"Betta? What happened? Where's the kylen?" I raised my head, slowly this time, and looked over at my friend. She crouched in her cage, no longer nude, but her clothes were in ruins.

"The mule took him. Others came, more Darkness. They hauled him onto a cart and took him. That was a few hours ago."

"How long was I out?"

"Half the day, a little more maybe. I think he'll be back for us at full dark."

"Fire and feathers!"

"Piper! You'll attract more of them. Who knows what's out here?"

I glared at her, my worry shifting to anger. "Why did you do it?" I asked, my voice low.

"Why did I leave? You'll think I've gone crazy."

"Try me," I said, sitting back against the bars and stretching my legs out in front of me as best I could.

She sighed. "The sea. It calls me."

"*I'm* the Sea mage, Betta. Moon mages are allergic to seawater."

"But tides on your seas are created by my moon."

"Technically, yes. Maybe that's why our magics work so well together."

"Do you remember the trip I was allowed to take to the beach last summer? I spent the days lying there watching the tide come in and go out. I could feel the moon in the sky like always, but I could also feel it *through the water*. It was different, Piper. I'm used to the moon's power waxing and waning over the month, but there at the sea, I could feel it changing with the *hours*."

"Fine. So we take trips to the beach every once in a while. *Guarded and sanctioned* trips."

"Last night was the spring tide." I nodded and she continued. "The *perigean* spring tide. I could feel the moon calling me, pulling me to the sea. I knew I had to leave then . . . or I'd never get to leave at all," Betta said, looking down at her torn clothes.

"Betta, I don't . . ."

"I couldn't stand the thought of living in a cage for all my life, no matter how exquisite. I wanted to be free. I know the Enclave is meant to keep us safe, but I am willing to give up that safety for a chance to see the world."

"That's a death sentence, and you know it."

"But the sea calls to you, too, Piper. I know it does. I can't imagine how strong the call is for you. A Sea mage. You might as well be a mermaid or pirate for all that you can resist it." She laughed, a short sound out of place in the cold of the darkening day.

"Yes. I understand the siren call, the desire. I never told you this, Betta, but when I came of age, I was hit with waves of intense desire. It wasn't linked to a seraphic overflight, though. During the full moon when the high tides rolled in, my body burned and ached with need, like a noncontagious mage heat. So I went to Samara, the only mentor I felt comfortable telling my secrets to. She made me an amulet that I could wear, charged with the power of the sun—an opposite force to dampen the heat. I don't have to wear it all the time, only during the full moon."

"Like last night."

"Yeah, it dulls the heat, but also makes me dead tired. I slept right through you leaving."

"We're littermates, Piper. Why is this the first time I'm hearing about any of this?"

"I should have told you, Betta. But it was embarrassing. And I could ask why you never mentioned your tide problem before."

"It was . . . oh, Piper, I'm sorry. I thought I could handle it on my own. I thought I was doing the right thing. It's all my fault you're here."

"You're damn right it is." I turned my head so that she couldn't see the tears that had started down my cheeks. "But what's done is done. Now we just have to figure out how to get out of here."

We tried to break open the cages, tried to tip them over, tried to cast every conjure we could think of. We tried everything. Nothing worked. All the spells we cast only worked within the confines of our cages.

Betta and I sat in silence as the sun moved across the sky, hints of warmth breaking through the tree cover and falling in shafts of golden light. It would soon be dusk.

"I wonder if the demon iron has extra spells cast on it," Betta said, breaking the silence.

"What do you mean?"

"I wonder if there's something that's keeping us from using our magic outside the cage."

"Could our powers be blacked out somehow?" I said at last.

"Is that even possible, Piper? I've never been the strongest mage—mediocre at best. If we get out of here and my magics are even more messed up, what will I do? I'm a freak." Tears spilled over the edges of her eyes and trailed down her cheeks. She slumped into a ball at the bottom of her cage.

I watched as Betta's shoulders shook, her sobs soundless in the still of the darkening day. Betta had always been the weaker of the two of us. And making friends didn't come easily for her. She and I had come from a litter of only three. Our brother was a Sun mage, so he hadn't spent much time with his Moon and Sea mage sisters. Besides, Moon mages were always considered a bit mystical and odd, and not just because of the way they shunned daylight.

I remembered the day she and I became friends and not just sisters. She'd sat on the ground of the play yard, much as she sat now, and cried.

She was alone, different. She was strikingly beautiful, even as a child, but different, almost angelic in her softness. I'd sat down beside her and nudged her with my elbow. "Y'know, nobody's playing on the swings around the corner because they're in the shade now and it gets chilly." She looked up at me, blue eyes rimmed with red. I stood, offered her my hand, and walked around the corner into the shade. We'd been inseparable ever since. Until this morning.

Betta looked up at me and wiped the tears from her cheeks. "I think I know what to do."

She held out the small wooden disk, identical to the ones I'd tucked into my bag before leaving the Enclave. She activated the charm and then smiled at me. "Catch this," she said as she reached through the bars and tossed the disk to me. I caught it—but only just—and pulled it inside. The *Warming* charm radiated heat inside my cage.

"Betta! That's it!"

"Piper, this is going to be risky. But it's the only thing I can think to do." She pulled out her prime amulet and held it in her hands. She looked at me, and fat tears ran down her face.

"What are you doing?" I asked, hoping she wasn't going to smash her amulet.

"We've always been stronger together, right? Well, we can't use our magic together while we're in here, so I'm going to send my magic over to you."

"No, Betta. That'll leave you too vulnerable!"

"It's my choice." She closed her eyes and released her breath, the pale blue of the rising moon shining on her as she cast. The words she murmured were unintelligible to me this far away. Blue light surrounded her, lifting her off her feet in the confines of the cage. And then she fell, crouching on the balls of her feet with the prime amulet in her hands. It pulsed with the azure coolness of the Moon magic within.

She tossed the amulet to me, a stroke of peace painting her face in porcelain.

I caught it and held it tight in my hand.

"Now we wait."

Night fell. The cold light of the moon filtered through the trees, but somehow its energy didn't make it through the bars to Betta. An owl hooted in the distance. We moved around in our cages as much as we could trying to generate body heat to keep from freezing in the April chill.

"That mule better come back for us soon," I grumbled.

"Speak of the devil and he shall appear. Look, Piper."

Betta's night vision was better than mine. The creak of a wooden cart reached me before I could make out the shape of the mule returning. "Are you ready?" I whispered.

"Yes," Betta's reply came, with a determination that I'd never heard from her before.

"Whatever happens, just know I love you."

"You too, Piper. And I'm sorry." Betta settled into the floor of the cage.

I took a deep breath and pinched my skin, careful not to draw blood. The pain brought tears to my eyes. Good.

"Betta, wake up! Don't die on me, Betta!" I sobbed as the mule drew closer.

He released the cart and went to Betta's cage, sniffing her still form.

"She's frozen. She's dying, mule!" I cried out. "She's no use to you dead." I spat on the ground at his feet and slammed my hands against the bars.

He pulled a key from his robes and unlocked her cage. He swung the door wide and wrapped a hand around Betta's ankle. As he leaned forward, she kicked out, striking him in the face hard enough to turn his head and throw him backward out of the cage. She scrambled to her feet and jumped on him, punching his face over and over again until she cried out in pain holding her bloody fist to her chest.

The mule lay still. She grabbed his robes and slammed his head against the frozen ground. Her actions were not the beautiful savage chi we learned at the Enclave. It was as if she was channeling the spirit of a street brawler from one of the musty Pre-Ap paperbacks we'd take turns reading aloud sitting by the fire in the great hall.

"Is he dead?" I whispered, although there was no one else around to hear me.

"I don't know," she said without looking at his body.

"Unlock my cage."

Betta stood to retrieve the key from the lock of her cage door—and the mule pulled a wicked blade from his robes and lunged at her. Betta started to turn and her eyes met mine as the curved blade sunk into her sternum. She only managed to get out a single word, "Pipe . . ."

The mule jerked the knife up, opening a wide space in the center of her chest. She collapsed against him, blood spattering onto his face. He drove her to the ground and lowered his head to her chest, sniffing at the gory wound. He reached a hand in and pulled out her heart. He held it up as the moonlight broke through the bars of the cage to shine on the mass of flesh. The heart reflected a pale blue light as if the moon were saying goodbye to one of its own.

I wailed and fell to my knees. I cursed, beating the floor of the cage as I watched him bring her heart to his lips and bite. Tears came as I gagged, heaving, though there was nothing left for my stomach to expel. I slumped over, a useless ball of mage puddled into a corner as the mule feasted on my best friend until there was nothing left but bones.

After he was done, the mule cleaned himself by the fire and chattered about his plan to please his master. "A bright, strong mage for breeding." He giggled. "Master will be pleased. The name of Machovy will no longer be banned from his halls." He sniffed at me. "Your friend was nice, but you'll be better. She was weak, odd. You'll be stronger."

"I won't let you take me alive. I'll die before letting you breed me with some monster." I crossed my arms over my chest and sat back against the bars of the cage.

"Oh no, mage. You'll be bred with the kylen. I have a debt to repay." He nodded and stood, stretching in front of the fire.

I watched him tug on the wooden cart, backing it up to my cage. Like a monkey, he climbed the side, looped a thick rope through the ring at the top. He jumped back to the ground and pulled at the rope until the cage toppled over onto the wooden cart.

I hit the side of the cage hard. I would be covered in deep purple bruises if, by some miracle, I survived this night. I rolled onto my back and looked up at the trees as the cart lurched along the forest floor, headed toward my death.

The stench of sulfur was strong as we rolled farther underground, deeper into the place where Darkness dwelled. I opened my eyes when the cart bumped to a stop. Creatures of the night swarmed around me, sniffing and poking, as if I were there for their amusement.

"Get the cage upright and take her to the kylen," Machovy commanded. The creatures obeyed. I scrambled to my feet as they righted the heavy cage. The mule unlocked the door and misshapen hands grabbed at me everywhere they could. I shrieked and pulled away, but there were too many. I was jerked from the cage. A burlap bag was thrown over my head and tied in place. Rough rope also bound my hands, and I was stripped of anything I could use against the Darkness—my knife, amulets, shoes, and belt—all but the items I'd hidden within my clothes. They led me down a dirt path, the occasional stone piercing the soles of my feet and stinging. I thought I could hear *things* following behind, lapping up the blood from my footprints.

I don't know how long, how deep we marched. Then heat started to build, a glowing ember low in my belly. The kylen was close. The sound of metal scraping against metal pulled me back from the enchantment of the glowing ember. The burlap was stripped from my head. I breathed in, gasped as I took in what lay before me.

The kylen was shackled to the stone wall at the opposite end of a cell. He pulled ineffectually against the chains encircling his wrists and his head sagged. Sweat gleamed on his skin in the firelight.

The heat exploded in me, and I fell to my knees, slumping in the mule's grasp. I *felt* as much as heard the kylen stand, his wings outstretched in his response to the heat sparking between us.

"Get to your feet, mage. Your mate awaits."

I was thrust forward into the cell, skidding onto the ground, scraping my palms on the stone floor. An iron door swung closed and metal clanged against metal as the mule turned the key, locking us in.

I scrambled to the corner farthest from the kylen and huddled there.

"Where's the other mage?" the kylen growled.

"Dead."

"You feel it, too?" he asked. I knew he meant the heat that coursed through my veins, burning me from the inside out.

I nodded.

"Then stay over there," his tone was harsh, dampening the heat like a wet blanket thrown over a fire.

"I'd planned to."

"They intend to breed monsters from us. We don't need to make their job easier for them."

I kept silent, my mind wandering to Betta, seeing her body fall with her eyes locked on mine.

"She was your friend?" the kylen asked.

"Yes. Sister and friend."

"There's nothing you can do for her now except save yourself. And me, while you're at it."

I looked up at the kylen. His eyes were dark, the light of the torch on the wall dancing in them.

"Call mage in dire. Save us both," the kylen said, his voice barely above a whisper.

"I'd rather die. I can't go back now. Betta's gone. It's my fault. Death would be better." I turned my back to him.

"You're an idiot," he mumbled.

Anger rose in my chest replacing the sorrow of only moments before. I turned back to him and hissed, "Why would I save you? What good would it do *me*? I'm not making it out of this alive. I left the Enclave without a chaperone. Do you know what they do to mages who leave like that? I'd rather die here than return and face a lifetime with her death on my hands."

"Lucky me. I am trapped in here with a suicidal mage . . ." He lowered his eyes, breaking contact with mine, signaling the conversation was over.

The kylen fell silent, sleeping perhaps, so I curled down on my side and closed my eyes against the darkness. I lost all sense of time without the sun, the moon, the tides to guide my hours.

Betta came to me in the darkness and spoke. "Piper, wake up."

I turned toward her voice, expecting the weightlessness of a dream, but instead winced with pain. I rubbed the sleep from my eyes and looked around. She wasn't there. It had been but a dream. I stretched and looked over at the kylen—still sleeping—before pulling out the prime amulet Betta had given me. *You know what to do,* a voice whispered from the remnants of my dream.

And suddenly I did. I activated the working stored inside, and the amulet shifted to pale blue, the color of Betta's magic. It was almost as if I could feel her with me though I knew her bones lay scattered in the woods.

I looked up, and she stood over me, white lace trailing from a long gown that covered her feet, her white-blonde hair glistening with the light of an impossible moon. Angelic, just as she had always been, but now bathed in the blue light of the moon.

I pulled myself up onto my elbows and scooted back to prop myself against the stone wall. I reached a hand out to her, but she only shook her head.

"Am I still dreaming?" I asked.

She didn't answer. Instead, she drifted to the other side of the cell and knelt beside the kylen. She laid her small, pale hand on his shoulder. He shifted in his sleep and his breath caught. She ran her fingers over the demon iron chains holding him to the wall.

I watched as the metal she touched began to glow, the same white blue that swirled within the confines of her cage in the woods.

The kylen's eyes flew open and he screamed in pain. He jerked his hands away from the wall, trying to escape the blisteringly cold iron. And the chains broke.

"What did you do to me, mage?" he hissed, crouching low, ready to pounce.

I scrambled to my feet, still pressed against the wall. "Nothing. I didn't . . ." I stopped and looked around. The ghostly image of Betta was gone.

"What the bloody hell was that then?" he said, blowing on his burns.

"I think it was a projection stored in a working, in this amulet she gave me before she died."

"Your dead friend?"

"Yes." I crept closer as I spoke, close enough to speak without my voice echoing through the cavern, but far enough away that the heat was bearable.

"They don't know you're free. Whoever comes in next, you take them out, whatever you have to do. I'll grab the key and make sure the door doesn't close on us. Then it will just be a matter of finding our way out of here. I might be able to do it, if the sea is close enough."

"You're a Sea mage, then?" he asked.

"Yes. I'm weak here, surrounded by earth. My sister, Betta, she was a Moon mage. She would have been just as weak. We liked to work together. It's been so long since I've conjured anything more than a few basic charms alone, I'm not even sure if I remember how." I laughed and wiped away a tear. My heart ached for my sister.

"That isn't a sound we usually hear down here," came a voice from outside the cell. "Making merry, little doves?" The mule came to the bars and looked at us. I crouched near the kylen; he'd positioned himself back under the shackles as if he were still chained.

"No. Not for you." The kylen pulled his feet underneath himself as he spoke. "You want us to breed? Get in here and make us, mongrel."

I braced myself, ready for the attack. The mule was in the cell and on the kylen quicker than I could see. He was faster than the mules I was used to in the Enclave. Perhaps the Dark ones were different.

"Now!" I screamed, as the kylen brought the iron manacles down onto the mule's head.

"I will not be part of your experiments, mule. And neither will he." I fell into a cat stance and drew my fingers into a shaking claw, the most effective move I could remember.

The kylen looped a chain around the mule's neck. "Get the blade," he growled as he pulled back on the mule's neck.

"I'm working on it!" I cried as I dropped my stance and moved, trying to catch the blade without losing a piece of myself in the process.

"Forgive me," the kylen whispered as he yanked the chain, the snap of the mule's neck echoing in the silence.

The body slumped at the kylen's feet, and I knelt to retrieve the knife from where it had fallen. I backed away when I saw the lust in his eyes. He stepped toward me and grabbed my arm, pulling me to him and sniffing, inhaling my scent.

I moaned, gritting my teeth against the heat exploding inside me. Summoning everything I held within myself, I jerked my arm away and turned toward the cell door. "Not now," I panted.

"Right." He closed his eyes and took a few deep breaths. "Now what?"

"We get out of here, I guess."

He nodded and knelt by the fallen creature. He said a few words over the body, perhaps asking for the Most High to have mercy on him. The kylen picked up the blade and handed it to me, handle outward. I wrapped my fingers around it. The memory of the blade sliding into Betta's chest came back to me, sudden and intense. The blade that may have stolen my best friend's life could be the only thing that saved mine. Guilt washed over me in waves.

The kylen took my hand. "It's not your fault."

The mage heat flared at the contact and we immediately separated. He stepped out of the cell and began walking up the tunnel. I nodded and wiped my face. I followed him out into the tunnels to find the light once more.

"I think we're going in circles," I said as we passed a now-familiar pile of bones for the third or fourth time. "We'll never get out of the maze this way."

"I was unconscious when they brought me down here. I didn't see how we came."

"They covered my eyes. I know we took several turns and kept descending, but that's all I remember."

"Why haven't we seen more spawn down here?" he pondered, kicking over the bones.

"Maybe they're waiting to ambush us."

"That's certainly positive thi—" His words were cut short by skittering noises. Spawn rushed at us in a massive, dark wave.

"Time to fight," I said, falling into a ready stance.

The kylen pulled a large bone from the pile at his feet.

I moved into a whirlwind move, the foul knife cutting a swath through the attacking spawn, my free arm blocking, keeping the spawn from my vitals. Whenever I cut left, the kylen's bone club would smash right. We weren't elegant or subtle, but we took down dozens.

I moved back and stumbled, my hand flying to my chest as I gasped. I felt something there, and then I remembered. The woods. The crystal vial. Thank the Most High I'd not stuffed it in my bag. I pulled out the vial and tugged out the cork. The water inside glowed faintly blue, Moon magic glimmering in conjunction with my Sea magic.

Smiling, I drew on the small amount of creation energy I'd stored in the vial and pushed my body to move faster, taking heads and removing limbs. My breath came in heavy gasps, and I landed with a grunt as one of the creatures jumped on me, knocking me to my back. I pulled on the last of the stored energy and cast *Blinding Flash*, sending the creature backward with his arms covering his eyes. I jumped up and sliced open his belly, gore covering me and the ground.

The kylen called out to me and I returned his call. He came to me and offered a hand. The last of the spawn had fallen. For now. He pulled me to my feet. "How did you do that?"

"It was a tactic Betta and I had worked out to use if we ever got in a situation like this. Except that *she* was supposed to cast the spell; I can't cast Moon spells. But somehow it felt right to try. And it worked." I thought of the pale blue glow that illuminated the vial, and tears sprang to my eyes. She'd saved me again.

"Are you all right?" he asked.

I nodded. "I'll be sore tomorrow, that's for sure."

"If tomorrow ever comes," he said, looking both ways down the tunnel.

"Hmm. Knock that wall over there," I said, indicating a place that glowed slightly with Dark energy, different from the rock on either side. He took his bone club and swung it against the wall. The rock was only inches thick and crumbled revealing another tunnel just beyond.

"Hence the going around in circles," he said as he stepped through.

We moved through the new tunnel, definitely upward now. Other spawn came from the darkest corners and we fought. Back to back, we parried and dodged, working in strikes as we could, battling the scourge. One by one they fell, and bodies littered the ground around us. The kylen grabbed my hand, pulling me farther up the tunnel. The remaining spawn gave chase, but the kylen pressed on, swinging his bone club and cracking their skulls. I buried the blade in the last spawn and went down, exhaustion overtaking me. The kylen lifted me from the ground and steadied me on my feet. A hint of heat blossomed low in my body, and I backed away. "Let's get out of here," I said, as I pushed down the desire and started upward again.

Too tired to talk, we soldiered on, the only sound our feet against the ground. After some time, I broke the silence. "I think we're almost there."

"Why's that?"

"Did you notice we haven't seen any spawn? We're probably very close to the surface."

"Hmm. You're right. Without their leader, they don't seem particularly brave. I never did figure out why the mule wanted us for breeding."

"I'm not sure either," I said. "He mentioned something about having a debt to pay to his master. That was after they'd taken—"

"Do you smell that?"

I turned my head, looking in the direction the kylen was pointing. "No . . ."

"The sweet smell of the winter air—it's freedom," he said, indicating a section of stone wall a few feet above us, no different than any of the rest. "The surface is *there*, mage."

"Give me a boost," I said.

He knelt, offering me his knee to step up on, and handed me his club.

I stood on his leg, grasping at the rough stone to steady me. His strong hands held my thighs, and my breath caught in my throat.

"Are you all right?" he asked, sensing me tense.

I didn't respond, my voice stolen by the intensity of the desire flooding my body.

Once I had my balance, he released the grip on my legs, and I felt creation energy build at my back. A brisk winter air whispered and then whistled through cracks between the stones. Pebbles fell to the ground and I could hear the larger stones groaning as they strained in place.

I stuck the end of the club into the widest crack. Using it as a lever, I pulled with both my hands. My strength and the kylen's conjure set the stones free, and I fell as the rock gave way taking my handhold with it, landing in a heap of kylen and stone.

"We did it!" he said, as he stood and pulled me to my feet.

"Why didn't you do that before?" I asked, hands on my hips.

He just shrugged. "I'm weakened down here—the stone, the stale air— it's too much. Just like you and your salty sea spray, your sister and her moonlight. But that sweet taste of the fresh air—it renewed me. And now I want more. Let's go!"

Using the fallen stone as makeshift stairs, we climbed up toward the surface and out of the hellhole.

We emerged into the end of a day, the sun descending through a watercolor sky. I stopped, transfixed by the fiery globe. I could smell salt in the air. "Race you," I said, as I took off toward the shore, mage fast. I smiled as I ran, dodging tree limbs, my feet trying to match the speed of my thoughts. Thoughts of the kylen, his strong, tanned body, his voice both a whisper and a scream, his hand in mine—thoughts of Betta, her form in the dream, finally at peace.

I closed my eyes for just a moment as I ran, feeling the call of the sea pulling me forward as I raced toward the edge of the woods.

The forest's edge broke and the kylen swooped in, grabbing me before I could run off the edge of the cliff. He pulled me to him, his body warm and strong at my back. I twisted in the kylen's arms and looked up at him. The sun had set completely, and his face was lit by the first light of the rising moon.

I clung to him as we glided out over the ocean, his wings carrying us through the salt air. I wrapped my legs around his, and felt the sea's power surge, igniting the mage heat, my body barely able to contain it. Waves crashed against the rocks below, and he set me down on the sandy shore, only yards from the rising tide. The sea spray tickled my face. I still held onto him. He looked down at me, eyes the deep blue of the Pacific. I raised up on tiptoes to meet his lips. Smooth as satin and tender as a young lamb. He kissed me. I melted into him and sighed.

"What's your name, kylen?" I whispered, my face close to his.

"Ezekiel." His eyes, heavy-lidded and growing darker with lust, sparkled in the moonlight.

"I'm Piper," I said as his lips met mine again. I tangled my fingers in his hair and breathed a sigh of relief against his lips.

I broke from the kiss and pulled back. He smiled, just a slight draw of the corner of his mouth. I was safe. I was alive. I had defeated a Darkness. And . . . I was in biiiig trouble.

The Best-Laid Plans
104 PA / 2116 AD

Faith Hunter

The deadminer lifted the saddlebags from his mount, unimpressed with Mineral City. Lolo had directed him here, aimed him like an arrow, to find the lost Stone mage, the girl hiding among humans, and become her teacher. He had resisted, fought the mage priestess long enough to search for and find the vanished city of Sugar Grove, buried beneath the glaciers of the mini-ice age. He had made a name for himself, become someone in his own right. Yet her resolve had finally conquered him, and he was here, saddlebags filled with dead-mined loot, items certain to interest a Stone mage who played at making jewelry.

He threw the bags over his shoulder, touched the amulet at his neck, making certain that his mule glow—energy patterns that coursed through the skin of the second unforeseen—was completely damped. Satisfied, long leather duster flapping in the wind, he strode across the ice-covered street, leaving his Clydesdale where it stood, head hanging in exhaustion. If he played his cards right, he'd sell the plunder, making a nice profit off of Thorn St. Croix, move his horse into the stable behind her shop and himself right into her bed, whether it was what he desired or not. He had his orders. It was what mules did best: followed orders, serviced, served, lived off of, and at the behest of, mages. That and fight Darkness. Sex and blood, the coin with which they paid their way.

The shop was neat and bright, taking up the ground floor of a refurbished stone and brick two-story building. Windows—real glass windows, when he had expected them to be boarded over to preserve the meager warmth inside—displayed jewelry, things made of stone and glass and intricate settings of gold and copper. He pushed open the door, jingling bells announcing him, his head nearly brushing the top of the doorway as he entered.

Inside, it was warmer than he had expected, and it smelled of tea. He felt his muscles instantly relax. The shop had been painted recently, and boasted a gas log fireplace, tables, upholstered chairs. Display cabinets ringed the central open space. To his right was a door, ajar, to reveal stairs leading up. Up to her home, he knew. Another door led to the workroom in the back. He had done his research.

A plain, brown-headed woman looked up from the center chair and set aside some needlework. Standing, she said, "I'm Jacey. Welcome to Thorn's

Gems." Though far smaller than he, she was too tall to be a mage, and he remembered that Thorn had partners, a human male and a human female. "What can I do for you?"

"I'm Audric Cooper, deadminer. I hope we can do business. I've got gold, some good quality faceted stones, and . . ."

A man stepped through the door in the back, his laughter filling the room as he turned and stopped. And Audric forgot what he was saying. The human was tall, some six feet, with long, jet black hair that caught the light and curled around his ears and collar. His eyes were black—or a blue so dark they looked black—and he wore an apron, heavy leather scored with burns and stained with chemicals that Audric could smell from where he stood, open-mouthed and mute. He was the most beautiful human Audric had ever seen.

The woman spoke, her voice laced with amusement. "Meet my business partners, Rupert Stanhope and Thorn St. Croix."

Rupert. Ahhhh. Their eyes met and held as Audric's world tumbled and shook and rearranged itself in an extended/instantaneous moment. When Rupert extended his hand, oddly shaped with a long index finger, Audric took it almost reverently. The flesh was unexpectedly hard, callused, as Audric held both it and Rupert's eyes.

And Lolo's plans fell away. He could feel his life shifting and resettling, remaking itself into something new and unknown. And frightening. Audric was aware of the little mage behind the man, and he thought he lifted a hand in greeting, but he wasn't sure. His eyes never left Rupert's.

"There's a Chinese place down the street," Rupert said, as uncertain as he. "You want to get lunch?"

"Yes," Audric said, knowing the single word agreed to much more than simply lunch.

"You boys go play," the human female said, "but unless you want to be gutted like rabbits, I'd wipe the sexual tension off your faces and pretend the lunch is business. At least until you see whether or not the town fathers will accept your—um," she faltered, clearly at a loss for words.

"Proclivities?" Rupert offered, his tone droll. "You have a point. One lone gay man is acceptable. Two could be, Realms forbid, an epidemic."

Audric blushed, the sensation shocking. He hadn't blushed since he was a child. Jacey laughed but he didn't care. Couldn't care for anything but the human man holding his hand.

"Put your horse in the barn," the mage in hiding said, "and you boys be sure to talk some trade over lunch while you flirt. The kirk is powerful here in Mineral City." She swatted Rupert across the butt in a familiar gesture, finally drawing his attention. "Be careful."

Audric tore his eyes from Rupert's and looked at the mage. She was everything and nothing like Lolo's description. Small, laughing, her mage attributes damped to human dull like his, her scarlet hair piled atop her head, a hunk of rough stone in one dirty hand. She thought he was human. The mage couldn't see past his glamour.

He wouldn't be sharing her bed. He'd be sharing another's. But at least he had found a stable for his horse. Unplanned laughter burst from him.

When they looked at him curiously, he shook his head and dropped Rupert's hand. "Lunch. Yes. That is, indeed, a good place to start."

Rogue Mage Anthology Vol. II
TRIBULATIONS

Introductions for TRIBULATIONS

From Spike:

When I was first asked by roleplaying game writer Christina Stiles to work with her on the *Rogue Mage RPG* back in 2007, I'd never heard of New York Times bestselling author Faith Hunter or her *Rogue Mage* trilogy of novels. In fact, nobody had gotten around to coining the "*Rogue Mage* trilogy" term to describe the books at that point, as the third novel hadn't even been released yet. But Christina and I had worked together on a number of projects, and I trusted her judgement and signed on to the project.

After some years of hard work, the roleplaying game was released—as the ROGUE MAGE RPG PLAYER'S HANDBOOK and GAME MASTER'S GUIDE, available in print from Bella Rosa Books and downloadable from Misfit Studios.

Then Faith asked me about the next *Rogue Mage* project. Faith had written a number of short stories and short-short vignettes for the game books, and she thought that they could be combined with an equal amount of new material to make an anthology set in the *Rogue Mage* universe, bringing those stories to readers who might not have seen them in the games, while providing new stories to please fans who wanted more. And she wanted me to edit the new material.

One thing led to another, and Rogue Mage: TRIBULATIONS (and the companion volume, Rogue Mage: TRIALS, that preceded it) are now double the size of that original conception. Along with the RPG fiction and a new Faith Hunter short story, Faith, her agent Lucienne Diver, and I assembled a group of other writers who we felt would enjoy writing in "the Faithiverse." Heck, even I got a chance to contribute, writing a handful of pieces scattered over the two volumes.

There are two things I've really enjoyed about working on these anthologies.

The first are the stories.

Rogue Mage: TRIBULATIONS isn't just about the adventures of Thorn St. Croix, "the rogue mage." It's about the entire *Rogue Mage* universe. The majority of the stories here, of course, feature Thorn and the supporting cast of the novels, but there are also stories set parallel to Thorn's adventures. In fact, all the stories of TRIBULATIONS take place in 2117, the same event-filled year as Faith Hunter's *Rogue Mage* trilogy—the novels BLOODRING, SERAPHS, and HOST. (TRIALS features stories that run from Biblical prehistory to just before the start of BLOODRING.)

The stories are set in other parts of the USA, in other countries, on different continents. They feature neomages, of course, but also kylen, humans, and others. There's humor, adventure, tragedy, romance, and some windows opened into what the reaction in the rest of the world is to Thorn St. Croix's activities in the USA. It was a challenge to make these diverse stories come together into a cohesive volume, and a puzzle sometimes figuring out exactly where each piece fit, but I think we managed to make it work.

And the second thing I've enjoyed are the authors.

I didn't know the majority of the writers of these anthologies before we got started, and there were some . . . disagreements between some of us. But in the end I've learned a few things, I think we've forged some relationships that will last, and, most importantly, I hope my editorial efforts have managed to take an assortment of stories that were already good in draft to excellent in print.

In the ROGUE MAGE RPG PLAYER'S HANDBOOK I couldn't imagine what the next project was going to be after that major undertaking. Well, now I'm here on the other side of the next project, and I wonder what we're going to do to top this.

—*Spike Y Jones*

From Faith:

For years I have been asked, "When's the next *Rogue Mage* book coming out?" and, "Is the series really over? It feels unfinished!"

And now I can say: The series isn't dead. Now you have TRIALS (you *have* read it, right?) and TRIBULATIONS, millennia of stories gathered in eBook format, fiction by some fantastic authors—including me.

The series is in your hands, *Rogue Mage* fans. Buy, read, review, and enjoy. And if enough of you still love the series and Thorn St. Croix, then there might yet be that long-awaited final novel, in serialized novella form. Fingers crossed!

—*Faith Hunter*

Unbidden Bonds
Late Winter 105 PA / 2117 AD

Faith Hunter

Kicking the snow from his boots, Zadok took a calming breath and faced the small house, trying to project the confidence of a seasoned healer, rather than the fear of an acolyte on his first solo cure. His smile was stiff on his frozen face, the air so cold and still that his flesh felt brittle, as if it would crack and fall from his bones should he move wrong.

The short trip had been brutal, his contingent of six guides and fighters more accustomed to the vicious cold and hard pace than a mage who had lived his entire life in the comfort and ease of the Seattle Enclave. He'd gained an appreciation for the humans who lived in the frozen wastes, losing his snide sense of superiority, which had been based solely on his mage abilities. He never would have survived the short trip without the assistance of the others.

He glanced at the human woman, Sarai. She'd saved his life when he'd stepped off the track and crashed through the snow into the creek beneath. The driving snow had already drained Zadok's mage energies dangerously low, forcing him to draw constantly on his prime amulet to protect himself, and he'd lost precious body heat to the icy water. Not even *his* amulets could fight off hypothermia. While Howard, a mule, started a fire, Sarai had activated all of his *Healing* amulets, stripping him down and crawling into a sleeping bag with him . . . naked . . . sharing her body warmth with him . . . offering her life energies.

He'd accepted the gift of her life, stealing the energies of a human in ways no Earth mage was permitted. Now she smiled at him, encouragement in her glance, seemingly hinting that some bond still lingered between them. Zadok nodded once at her and opened the door of the fortified building.

Stepping inside the thick stone walls, he took in the dwelling with a sweeping glance. Perhaps twenty humans were gathered around a huge fireplace in the large room. Except for a table before the fire, the furniture had been shoved against the plastered walls. On the table was a blanket-covered form, a body racked by shivers. The gathered humans looked up, fear and stress grooving their faces. Zadok took a second calming breath and the stench of rotting flesh, old urine, and feces met him. Fear threaded through him, knotting his muscles, causing him to pant. *Am I too late?*

He gulped, frozen on the threshold. Gently, Sarai pushed him into the room and closed the door behind them, leaving the others to set up peri-

meters. As if she were his servant, she took the satchel from his numb
fingers and whispered, "You can do this. I have faith in you." Louder, she
said, "The healer Zadok has arrived from Seattle Enclave to work an incantation of healing on your kirk elder, Judith. He requires a surface for his
implements, a cup of warming chai, and space to work." Within moments,
the humans had helped him from his winter gear, brought him hot chai
laced with brandy, placed a table before him for his mage amulets, and
eased the body from the tabletop to the floor, creating a space wide enough
for him to work a healing circle.

Fortified, Zadok thanked them, his hand resting on Sarai's shoulder a
moment, for a thanks more personal and heartfelt. With her help, he folded
back the mounds of blankets and inspected his patient. The stench of death
was caught in the blankets, and Zadok tossed them aside. "Burn them," he
said, curtly, "They contain the taint of Darkness." Beneath the blankets,
Judith's skin was feverish and tight, stretched like the desiccated tissues of a
mummy. Spawn bites were ragged holes in her flesh, covered by bandages.
The bites had become infected, the pustules suppurating.

Infection had been wiped out in the plagues. Humans no longer suffered
from bacterial infection except as a result of spawn attack, and few spawn
victims survived the immediate shock and blood loss long enough to suffer
the infection of the Dark. Zadok had studied medicine from Pre-Ap
medical books, and had seen photographs of similar diseases. His obscure
course of study, and his creation of a new series of amulets, was the main
reason he'd been chosen for this mission.

Steeling himself, he placed one of his diagnostic amulets on Judith's
stomach. In moments, he had an answer. She had a medical condition
called septicemia, caused by a bacteria once known as *Staphylococcus aureus*—
but a more virulent, Dark-mutated version of the germ. It had resulted first
in kidney failure, and the amulet indicated she now had pneumonia, liver
failure, and an infection of the lining of her heart. Organ by organ Judith
was dying. There was nothing that could be done for her. Nothing. It was
too late. He backed away from her sickbed.

Sarai knelt beside him and took his wrist, her fingernails digging into the
tender skin above his thumb. "You may draw on the energies of the
forest," she whispered. "You may draw on the energies of the mules who
escorted you here. You may draw on the life force of the earth itself." He
knew this. He knew it all, but his mage gifts seemed frozen inside, petrified
by fear. What if he failed?

Her fingers dug in harder. "These are legal uses of your gift. I *know* you
know how." She held his gaze with her fierce one, reminding him that he'd
stolen her own essence in extremis. "Try."

Zadok nodded and she eased away, turning to the low table set with the
implements. "Salt for the healing ring?" she asked. When he nodded again,
she placed the bag of salt in his hands. Five pounds of pure earth salt, dug
from deep underground, enough for a very heavy salt ring. He stood and
paced around the patient, evaluating her and the situation. The forest had

the best chance of surviving the removal of life energies, the bleeding of power necessary for a healing of this magnitude.

He walked a slow circle, a circle large enough to accommodate Judith's pallet, his implements, and himself. As he walked, Sarai followed, sweeping with a broom to clean the surface of the floor. She had clearly worked with mages in the past, or perhaps she studied the Internet sites dedicated to his species and knew what was needed. She was still acting as his servant, which made Zadok uncomfortable. But her presence and her actions were calming to him, so he let her continue. When the circle had been walked once and swept clean, he walked it again, Sarai on the outside now, the bag of salt upended, pouring a thick ring. When it was finished except for a narrow opening, he brought in his implements.

"I need a living bough from the forest," he said, "a cup of water drawn from a deep well, a cup from a running stream, a cup of snow, and a cup of dirt from near her home. And I need something from the fight when she was injured: the claw of a spawn, a weapon still bloodied with their blood—anything will do, but it must come from the actual battle."

Zadok turned to the oldest of the humans. "These are the words the townspeople must chant from the moment the blood of sacrifice is drawn: *Thus saith the Lord, the god of David thy father, "I have heard thy prayer, I have seen thy tears. Behold, I will heal thee."*

The old man nodded, tears in his eyes. "We will not fail Judith. It shall all be as you command."

The Earth mage looked at Sarai as the townspeople scurried into the storm to bring him what he required. Zadok placed a small silver chalice in her hand. "I need a cup of mingled blood from the townspeople, a gift of their love, gathered by self-inflicted wounds in her honor. Hold the cup thusly." He encircled the cup with her fingers so her body would keep the blood warm. "Nothing must be spilled. Every drop that falls must fall into the cup, nothing lost. Understand?"

She nodded. "I am honored to bear the cup of sacrifice."

Zadok opened a vial and poured a clear liquid into the cup. It was an anticoagulant that would keep the blood a liquid, not allowing it to clot. "You must swirl the cup as it is filled to keep it well-mixed. Hurry," he said. "Judith will not live through the night."

When all the items he'd requested were gathered in the salt circle, Zadok opened a vial of holy oil and poured it into a silver bowl. He nodded at Sarai. "Begin."

Sarai stepped to the first three townspeople. They each washed their hands, dried them on clean cloths, and drew their long belt-knives. Without demur, each pressed his or her blade to the clean flesh of a finger and held the digit over the bowl. Soft plinks sounded, mixed with the uneven breathing of the patient, and the murmured chanting of the townsfolk.

As the gifts of blood were collected, Zadok sat, crossed his legs into a comfortable position, placed the carved amulet that allowed him to access the power of the Seattle Enclave on the floor between his legs, and began his calming chant, one adapted to the use of Earth mages from the oldest of times. "Fir and fire, water and blood, life and kin prevail. Wings and shield, dagger and sword, life and kin prevail." His heart rate slowed, his breathing steadied. Calm descended on him and his chi strengthened.

He opened his mage sight, seeing the power in each of the cups of water, in the fir, and in the energies of the people in the room. Gently, he reached into the fir branch and, through it, into the forest, drawing on its creation energy. Holding the living power steady, he drew from the cup of well water, pulling the energies of the deeps of the earth into him, and into the cup of running water, harnessing nature to his need. Instead of extracting great gulps of energy the way other mages did, Zadok pulled in small sips of the power each offered, shallow tastes, slowly growing in strength. To take too much was to risk becoming a death mage.

When he was ready, he opened his eyes and looked directly into the calm gaze of Sarai. She was kneeling at the opening to the salt ring. He held out his hand and she carefully placed the silver cup in it. He set the cup of sacrifice beside the holy oil, the water, snow, and soil, and with a last handful of salt closed the circle. Power from the forest crawled up his legs through the floor like vines. Power from the earth misted from the snow on the ground outside and joined the air he breathed, becoming one with the water of life in his body.

"Fir and fire, water and blood, life and kin prevail. Wings and shield, dagger and sword, life and kin prevail." Chanting, he dipped his fingers into the well water and splashed it over Judith. With each splash, he drew on the forest, the earth, the water of his own life, and poured energy into her, first supporting and stabilizing her heart, encircling the beating muscle and searching out the bacteria that infected it, hitting each with a little jolt of electricity, killing it, and adding the life energies to his own.

When Judith's heart was stable, Zadok poured the cup of earth onto her belly and went to work on her lungs. Here he used the knife crusted with spawn blood. It was a powerful sacrifice.

Hours later, Zadok was exhausted, sweat soaking his clothes, his brow dripping with it. His fingers vibrated with fatigue, and he was so near to collapse he'd feared he wouldn't make it to the end. But at last Judith was stabilized.

Certain that she would live through the night, Zadok eased his mind away from her. He placed the amulet that offered the energies of the Enclave on her abdomen along with three of his own *Healing* amulets: a piece of petrified redwood carved in the shape of a lily, a sliver of thorn from an acanthus bush that crawled over the roof of his house, and a vertebra said to be from a dinosaur. Gently he aligned the energies of all four and withdrew.

Too tired to move, he fell across the salt—breaking the power of the healing circle—right into the arms of Sarai.

Bones
Late Winter 105 PA / 2117 AD

Faith Hunter

David lifted the large crystal. On first glance, it appeared to be a huge chunk of amethyst, gem quality, smooth to the touch, but it contained a luminescence that looked biological rather than mineral when he placed it under a microscope. It looked like *things* were swarming inside, creating purple light. He had no idea where the rock had been found—or even if it was true rock.

Though he had done it a thousand times already, he rubbed a thumb across the stone and inspected the pad of skin. Nothing rubbed off.

With a chisel, he scraped along one smooth facet of the natural crystal, collecting the rock dust onto a glass slide. He lowered the 100X microscope lens. The dust sprang at him through the oculars, glowing. Then the luminescence dimmed, the motion that he could almost—almost—see slowed. And the faint light went out. Just like always.

David removed the slide from the scope and carried it to the workbench. With tweezers, he eased off the cover glass and scraped half of the rock dust onto a petri dish. The other half, he carried back to the crystal. He pressed the start button on a stopwatch as he shook the dust back onto the rock. He watched as it was reabsorbed. Clicked the stopwatch. 8.4 seconds. The first time he had done the test, the dust had taken over twenty-four hours to reabsorb. It was as if the rock had learned a new task, and now excelled at it.

David closed the crystal up in its metal box and entered his notations into the computer file. An Earth Invasion Heretic and a self-taught scientist, David was also a blasphemer. Not an atheist—not exactly. He believed that the being the seraphs referred to as the Most High did in fact exist. He just didn't like him very much. He didn't like what the seraphs and the MH (a glib abbreviation he was careful never to voice among his kirk-employed co-workers) had done to the Earth or to its people, so he had joined the EIH to prove that the Most High (whatever it was) could be defeated. And now the EIH had joined with the orthodoxy to study artifacts and find a way to defeat the Dark. It was an uneasy alliance, and David imagined that when the Dark was conquered the coalition would fall apart—messily.

His curiosity unsatisfied, David locked the lab and walked down the hallway to check on his most recent experiment. The seraph. Well, the watcher—a fallen seraph. This one had allied with the Light in the Last

War, and was wounded in the battle over Mexico City nearly a hundred years ago: burned to a crisp, sixth-degree burns over his entire body, leaving only bones. But he hadn't died. Not exactly.

The bones and associated connective tissue and five charred feathers—along with a blackened seraph sword, a warped shield, and some jewelry—had been gathered up, shipped north, and stored in a box in the EIH storage locker. The bones and traces of tissue had been tested several times over the intervening century and had shown no evidence of either deterioration or regeneration. Until last month.

Two days after the weird purple rock had come in the mail, a technician had noticed a strange light in the cubicle that held the box of seraph bones. When she opened the box, she discovered that the bones were covered with pale scarlet fuzz, like mold.

David had taken over. He had looked at a scraping under a scope and saw what appeared to be blood cells. Remarkably like young, active, dividing blood cells, like human bone marrow. Since then he had put the cells through a series of tests. All were still viable—sitting in a test tube, without a preservative, *still viable.* And growing. And so were the bones. He had laid them out on a table in the morgue, more or less in the proper position, with a camera monitor on them 24/7. He had changed out the camera three times before he realized they weren't defective cameras; the film was being damaged by the bones and the weird radiation they were emanating.

There weren't enough trusted techs to keep watch over the bones, and without a camera's monitoring eye, there had been no way to keep track of the bones' alteration. When no human was present to see, the bones had re-attached to one another. The seraph was healing. Not like a spiritual being would heal, not magic or miracle, but like a biological organism. Which said to David that seraphs weren't angels—not spirits of light. They were a race of beings. Biological. Like the damn crystal.

Checking the radiation monitor beside the door, he unlocked the morgue. The radiation was unusual. It measured on the particle emission testing gear, but not on a Geiger counter. They needed military equipment to do more testing, but the military would simply confiscate the rock and the watcher. Not going to happen on David's watch. For one thing, the radiation had another effect besides fogging film.

Humans didn't get cancer anymore—not since the plagues. But David was an exception to that rule. He had developed what the medics called melanoma. It was killing him, slowly and painfully. Until the purple glowing rock and the seraph bones. His cancer had vanished over a two-week period, and there hadn't been a sign of the disease since. It was a mystery how it had happened. Almost as big a mystery as why he was the only person on Earth to get cancer in decades.

He turned on the lights. The bones had now formed a body, the flesh on them beginning to fill out. The left wing was nearly whole, covered with a bright green down. Unable to help himself, David stroked the down and inhaled the incense of the watcher's scent. He hated seraphs, but like any human, he was susceptible to their pheromones and their allure. He stroked the newest fleshy parts of the being, pressed and prodded. Tested for blood pressure and pulse—nonexistent. Checked the eyes under the thin lids. No more than gelatinous orbs yesterday, there was now a pupil and a hint of iris. He thought it might be green, the shade of the feathers. He extended a wing. The joints of the wing bones moved smoothly now, and the wing opened to its full length: over twelve feet.

Settling the wing back against the seraph, David gathered up the strange seraph jewelry. So far, he had found uses for three of the four pieces.

One was a curative instrument that, when activated, sped up the healing of the burned seraph. He had used it twice and found measurable improvement in the being.

One was an energy device that could attach to a third apparatus—an energy sink; most likely a weapon. His captive mage had told him that just before she went into a mating frenzy and attacked him. They had not found a way to make the weapon work.

One tool could be a communication device. If he held it just right, he could hear bells in it. Seraph bells. The bells were a form of speech.

The pieces of jewelry were devices, and devices spoke of technology, not miracles, making the seraphs high-tech invaders, not messengers of God. When the burned seraph was healed, David was going to interrogate it. Most thoroughly.

The visiting superior kirk elder disagreed with his plan. He still thought the seraphs were holy, but simply had a physical form as well as the pure energy that fulfilled the concept of a spiritual being. The kirk thought the devices were created things used by the Almighty. David believed the human race had been duped, invaded, and conquered. Only the living rock gave him pause. If the rock was alive, were the amulets alive as well?

Even after all these years spent studying the seraphs, he still didn't know quite what they were. But soon he would have a seraph to test and experiment on, and then—then he would know.

Carefully, wearing padded gloves, he lifted out the demon iron shackles and fitted them above the watcher's fully-formed ankles.

River Bones
Late Summer (Southern Hemisphere) 105 PA / 2117 AD

Jean Rabe

The trees along the river had been as big around as grain silos—a long time ago. Agata D'Cruz had seen pictures of the rainforest in books in the convent's library. The Amazon basin was still thick with green as far as she could see, but the decades since the Apocalypse had slain the giants with their foliage so dense it had blotted out the sun.

Z would be easier to find without them in the way.

Much had been harvested for building materials and medicine, cut down and burned for farmland, before the Apocalypse and since. Good that a drug cartel controlled the land now, Agata thought, so the forest could return to its ancient majesty—just not before she'd finished her business here. Armed with expensive Chinese weapons and trained to fight, the cartel soldiers kept the harvesters at bay while traveling between transient forest camps and the cities and villages, pedaling their murky wares and instilling fear.

But the cartel hadn't managed to keep her out.

She'd deftly avoided them so far, though there had been a couple of too-close-for-comfort episodes, and one that sent her braving the caimans by hiding in the root-tangled river shallows. Just enough to get her heart hammering wildly; not enough to prevent her from coming back. The prize was too great to give up on.

The maps of the basin she'd razored out of the convent's books had proven valuable. They'd led her to the old places where people lived before the divine conflagration and to where they'd left behind curios and ornaments—not terribly far beneath the surface—in demand in the coastal cities. She'd amassed enough wealth that she no longer needed to risk the cartel's patrols to scavenge, but she came back to the river anyway. Agata liked to dig in the dirt and reveled in the surprises she unearthed. More than that, she dreamed of the singular find that would make her famous and take her anywhere in the world she wanted.

Z.

She'd been searching for it for the past three years. Today she would find it. All the clues had fallen into the right places.

Today.

There was a beautiful sameness to the rainforest—all the shades of green run together like watercolors in one big smear, reaching up to touch a sky that today was ash-gray and domed the world with a bleak and unforgiving pall. A storm was coming, and soon; the air had that wonderful teasing scent to it.

Rock formations were scattered along her course, stones brought to the surface a century or so ago when the forces of Darkness fought the seraphs even here. Harsh winds and pounding rains helped sculpt the formations, and man-made explosives had contributed, creating twisting spires that looked like the upraised limbs of giant corpses.

River bones, Agata called them.

"*Earth rais'd up her head*," Agata quoted from a poem she'd committed to memory as a child. William Blake had been one of her favorite studies. She stared at a tall, artistic-looking rock that pressed against the trunk of a possumwood. "*From the darkness dread and drear. Her light fled. Stony dread!*"

Agata adjusted the large pack on her back, froze, and listened. The birds had stopped singing, so she crouched behind a big fern growing bush-like on tree bark. Maybe a predator was around, a large cat looking to eat monkeys. Maybe a cartel band. Her legs cramped, but she didn't move. Sweat ran down her brow and into her mud-brown eyes. It was a hotter than usual August.

After a handful of heartbeats she saw it, some type of animal-meld creature, looking mostly like a tiger, although there were no such cats in the basin. Twice the size of a jaguar, with an orange and black overlarge head and tall pointed ears that swivelled as it prowled. Its tail was serpentine, twitching slowly, and along its back and on its back legs were dark greenish scales. It looked dangerous.

She breathed shallowly, her hand in her pocket, where she kept a switchblade. The cat-thing crept out of view, and she relaxed. Minutes later the birds resumed their songs. Agata caught sight of a scarlet macaw pair flying lazily overhead. Whatever threat the hybrid posed had passed.

"*How sweet I roam'd from field to field*," Agata mused as she stood and worked the cramps out of her legs. "*And tasted all the summer's pride.*" She tipped her face up, the sweat running away from her eyes. There was no breeze to cool her. Maybe the coming rain would help.

Agata paced out fifty steps from the twisting rock. She couldn't see the river from here, but she was parallel to the bank and could hear it—comforting. Kneeling, she fumbled in the large pack, retrieving a top-of-the-line pre-Ap handheld metal detector and one of her prized map pages. She'd studied this particular map so often in the past several weeks that it was practically engraved on her brain. Still, she scanned it one more time, double-checking her notations along the borders.

"Should be right about here. Everything points here." All her research, her time searching. "It is here." But the metal detector picked up nothing. Maybe it *was* here—the lost city—and all of its gold had been discovered and removed centuries ago. But she would have read about that, right? "No. It's here. Here here here."

Agata turned south, paced off another fifty steps, and tried again. "Suck toads." Nothing. Five paces west, around a thin palm, more pacing—a grid search pattern. A little black-and-white monkey followed overhead. She retraced her steps and paced out seventy-five, parallel to the bank. The metal detector finally clicked. The screen showed a weak reading of precious metal down ten meters, and a stronger one at the fourteen-meter mark—a lot stronger. "Suck toads and back again!" she hooted. The monkey chittered and hopped as if sharing her happiness.

Most of her previous finds she'd been able to hand dig with just a shovel, a meter or two at most. Admittedly those expeditions had been just to fill time and her pockets while she researched and pursued her true goal: finding more wealth than she could spend in a thousand lifetimes.

Agata pulled a two-stage directional charge out of her pack, attached the detonator, and pressed the charge into the loam, spinning her shovel around to use the handle to shove it deeper. She skittered back several feet, taking cover behind a shagbark, and pressed the remote activator. The forest floor shuddered and the double-explosion spooked parrots, which shot out of the branches, screeching. Her monkey shadow screamed and fled, and after a few moments everything went eerily quiet.

But she could still hear the river.

The hole created was roughly three meters deep and a meter and a half across. The mud and detritus spat up was plastered against tree trunks and scattered in the undergrowth. She withdrew a long, thin rope from her pack. Tying it around the base of the shagbark, she clipped it to a belt hook, tested it. Then she pulled out another charge, slipped down the hole, and placed the charge. Even with the rope, exiting the hole was difficult, making hand- and footholds in the soggy earth, slipping, grabbing onto roots, and finally pulling herself over the edge. She took cover behind the shagbark. Another double-thump, this one softer.

Another three meters down and a bit wider.

It was risky, making noise like this, especially repeatedly. But the adrenaline was pumping and she couldn't bear to put this off. She only prayed the cat creature wouldn't return to investigate.

Her breath came faster and the air smelled sweeter, though she might have just imagined the latter. Agata waited, the silence prolonged. She listened carefully, and when the birds started to converse, she set one more directional charge. Not wanting to be too weighted down, she'd only brought four of them, plus a few sticks of TNT. The TNT was too nonspecific for delicate jobs like this, but could pull double duty against cartel soldiers.

Safe on the surface again, she set off the third explosion. Then back to the bottom of the hole. Agata pulled out her metal detector. The reading of precious metals persisted—a meter to go—as did the much greater reading nearly four below that. Maybe there was a cavern between the readings; her detector hinted at that. Too risky to expend her last shaped charge for only a meter of dirt. She'd already made too much noise, and she didn't want to risk damaging any treasure.

The ground trembled, and for a heartbeat Agata thought someone near-by was using explosives, too. But then rain started to fall. Thunder. She'd been looking for the lost city too long to let a summer storm delay her.

A manuscript Agata glimpsed a handful of years before during a visit to the national library in Rio de Janeiro claimed a Portuguese explorer had found a lost city in the rainforest in 1753, but he gave no precise directions and no notes other than that there was more wealth than he could remove. Intrigued, she researched further in the years after that. She found other reports from centuries past, some in the convent's archives, others in city libraries or on the Internet when it worked. One of the most detailed accounts was that of a British surveyor named Percy Fawcett, who called it the Lost City of Z, and searched extensively but futilely for it in the early 1900s. Agata spent many hours after abandoning the sisterhood piecing together these and other legends and plying archaeologists with ancient pottery in exchange for information.

All of those efforts and more had brought her here.

Agata hung her night-vision goggles and infrared illuminator around her neck. She put a flashlight in a pocket and climbed to the gloomy bottom of the hole. She lost scent of the river here; it was all musty dirt mingled with rotting wood. She started digging, the rain pattering against her head.

"*Does the Eagle know what is in the pit? Or wilt thou go ask the Mole?*" Again, she quoted Blake. She fanned the air in front of her face, a futile endeavor to keep the earthy odor from settling at the bottom of her lungs. "*Can Wisdom be put in a silver rod? Or Love in a golden bowl?* And can I find me the lost city and more golden bowls than I can carry?"

She dug until her shovel clanged against shale.

Agata was sodden from the rain. She couldn't hear the birds anymore, but she could hear her heart beating in anticipation. She chiseled at the shale with the tip of the shovel for quite some time, until her arms were so tired they felt like lead weights she could barely lift.

But then the shale cracked through, a piece falling away into darkness. She shone her flashlight through the hole, revealing a cavern below.

All shiny.

She blinked her eyes and stared.

The floor where the circle of light hit it was littered with gold.

She sucked in a breath and rubbed furiously at her eyes, smearing mud all over her cheeks. Closed her eyes and counted to ten. Opened them and the gold was still there. A little more than four meters below her. It was a veritable carpet of gold coins, jewelry, figurines. She had to get a close look at it. Now.

She broke away more of the shale, opening a hole wide enough for her to squeeze through. Agata nearly jumped down, but a part of her brain held her back. The underground was ruled by Darkness. She stuck her head into the hole and breathed deep. Stale air. Her heart leaped at that—stale, not the putrid odor of carrion that would signal that spawn or other Dark creatures had been this way. The cavern below would be safe.

Agata climbed up and retrieved some folded canvas bags from her pack—for her first trip. It would take dozens of trips to remove everything, and most likely she wouldn't be able to claim it all. Maybe she should be selective and only take the choicest pieces. Agata couldn't leave and bring back a car or truck; probably couldn't navigate through the weave of trees. She could bring a boat down the river, tie it up, and come inland. The river was so close. That thought stuck; a nice flat-bottomed boat. She couldn't look to others for help—there was the issue of sharing and the probability of being backstabbed. So she'd take the dozens of trips, cover the hole in between, sell the gold in different markets to avoid drawing too much attention.

Agata's mind danced with all the possibilities.

She lowered herself down the rope to the floor of the cavern. The walls of the great room were painted with faded images of fantastic beasts. The ceiling was plated with gold, explaining her detector's initial reading. The floor—that was the heart stopper, and she sat amid the wealth and ran her fingers over the treasure. The light from her flashlight set everything a-glitter.

"Is this real? Am I dreaming?" She squeezed her arm and felt the pressure. Agata sobbed with happiness. "Saints be praised, I've truly found it."

When she swung her light the beam reflected from a smooth sheet of metal, pitted in a few places, attached to something larger that was embedded in the wall.

Agata crept toward it. Her light struck the mirror-smooth metal and she blinked. It was a throne.

She cocked her head, hearing something. Thunder, muted so it sounded like the ground whispered. Something else, too. She returned to the rope. Music? Voices? Would have to be loud up top for her to hear it this far down. Maybe it was nothing—her imagination. Best to check, though.

Agata clipped the line to her belt and pulled herself up. Near the top, she slowed. As stealthily as she could, she raised her head until her eyes were just above the lip of the hole—and saw them.

"*Mira! Una sorpresa!*" A short, broad-shouldered man in fatigues shouted from a couple meters away. He waved a rifle in her direction. Harsh, dissonant music flowed from a player attached to his belt. He thumbed it off.

"You were right, *amigo*. Someone was down that hole. A dirty little woman! And one with explosives to do her digging. I wonder what the dirty little woman was looking for." It was an ugly voice attached to an ugly person. Agata assumed he was in charge.

She could see six of them, all soaked by the rain. Definitely a cartel band. They wore camouflage fatigues and each carried a rifle and had a second slung over a shoulder.

"C'mon. Out of there! Out of the hole!" the ugly one snapped, free hand on his hip, scarred chin thrust out, sleeves rolled up showing tats of serpents. There was anger and hunger in his eyes. He sneered, "She's a scavenger. Soon to be a dead one."

"Maybe we should have some fun with her first," another suggested.

"In this rain?" Ugly spat a gob of something he'd had stuffed in his cheek.

Agata climbed out to stand in front of him, her thoughts swirling. She had a gun, but it was in the pack. Idiot! She'd never been stopped by a cartel patrol before. She'd seen them, always avoided them. They'd heard her explosives and come to investigate, and now they were going to kill her and claim Z.

Maybe she could find her way out of this and still net at least some of the treasure. Or come back with friends and lots of weapons.

"You're gonna need me," she said. Buy some time, work things through.

Why hadn't she waited until night to plant the charges? In the darkness, they wouldn't have found her. Her impending demise was her own fault, but she could fix this. She could— "Yeah, maybe need you for some fun," the leader said to his fellows. To Agata: "Whadya find there, dirty little woman? Something valuable in that hole? Something from before the Apocalypse? There's ruins in the trees. We know."

Agata needed to give him some answer, but—

"Won't talk?" he persisted, taking a swaggering step forward. "I can make you talk."

"She won't talk, huh?" One of the six was a woman. She'd been hanging back until this moment. The woman soldier had dark hair, unnatural—it was an intense, shiny purple that looked like plastic. "*Mujo poco sucia*. She's a digger, Karlo, a thief or archeologist. Same difference, eh? Didn't think we'd be out in this weather. I think she won't talk 'cause she doesn't want to tell us what's in her hidey hole."

"*No importa.* Doesn't matter what she is," Karlo returned. "We'll find out ourselves what's down there. *Tesoro cártel.* That's what's down there, Maria. From some Mayan ruins."

"It's not the cartel's treasure," Agata growled. It's older than Mayan. "It's—"

"Ah, *sucia*, you answer after all," Maria said. She tilted her head, the purple hair twisting unnaturally against her shoulders.

"Something good is down there," Karlo said. The others nodded when he looked over his shoulder at them. "Maybe drugs. Maybe she's planting drugs she stole from us. Would explain what's gone missing. Maybe Mayan trinkets. Trinkets, dirty woman?"

"Trinkets?" Maria said. "Something better than trinkets. Too many holes dug along this river. She's been looking for something. I think you guessed right, Karlo. Something from before the seraphs."

"No trinkets," Agata admitted. "It's Z."

"And what is that?" Maria shook her head and aimed her rifle at Agata, making the pretend motion of firing.

"Nothing you would understand . . . or deserve," Agata returned.

"Urlo!" Karlo barked.

One of them stepped forward. He was tall, thin. His faded green pants hung low on his hips, the pant legs too short, striking about mid-calf and contrasting with his parchment-white skin.

"Urlo, go find out what the dirty little woman is hiding from us."

The lanky man stepped toward the hole. He stopped and looked at Agata. She saw his face, all planes and angles, and when he grinned, his eye teeth extended in vampiric fangs. A daywalker—apparently they weren't just rumors.

His gaze turned into a stare, as if his glowing violet eyes were trying to peer into her brain. Agata shivered.

"Maria, you look in the pack. Maybe there are more explosives. Maybe we will blow up the dirty little woman." Maria obliged, although the look on her face suggested that she didn't like being ordered around.

"You've no right." The words hissed out between Agata's clenched teeth. "The pack is mine. Be careful with it! You don't understand what you're doing. You'll need my help to—"

"Oh, we understand, all right," Karlo said. "We're dealing with a trespasser."

"You don't own the forest." But Agata knew that in the way that counted the cartel did.

"Urlo! See what's down there, I said!" Karlo snapped. "I will not tell you again."

Looking at the size of the hole, the daywalker stripped off his bulky pack and rifle, and leaned them against a tree. Then he unhooked the clip from Agata's belt and fastened it to his own. A heartbeat later he disappeared into the hole; Agata didn't see a light turn on below, but after a few minutes Urlo hooted up that he'd found gold.

"Let me go," Agata said. Z lost to her, at least for the moment, she needed to get away to think, to come up with a plan. "You've got the gold. You don't need me. Leave me—"

"You're mad as a rat if you think I'll let you go."

"I won't tell. I—"

"Karlo," Maria cut in. "Maybe others already know about it. Other diggers. Maybe more are down in that hole. We saw signs along the river of digging. Maybe—"

"No. She is alone." Urlo was sitting on the shale roof of the golden chamber, his legs dangling in the hole. "I smelled only her. It is a ruins down there. Ancient. Well before the Apocalypse."

"Ancient?" Karlo raised his chin and let the rain splash against his face. He laughed loud and long, the sound odd and grating in this place. "Gold for the cartel!"

"She's got a gun in the pack," Maria said. "And a bunch of maps." She stuffed the machine pistol in the band of her pants, pulled out the maps and dropped them, the rain smearing Agata's notes. Next, she removed a stick of TNT, waved it in the air, dropped it on the ground, too, and then pulled a grenade from her own pocket. "I say we blow her up real good."

Karlo drifted so close to Agata that she was forced to share his foul breath. She coughed, and he grinned as if pleased he'd offended her. "Digger, tell me *all* about the treasure hole. How did you find it? Who else knows?"

"No." There was no force behind Agata's voice. "I'm not going to tell you anything. You'll need my help, to tell what's valuable, what's—"

"I need nothing from you, *perra*."

Agata jerked the switchblade from her pocket, flicked open its four-inch blade, jammed it into Karlo's gut. If they were going to kill her, she'd take this one's soul to a dark place with her.

The daywalker's unattended rifle was an arm's length away, and she used the moment of surprise to snatch it up, swing it around, and fire at Karlo, who was grabbing at the knife in his belly, a spreading blossom of blood around it. "*Perra*! Shoot—" A second shot from Agatha finished him.

Maria howled, dropped Agata's pack and raised her gun one-handed, grenade still held in the other. Agata was still firing, and a bullet tore into Maria's leg.

Maria screamed, parrots exploded from the trees, and something large snarled.

Everything else happened at once. One of the thugs swept his rifle around and fired, Maria, the farthest away, fell to her knees and dropped her gun so that she could pull the pin from the grenade. As she raised it to throw, the cat creature sprang through the foliage. The grenade tumbled from Maria's fingers as the cat slammed into her.

Another soldier fired. Agata's arm felt like it'd been speared by lightning.

A strangled "Help!" came from Maria.

The grenade rolled on the ground.

An arm reached up from the hole, a hand grabbed Agata's ankle and yanked her downward . . . just as an explosion tore through the forest above.

It was a painful tumble, bouncing from side to side down the vertical shaft, dead roots tearing at Agata's clothes and hair, mud filling her mouth. A weight landed on top of her. She spat out the mud and struggled to get up. There was another explosion up top, and another. Then the stone beneath her, the ceiling of the chamber below, collapsed. She hit the floor hard on her back.

Then everything was black.

The weight—the daywalker was no longer on her, and she heard him nearby. She could see the glow of his eyes moving around her in the darkness, appearing and disappearing. Agata couldn't move, couldn't feel her fingers, couldn't hear anything through the ringing in her ears. The explosion—the fall—did she break her neck? Was she going to die down here, her corpse eating itself and her skeleton becoming river bones?

The great river wasn't far away; the familiar smell of it came faintly to her. Or was that her imagination?

Agata felt the strap of the night-vision goggles around her neck and wished she had them on, desperately needing to see *something*.

It hurt to breathe.

Another scent intruded: the stink of dirty clothes. The daywalker was nearby. She could hear him say something, but she couldn't make it out.

So tired. So hard to breathe.

Just die, she thought. Let's see what waits on the other side of life.

Instead, she saw a beam of light—her flashlight thrust in her hand, her fingers forced to wrap around it.

"Urlo," he said, the word sounding rich like a musical note. "My name is Urlo."

"What—"

"Your back was broken. A bullet went through your arm. I have cured your maladies. You are welcome."

"I didn't say thank you." Agata tightened her grip on the flashlight and pain flickered down her arm. She cautiously pointed the flashlight toward the voice. The beam caught the striking face of the daywalker.

"Then you have poor manners."

"I wouldn't have needed—" she stopped herself, didn't finish the sentence: *I wouldn't have needed healing if your band of thugs hadn't come along.* He'd knit her bones together, healed her wounds. The daywalker—Urlo—could have easily let her die, but he'd saved her.

"Agata," she said after a moment. She still smelled his sweat and the stink that clung to his clothes. She also smelled the old fustiness of this chamber, and still, faintly, her beloved river. That hadn't been her imagination. Deep below ground, she still smelled the Amazon. It was a deep river with so many tributaries, some part of it was close. She tried to focus on that favorable scent. "My name is Agata D'Cruz."

She expected him to quiz her: what she was doing in the rainforest, where she'd come from. Instead, he looked away, worried at a thread on his shirt. She thought of questions for him: how a daywalker came to be with a cartel band, why he'd spared her, what other magic he possessed. She tamped her curiosity down; the less she knew of him, the better.

"How long?" Agata held out her free hand and he pulled her to her feet. She ached all over. "How long was I out?"

Urlo angled his face away from her light and shrugged. "A while. One hour, perhaps." He brushed at the caked dirt on his pants. His head was in constant motion, and then he glanced up too. "That is no longer a way out."

Agata shone the flashlight beam up. Broken tree limbs, dirt, stone, and other debris had fallen through the hole in the ceiling, sealing it. The multiple explosions she'd heard. And it didn't sound like anyone was trying to dig them out.

Playing the light around the chamber, she saw a dazzling assortment of gold objects. They didn't seem quite so shiny given her predicament.

Agata set the flashlight down.

"My companions are most likely dead," he said.

"They were cartel thugs." She didn't add that he also was a cartel thug. Did his face, in the dim light, take on the slightest hint of color? Ire?

"We are not thugs. We are survivors," he returned. "We do what we have to. We . . . they—"

"Are most likely dead, as you said, and so no longer of any consequence. To the explosives, to the bullets, to that . . . that . . . cat creature. Dead."

"Animal-spawn crossbreed," he corrected. "It appeared to be a mix of tiger and caiman."

"No tigers in the basin."

"It looked like—"

"Yeah, well, whatever it was, Urlo, I'd call it mean and hungry." She closed her eyes and recited her favorite Blake poem, an exercise to center herself. "*Tiger! Tiger! burning bright, In the forests of the night. What immortal hand or eye, Could frame thy fearful symmetry?*"

"*Did he who made the Lamb make thee?*"

Her eyes opened in surprise at the daywalker quoting a line from the poem. Scholars of ancient English literature referenced it, but a hellhole-raised Dark half-breed?

"Quoting a centuries-dead poet will not get us out of here," Urlo said. "This will be our coffin if we cannot get closer to the surface where the few conjures I know might help." He dug the ball of his foot against the floor, displacing some of the gold. "The cartel may find the fallen above—"

"But they might not think to come digging," Agata finished. She didn't want them to come digging.

"What is this place, Agata D'Cruz?"

"Z. Like I told your buddies up top. It's called Z." She gave him a brief account of her years of work to find it. "And I'm taking some of it with me." One of her sacks was still tucked under her belt. She pulled it out and began grabbing up gold figurines, pieces of jewelry, things that looked exceedingly valuable and small, things with inscriptions she didn't have the time to decipher, stuffing them roughly into the bag.

"We need—"

"Yeah, to find a way out. We'll do that. This won't be our coffin. But we're not leaving 'til this bag is heavy." As she made a circuit of the room, she studied the walls, noting the painted figures, not Aztec or Incan or any of the other Meso-American cultures she'd studied. She stopped cold in front of one. It was an image of a winged warrior—a seraph. Farther along was a second one, darkly colored, in battle with the first. Behind the second seraph was a third figure, a man with snakes writhing from his hands to threaten the dark seraph—a neomage casting a conjure? Under the bright seraph's feet was a defeated figure: an animal-man with prominent fangs—a nightwalker?

"Not possible," she whispered. She knew the Light and the Dark came to Earth before in Biblical times, but this was more recent; the Amazon basin had no such civilization in 3000 B.C.

Had there been another Apocalypse, completely forgotten? And because mankind had forgotten, had it brought about another wave of divine retribution centuries later? She tentatively touched the wall, her fingers tracing a design, registering the smooth gold, coarse ceramic, and the fish-scale feel of ancient paint.

Some of the faded images looked tortured: buildings in ruins, a sun blazing, the moon cracking, trees burning, people running. A sprawling scene on one wall clearly illustrated an epic disaster.

Had Z been buried in an earlier Apocalypse? If Z was destroyed in the Apocalypse, was this mural painted afterward? Agata knew she'd be pondering this for a very long while.

She needed a camera and more time. But right now, she needed to get out of here with what she had.

Agata looked for Urlo. He sat on the throne against the opposite wall, studying her.

"Over here," she said, approaching him. There was a gap between the throne's back and the wall. "I smell the river strongest behind the throne. Help me move this," she said, gripping one of the armrests, but Urlo casually shoved the heavy chair aside. There was a slash in the wall behind it. "It's a passage. A tight fit." She'd barely be able to drag her overstuffed bag through it. Maybe it led to another chamber, a gate, a way out. The Lost City of Z must have had many buildings, and the Light Father had been so gracious as to let her find one filled with treasure. If she could find her way out, she'd come back and back and back, exploring, pillaging. Agata felt drunk on what the future could hold.

If she could get out.

The beam from her flashlight failing, she put on her night-vision goggles and slipped into the crevice. "I'm leaving," she told Urlo.

"And I will make sure no one disturbs this place again." She spotted him against the wall with the images of the warring angels. "Your lost city should stay forever lost."

We'll just see about that, she thought to herself.

The crevice opened to a twisting natural tunnel. From the smoothness of the wall, it appeared to have been carved from the rock a long time ago by running water—a tributary of a prehistoric Amazon. There were spider web-fine veins of silver threaded through it. Another poem sprang to Agata's mind: *"And by came an Angel who had a bright key, And he opened the coffins and set them all free; Then down a green plain leaping, laughing, they run, And wash in a river, and shine in the Sun. Then naked and white, all their bags left behind, They rise upon clouds and sport in the wind; And the Angel told Tom, if he'd be a good boy, He'd have God for his father, and never want joy."* More Blake.

Agata prayed this passage would lead away from the treasure-filled coffin. Lead away so she could come back.

Urlo followed, scraping his shoulders at first and then somehow making himself smaller. The sharp angles of his face smoothed. He'd adopted a human guise. The fatigues fit that form near-perfectly.

He prodded her shoulder with a finger. "My spell is finished," he said. "You had best pick up speed."

"Spell?"

"Some such castings have names. This is called *Seismic Shock*. I put everything into it, Agata D'Cruz. It would be advisable to move faster."

Agata heard a jarring, crashing sound far behind them. A gust of dust-laden wind from the same direction banged her into a wall.

"What did you do?" she hollered.

"Keeping your lost city lost, I say again."

The rumbling behind her continued, so Agata took off along the passage. The tunnel twisted and turned, rose and fell. Side passages too narrow to navigate branched off from it, but they continued along the main tunnel. At one point it opened into a small natural chamber, and she paused to catch her breath. "You had no right," she panted. "Damn you to—" she stopped herself. Curses carried real meaning, and Urlo was a creature of Darkness.

"No one needs to know if there was an earlier reckoning. They are paintings that do not matter now."

She was too tired to argue. She felt like she'd been moving for hours. She was exhausted, wanted to rest, just a brief sleep. But the daywalker kept moving, and if he got far enough ahead of her, he might collapse the tunnel behind him, trapping her. She pushed on.

Some time later, after another complicated downward twist in their path, Agata's hopes flagged as low as her energy. "The tunnel . . . it could go on for miles."

"It does. But it will come to an end."

If Urlo had meant to encourage Agata, he hadn't succeeded. But the scent of the river was stronger. And that gave her the strength to continue.

They struggled forward, the cleft in the rock angling steeply up now and narrowing. Agata struggled to squeeze both herself and the gold through it. She looked over her shoulder, seeing Urlo press his hands against the rock, words she couldn't understand tumbling over each other out of his mouth. The tunnel behind them collapsed. Tremors persisted for a few moments, the ground groaned, and then there was silence.

"You . . . are . . . a . . . fool," Agata hissed.

"Blake does not have a poem about fools," he said.

"Odd that you know his work so well." She edged forward.

"Ancient poetry is my friend," he confessed. "In an . . . earlier time, I found comfort in Blake. Shelley, Keats, Tennyson. I have a very old book among my belongings, *The Norton Anthology of English Literature*. The pages are as thin as fog, and there is not much left of the binding. It is worth more than all the gold in your sack."

"Wait. I feel a breeze."

"Yes. The rock breaches the surface ahead. I have opened the way."

"Opened . . . you mean you could've made a tunnel to the surface for us any time you wanted to? But you—"

"My magic can only affect stone . . . and a few other things. I was unable to help us until there was no dirt overhead to bury us. I didn't seal the way back down until we were assured of a way out."

They returned to their climb, Agata mentally calculating what equipment she would need to reopen the site in a month or two when the cartel had given up on the area.

Minutes later, the passage widened, jagged, newly shattered rock littering the tunnel floor, fresh air swirling around them; they'd reached the surface. Agata collapsed, thoroughly spent. She'd been underground for hours. It was night, and the moon and stars shone down on the river. The pale light grazed stones that had been blasted up at odd angles to jut between the larger trunks—river bones.

Urlo's face was pointed up at the stars. It was parchment white again, angles and planes, his daywalker form regained. When he glanced down at her, his eyes took on a distant, almost sad, cast.

"I should kill you," she said, "for what you did to that chamber."

"This is Blake's forest of the night," he returned. "But you are not a tiger, and I am not a lamb. Be content that the cartel will not gain the gold. Be content that you have enough of it." She noticed that the pockets of his trousers bulged. He'd taken some of the treasure, too.

"Agata D'Cruz." When she looked up at his face, his violet eyes caught hers, held hers. *"Past the new meadows, over the still stream. Up the hill side; and now 'tis buried deep, In the next valley-glades: Was it a vision, or a waking dream? Fled is that music—Do I wake or sleep?"*

"That's not Blake," she said, fighting sleep, "that's Keats . . ."

Agata closed her eyes and unwillingly drifted off to sleep.

She awoke some time after dawn, someplace that wasn't where she'd fallen asleep. There was no sign of the daywalker, no sign of the tunnel. The sack was there, and still full. But when she inspected the treasures, there were new pieces she didn't remembering taking. As for the rest, everything was golden, bejewelled, and obviously valuable, but there was nothing spectacular, nothing that would take the art world by surprise. Nothing with an identifying inscription or an incised Apocalyptic scene.

Her pack was somehow on the ground next to her too, despite the distance they'd traveled from the dig. It was spattered with mud and other stains, ripped by shrapnel, but a few things survived intact: food, flashlight batteries, even some of the detonators and one of her explosive charges. Not her maps and notes.

"That's a setback," she said to the birds, "but not a major one. I can just go back to . . . back to . . ."

She couldn't remember. She recalled the blasting, the digging, the encounter with the cartel soldiers. She could vividly visualize the chamber, the murals, the tunnel, and Urlo. But when she tried to picture landmarks on the way to her find, picture her annotated maps, picture the landscape near the river where their tunnel had reached the surface, everything went hazy. The more she concentrated on them, the more indistinct they became.

"Was it a vision, or a waking dream? Fled is that music—Do I wake or sleep?"

Urlo had left her gold, but had taken her treasure, her dream from her. But she'd found it once; she would find it again. Somewhere within scent of the river.

A Wing and A Prayer
Early Spring 105 PA / 2117 AD

Faith Hunter

Evan looked at the mage in disbelief. "You want us to go in a hellhole? With no recon? No intel? Are you out of your mind?"

"Yes, yes, yes. And no. I'm quite sane," Marc said, answering each question in order, fingering his gaudy amulet necklace. It was made of blackened steel links and dangling steel and copper leaves so finely made they whispered and tinkled at the slightest movement or breeze. And probably held the destructive power of an armored battalion. Enough to destroy a dragon, if he could get close enough. For which he needed the Army.

The steel and copper leaves meant Marc was a Metal mage of some kind. And mages made the back of his neck itch. His dad used to claim mages were responsible for all the plagues. For all Evan knew, the old bastard was right.

"I'm not leading my men underground—*underground!*—without intel, I don't care what you think is down there. You get me some intel and we'll talk." Evan hooked his thumbs into his belt and waited, knowing it wasn't over.

"If I get you the data," Marc said, raising his head, his hair falling forward in a slow wave, "then what? Then you'll tell me if you have a nuke? Then you'll give me men and weapons and go with me to take the cavern?"

"Then we'll talk about it."

"And meanwhile the seraph and the mages that the dragon captured will suffer and bleed and die. My *wife* is down there!"

"Not my problem." Mage women—whores, every one of them. And seraphs could burn to ash for all he cared.

"Even if I can bring a kylen to work with us? A kylen who can control his sexual urges in battle?"

Evan raised his eyebrows, watching Marc's face clenched in hope and fear. Evan should have been irritated with the offer, but, instead, he considered. He'd fought beside a kylen once, when he was kid. Next to seraphs themselves, kylen were the best warriors on Earth, and having one on your side meant a better chance of victory, without the risk of humans dying by the hundreds afterward from the effect of the sword of judgment a seraph carried. Some kylen could draw on the same energy sources that the seraphs could. "You bring me the kylen and a map of the maze down there, and you got a deal."

From his cloak, Marc pulled out a wad of papers and handed them over, a grin on his face. Realizing he'd been outmaneuvered, Evan sighed and looked at his adjutant. The man drew to attention, his face going white. He'd searched the mage and still let the papers through? Evan fingered the papers. They had to be glamoured.

Evan sighed. Having stars on your lapels meant you had weapons, ordnance, and soldiers at your beck and call. It meant that you could kill Darkness better than most. But it didn't stop you from being conned by the damn mages.

The rising sun hidden by falling snow, Evan and Marc stood before a hellhole, inhaling the stink of sulfur and rot. The entrance to the dragon's lair was right where the mage had claimed, which made Evan a bit happier about the entire event. And the screams of the tortured could be heard all the way up in the surface, which made the intel the mage had provided look credible.

Evan looked back, checking the armor on his men. It was the latest stuff out of DuPont R&D. They called it Diamondtuff. Harder than diamonds, actually. Evan had been itching to try it out, though he'd never tell the mage. And the new fléchette rounds—Diamonite—that the men had been issued should make the darkuns' body count rise. His men, dressed for battle, looked like something out of an old Pre-Ap movie. *Star Wars*, maybe. He snorted at the thought.

Now, if the kylen showed, and if the feathered wonder and the mage didn't fall on each other and screw each other's brains out before the battle got started, it would be a pretty good start to the day, Murphy's Law notwithstanding.

Suddenly Marc shot up his head and sniffed. In a motion so fast Evan didn't see it, the mage pulled his swords. Then he began to dance around in martial art forms, as if warming up. Marc locked eyes with him over the swinging swords and said, "He's here, just like he promised."

Out of the low-lying fog walked a winged warrior—a kylen. Evan's men began to whisper, and Evan shot them a glance. Instantly they settled, but every eye was on the newcomer. Like the mage, he carried two swords, with small throwing blades belted around his thighs, a spear in a sling on his back, and a shield that Evan knew was magical. Kylen were damned hard to kill. Unless a Darkness was mighty lucky, most kylen could heal back from almost any wound, though it might take a while.

But they had weaknesses. Overconfidence. Inability to sitrep—read a situation and change a plan accordingly. They were unable to adapt to changes in situation too. And then there was the likelihood that they would be called back without notice to whatever Realm of Light had let them loose. They were virtual slaves, had to obey the seraphs, and had no personal freedom; it had to suck.

But living like they did had compensations. Human women found them irresistibly attractive. And if they happened on a mage without one of the new seraph stones that stopped mage heat, the resultant rut was said to be a freaking amazing bang—with love-'em-and-leave-'em benefits.

"I am Nireonel," the kylen said.

Evan sipped from his coffee cup, considering the kylen.

"I am here at the promise of Achaiah the seraph, the discoverer of the secrets of nature. He sends me to bring back Avena, the mate of Marcus Walker." Marc lowered his head in a kind of formal acceptance.

Evan studied the two and shook his head. It was all a bunch of mage crap. The kylen looked like a pretty-boy—too . . . delicate . . . to fight, too fragile to be a soldier. But the scars across his shoulders and the leathery patches on his wings where plumage had burned away suggested he was no neophyte, but a battle-hardened warrior.

Nireonel spread his wings and snapped them down tight. The mage closed his eyes and breathed deeply of the agitated air. He looked drunk. And horny. Crap. Time to get this show on the road.

Evan spoke into his throat microphone and the soldiers under his command moved forward, checking weapons, adjusting radios. There was a spike of adrenaline in the air that even Evan could smell before he pulled the gas mask over his head, adjusted his night-vision goggles and his automatic weapons. He nodded to the mage. The man lowered his head and called up his magic—his creation energy—whatever the hell they called it. The kylen lifted his head to the cloud-shrouded sky and prayed aloud. Evan ignored the kylen's words. He didn't hold with EIH, but he wasn't a religious man. His men were, however, and he heard them murmuring "Amen" to the kylen's words.

Instead, Evan considered the battle. By nightfall, the walls of the quonsets would be decorated with spawn and dragon parts. And, if Marc was to be believed, they might have saved a mage princess and earned kudos from the Most High for saving one of his winged warriors. There was gold and a place in the history books for that alone. Blood, guts, and glory, huzzah!

Together the mage and the kylen turned as if it was a dance, clanged swords together in a ringing salute, and shot forward toward the hellhole. They moved faster than Evan's eyes could follow. Behind him, Evan's men screamed their individual battle cries, Scripture each had chosen as his or her own personal mantra. And they gave chase.

Evan was human, which meant he didn't get lost in bloodlust like mages, but the adrenaline rush and endorphins were nearly as good. He shouted "Victory of A'albiel!" and slung his weapon from rest to ready, flipping the safety to "off" at the first hint of the stench of brimstone and the reek of old blood.

It wasn't full dark yet, but he heard the skittering of spawn close by. Spawn were fully nocturnal unless a major Darkness inhabited the hellhole with them. Then spawn could wake at any time, though they were still bound to the deeps as long as the sun shone. Their chittering rose to a roar; a fact that meant their master was a BBU—a big bad ugly. Ahead, the kylen and mage had stopped, standing battle-ready, weapons out to their sides, as they shouted Scripture and challenged the Darkness.

The spawn came into view—a huge swarm of red-bodied, clawed beasts, visible beyond the mage and the kylen, whose wings were fully extended, partially blocking the tunnel. At the last second, they leaped, landing on the small armored car behind the first row of troops. The second rank soldiers opened fire. Automatic combat shotguns blasted. The pellets ripped into the beasts, quickly eliminating the first spawn wave.

The first rank didn't break discipline to witness the carnage occurring behind them, so they were braced when the next wave appeared at the tunnel mouth. The stench of Dark blood and burned gunpowder filled the air as spawn fell by the tens. The hundreds. Maybe thousands.

Evan waited until the first rank soldiers were each down to a single spare ammo magazine and then ordered the second line of troops forward. They took up positions behind the front line, then each tapped his front-rank partner on the shoulder and slipped forward into the line. Once the new trooper had started firing, the relieved soldier lowered weapons and stepped back. Now to the rear, first-line warriors checked for heat-related weapon failure and stocked up on fresh magazines, prepared to move forward again when he gave the word.

The spawn were dying so fast they didn't have time to eat their own wounded, leaving twitching heaps in front of the soldiers. There wouldn't be time for the darkuns to heal and return to the fight before the mission ended, and he had a holy-oil-fire exit planned that would burn the bodies to ash. And maybe the carnage would encourage the torturers to leave off their fun and games and come to defend their territory. It wasn't much of a plan, but Evan had gone into battle with less.

After an endless ten minutes more of firing and trading places and firing again, Evan saw the flow of spawn into his killing field slow to a trickle. He barked into his mike. "Hold fire. Phase two."

The two lines moved back, parting into equal-sized groups on either side of the entrance. The shooters would hold the hellhole open for the party that would descend into the hellhole, stopping any egress of the Dark to lay a trap, covering their retreat, and keeping open essential communications.

The armored car ground gears and inched down the incline, into the maw of the hellhole. Perched on and behind the armored car came the shock troops, four mules and six humans, an assortment of ethnicities, male and female and questionable.

Evan grimaced. He didn't like working with the mules, especially the jenny mules. Women should be women. Not . . . whatever the mules were. But he had to admit they were damned fine fighters.

Evan, the kylen, and the mage followed the special forces soldiers. The screams of human pain had died away, and now there was only an eerie silence marked by echoing *plinks* of water or perhaps blood.

From a side corridor, a blurred form raced at them, a dragonet, two, three, wings making the *zzz* of buzz saws. Evan got only a glimpse but he catalogued the traits. One was scaled, one was covered in knotted and snarled hair, and the last one looked as if human DNA had gone into the bizarre mix, putting human skin on a snake-like body, and human hands instead of pincers near its insectoid mouth.

All three landed between the shock troops and the trio of Evan, Marc, and the kylen, who all crouched instinctively. Unable to use firearms without hitting the troops in front, Marc shouted "Orbs!" and tossed a half dozen metal balls at the monsters. He and all his men hit the cave floor.

Muted explosions concussed the air, detonating at exactly three feet off the ground. He rolled and came up fast, his weapons ready, but the dragonets were obliterated. Dark blood burned on his uncovered skin. Around him, his men were shaking dragonet splatter off themselves and a couple saluted, a casual half-wave that meant, "Good job, boss. Got them without getting any of us."

Marc looked up to him, his skin doing that weird thing mage skin did, glowing like pearls. "My wife is near. According to the map, to the right is a branching corridor with a small series of rooms. Cells?" The armored car would have to be left behind in the larger tunnel.

"You," he called to the kylen, "Winged wonder, you go first." It was a sound move. A kylen would have a good idea where any mage was. The mating instinct would be better than bloodhounds.

The kylen nodded and positioned his shield, sword at the ready, held low across his body. Marc moved to his left. The small cadre of special forces followed.

With a screech, a creature burst from the cave shadows, taking down half the shock troops with one slash of demon iron, some missing limbs, two bisected.

The dragonet—greater dragonet—was now in the clear, however, and Evan threw a CC24. His men hit the deck again at the familiar whistling sound. With a *whump* that he felt in his chest, the device went off. The dragon exploded.

Evan called the surface on the com unit. The unit was starting to have static, the result of being around mage energies. He just hoped the coms lasted long enough to get through this. Moments later medics swarmed in, patching up the ones who could be saved and loading them on the armored car to return to the surface. The kylen tossed amulets at them and a weird energy pattern opened over them. It was pink. Nireonel smiled at him. "A gift from the High Council of the Seraphim. Healing domes."

"And the captives?" Evan ground out.

"I sense three. They are close."

Marc raced from the dark. "Third cell on the left," he gasped. "My wife."

Evan followed, hearing the crackle of disconnect in his com unit. Damn mage energies. Between the demon iron bars of the cell, he threw an illumination sphere, a human device powered by human batteries running on energy gathered by a Sun mage. In the sudden burst of light, he saw a woman, a female mage, chained naked to a wall with demon iron manacles. Blood pooled beneath her; long gouges were ripped into her flesh. In the cell with her was some sort of human-dragon crossbreed, its scales the patterns of a diamondback rattler, if rattlers were red and orange. It hissed at them and spread its wings.

Marc shouted to his wife, "Avena!" The woman looked up, seeing through strands of oily hair. "Your belt!" With an underhand toss, he threw a mage-spelled silver chain through the bars. It tore through the thin dragon skin of a wing and landed at Avena's feet, touching her toes.

She bared her teeth and, Evan would swear later, growled at the dragon-man. Power flared up from the silver links into her body, and she glowed so bright Evan had to squint against the glare. "Frozen iron demolish," she said. Ice rippled over the manacles and they shattered, freeing her. At the cell mouth, Marc hit the bars. They too shattered into brittle shards.

Avena bent and took hold of the silver belt and held it toward the dragon-man. "You wanted children from me? For that, 'Blades and shock and blood there be, burned near death 'til eternity,'" she spat. A burst of light came from the belt and seemed to meld with the mage. Purple energies whipped around her, offered by Marc. And the crossbreed went up in flames, his death screams tearing at them.

"Son of a goat," Evan swore.

The kylen turned to him. "Yes, it was. And the seraph is next door." He raised his head and wings. "Jehovah! To war!" he shouted.

The Magnificent Seven
Spring 105 PA / 2117 AD

Faith Hunter

Ramah and the other five second unforeseen stood in a clearing surrounded by stunted trees. Each of them was a battle mule, the best of the best—heavily armed and ready to fight. Each was sworn to her, well-trained and prepared for war, groomed to be bonded to a seraph. Eliab, Abinadab, and Shammah were jacks. Simone, Kaylie, and Ramah were jennys. Together with a seraph, they would make a troop of seven, an auspicious number for defeating Darkness. For four months since Ramah had been bonded to the seraph Yarashiel they had trained together, working day and night to become the perfect fighting unit, to purify themselves, and to prove themselves acceptable to the seraph.

Now, a cold wind blew off the ocean and whistled through the twisted myrtles. They waited with Ramah for her liege seraph to appear. Together they chanted the Scripture they had chosen as their battle mantra. It was longer than most, but they'd agreed that it was perfect for their cadre. "Thou comest to me with a sword, and with a spear, and with a shield. But I come to thee in the name of the Lord of Hosts, the God of the armies of Israel, whom thou hast defied."

Yet Yarashiel still did not appear. The tide came in and began to recede. The moon rose to brighten the darkest part of night. Still they chanted. And still they were alone. Ramah knew he would come. Her dream had been too intense, too sharp, and too foreign to be just her own imaginings, yet she was beginning to worry—to wonder. *Had* she imagined it all? Had it all be her own longings, and not a true call to battle? Was that possible?

The dream had been one of gore and the stink of spawn blood, rank with death and the stench rotting meat. Swords had flashed. The boom of weapons had been deafening. And Yarashiel had stood beside her, his wing behind her, flight feathers touching her back, fighting shoulder to shoulder.

A light brightened the sky and Simone pointed. Excitement filled the small group, swirling around them like mist. "Yarashiel comes," Kaylie said, a thrill in her voice. She drew her two-handed longsword, huge and well-balanced, perfectly suited to her bulk. "He comes." The rest pulled their weapons free, battle-ready the instant the seraph appeared, yet all still chanting their mantra.

The light grew in the sky, brighter than the moon, and Yarashiel swept over them, his wings the bright yellow of a bunting but far more fierce, the tips of the flight feathers edged in black, with wide scarlet triangles at the nervure. Down covered the underside of his wings, his chest, stomach, and along his arms and legs. His fighting armor was translucent, revealing his black and yellow vestments and downy flesh.

The cadre had, many times, viewed the ancient video of the seraph fighting, and the magnificence of Yarashiel rivaled even Michael, the Archseraph. Now he dropped into the midst of them, touching down lightly, bare feet visible through clear boots, his wings folding with a soft snap. His eyes sought out Ramah and he smiled. Simone sighed, holding her weapons across her body; almost a protection. Abinadab, who was known to prefer the touch of male flesh to that of female, fell to his knees, staring with near rapture. Kaylie fell back, staring. Their chant fell into silence; the hiss of surf and the whistle of wind were the only sound.

With eyes only for Ramah, Yarashiel cupped her chin. "You are well and strong," he whispered. The seraph's scent filled the clearing, dancing on the breeze, the top note of yellow roses, buttercups, and rich cream, the almost-bitter base note of lemon mint.

Ramah pulled in the fragrance, remembered from her healing. "Yes. Thanks to you."

"I am pleased. And you bring warriors to fight with us?" Ramah kissed his palm. Yarashiel dropped her face, walking in a small circle, studying each of them—a long, probing evaluation. When he reached Shammah, the seraph frowned and cocked his head to the side. "You are not well. You have torn shoulder muscles and scaring beneath your shoulder blade. Do you desire healing?"

Shammah's eyes went wide. "I have had pain here." He lifted his left arm over his right shoulder and patted his back. "I thought it only a pulled muscle. Yes, heal me, Holy One."

"I am not holy," the seraph said, "but I give what I have." Shammah dropped to his knees beside Abinadab, and when the seraph touched his shoulder he quivered as if from an electric shock and fell to the ground, twitching.

Yarashiel looked at Abinadab. "You will be his wing mate, fighting at his side." To Simone he said, "You will fight near Eliab. Kaylie will fight to my left. And my chosen one, Ramah, will fight at my right side. We battle in the name of the Most High. We have been charged to find a seraph taken captive by a Darkness whose name shall not be spoken. And the Most High has gifted us with transportation. He has provided *ophanim*."

Overhead there was a clap of sound and light like lightning and thunder in a terrible storm. The concussion threw them to the ground. When they raised up, above them, sitting serenely in the sky was an ophanim—a wheels, the fabled ship of the cherubim. A lion's head bent over the gunwale, perilously close to the spinning rotors that circled the ship like the rings on a gyroscope. The ship was the yellow of citrine, flashing with light and holiness.

"She will take us to the hellhole," Yarashiel said. "There now fight a contingent of the second unforeseen and mages, part of the human army. And they have discovered a seraph, chained to the wall on the sixth level and shorn of his wings. The Most High tells me that they are soon to call mage in dire. We will assist with the battle and rescue Schachlil, an angel of the sun's rays. Gather your gear." Looking up, Yarashiel shouted, "We mount up with the wings of angels!"

In an instant the cadre of mules was aboard the ship, dumped onto the deck like so much cargo. And with g-forces dragging their skin back, forcing them to the floor of the wheels, they were in flight.

A Start
Spring 105 PA / 2117 AD

Spike Y Jones

Step.
Step.
Pause.
Step.

Every step he took was deliberate, his feet placed precisely on the ground so that he didn't make excess noise, didn't leave an easy-to-follow trail, didn't leave his scent on bushes and bracken or in the scattered snow along the way.

The trap lines had been a mixed bag. Hardly anything caught in any of his snares, but no blood stains on the ground to show that he'd caught something that had then been eaten. There should be more game at this time of year. He'd seen it before: Devil-spawn had eaten the area clean. But he'd caught *some* game, which meant that the spawn weren't here *now*. He hoped.

But two rabbits weren't going to feed the family. So John had dressed and packed his kills, pulled up the snares, and gone looking for bigger prey.

Step.
Pause.
Check the wind direction.
Step.
Scan the ground.

His movement wasn't slow. It was *natural*. Animals didn't race through the woods unless they were trying to get away from something. But they also didn't dawdle; if they moved slowly, it was because there was something nearby that made them *want* to move slowly, like food to graze. John moved at the pace of an animal that was neither afraid nor distracted, an animal that was looking for something but hadn't found it yet.

He'd heard someone say that a hunter had to become his prey, had to become the deer or the rabbit. He told his grandfather that one day. "Crap! Whoever told you that buys his game off the back of a pickup truck. Does the wolf become the deer? Of course not. He becomes a wolf. I don't know why you listen to those friends of yours."

Sometimes John's grandfather had been wrong. John wasn't a deer, but he wasn't a wolf either. What made man a great hunter? Knowing *when* to think like a deer, *when* to think like a wolf. And when to think like neither of them.

Step.

If a hunter didn't have the senses of a wolf, he found deer by thinking like a deer. If there were deer in these woods, where would they want to be?

A deer could roam anywhere looking for food—too much ground to cover. But eventually it would need water. Not just water, but also a safe place to drink. John continued until he came to a melt-creek. The stream was small, but the banks were too steep to tempt a deer, so he started upstream, paralleling the bank from far enough away that the gurgle of the creek wouldn't prevent him hearing the noises of the woods around him.

Step.

It wasn't long before he found what a deer would consider an ideal watering hole. The creek curved outward, leaving a sandy slope in the lee. There were clear sight lines in all directions, so animals would feel safe drinking there.

In the sand, John saw numerous prints: porcupine, fox, some birds, an old print that could be a wild pig. And a single deer hoofprint. The edges were sharp. The indentations not yet filled with seeping water. Less than an hour old. With nothing to scare it away, it wouldn't have wandered far in its foraging in an hour.

It hadn't left any other hoofprints in the sand, but there were only a couple routes it would have used to approach the watering spot, and it would have left along those same routes. Picking the likelier one, John began walking back into the woods.

Step.

Scan the ground. Always scan the ground.

Step.

A bit of fur on a branch beside the path. Whitetail. He'd picked the right route.

Nock an arrow to the bowstring.

It was a good Pre-Ap bow. Not a modern bow with complicated pulleys that could freeze up in the winter, but a strong traditional bow passed down for generations. Although its origins were certainly in a sporting goods store maybe a century ago, not somewhere in the mists of tribal prehistory or any of that hokum.

Of course, he had a rifle strapped on his back. He wasn't an Old Ways idiot. But with a rifle, you got one shot, and if you missed your target, the noise would scare all the nearby prey away for a good long while. And right now, just the sound of chambering a round would ring out in the quiet of the forest. Sometimes, in some situations, the old ways made sense.

Step.

Ahead of him. A flash of ivory through the branches. Angular. Antlers.

Too far away to get a clean shot. He continued moving forward, careful to stay downwind, to keep a clutter of trees between him and the buck, keeping his movements *natural.* John Sawatis *belonged* there in the same woods as the buck.

His grandfather had claimed to remember places called Canada and New York. He said that when the glaciers had forced them off their northern reservation land, the family had chosen to live free in the woods, instead of going southwest to beg for space on another tribe's reservation or south to take over the homes of dead people in the cities. Grandfather Joe remembered some of this uncles and aunts struggling and failing in the forest—they may have been living on a reservation in upstate New York, but they'd been city folk for all that. His grandfather had grown up practicing survival skills with *his* father and grandfather, so they'd made the transition better than most.

John Sawatis had lived in the Tennessee woods his entire life. He was *a part* of the forest, *a part* of nature. Just like the buck.

Step.

Closer.

The buck was walking slowly through the brush, browsing on the fresh greenery poking through the melting snow. Then it paused, alerted to something. John paused. Made a low grunting noise. Started moving forward again. Nobody here but us wild pigs. Satisfied, the buck returned to its grazing.

Closer.

It was odd that the buck still sported antlers this late in the year. They usually dropped off before spring—sometimes in the middle of the winter. A rare doe or an underage buck might keep them late, but the depth of the hoofprint said this was a heavy deer—a mature male. But the winter had been *different* and spring had come early this year; maybe that confused the animal's internal clock.

Closer.

Close enough. John drew back on the string, sighted along the arrow at the deer. The brush screened it, but the low foliage was thin enough that it wouldn't turn the arrow. He released it. The arrow streaked across the clearing.

Crash! The deer was off.

Run!

John angled his sprint to pass through the spot where the deer had been standing. No arrow sticking out of the ground or a tree; he'd hit it.

Now it was time for him to think like a wolf. The buck could run faster than a man or a wolf, but not forever. He had to have patience, keep on its tail, keep the pressure on it to make it exhaust itself, keep an arrow ready in case he got a chance to hit it again. He didn't have to keep the deer in sight; so long as it could still sense him somewhere behind it, it would keep moving.

Run!

He wasn't stalking anymore; time to make noise. John yelled as he ran. Not words; barking noises that would evoke images of wolves in the deer's instinctive brain.

Run!

John saw it ahead of him, its path curving to follow the lay of the land, the path of least resistance and maximum speed. A longer shot, but still doable. He loosed another arrow at the buck, hit it again.

Run!

He wasn't aware how long he chased the deer. Time was meaningless. There was only the buck and running.

The buck was slowing down. Another arrow. A miss, but he kept the pressure on the injured beast.

Run!

Finally the deer couldn't run anymore. It collapsed to the ground. John came in cautiously, long knife drawn for the kill, but careful to ensure that the buck couldn't gore him with the last of its strength.

His arrows had caught the buck in a haunch and in—John hissed through his teeth—in the pink, hairless flesh below one of its arms—one of its human arms on its human torso. The "deer's" antlered head and neck blended seamlessly with the pink torso. So did its furred legs.

Another monster from the headwaters of the Mississippi, up where St. Louis used to be. Either John had strayed further north than he'd thought, maybe to Kentucky—although lines on the maps didn't matter much on the frontier—or maybe the ice was still advancing, forcing . . . things like this further south. Or maybe the monster population was growing, like it did in his grandfather's day, expanding in all directions.

It didn't matter. He'd have to burn it. Didn't want the local predators to get a taste for human flesh.

Holding the thing's head down with a foot on one antler, John slit its throat. He hung the body over a stream to bleed out. The blood would dilute in the running water, and the body would burn more quickly; he wouldn't have to gather as much wood for the pyre.

As he searched for tinder and fallen branches dry enough to burn, John's thoughts drifted to discussions around the campfire with his father and his grandfather. Damn them all. Let the seraphs kill the dragons or the spawn kill the seraphs. Let the mules die fighting the kylen or the mages die screwing them. Let the orthodoxy wipe out the EIH. Let the cities burn. Let the ice take them all. He didn't care. When they were all gone, the land would be given back to The People.

It was almost sunset with he finally got the pyre built and the fire started. He had no prayers to offer over the abomination's burning body, but the flickering flames brought to mind a joke John's grandfather used to say. He must've really liked it, because he'd said it often enough. He'd repeated a lot of things in his last couple years. "Whadaya call an alien invasion, a plague, a world-wide religious war, and an ice age that kills three-quarters of the world's population?"

"A start," John Sawatis said aloud.

Girl Loves to Shop
Spring 105 PA / 2117 AD

Faith Hunter

Zerah strapped on the ES24, the electronic shield devised by the R&D department of the Pentagon. When she flipped the switch, the unit buzzed against her skin like angry bees—she had an urge to scratch an itch that wasn't there.

The ES24 would allow her to use the satellite uplink communications and her new miniature computer while in the presence of neomages . . . at least for a time. Not even the Pre-Ap electromagnetic shielding designed to thwart atmospheric detonation of a nuclear warhead was proof against mage energies. And the military still didn't know why, Zerah thought sourly. But at least they were getting a handle on it.

Once activated, the ES24 would give her four hours of electronic stability. After that it was a crapshoot. And there would be five mages on this mission. Five freaking mages. She flicked the switch down, deactivating the unit, saving it for when she *really* needed it.

From the EWU, the electronic weaponry unit, Zerah strode down the long hallway to the StandRep, the standard hardware repository. She had carte blanche here: permission to sign out any weapon she wanted, up to and including the T-47, the howitzer capable of launching the new .502 mage-inspired ammo, each round loaded with seraph steel and salt from the Holy Land. She'd been tempted to take a T-47, but had no transport for the massive unit. Zerah had seen the demonstration on captive spawn. Damned effective against the damned. Her grin hardened, showing teeth and fury.

Once, only beheading, burning to ash, being eaten by its own kind, or processing through a meat grinder had been permanently effective against devil-spawn. Now the good guys had ammo that kicked major Darkness ass, and swords were finally beginning to fall by the wayside. Of course, swords didn't run out of ammo, which gave them an undeniable edge, though she balked at the play on words.

She shoved open the StandRep door and it banged against the wall behind.

"Morning, Cap'n," the gunnery sergeant saluted. He didn't rise, but she didn't expect him to. He was sitting in the cockpit of the mobile armament retrieval vehicle, affectionately referred to as Morry, and only one arm was free of the straps and electronic sensors that married him to the unit. "Watcha need?" he asked around a mouthful of chaw—either that was some of the low-quality tobacco that grew here and there in the U.S. now-adays or the job paid better than Zerah thought.

"I want something that'll knock a hole in a dragonet big enough to dis-able it so I can kill it before it regenerates. And I want enough ammo to repeat the process for a hellhole full of 'em." Her anger had been hidden, pressed down deep inside her for years, but in the silent, dark places of her soul that rage had continued building and growing. And finally she was go-ing to set it free, the decades-old fury that that had shaped and formed her. She forced herself to relax, and stood at parade rest, fighting the tremors, the demand for fight-or-flight in her limbs. She watched Morry and its driver.

Gunny muttered under his breath, his eyes roaming his arsenal. He shook his head and activated a foot pedal. Morry, made of reinforced tubular mage steel, pulleys, a long-life solar battery powered by a Sun mage, and protective mesh in the event of a gravitational mishap—the military's way to describe stock falling from high shelves—moved smoothly forward on its wide tires. He shifted his left arm, sheathed in a Pre-Ap sensory glove, and Morry's retrieval arm raised, extended, and sought a wooden box on a shelf marked "AR." The pincer at the end of the arm opened and closed on the end of a medium-sized box and began to slide it forward. With a series of complicated hand motions, Gunny maneuvered Morry's pincer along the long box to its midpoint, and then lifted it and carried it to the floor. The box was marked "AR-82."

The AR-82s were lightweight, shoulder-mounted, practically recoilless, wildcatted .470 semi-automatic dragon-guns. With a velocity of around 2,000 feet per second, and increased range and penetration over their black-powder, elephant-gun forebears, the ARs were a dragon-hunter's wet dream.

"Oh yeah," Zerah murmured. She took a pry bar from the desk and opened the box. Sighing with pleasure, she removed one of the two sleek, black units from the molded foam padding. Expertly, she broke down the weapon, inspecting it thoroughly and minutely. Satisfied, she nodded at Gunny. "I'll take seven of them and as much ammo as a WetBetsy can carry." WetBetsey's were armored personnel carriers based on the same design as Morry. They were created to penetrate hellholes and carry troops and weaponry deep underground. And they cost a freaking fortune. Zerah knew she would be court-martialed if she came back without it.

Gunny's brows rose in surprise. He opened his mouth to question, but spat into a cup instead. He closed his mouth, pursed his lips and spat again, and had Morry bring down another box. While he worked, Zerah remem-bered to breathe, and meandered to the steel weapons cache. She chose seven human-forged steel swords and fourteen throwing knives, each with its sheath or scabbard. From the aisle dedicated to handguns, she gathered seven Smith & Wesson 9mm semiautomatics, a couple pristine originals and some newer models built from the original patterns. They were useless against spawn, but they worked against Dark mules well enough.

When she glanced back, all the AR cases were on the floor and Morry idled. His eyes narrowed, Gunny watched Zerah, making her itch between her shoulder blades almost as intensely as mage-shielding did. It was as if he knew she was here with forged papers—as if he knew she was going off the grid, into the wilds, on her own. Just Zerah, her handpicked troops, and five battle mages, chasing after the dragon who had killed her family. It had taken her twelve years of careful and clandestine accumulation and analysis of data to pinpoint the region where the dragon's hellhole was situated, and now, finally, she was going after it. And no sergeant was going to stop her.

The door to the hallway opened, and six black-clad second unforeseen walked in, their battle boots oddly silent on the concrete floor. Each saluted her, nodded to Gunny, and began to inspect his or her weapons, strapping on the blades and shouldering the ARs. Without a word, they left, one at a time, slipping from the room.

Gunny spat again and smiled, his big horse teeth coffee-brown in the sterile light. "Good luck, Cap'n. Bring me home a claw for my part in this little . . . *run*."

Zerah tensed. It sounded like blackmail. Claws were expensive items on the black market. She studied the sergeant, wondering if he would report her, set an alarm, call the general and have her stopped at the gate. *I should take him out.*

Gunny tensed his fist. The huge pincer swung—hard, fast, right at her. Zerah whipped back her head. The pincer stopped a bare inch from her chin. She froze.

"What?" he barked. "You think you're the only one who lost family to the Dark? Think you're the only one who goes after them when they find the hellhole?" Gunny relaxed his hand, the pincer easing away from her face. Zerah remembered to breathe. "Just don't bugger up my guns. And try to get them all back to me. It's a pain in the ass to balance the paper-work."

Zerah back-stepped slowly to the door, her eyes hard on the sergeant.

Gunny grinned. "Don't forget that claw." He pointed with his chin, and Zerah looked to the corkboard on the wall. There were five claws hooked into the board, each holding a photo of a dead dragon. Before she could react to the sight, he added, "I got good odds on you making it . . . all of you. The general thinks you'll leave your men's blood on the ice. Don't make me lose my pocket money." The breath stopped in Zerah's lungs. Gunny just laughed.

Beauty and the Beasts
Late Spring 105 PA / 2117 AD

Faith Hunter

Reimei watched from his cell, standing well back from the demon iron bars so he wouldn't get singed. The stone at his sides and under his bare feet burned badly enough as it was. A Stone mage might have drawn power from it and found freedom, or at least taken out some of the swarming spawn in the hellhole. But deep beneath the ground, there were no winds to draw on, no weather patterns to siphon energies from, and his own meager stores were long-depleted. An Air mage was useless down here.

The captive neomage had no idea what the dragon intended for him, but whatever it was, it would be far worse than being eaten alive by dragonets. Eaten alive—Reimei, neomage of a litter of eight, chuckled to himself, the half-mad cackles bouncing sickly off the stone. It was a strange day when being eaten alive would be the lesser of two evils.

In the passageway outside his cell, he heard rustling—not the beloved rustling of leaves in the wind, but the dry slither-rustle of scales and chitinous feet on stone. Reimei took an involuntary step back, his shoulder blades only millimeters from the cold rock wall.

The dragon stopped outside his cell and peered in. Chorael was small, only eight feet tall, and so stood straight, not hunched, when he paused outside the cell door. Chorael pulled his leathery wings close around him, leaving only his misshapen head, his haunches and lower feet, and his long tail visible above and below.

The dragon's eyes were the shade of the finest pearls, matching the rows of pointed teeth and the silvery horns extending back from his head. His tongue licked forward, moistening the black lips that outlined his mouth. Chorael was beautiful in his dragon form, his skin glowing like the sea on a balmy day, and his wing tips appearing frosted like whitecaps kicked up by the wind. The scales swirled down his body, darkening in color as they formed a distinctive geometric pattern across his belly and then cascaded chaotically over his thighs and lower legs. His feet were emerald green, with even darker claws. Chorael's skin would make a beautiful wall hanging.

Early on in his confinement, Reimei had hoped to see the skin on a wall in the New Orleans Enclave, or perhaps even as a canopy over his bed. He still harbored hope that his litter-mate Melina was alive somewhere in the hellhole's depths. If so, she might yet find a way free, and perhaps even bring help to rescue him. It was a faint hope, but the only one that kept him going each time he woke.

Chorael's stare and silence were unnerving, and Reimei hunched his shoulders, tucking his hands into his armpits to warm his fingers. Chorael shifted, his form blurring and flowing until a human-looking man stood before him, a man with pale green skin and flowing white hair, green-green eyes and silken clothes, a cape tossed back from his shoulders. The fallen angel leaned into the bars and gripped them with elegant fingers. "Have you reconsidered my offer?"

"Many times," Reimei said. "But I will not willingly mate with your Dark mage. Not now. Not tomorrow. Not ever."

"I will not force her on you. But look upon her face one last time."

Last? Reimei thought. "So, will you kill me now?"

Chorael smiled, his expression kind, almost angelic. "You are too valuable to feed to my spawn. Far too valuable to me." Chorael gestured to his side and a neomage slid into the crook of his arm. Dark mages had been considered mere myths until recently, when that new consul-general, Thorn St. Croix, fought some on the hellhole mountain near her home. Now they were feared because their powers were less tied to external elements than mages of the Light. The only good things about Dark mages were that they didn't have formal savage chi and savage blade fighting techniques, and they were untrained in the use of their magics. But raw power—they had that a-plenty.

"You remember my Jasmine . . ." Chorael crooned.

Jasmine was beautiful, a tiny, pale-skinned woman with glistening black hair and eyes, her body emblazoned with Dark mage tattoos. A River mage apparently, she was dressed scantily, a length of silken cloth tied at one shoulder. Her flesh was swirled with the blues of ponds, the burbling green foam of streams, and the near-black of subterranean rivers. The skin art was magic—elemental conjures tattooed into her flesh, giving her an attachment to Chorael, allowing her to use him as a power sink, giving her almost unlimited power.

Reimei could smell her heat, his body reflexively reacting in ways that strained his bonds of self-control. He swallowed convulsively. Since she was in heat, the dragon had to be holding a kylen or seraph prisoner. The rumors were true—not that knowing it for certain gained Reimei anything but another reason to despair.

Chorael untied the knot holding Jasmine's clothing in place. The cloth slithered down her body to pool at her feet. She stood before Reimei, her body firm and perfect, her tattoos churning, whirling water patterns seeming to froth up and out from her navel. The waves curled around her tiny breasts, to splash over her nipples.

Reimei clenched his eyes shut, blocking the Dark mage's image out.

In the passageway, Chorael sighed. "You make this difficult, mage."

Reimei heard the receding patter of feet. Jasmine had been sent away. He shuddered with relief. And then he heard a sound from the door. Reimei opened his eyes to see two dragonets entering. He'd seen parts of

Thorn St. Croix's battle on SNN, as had most of the rest of the nation, and these new Dark creatures had drawn much commentary.

They were smaller versions of those things, each only about three feet tall—or three feet long.

The long one was built like a centipede, with an articulated body and multiple jointed legs. The creature had long forelegs that jutted up and then down, like arms, with pincers on the ends. The smaller feet had tiny hooks at their heels. It had scarlet hair in tufts on its head and sparsely across its back. And it had faceted pink eyes, eyes that held him in their sights.

The tall one was part human, standing on human feet, with human legs and human genitalia, but with the upper body of a hyena, snout filled with serrated teeth designed to rip flesh. And his hands were taloned like a bird.

Reimei backed up against the cave wall, the stone an icy ache along his spine, but nothing compared to the frozen fear he felt at the sound of the cell door swinging closed.

And the stone at his back heated, a sudden burst of energy that healed his pain. He gasped.

From the hallway, he heard a long gurgling breath as Chorael shifted back to his dragon form, and a dragon scream that tore at his eardrums. "To war! *To war!*"

The dragonets whirled and sped from the cell, following their master. And the cell door did not clang shut.

Two Mules for Brother Hope
Early Summer 105 PA / 2117 AD

Christina Stiles

When the sun finally rose after the long, hellish night, its light revealed the true extent of the damage. The kirk was gone, destroyed by fire. Most of the shacks the indentured townsfolk had lived in were likewise burned or had been leveled by the larger monstrosities. Even bossman Lawrence Decker's brick mansion had been gutted. Only the stone-built town hall stood unscathed.

The survivors were gathered in the town hall. "Only sixty-two sheep, Oh Lord," Brother Leon Hope said aloud. Trinity's population had been roughly three hundred before the attack. "I am their shepherd. I will protect those you've given unto my care." Brother Hope clasped his light brown hands in prayer and looked skyward.

Nearby, Reasha Zhane, the beautiful, dark-skinned Earth mage on license from the New Orleans Enclave, moved another mound of dirt with her magic, dumping it on a burning building. The weight of the earth collapsed the structure entirely, but extinguished the fire. That accomplished, she fell, exhausted, to the ground. Michael Eagleheart, her bodyguard, was beside her in an instant and lifted her tired body into his arms.

He walked with her to Brother Hope, interrupting the kirkman's prayer. "She's spent, kirkman," Eagleheart said. "Don't expect Reasha to put out more fires today. She faced the Darkness with the rest of us. When the battle was over, she dug the grave pit and buried all the dead. Then she fought the fires and built the firebreaks to save what she could. I don't care what else needs to be done, she needs to rest."

"Yes. You're right. We all do." Brother Hope replied. "After that we'll need to prepare defenses for when the creatures return."

"About that, Hope. We need to talk."

Reasha Zhane lifted her head from Michael's chest. "You think they're coming back?"

Brother Hope saw the terror in her eyes. She was from the posh New Orleans Enclave. She'd led a pampered existence before Decker had hired her. Her encounters thus far with spawn, succubae, dragonets, and Dark mules had left a scar on her soul, one from which she might never recover. Reasha was handling the shock better than he'd expected. She was stronger than she realized. If he'd had more time to counsel her, Hope was sure he could have made an ally of the Light of her and her companion. The Most

High needed people like them.

He didn't know if he could save Jesse Holder's soul, though. Jesse liked to fight, but didn't care why she fought, only that she was paid for it.

"I'm sorry, Ree, but they most certainly will be back," Eaglehart half-whispered to her. "They know there's food here, and devil-spawn are walking hunger. They won't stop hunting here until there's no one left."

"Didja tell him?" said a gruff female voice from behind them. They all turned to see that Jesse Holder, bossman Decker's former enforcer and lover, had joined them. She held a pistol in each gloved hand. "Seraph balls, but we are in one *serious* load of spawn shit here, boys."

"Please stop the cursing, Jess. We don't need to add divine judgment to our . . . troubles."

She arched an eyebrow at the kirkman, and then said, "Seraph balls. Ser. Aph. Balls. Why should I be afraid to curse your so-called Most High and His so-called host? His seraphs might hear me and take offense? Not bloody likely. There aren't any seraphs listening, there aren't any seraphs coming to punish me, and there certainly aren't any guardian angels coming down from the heavens to help you save your spawn-bait congregation!"

"Forgive this woman, Most High. She knows not the power of her words."

"Screw that, Leon. If your God is so almighty, why did He let this shit happen to this town? These folks were innocent enough. They did a good day's work and prayed with you on Sundays. So why did your Most High allow Decker and Yates to enslave them all that time? Why didn't He send His servants to blast the Dark creatures to oblivion when things got really bad? Those invasion theorists got it right: Those seraphs we see on the TV are just aliens using our world as a proving ground, and we're damn well stuck in the middle of their crazy war with the other aliens that followed 'em here. This shit sucks seraph balls! Eagleheart is right."

"Right about what, Michael?" he asked, turning toward the neomage's protector.

"Uh, we've been talking, Leon," the big man said, uncharacteristically hesitant, "and we've decided to leave."

"A lot of the townsfolk are injured or too weak to walk any great distance."

"*Screw* them, Leon," Jesse spat. "I'm not worried about them at all. You are bat-shit crazy if you think we're moving them. We can't take them all with us—and we *won't*. We have to look out for ourselves, preacher man. They'd slow us down and be a huge target, and in the end we'd all get killed. There's a pickup truck at Decker's manor house that Lizbeth should be able to get running in short order. It'll be big enough and fast enough to get us—just us—to Atlanta. Yates, too, so he can stand trial."

Eagleheart, softly spoke. "Maybe they can scatter into the hills, find defensible locations to hold out for a couple days. Once we're back to civilization, we can report the problem to someone. The authorities, the Army, the neomages will know what to do about the growing Darkness."

"But we have a duty—"

"I am sworn to protect Reasha, not these people, kirkman," Eagleheart interrupted. "I have to get her safely back to the New Orleans Enclave, or at least to the Embassy in Atlanta. That is *my* duty." After an uncomfortable silence, he continued. "I'm taking Reasha inside to rest now," and he turned away with the neomage.

"Yeah, we'll need her at full strength for the trip," Jesse replied. "Tell Lizbeth to get out here. I need her." To Brother Hope, she said, "So, while Lizbeth is fixing up the truck, the rest of us should be gathering food and supplies. We should try to get the hell out of here no later than two o'clock this afternoon so we get a good start under daylight."

Hope shook his head. "I'm not leaving my flock. You all are free to do what you wish, of course, but the Most High has given them into my care, and I will lay down my life in His service. Make sure to leave us food and supplies."

Jesse stomped a booted foot. "Damn it, quit being all high and mighty and *stupid*, Leon," Jesse said. "We can't save them. They're going to end up as spawn vittles when that horde gets here."

"I will protect Trinity with my last breath. I am their shepherd."

Jesse huffed. "Then you'll be food, too, kirkman."

Despite the warmth of the early summer day, Trinity's survivors huddled together in front of the fireplace in the town hall under coats and blankets they'd managed to salvage from their homes. Beside them lay a few other possessions reclaimed from the smoking debris. Brother Hope watched Lizbeth James walk from person to person, handing out emergency rations and bottles of water from the stock room. Decker's town administrator, Jacobin Yates, visibly cringed at the loss of such valuable items.

The townsfolk were unnaturally quiet, their eyes glazed over from the trauma of their recent encounters with Darkness. For the first time in Brother Hope's life the desire to sing to bolster the courage of those around him escaped him. He took a deep breath and exhaled loudly. Although he couldn't muster a song, he would still be the rock that these people needed him to be. He rejected every doubt that crossed his mind. The Most High believed in him, and the Lord never gave a person more than he could handle. Adversity built strength of character. His flock would survive. They would rebuild. They would flourish in Trinity. These were the truths that he believed.

And if he had to lead them all through this tribulation alone, he would do so. It was necessary.

Resolved, Brother Hope waited for Lizbeth to finish distributing the food before he approached her. She had been a good friend. He would miss her.

"Lizbeth," he said, quietly.

She looked up. Dried blood still streaked her face, and a few patches of her skin and clothing had been eaten away by the acidic blood of the Dark minions.

"Did Michael give you Jesse's message?"

"No. He came in and put Reasha in Yates's bed, and then he went out. He didn't say anything to me."

"Jesse wants your help in getting Decker's truck running. She wants you all to be ready to leave as soon as possible. They don't want to be here when the devil-spawn return."

Lizbeth stared at him.

"Did you hear me?"

She blinked. "I did. But I didn't hear the part about *everyone* needing to escape this town. What's the plan to save *them*?" she glanced toward those crowding the main room.

"Jesse isn't taking us with you. She will take Jacobin Yates, though. To bring him to justice."

"Oh, yeah? She intending to walk? I'm not fixing up anything unless we all get a ride to safety."

Brother Hope laid his hand on Lizbeth's arm. "Be charitable, Lizbeth. Michael promised to alert someone in Atlanta or New Orleans to the problems here. He'll do that as soon as he gets Miss Zhane home. I trust him. He has proven nothing but honorable since we started working together."

"I can't say the same about Jesse," she said.

"It will be all right, my child."

She laughed. "Child? You aren't any older than I am."

"Sister?" he smiled.

She held his gaze. Her voice dropped to a whisper. "No. I don't want to be your sister, Leon. My thoughts about you are often . . . impure."

He arched an eyebrow at her and released his hold.

"What? Kirkmen can be sexy."

A smile reached his eyes. "You flatter me, Miss James."

"'Miss James'? What happened to 'Lizbeth'?"

Brother Hope noticed the survivors starting to stare at his exchange with Lizbeth. Dirty faces watched their every move.

"Were we not in such dire circumstances," he whispered, "I'd explore what future we might have. But alas . . ."

He cleared his throat and stepped back to be more circumspect. "As I was saying, Jesse needs your help. Please help them get Reasha Zhane back to the Atlanta Embassy. Her seraphic visa will only be active for two more weeks, and it's dangerous for a mage to be out and about without one. I wouldn't want anyone to go through what I've heard rogue mages suffer. Nor would I want to risk the Darkness capturing her—that could be much, much worse than death."

"Back to business, huh? Okay, kirkman. I'll fix their truck, but I'm not going with them. I can help save this town. We kinda owe it to them after we screwed up in the mines."

Brother Hope and Lizbeth James helped the others pack the pickup truck with supplies from the town hall's storeroom, while the townsfolk spent the day gathering weapons and shoring up the block building as best they could, boarding up the windows, leaving spaces between some of the boards for the defenders to shoot through. If they'd been interested, Jesse and Eagleheart could have done a better job of setting up defenses. As it was, Brother Hope relied on the Army training he'd received before he'd heard God's call and changed careers.

"The boss isn't going to be happy about you taking all his stuff," Yates grumbled during the loading. He'd been pacing and muttering to himself the whole time. He didn't seem glad to have a seat on the only vehicle leaving town.

"Neither you nor your absent boss have a say in it," said Lizbeth. "I don't think he plans on coming back. And once a judge hears about what you've done, I doubt you'll be coming back any time soon either."

Jacobin Yates stopped his pacing, and leaned into Lizbeth. "It wasn't supposed to happen like this. The neomage was supposed to be an appeasement to the ones Decker pissed off! You ruined the exchange!"

Lizbeth pushed her face toward his until they were eye to eye. "You mean to tell me that he *wanted* the Darkness to take Reasha and you knew about it all along?"

Yates straightened up with a jerk. A glint of madness and hatred shone in his eyes. "Yes! Yes! And you screwed up everything! Now, they'll be back for sure!"

Coming around the corner, Jesse Holder overheard Jacobin Yates's last exclamation. Moving fast, before anyone could react, Jesse drew a pistol. Stepped to the side. Shot Yates in the head. The angle of the shot blew brain tissue across the far wall. Yates's body crumpled to the ground, arms still extended outward, his mouth open as if he had more to say.

"What in the world did you do that for?" Brother Hope yelled at her. He bent down to examine Yates's body, but there was nothing anyone could do to save the man. "No one liked Jacobin Yates, but you didn't have to kill him!"

"I'm the law in this town. The man was a confessed criminal."

"He deserved a trial," Lizbeth muttered.

"He just had one. I'm the judge and executioner here too."

"Yes, you served Lawrence Decker as law enforcement here for several years, but Decker's gone," Brother Hope replied.

"What can I say? Old habits die hard," Jesse said with a shrug. Turning, she yelled, "Hey, Michael, put the body in the back. We're going to take this sorry sack of shit with us, dump it somewhere away from town." She faced the stunned Brother Hope again. "That might gain you a little more time to finish your prep for the devil-spawn."

Without a word, Michael Eagleheart lifted the dead body into the back of the truck, and then climbed into the cab, taking his place beside Reasha Zhane.

Brother Hope said a prayer over the body and turned toward Jesse. "Your soul is tainted, Jesse. You need to make right with the Lord and cleanse this evil from you, else you'll be joining the Darkness yourself."

"Yeah, well, I don't plan on working for those ugly guys. I do a little good here and a little evil there. It all balances out in the end."

"Don't believe it. The scales are tipping in the wrong direction. Cleanse your soul, Jesse. Make right with the Lord."

"Perhaps another day, kirkman. I've got things to do, and I get by okay." Then Jesse turned to Lizbeth James. "Sure you don't wanna come along? There's room for one more."

"No, I'm needed here."

"Suit yourself," Jesse said as she climbed into the truck, cranked the engine, and headed down the road to Atlanta. Michael, Reasha, and Jesse had left the mining town behind, and Brother Hope sent up a prayer that they would safely arrive at their destination.

As the truck disappeared in the distance, Lizbeth held out her hand to Brother Hope. He took it, a little unsure of what she was doing.

"It's been a great run, Brother Hope," she said, giving his hand a good shake, and not letting go. "I'm happy to have met and worked with you. I wish we'd had more time together. I'd like to have had the opportunity to get to know you much better." She shouldered a rifle and a pack.

"I thought you were staying."

"Oh, I am. But I'll be more use to you outside. I found a cache of grenades, and I have as much ammo as I can carry. I'll try to keep them off your door. Hopefully, they'll settle for my kills as supper."

"I don't think that's wise."

"I'm best at sniping, Leon. I have to follow my talents on this one."

"I don't want you to go out there, Lizbeth." He brought her hand closer and looked down at it. "Please don't go out there."

"It's getting dark," she said, pulling away. "The devil-spawn will be here soon, so I need to set up on the roof. Lock up behind me, and send up a prayer and a few battle songs." She kissed him on the cheek, and then drew on a pair of low-light goggles. "I'll either see you later or on the other side, Leon," she said, and then disappeared. He bolted the door after her.

It was deathly silent in the town hall, the only noises being occasional coughs from the town's nervous defenders and the hum of the generator powering the lights. The smell of fear was thick in the room.

Brother Hope gathered his flock, and began a prayer. "I am in the midst of lions; I am forced to dwell among ravenous beasts—men whose teeth are spears and arrows, whose tongues are sharp swords."

The townsfolk formed a circle, held hands tightly, and watched Brother Hope's face.

"Be exalted, O God, above the heavens. Let Your glory be over all the Earth."

He knew they believed in him. Ever since he'd come to Trinity, the people had gravitated to him, even those who'd been too downtrodden and depressed to believe that an Almighty God watched over them. Little by little, even the faithless had come to accept him as a faithful servant of the Lord. Just weeks ago the attendees had outgrown his little kirk, and they'd had to start gathering in the town hall to accommodate everyone. The people of Trinity were like family to him now, and the Darkness had killed *a lot* of his family.

"They spread a net for my feet—I was bowed down in distress. They dug a pit in my path, but they have fallen into it themselves."

A shot rang out from overhead as Brother Hope's prayer built to a crescendo. *Lizbeth.* More shots followed.

"They're here!" Lizbeth yelled down. "Lord be with us, but they're here! Ten devil-spawn coming this way! Probably more to follow."

"Get your weapons ready, everyone." Hope ordered. "Shooters, take positions at the firing slots in the windows and take out as many spawn as you can. When you run out of ammo or if they break through, fall back. Then those who're good with knives and swords take over the battle. These windows and the front door are the only entry points to worry about, so keep the creatures log-jammed here—and don't let them get to the inner room, to our friends and families."

Hope grabbed his own gun, and moved to an opening. He felt a song growing inside him. The Lord was with him. He began belting out a battle hymn, one written about Mole Man, the Carolina mountain-country hero. A few others mumbled the words along with him, fear keeping their voices subdued.

Above them, Lizbeth continued to fire, the sound of her rifle cracking rapidly. They could hear growling as the spawn fought over their own dead. The sound, a wet, tearing noise amidst the snarling, was chill-to-the-bones terrifying. Kol, one of the townsfolk, dropped his weapon, fell to his knees, and put his hands to his ears. "I can't do this! I can't do this!"

"Have faith, Kol. The Most High is with us this night," said Brother Hope. Kol rocked back and forth.

Then came growling and scratching at the shutters. A three-fingered hand burst through a board and withdrew. Another board splintered and the hand returned, grasping for one of the humans. The spawn's rat-like face appeared in the hole it had made. Several inside the hall screamed.

"Fire," Brother Hope shouted. The defenders began shooting at the attacking spawn, and Hope turned back to the man cowering on the floor. "You can do this, Kol. We need you. Trinity needs you." Hope's voice was calm and inspiring.

"Join me, Kol. Join me in prayer." Hope knelt next to Kol, gently pulled the terrified man's hands away from his ears and held them. Raising his voice over the gunshots, he began reciting a familiar psalm. "The Lord is my shepherd . . ."

Kol joined in almost out of habit, ". . . I shall not want. He maketh me to lie down in green pastures. He leadeth me beside the still waters. He restoreth my soul. He leadeth me in the paths of righteousness for His name's sake."

Gunshots continued, both from the roof and from within the town hall, but Brother Hope ignored them, concentrating on the man in front of him, holding Kol's attention with his unwavering gaze.

"Yea, though I walk through the valley of the shadow of death, I will fear no evil, for Thou art with me, Thy rod and Thy staff they comfort me. Thou preparest a table for me in the presence of mine enemies. Thou anointest my head with oil; my cup runneth over. Surely goodness and mercy shall follow me all the days of my life, and I will dwell in the house of the Lord forever."

Kol stopped rocking, looked into Brother Hope's eyes. "Yes. Yes, Brother Hope, I can do this," he said, pulling himself unsteadily to his knees and grabbing his rifle. He got up, returned to his assigned defensive position at the window, pointed his rifle through a firing slot, and fired—shaking, without aiming, probably not hitting anything, but a part of the town's defense.

More devil-spawn rushed the town hall, clawing at the boards and shutters. Some ripped wood away and burst through the remaining glass. As bullets struck one creature, its corrosive blood spattered outward, hitting Lewis, a miner who was closest to the opening. He shrieked in pain, as the blood sizzled on his neck and face.

Another defender shot the creature in the head. It stumbled backward, but two more advanced to take its place. "Incoming," Lizbeth yelled from above.

Brother Hope took steady aim and blasted one devil-spawn in the face. Another pulled itself into the room. Grady rushed it with his axe, scoring only a glancing blow to its arm. A newcomer to Trinity, Grady still had some heft to him, muscle that hadn't yet been sapped toiling in the mines. He towered over everyone in the room. But all that meant little facing the speed and reflexes of the darkun. The other humans, still shrieking, backed against the wall, behind Brother Hope and the few who were proficient with weapons.

Another wave of spawn swarmed toward the hole. A grenade exploded in their midst—dropped from above by Lizbeth James, Hope knew.

Grady took another swing at the devil-spawn trying to get past him, but missed wildly, lost his footing, and fell. The creature jumped on him, tearing at his neck, teeth snapping for his throat. Brother Hope placed his rifle against the spawn's head and fired. The creature toppled to the side.

"Are you hurt badly?" Brother Hope asked, holding a hand out to Grady.

"More scared than hurt, I think," Grady replied.

The kirkman scanned Grady's bloody neck. "Doesn't look deep," Hope said. "Someone bandage him up."

An explosion went off. Grenade.

Another.

Then a third.

These weren't detonating near the town hall like Lizbeth's grenade. They were further away, some distance down the road.

Brother Hope heard whooping and hollering. Yells of, "Watch your back! Get that one! Nice job, brother!"

"What on Earth?" He noted that Lizbeth was no longer firing from the roof, and wished he had a comm link with her to learn what was going on. Jesse and her crew had taken the last comms—she didn't think he'd be needing them, after all.

"Keep your guns ready," he yelled to the people manning the windows. "Not you, Kol. I want you to guard the door. I'm going to step outside to see what's going on out there." Kol seemed surprised to be called on, but quickly took up his position at the door, a look of resolve on his face.

Brother Hope unlocked the door, and scooted by the man.

Outside, more explosions went off. Briefly, he saw a flash—the glint of a blade? Although he had only human night vision, in the available moonlight he thought he could see limbs propelled across the street, making squishy thuds against what remained of a burned-out building. There were figures running in the distance, and beyond them fires burned.

Above him, Brother Hope heard a scrabbling sound, and he instinctively raised his rifle to shoot.

"It's me," a female voice called. Lizbeth lowered her body down a rope from the roof, as he pointed the rifle away from her. "I didn't mean to startle you. Sorry."

"What did you see? What's going on?" Hope asked.

"Two men," she said with joy in her voice. "Two brawny men, I should say from their outlines. And, as Jesse would say, they've killed a shitload of devil-spawn. They seem to be enjoying themselves, too. It's like they're playing with them. And they appear to be walking this way. Should we greet them or hide?"

"Take your dead and run, you dogs," one of the men yelled. "Git. There'll be no snacking on the fine citizens of Trinity tonight. Not on my watch." Another grenade went off, and something went up in flames.

"Wow, the devil-spawn seem to be obeying—what's left of them. I see them dragging a few of their fallen off," Lizbeth said, craning to see from ground level.

"Take off the goggles."

Lizbeth did so, and Brother Hope leaned into her. "I want to see who we're dealing with."

Brother Hope barked an order to those inside the hall, "Hit the outside lights." Light spilled out from the building, illuminating the surrounding streets.

"Hey, now! A little warning next time," a male voice barked. "Don't blind a guy who's trying to help."

"Yeah, whoa there!" the other man exclaimed, shielding his eyes, and moving inhumanly fast to the corner of a still-standing wall, taking cover.

The first one seemed less concerned. He stood in the light, and scraped devil-spawn goo off his sword with a cloth hanging from his belt. It sizzled a bit as the blood burned through it. The sword didn't seem to be affected, though sections of his arms showed acid burns.

"Who are you?" called out Brother Hope.

"Your rescuers, obviously," the man in the center of the road replied, with a short laugh. He sheathed his blade and made a gallant bow. "I come in peace. May I approach, Trinitiean? Trinitarian? Trinite? Oh, whatever you guys call yourselves."

"You may," Brother Hope responded. With a hand behind his back, he motioned for Lizbeth to train her gun on the man. "My friend has you in her sights, so keep your hands up. Tell your partner there to do the same."

"Sure. Hey, Colin. Come out, you freak."

Both men held up their hands and approached. Their arms were bare but they seemed perfectly comfortable, though the cold wind from the mountains made Brother Hope shiver. Between that, their size, and their inhuman speed, Hope guessed they were mules. Brother Hope placed one hand on Lizbeth's barrel, pointing it toward the ground. "There's no real use in threatening these two. They could kill us in a heartbeat."

"But we're the good guys. We wouldn't do that," the first mule said with a broad smile. They were both tall, broad, light-skinned, blond, and handsome.

"Yeah," the other seconded.

"Are you?" asked Brother Hope. "Are you agents of the Light?"

"Well, I wouldn't go that far. Let's just say that we're grey," he laughed.

Brother Hope and Lizbeth stared at them.

"I'm sorry. My friends say I tend toward humor when seriousness is required," said the first mule.

The second mule, the mirror image of the first, now that they could see him clearly, nodded. "Yeah."

"And you can shut up." He returned his attention to Brother Hope. "No, we aren't with the Light, exactly, though we do fight the Darkness."

"Again, who are you?"

"I'm Davey, and this is my brother Colin. We were sent here to help someone named Brother Leon Hope. Would you happen to know where we could find him?" he said, still holding up his hands. "Plus, may we put our hands down now? We already killed the things we came to kill."

Brother Hope nodded and the two lowered their arms.

"So, is one of you guys Brother Hope?"

Lizbeth looked at the kirkman's robes and then down at herself. "You're joking, right?"

"Yeah. There's that sense of humor again."

"I'm Brother Hope. Who sent you?"

"Ah, Brother Hope, good to meet you," Davey said, dropping to one knee and bowing his head. His twin mirrored his actions. "Jeep sent us."

"Yeah, Jeep."

Brother Hope shook his head. "A vehicle sent you?" He shot a quizzical look at Lizbeth.

"Nah. Nah. Jeep is a jenny. She and Alaska Stanhope sent us. They heard there was trouble brewing up this way, and they sent their best," he tapped his chest, "and him," he thumbed at his brother.

His brother scowled.

"We are yours, Brother Hope. Jeep said you have the authority to lead us where you wish, and that we should listen to your wisdom. You are our new master."

"I am no one's master," Brother Hope snapped. "I do not own people. I am a servant of the Lord. Please stand up, gentlemen."

They rose quickly.

"Jeep gave us to you. We are yours. We are to serve the servant of the Lord in his fight against the growing Darkness. Mules serve."

"Well I'll be," Lizbeth said. "I never thought I'd see the day when a kirkman became a slave owner." She burst out laughing.

"This is *not* funny! Let's all go inside and talk this over. I am *not* your master. Let us in, Kol!" he yelled, knocking on the door.

The mules looked at each other and shrugged. They followed Brother Hope and Lizbeth into the town hall. The people inside stared as the cheerful, gore-covered warriors sauntered in. The mules lifted hands in friendly, short waves in response to the onlookers. Then they turned back to Brother Hope, as if waiting for an order.

"Everyone, this is Davey and Colin," said Brother Hope. "They're here to lend us a hand against the Darkness. They must've killed dozens of devil-spawn between them."

"Hundreds, your lordship," Davey interjected.

"Please see to it that they get some food and drink."

"Oh, we aren't hungry yet. We could go hunt some devil-spawn down, if you want us to. Blast the entrance to the hellhole. It's not a long-term solution, but it would slow them down some, master."

The attention of Brother Hope's flock shifted to him on hearing the term "master." Grady, in particular, raised his brows. "Are you planning on picking up where Lawrence Decker left off and making us into slaves?"

"No! By no means! These men are simply confused."

Colin nudged Davey.

"What?"

"Supplies."

"Oh, yeah. Jeep sent a truckload of supplies, too. We abandoned it to fight the spawn, but we can go get it and unload it wherever you want it, master."

"Stop calling me that! I am not your master."

"Mules must serve," Davey repeated, looking surprised. "We're bred to serve."

Brother Hope sighed. "We could use your help through this ordeal, but you can certainly return to your home afterward."

"No can do! Jeep said you'd try to get rid of us. She told me we couldn't return to her service or Alaska's. She won't take us back. She told me to tell you that you are absolutely stuck with us! What Jeep says is law."

"Then she's obviously your master."

"Used to be, yes. Now you are. But we can't return. We are Trininites . . . Trinistasians . . . Trinities . . . now," said Davey.

"Yeah," Colin echoed and nodded.

"Didn't I tell you to shut up?"

"I do not know who this Jeep person is. Or this Alaska. I have no idea why they would send you to serve me."

Davey shrugged. "I guess you'd call them freedom fighters. They live out with the nomads. They've been fighting the Darkness for almost three decades. We all have, since we were kids. We were trained to fight, you see. When we all escaped Colonel Suarez's training camp, we decided to choose our own side of the battle. And you'll be happy to know that we chose yours," he smiled.

"If you choose sides, then it sounds as if you're autonomous individuals, not servants," Brother Hope replied. "If you'll both just continue to do what you did when you got here—help us, that is—then that is all I ask. You're free individuals otherwise."

"As I said: Mules must serve."

"Yes, you've said, Davey. And Jeep is a mule too?"

"Yes."

"But you served her? She must be autonomous, then."

"No. Jeep serves Alaska Stanhope."

"And this Alaska, is she a mule?"

"No. I honestly don't know what she is. She isn't a mule or a neomage. She's something different. She has some powers we've seen. Things we can't do. She's just weird."

"Well, there went that argument," Brother Hope sighed. "Help us, and don't call me master, and you can gladly stay with us."

"Yes, master . . . I mean, yes, sir . . . mister . . . uh, Brother Hope."

Brother Hope shook his head. "So, besides you two, who did this Jeep send to help us hold the town? And how did she know we needed help?"

Davey shook his head, "Nobody but us. As for how Jeep knew to send us, a watcher named Rama told her. He knows just about everything that happens around Kings Mountain. He said there's a hellhole nearby, and that something *powerful* was unleashed in the mines."

"Yes," Lizbeth said, looking around her, "we're aware of that."

"Yeah. Well, there's a lot of things like that happening, but we don't get involved in all of them. Rama must have had some special reason to be interested in you guys. So Jeep sent us to do what we could. Our transport truck, minus the boxes, is big enough to carry your wounded. If you want my battle-hardened opinion, I'd say we move out at first light. Right, brother?"

Colin nodded.

"This is our home. We're not abandoning Trinity."

The mule stared at the kirkman, but saw no weakness or doubt in his eyes. "I'd suggest you pray on that one tonight, Brother Hope. But Jeep said to follow your lead. In the meantime, we need to secure the supplies we brought. We should be safe enough out there now. Any spawn that we didn't kill will be too scared to pull anything more tonight. You have some folks you can spare to help us?"

"I'll go with you," chimed in Lizbeth.

"We'll both accompany you. Grady and Kol will look after everyone here while we're gone," said Brother Hope. "Got that, Grady?"

"Yes, Brother Hope," Grady said. "I'll keep them safe." Kol nodded his agreement.

"We left the truck just outside of town, and fought our way in from there," Davey said, as the group closed the door behind them and they walked into the street. "We've got weapons, food, clothes, medicine—everything Alaska and Jeep thought you might need. We'll take point."

Brother Hope carried a lantern in one hand, a handgun in the other. A half moon low on the horizon provided additional illumination. Beside him, Lizbeth scanned the area with her rifle. She kept her night-vision goggles around her neck, in case she needed to separate from Hope during a fight. The brawny mules held huge swords in two-handed grips, ready for anything that might leap out at them.

Not needing the lantern's light, the brothers ranged forward, quickly outdistancing the humans. Hope and Lizbeth moved more slowly, their boots crunching, revealing their presence further. They couldn't hear or see the twins, and so crept down the road.

At the edge of town, they saw vehicle lights ahead. There was more than one pair.

"More than one truck. Did Davey's friend Jeep change her mind and send more help?" asked Lizbeth.

"He sounded pretty certain that it would be just him and his brother." He strained to see anyone behind the lights.

Three shots rang out from the direction of the vehicles, a pistol blasting away the silence. Brother Hope and Lizbeth fell flat to the ground, and Hope turned off the lantern.

"Looks like your man is rusty, Harper!" Davey yelled out. "Couldn't hit the nut sack of a large dragon, that one."

More firing followed. The handgun and a few rifles this time.

"Oh, that's terrible, fellas. What's Suarez teaching you guys nowadays?"

One of the twins tumble-rolled in front of the headlights and rushed to the doors of the truck on the left, pulling it open. A man screamed and was thrown into the night.

Brother Hope glanced at Lizbeth. "If we're going to be any help, we have to get out of the glare of those lights."

Lizbeth leaned over to kiss his cheek. "You should find some cover and do what you do best, Leon: Inspire us with the Light—and take a few shots. Give me a prayer and keep yourself out of trouble." She pulled on her night-vision goggles and took off at a jog to the right, away from the lights.

Swords clanged as Brother Hope low-crawled by moonlight toward cover: a broken-down cart to crouch behind. "Be safe, Lizbeth," he whispered and started a prayer. "Be merciful unto me, O God, for my soul trusteth in Thee. In the shadow of Thy wings will I make my refuge, until these calamities be overpast. My soul is among lions, and I lie even among them that are set on fire, even the sons of men, whose teeth are spears and arrows, and their tongue a sharp sword."

He let his eyes adjust to the light conditions, his Army training coming back to him. Finally, Hope saw at least five people moving near the trucks. Some were as inhumanly fast as Colin and Davey. Mules, no doubt.

Then he saw the source of the clanging. Moving in and out of the light, one of the twins—Colin he guessed, from the lack of chatter—artfully danced in savage-blade style, his sword swinging, fighting two dark-haired, similarly skilled opponents, weaving in and out of their attacks. Colin's dance was beautiful, and he cut one with an upward thrust as he did a split to the ground and rolled up to meet the other. The blond lifted his sword to block a blade, and tumbled a few feet away. Trusting that Colin could hold his own for the time being, Brother Hope aimed his rifle at a pistol-armed attacker who was lining up a shot at Colin.

"They have prepared a net for my steps; my soul is bowed down. They have digged a pit before me, into the midst whereof they are fallen themselves." Brother Hope fired. The attacker with the handgun jerked. He fell forward with a crunch, blood spouting from his chest.

"I will praise thee, O Lord, among the people. I will sing unto Thee among the nations. For Thy mercy is great unto the heavens, and Thy truth unto the clouds," Hope thundered, aiming and shooting one of Colin's attackers through the throat.

Hope heard a shot from the direction Lizbeth had run off to. It struck the leg of the other swordsman fighting Colin. Provided an opening, Colin quickly finished off the wounded attacker and darted away.

His hiding place compromised, Brother Hope dashed to the cover of a burned-out building. From this new vantage, he could see the other combatants.

Further down the lane, Davey approached another man. The other man shouted, "Hold your fire, boys. This one's mine!" Hope could see light reflecting off the man's bald head as he faced Davey with sword in hand.

"I hope you won't run this time, Harper," Davey said. "Our unfinished business needs, uh, finishing—with your death, that is."

"You can stop your trash-talking, deserter. It's not my day to die. In fact, today's the day I bring your head to Suarez. Your brother's too."

"You always were a dreamer, Harper," Davey said, moving mule-fast to attack, slashing his blade at Harper's head. Harper parried the attack with his own sword, ducked, and swept a leg to take out Davey's, but the blond mule jumped, avoiding the sweep. Judging from how the man's movements mirrored Davey's, Hope guessed that the other man was also a well-trained fighting mule.

Brother Hope crept along the wall of the building, trying to get close enough for a clear shot at Harper. Just as he got settled, Hope saw Davey strike Harper across the temple with his sword's pommel. A cut formed, and blood oozed from Harper's forehead, blood that looked black instead of red in the uneven light. Pressing his advantage, Davey cut, cut, thrust his blade into the off-kilter mule's torso, yelling, "For Jeremiah!" even as Harper's head wound stitch itself together into smooth flesh.

"What the—" Davey exclaimed, echoing Brother Hope's thoughts.

Harper rose from his squat, looked down at his chest, dark fluid leaking out of the punctures. The mule stepped fully into the lights from the trucks, and Brother Hope could see that the blood on his chest and head really was black. The bald mule smiled. "Suarez made some improvements to his favorites since you and I last met, Davey. We've received infusions from our master. I heal much quicker now," he said. His chest wounds were knitting back together before Brother Hope's eyes. "I'm stronger, too," he said, "and faster." Hope could hardly follow Harper's movements as he stabbed Davey in the gut, punched him in the face, and knocked him to the ground before the twin could react.

Harper stood over the prone form. With both hands on his sword's hilt, he brought the weapon above his head and was about to thrust it into Davey's neck when the sound of a rifle rang out, and Harper yelped in pain. Then he shouted something at the top of his lungs, words that Brother Hope didn't recognize, but that felt *wrong*.

"My soul is among lions, and I lie even among them that are set on fire," Lizbeth yelled from underneath one of the trucks. "I learned that one from you, Leon. Plus a little Dead Sea salt to stir up that evil blood. Ah, what the heck; have another." She pulled the trigger again, a second bullet striking Harper in the center of his back.

Harper jerked as the blood oozing from the bullet holes burst into flames. Davey dragged himself away. The flames spread to engulf Harper, who screamed and dropped to the ground, but Brother Hope saw that the mule's rolling in the mud and dirt did nothing to put out the purifying flames. Harper's struggles slowed and then his voice emerged from the roaring flames, distorted by pain and the sound of the holy fire, "Enjoy your little victory, deserter. I called; more spawn are coming. If you survive these, Suarez will just send more—they breed quickly and the mountains are full of them. And he has plenty more combat teams to send. You two—and this place—are goin' down." He grunted and stopped moving, laying face-first on the watery earth, his body still burning.

Brother Hope heard a noise and scrambled to a new position to look. Colin was battling two more fast-moving opponents, and looked to be suffering from a number of minor wounds. One of the attackers was staring at Harper's immolation, so Colin launched into a series of unorthodox moves that left his own body momentarily vulnerable but took down the distracted one. The other attacker rushed at Colin's exposed back, sword high.

Two rifle shots cracked the air: one from Hope and the other from Lizbeth's direction. The enemy mule dodged one bullet, but his momentum threw him into the path of the other. The sword-fight continued, with no opportunity for Hope to safely fire into the fray, but with a few more dance-like parries and thrusts that the enemy mule had trouble following, Colin's opponent fell dead.

There was silence except for the breathing of the twins, the crackle of the dying flames consuming Harper, and the staccato thumbing of Hope's heart.

Brother Hope rose from his position and walked toward Colin. He began to sing his favorite passage loudly into the silence, "I will praise Thee, O Lord, among the people. I will sing—"

"Incoming," Colin interrupted. Brother Hope didn't hear or see anything.

Lizbeth crawled out from under the truck. "They're here!" she shouted. "Lots of them. Over that way," she shouted, pointing her rifle into the darkness.

"They're everywhere, actually," Colin said.

Then Hope heard it: growling around him, the pattering of feet from every direction. "Get your back to the truck! Don't let them surround you!" he yelled at her, racing for the safety of the trucks.

The mules reached Lizbeth and the trucks in seconds, but three devil-spawn rushed out of the night, grabbing at him, before Brother Hope could get there. Lizbeth reacted with a quick shot that dropped one of the spawn. The twins darted forward. With a swing each, they lopped off the heads of the two spawn, spraying blood sizzling onto both mules and the kirkman.

Freed, Brother Hope resumed his rush to safety—and saw devil-spawn swarming toward the truck. Spawn were also crawling *under* the truck. In an instant, the creatures were all around Lizbeth. Before Hope could react, Lizbeth dropped her rifle, yanking out the hatchet that hung from a loop on her leg. The creatures rushed her, claws slashing, cutting through her clothing to her flesh. She hacked at them, but they crushed her beneath them, pushing her to the ground. The axe fell from her hand.

Brother Hope fired, killed one, but there were too many, too close to Lizbeth.

Davey was on Lizbeth's attackers in a flash, cutting through them in a near-frenzy.

Colin joined Brother Hope. "Put your back to mine, master, and follow me toward them," he said, gesturing toward Davey and Lizbeth with his sword. "I'll take their attacks and protect you. If you have a handgun, use it."

"Yes . . . yes." Brother Hope gulped, looking at the growing numbers of spawn on all sides. "Thy mercy is great unto the heavens," he began praying.

Colin started forward with his sword swinging. Brother Hope could hear the creatures clawing at the mule's bare torso, but it didn't seem to slow the big man. Keeping up with the mule while facing backward wasn't easy. Hope held onto Colin's belt with a hand behind him, and the mule pulled him along. The jostling movement didn't help Brother Hope's aim, but when one spawn got past Colin, Hope fired three shots and it dropped. One of how many? Were there more than fifty? And had the things surrounded the town hall, too? What was happening to his flock?

Two spawn grabbed Brother Hope by his clothing, and started pulling him away from Colin. He tried to hold onto the mule's belt, but his grasp slipped, and then he was down, beneath the slobbering creatures. They were biting him. Clawing him. Blood flowed from numerous cuts.

Colin twisted around, and with a growl, he jumped to defend Brother Hope, his blade flashing through the creatures. Behind him, several others leapt onto the mule's back. Their weight didn't knock Colin down, but they dug their claws deep into his flesh and their serrated teeth into his neck. He grabbed one from over his shoulder and flung it away like a rag doll, but the others were inaccessible.

"Hold still," Brother Hope yelled over the din of battle. Hope staggered up and shot the spawn, one after the other, at close range, careful to angle the shots away from the mule.

More rushed in. A quick glance showed a blood-covered Davey fighting above Lizbeth's unmoving body. His blade was flying furiously, but it was slowing and he was about to be swarmed.

A grenade exploded behind the swarm. Then another. Fire erupted from the explosion sites. The high-pitched squeals of burning devil-spawn filled the air.

Who had come to their aid, Brother Hope wondered. "God bless you, whoever you are!" he exclaimed. Though wounded and tired, he found new reserves of energy to keep up the fight, firing round after round from behind the protection of the twin mules.

Trapped between two sets of attackers, some of the leaderless spawn continued to fight Davey, Colin, and Brother Hope. Others rushed toward the newcomers, only to be mown down by concentrated firepower. Some dragged away the bodies of the dead Harper and his men and retreated into the night.

Slowly the two forces worked their way toward each other. Eventually Brother Hope could make out the new fighters in the moonlight: half of the armed defenders of Trinity, led by Grady standing tall above the swarm, swinging his axe with great strength and even greater courage. The sight bolstered the kirkman, and he sang out praise to the Most High with verve.

By the grace of God, they would survive this day.

It was hours before the last of the devil-spawn was killed or chased away, the last of the dead creatures burned in a pyre at the far end of town.

The remainder of the night was spent healing wounds and sending up prayers to the Lord. Miraculously, not a single Trinity citizen had died in that night's assaults, but many were wounded and Lizbeth was barely alive. She'd lost a lot of blood, her pulse was thready, and she was showing the signs of spawn virus infection.

Brother Hope wished he could help with her care, but he was trying to sit still while his own wounds were treated. Sitting next to him in the town hall was Grady, still looking heroic despite—or maybe because of—the bandages covering easily a quarter of his body.

"What made you come out?" Hope asked him. "You were supposed to stay in the hall and look after everyone."

"'Everyone' includes you too, you know," Grady replied.

At dawn, Brother Hope sought out the twin mules. "I prayed on it," he said, clapping Davey on the shoulder, "and I think you're right about seeking out the help of those who sent you. Although you say your people don't serve the Light, you *are* fighting the Darkness. My people should be safe with yours, and they have skills that can probably help your community. Let's get everyone to safety, and then we'll see about coming back to take care of the hellhole and the unleashed Power." He paused, dropped his voice. "My friends and I failed to prevent the Darkness being released. With your help, and the help of others, perhaps we can do something to defeat the blight there."

"Fighting is absolutely what we do best, ma . . . Brother Hope." Davey said, smiling.

"Yeah," Colin agreed.

It took only a few hours of preparation before the group loaded themselves onto the trucks: Harper's and the one the twins had arrived in. With Davey and Colin, Grady, Kol, and Brother Hope standing on the running boards to free up space inside, they managed to get all of the townsfolk wedged into the trucks. Hope positioned himself so he could see into the back of the truck, keeping an eye on the bandage-wrapped Lizbeth James.

"Be merciful unto me, O God, be merciful unto me..." Brother Hope prayed as the lead truck out from the fallen town, carrying the heart of Trinity—its people—down the road that would lead them to Jeep . . . to Alaska . . . and to whatever destiny awaited.

Note to the Reader: "Two Mules for Brother Hope" features characters and locations from the *Rogue Mage RPG Game Master's Guide* and free adventure downloads "Supply Run" and "Trying Times in Trinity" (available in print from Bella Rosa Books and downloadable from Misfit Studios or rpgnow.com).

Trading Debts
Early Summer 105 PA / 2117 AD

Faith Hunter

Homer crossed the wood planks into the dark opening of the boxcar. The Friesian went without complaint, unconcerned by the hollow sound of his hooves on the boards of the ramp. The open sliding doors looked a lot like the entrance to his barn now that its doors were gone, burned off during a spawn attack before the start of spring.

The boxcar was hitched just behind the private railcar I had commandeered to take me southwest to the New Orleans Enclave, to the command performance I could no longer disregard. I wouldn't be traveling alone, of course. As the neomage consul-general of the Mineral City Battle Station Consulate, it was assumed I would travel with a retinue, and I wasn't being allowed to flout that expectation. When the train finally pulled out of my home town of the last decade, I would have an entourage consisting of a kirk representative who was also a prophet of the Most High and six champards: a kylen, my ex-husband, a double agent of the Earth Invasion Heretics and the Administration of the ArchSeraph, a child who had the uncanny ability to use a seraphic amulet and who now glowed with seraphic energies, an offspring of a mage-human mating called a mule, and a human who wanted to become my lover and wasn't averse to sharing me. I also traveled with a death mage, and my very own personal protocol officer/scribe/assassin. It was a gathering that seemed destined for chaos and havoc, if not the death of us all.

I followed Homer into the boxcar and inspected the makeshift stalls, each large enough to hold an oversized workhorse, his tack, food and water troughs, and still leave room on one end of the car for hay, feed, and our baggage. Lots and lots of baggage. It was piled from floor to roof, strapped to the walls with heavy cable. Some enterprising person had strung two hammocks in a corner. Smart, considering the size of the beds in the private car. Even thought I was naturally small in stature, I was unhappy at sharing sleeping quarters with six others. Maybe I could confiscate one of the hammocks.

I heard the rumble of hooves again and jumped onto the railing between stalls, getting out of the way as Audric led his Clydesdale, Clyde, into his stall. Blond Clyde and pitch black Homer made an interesting pair, both horses tranquil and undaunted by the accommodations, each standing nearly six feet at the shoulder. They were big, *big* horses, a fitting size for my senior champard, but ridiculously oversized for someone like me. Audric was a giant, a dark-skinned, bald-headed death machine, a master of savage chi and savage blade, and my teacher in the martial arts. And once upon a time, my friend.

As if he didn't see me, he turned once in a circle, inspecting the mobile barn before turning back to the animals. I watched silently as Audric gentled his mount and checked the water supply. Inspected his workhorse's feet. Made sure his tack was secure. Rechecked the water. When Audric had occupied himself as much as possible, and couldn't put off the inevitable any longer, he turned to me, eyes lowered as if in respect.

My heart ached, a familiar pain; it wasn't his deference I wanted, but a return of his friendship, and I feared I had lost that forever by being unable to save the life of his partner, my best friend, Rupert. Audric had remained aloof and cool as the glacier atop the nearby mountains since the death. Though it was summer, and the temperatures reached the seventies at midday, I shivered in his presence, and wrapped my arms around myself.

We both suffered and grieved, but alone. It would have been bearable, perhaps, had we been able to console one another, but between my guilt and Audric's blame, there wasn't room for comfort.

"Mistrend," Audric said, bowing, formally. As if he could sense my rising misery and wished to circumvent my response, he said, "Our mounts will travel well."

I swallowed my hurt. "Better than we will," I said, "crammed in like sardines." I laughed, a forlorn sound, and saw my pain reflected in his eyes. "Audric . . ."

He whirled and faced the opening of the boxcar, his weight balanced on wide-spread feet, his stance the unarmed version of the crab. I caught my breath. A peculiar silence seemed to spread over the world, an encroaching quiet that made the slightest sound brittle and echoing. I swung from the rail to the floor, landing lightly on the straw. The horses at my back moved restlessly, their breath stertorous in the confined space.

I breathed deeply, sending out a mind skim, drawing in the physical and psychic scents carried on the wind. Horses, manure, hay, feed, leather. Audric, soap, sweat, and beer. Tension. Farther off, smoke. Fear. The stink of brimstone, acid, rotten meat. *Spawn*.

Audric instinctively reached for a weapon that wasn't at his side. He had been working all day, using his brawn to carry stone, building a house for humans, to protect the citizens of Mineral City, the people under my care. He'd been working, unaware of the passage of time, and now it was near dusk. There had been no hint of the Dark for two months. He had become lax. As had I. "Damocles," he said. "What weapons you can find. Now."

Without a thought about who was the titular superior, reacting instead of consciously acting, I whirled, erupted into mage speed and burst through the door between train cars. I flew over the segmented wooden bridge that jacketed the coupling between cars and ripped at the door to the private state car, slamming it back on its hinges. Inside, Eli looked up, his head moving human-slow.

I raced to the pile of my luggage and jerked the weapons case from the center of the stack. The baggage began to slide, a sluggish, ponderous response to gravity, unimportant to a mage. I ripped the case open and unstrapped my newest weapon, the sword of Damocles, pulling the blade from its soft sheath. Before it snapped free, my left hand had liberated the kris-knife and slipped it into my belt.

Still moving faster than a human could focus, I scrambled over the falling luggage, spotting Audric's weapons case, a plain, supple, leather bag, long and narrow, menacing in its simplicity. Without a thought I upended the bag. As the pile of luggage hit the floor of the railroad car, I pulled Audric's twin swords free, jumped to the floor, and raced back.

"Thorn?" Eli's question trailed behind me.

In the doorway of the boxcar, I slapped Audric's katanas into his hands and followed him down the ramp to the cracked asphalt road. My heart raced, uneven thumps of adrenaline rush. My breath came fast as I studied the town spread uphill before me. Stone buildings lined Upper and Lower Streets. Humans hurried along them, dressed for summer in thin clothes, unarmed, children at their sides.

The sun was a splinter of light on the horizon, casting long shadows, obscuring faces and identities, not that it mattered who they were, friend or uneasy ally. They were all under my protection, had been since I claimed the town as a battle station against the encroaching Darkness.

I heard the boxcar doors roll closed, and Eli appeared at my side, strapping his flame-thrower on and closing a sat phone. "What we got?"

"Spawn-scent," Audric said. It was a fact that spawn didn't move until full night. Of course, the last few months had convinced us that facts were things to be disproved.

Eli sniffed and shrugged. "You supernats got noses like dogs."

"Wolves," Audric corrected. "We are not domesticated."

"Stop," I said, when Eli showed an inclination to argue, or to defend dogs. The two had been sniping at each other for days. "Have you . . ."

"Called the town fathers and the EIH? Yeah. They're on the way. Ciana is standing at the door to the shop with the amulet to bring up the wards, people are pouring in, and the bell"—over his last word, the sound of a brass warning bell began to clang—"over the new town hall is ringing. We got people watching the hills and warriors heading our way." He slapped the last strap in place and pulled a 12-gauge, double-barreled shotgun from the long holster strapped to his back, breaking it open to check the load. The gun held four rounds, each filled with holy oil, salt, and fléchettes of mage steel. It was his own design, put together with the expertise of my pet assassin. There had been no incursions of the Dark since the big one that destroyed the town; Eli had been eager to try them out.

As if aware that my thoughts were on him, Eli slid a palm around the back of my neck and pulled me to him. I opened my mouth to say "Stop," but his mouth landed on mine in a cold, hard kiss that tasted of human and beer. I felt my knees soften, which was really stupid considering the spawn. But I leaned into him, just for a moment, and wrapped my sword arm around his waist, Damocles pointing to the sky. I kissed him back. His grip on my neck softened, and he eased away a fraction. "Luck," he said against my lips, his amber eyes wicked and laughing.

Eli wasn't dumb. He knew I'd been fighting my response to him for weeks, and he was doing everything in his power to make sure I lost that battle. Releasing me, he cocked his brow at Audric. "Dogs," he said. "Cute little lap dogs."

Audric bristled. And ducked. The near silent whirr of wings was the only warning.

Dragonet. Damocles was out of position, my grip weak. I stepped into Eli, shoving him down, and spun, twisting my body and the battle sword around, up in a spiral. And impacted the scaled legs and body of a Darkness. Ichor flew. Splattered my cheek, burning like acid, as it flew away, not unharmed, but not near death. The blasted beasts had far more than the nine lives of cats.

Eli swatted my backside, a look of approval on his face—of the move that saved his life or of my butt, I wasn't sure.

I whirled the sword, grimly pleased. I tossed the blade up and caught the hilt. Audric rolled his eyes at the theatrical move. The sword, which had hung in the town hall for less than two months, had been gifted back to me by the Elders for use in the town's defense. And as it turned out, I needed a good sword. Though I had thought I would hate the weapon, its perfect balance and the zing of power I felt each time I touched it had grown on me in practice sessions in the last months.

Spawn raced down the street in a swarm. The sound of their chittering and squawking, so much like a bizarre language, rose on the cooling air. They sprinted from alleys and side streets, the swarms meeting like the eddy line of the tide and an inland river, crashing together, merging. There were thousands. Someone started to scream. "Get it off, get it off, get it off me! Noooo—" the scream cut off in mid peal, gurgling, choked as if the screamer's throat had been bitten away. Audric danced up the street and dove into the wave of spawn.

In the distance, I felt my twin lift her head and stare into the distance, aware of my emotions, my fear racing through her. *"Thorn?"* she thought at me.

"Dark!" I thought back. Rose reached for an amulet. I saw/felt her hands close on it. A spawn lunged in, clawed hands razor sharp. My mind engaged, I failed to respond. The shotgun boomed beside me, opening a wide swath in the attacking Darkness. Leaving a mist of black blood hanging in the air, body parts of the long-legged beasts littering the ground.

"Hot tamales, it works," Eli said, clearly stunned. The new ammo was a success.

I shook off Rose's reactions and preparations, and whirled the long-sword. The battle blade took the arms off of a shocked spawn, standing nearly inert with astonishment.

Eli screamed, "Yeeeeehaaaaw!" and depressed the trigger of his other weapon, shooting burning holy oil at the Dark charging in to fill the void. The flame was a long, horizontal stream of fire, rising in the falling night. Spawn sizzled, crackled, and screamed. "Feel the burn, baby!" Eli shouted. To me, he reminded over the sound of battle, "Herd them toward the old church."

I nodded and lunged into the swarm behind Eli who fired the shotgun again, clearing a path in the oncoming Darkness. My heart settled, beating hard and steady, my battle sword and kris flashing with the confidence of two months of intensive training.

I centered myself between my champards. Nine feet from either man, I whirled the swords, hacking off spawn body parts, leaving the mutilated beasts in the street. We no longer dispatched spawn left alive behind on the battlefield. Once upon a time, spawn would crawl away, heal, and come back to fight another night. But there was little game on the mountains; all the deer, elk, rabbits, turkeys, and moose had been devoured by the Dark. Now the spawn were hungry, starving, and ate their brethren when injured. Around us, spawn began to pull away the wounded and feast.

I cut into a spawn eating its kin, Damocles' edge slicing true and clean, so sharp it was like cutting warm butter. The mole-like body of the minor Darkness halved and toppled. I was cutting two more before it reached the broken pavement of the street. I had already blown through my energy reserves, and drew on my single remaining prime amulet to power the mage speed, knowing I couldn't keep up the pace for long without it. And I didn't want to drain power from the new power sink up the hill. I needed that for other things.

Ichor and spittle burned through my street clothes and I again drew on my amulets to provide protection and to speed healing. The night air was chill, even in the middle of summer, and goose bumps rose on my burned and exposed flesh. None of us were dressed for battle, and according to the U.S. military, spawn were developing more toxic blood and body fluids. If the burns on my arms and face were any indication, the military was right.

The roar of battle pounded against my ears as the minutes turned into the first hour of battle, the exhausted men to either side grunting with hoarse breath. I smelled their burned flesh and the pheromones of pain. They were in trouble. But there wasn't time to pull amulets for them; the spawn were closing in, ready to overwhelm us by sheer numbers.

I opened mage sight as full night fell, and the carnage emerged in bursts of mustard yellow and dazzling motes of black light for the Dark and dull blue, pink, red, and gold for the humans. Audric and I were the sole glowing mage attributes in the battlefield. Cheran, the assassin, was . . . elsewhere. As usual in battle. And Rose . . . was busy. Preparing.

EIH warriors and several orthodox kirk acolytes appeared up the street. They battled side-by-side, the acolytes praying from Deuteronomy 7:23 with each death-stroke. "The Lord, thy god, shall deliver them unto thee,

and shall destroy them with a mighty destruction, until they be destroyed."
The heretics shouted the Scripture of their choice, one that repeated the
ancient words of an enemy of the Most High, Exodus15:9, "I will draw my
sword, my hand shall destroy them!" The phrases rang out, pealing with
power.

The Dark fell before the words of both parties, the might of Scripture
and prayer increasing the efficacy of each sword stroke and shotgun blast,
no matter what the original import of the words had been. But there were
thousands of spawn and at least six dragonets. I stumbled over a body and
glanced down to see a human and three spawn. The beasts were eating. The
man was still twitching. I redirected the downward motion of the sword
and killed two of the beasts. My kris took the third one through the eye.

Their deaths created a moment of calm around me. Wiping the dripping
kris clean on a patch of grass and sliding it into my belt, I pulled *Healing*
amulets, ones made by Cheran and me working together in uneasy alliance,
each amulet imbued with a sliver of cherub/wheel amethyst and a drop of
the assassin's gold.

"Eli!" I shouted. When he glanced my way, his smile wild with battle
glee, I ducked in under his arm and dropped an amulet into the open neck
of his shirt. He sighed, the amulet easing his agony. The scent of flame-
thrower—eucalyptus and rosemary—and roasted spawn were harsh about
him as he curved an arm about me, pulling me tight against him. Eyes
sparkling wickedly despite the battle, he said, "You're a ministering angel.
Wanna play angels and mages, and make hot monkey sex?"

I rolled my eyes, rotated out of his embrace, and shouted Audric's name,
repeating the process. My senior champard offered no thanks. Treating his
wounds was part of my job as mistrend—I knew that—but appreciation
would have been nice.

Taking my irritation out on an unlucky dragonet, I beheaded it, sliced its
legs and wings off and cut it in four near-equal parts. It wriggled and died,
the division too much for even its regenerative powers. I spotted a second
group of soldiers entering opposite from the kirk elders, moving uphill
from Crystal Street. We were beginning to get into position.

The battle lasted almost two hours before all the combatants were in
proper position for the little surprise Eli, Audric, and Cheran had cooked
up between them. Ten handpicked fighters had converged at the remains of
the old Central Baptist Church, hacking and shooting through the melee.
Other warriors had herded spawn onto Upper Street.

The few walls of the old church that still stood had been reinforced with
timbers, and now concealed two, handmade, muzzle-loading mortars. Their
ammo, like Eli's personal ammunition, was filled with salt and mage steel
fléchettes—fléchettes Cheran had worked with his magery. Into the mix
had gone well-used earth salt charged from previous workings with leftover
creation energies. The blend had then been prepped with an incantation
Cheran had dreamed up in his murderous little mind. We hoped the combination would provide a nasty surprise for the spawn.

When we gained the walls, five men slung weapons across their backs while everyone else protected them with covering fire and flashing blades. They pulled concealing branches and tarps from the mortars. The rest of us formed a semicircle at the opening in the stone, holding off the invading beasts, killing just enough to make it look like the tide of battle was against us. Letting them come to us, bunch into us, ready to overtake and overrun us. If the weapons didn't work, it would be a lethal plan—lethal for us.

Clearing a path with the swan wing, I looked down, assuring myself that my part of the plan was still in place—the ring of stones half buried in the earth. A spawn took a bite out of my left arm, ripping muscle, scoring bone. Lightning pain lanced up my arm. I screamed. I'd been a fool. The plan was to make them *think* they were winning, not to *actually* let them win. I impaled the beast and shook it off. My blood pulsed into the night. It had hit an artery.

With stiffening fingers, I slid the kris into my belt and activated a new amulet I had made. The blood stopped spurting as a sensation like a tourniquet tightened around my arm above the wound. Fighting with only my longsword, I scrutinized the battle and met Audric's eyes. He nodded once, agreeing with me. "Back," I shouted as if I was calling for retreat. "Behind me!"

The fighters drew closer together and stepped to the rear. Spawn surged in. When we were all behind the stones, I lifted my head. "Now, Audric," I shouted, "Now!" I activated the small relay on my necklace. A narrow *Shield* rose from the stones in the ground—a thin band of energy ten feet high and fifty feet long, curving around us. Locking us in with a few dozen spawn, locking the rest out.

"Down!" Audric shouted, his voice bellowing over the screams of battle.

We dropped to the earth, blades cutting legs from the spawn nearest. As they fell, we stabbed and cut, killing and maiming. I held my injured arm curled into my chest, slashing with Damocles.

Above us, the big-ass guns boomed. The earth shook. The shells whistled downward and exploded—thankfully on the other side of the barrier. A wide swath of bloody ground opened up before the energy shield. Shredded flesh arced over the barrier, mostly falling behind us, although a burning mist of spawn blood filled the air. Slowly, glancing back to make certain there were no more shots ready, shaking my head to clear my concussion-damaged ears, I rose to my knees.

It was full dark, but I had been fighting with mage sight, and the carnage of dissipating energies was . . . startling. Drenching the ground, clouding the air, was black spawn blood. But the spawn were . . . gone.

The beasts at the far edges of the battle stood frozen. As one, they swiveled on four legs and took off for the Trine, the mountain north of town where they lived and bred. "Down," Audric shouted again. "Fire!"

We dropped and the guns boomed. I covered my ears against the concussion, though I could tell it was too late to save my eardrums. I had made a fairly sophisticated amulet to regain hearing after battles, and I thumbed it on as the echo of the mortars died. We raised our heads.

Eli was propped on his elbows beside me. "Holy smoking angel crap," he whispered, his breath billowing in a cloud. Elder Jasper ignored the mild profanity and murmured a prayer of thanksgiving to the Most High. The rest of us just stared.

The mortars had medium to high trajectories, and the six-inch shells had risen over the heads of the attacking spawn and descended sharply to explode on impact, scattering steel and salt in a wide arc, far enough out to not harm us so long as the horde between us was dense and so long as the *Shield* held. The incantation within each then sent a shockwave out, spreading into the mass of spawn along the street and down the alleys and into the air above. Upper Street was clean of living spawn.

Looking up, I saw my twin standing atop the rebuilt three-story town hall and library, beside the warning bell. Rose glimmered and burned with cruel might, absorbing the death energies of both spawn and humans, and directing them into the forest a mile south of town, across the Toe River, storing the power in the living trees. Her mage attributes glinted like green fire and sparkling garnets. Though it was too far for us to hear one another, I felt her attention on me, her mind touching the edges of mine. *The* Shield *is mighty. The town will be safe when we are gone*, she thought at me.

I worked to hide my fear of her, locking down on the dread. *Good*, I thought back, knowing it wasn't good, not completely. Energies stolen from the dying never are. But she was right, in that it would have been impossible to collect and store enough energy to shield the entire town any other way. For that it was good. For that the sacrifice of humans was . . . worthwhile. The word was bitter in my thoughts.

You're injured, she thought at me. Instantly heat and electricity and a burning like the sting of fire ants buzzed over my skin. I gasped and looked down. The bleeding from the spawn bite clotted over. The edges of the wound began to close together. The pain dissipated. I felt Rose smile with a cold satisfaction. Before I could disengage from her, spawn raced in from the night. And leapt over the *Shield*. So much for safety.

Eli, ever at my side, killed a dozen with his shotgun and pulled me to my feet. With a yelp, he jumped back, eyes wide. He looked at his hands, only recently bleeding from a dozen small cuts, and wiped at a deep laceration. The bleeding had stopped. His mouth twisted into a frown. "Rose?" he asked. I nodded, still catching my breath. He turned away so that I wouldn't see his disgust, but I felt it.

"Down," Audric shouted again. We fell. The mortars boomed. Advancing spawn vanished in a cloud of acidic ichor. Two dragonets fell, mangled and dead. We jumped up and made quick work of the spawn on our side of the barrier.

I closed the *Shield* and the fighters around me released the brakes on the portable weapons and pulled them down the street on protesting wheels, their squeal oddly similar to the screech of spawn. We followed, protecting their rear. It was over, except for the mopping up and rooting out of any hidden pockets of spawn. Now that the Darkness knew about the guns, we couldn't leave them out in the open. The element of surprise was gone. They'd be stored in the old firehouse, with the even older fire engine.

The townsfolk hunted Darkness and fought through the night, taking out several thousand remaining spawn and the last of the dragonets. When dawn came, pale golden light arching over green oak, maple, chestnut, and the darker greens of conifer, the last of the spawn slinked away, up the mountain. We had won. The big guns had done their job, turning the tide of battle for us, and had achieved a place of glory in the town's arsenal. And a power sink big enough to power a *Shield* around the town for six months had been created. The town would hopefully be safe until I returned.

The summer air was beginning to warm. Shadows stretched along the broken asphalt. Warriors gathered close, a mismatched group, all of us wounded, all of us bleeding. Half-eaten bodies, human and spawn, were piled in small mounds around us. Blood soaked the ancient asphalt. I counted over twenty human dead just on Upper Street.

Audric, holding the two katanas he had fought with, stood tall in the dawn, like a black prince, his bald head catching the early rays of the sun. His dark flesh was slicked with sweat and blood, and blistered with second-degree burns. "Wounded?" he asked, succinct as always.

"All of us. Maybe twelve badly," a voice called from a side street. Elder Jasper strode uphill, his brown kirk robes fluttering in tatters as he rounded the corner of the town hall. "They're being taken to the consulate for . . ." a shadow covered him. Fell upon him. Faster than I could react. It crushed Jasper to the earth. I had a glimpse of a dragonet, scaled and horned, multiple wings fluttering, carapace barbed, with razor sharp edges.

At full speed, Audric and I raced in, me to the left, out of the way of his longer reach. Before we made five steps, the dragonet wrapped its sinuous body around Jasper and hissed.

It opened its mouth. Bit down. The crunch of bone and Jasper's screams echoed. The kirk elder's bloody hand rolled into the street. Blood spurted from the stump. Jasper's scream gurgled away with shock.

The beast took the elder's head in his mouth, speared us with four of its eyes. A clear threat. Audric and I froze. Waiting.

A glimmer of mage energies slipped by at the edge of my sight. *Cheran.* Watching. Doing nothing. As always.

I reversed my kris to a backhanded grip, and dropped Damocles to the street. "Stairway to heaven," I said sotto voce, gathering my energies to me. Audric grunted once and dropped one knee toward the ground. With a finger, I activated a new amulet and raced at my champard. His knee touched the street. I toed to his thigh, his braced arm, and raced to his shoulder.

As my body stretched from a crouch, Audric pressed an identical amulet and launched himself upward. We both appeared no more than mist, invisible. I hoped. Using the momentum of Audric's leap, I sprang across the intervening space and landed on the dragonet.

I caught the beast's carapace at the juncture of neck and head in one fist. Wrenched it back with force. And thrust down with the kris, into the joint. The blade lodged tight. Audric's katana, hidden in the misted energies, sang through the air.

The beast writhed, ducked, and whipped out its tail. The barbed stinger pierced the mist. Audric exhaled, pain in the single, soft note he breathed. "Thorn?"

The stinger reappeared from the mist and thrashed the air. It turned toward me, Audric's blood coating the deadly tip. I bent my elbow down, laying all my weight against the hilt, forcing the kris up at a sharp angle, and jerked the blade to the side.

Blood gushed. I ripped the kris to the other side and pulled the opposite way with my hand in the neck joint. The dragonet's head creaked and cracked. It came free in my hand with a torrent of black blood. The gore flooded over my hand and I hissed with pain.

Battering the street with legs and tail in its death throes, it slid from Jasper. I jumped free, deactivating my amulet with a touch. The warriors rushed in, hacking the Darkness. Rose knelt beside the kirk elder, the death energies she had absorbed during the battle making her glimmer garnet and green. I clamped down on the mental shields I had learned to use, not wanting her in my mind. I drew on a *Healing* amulet, hiding my blistered hand from my sister's sight.

Jasper was white-faced, his blood pooled on the street. It still dribbled weakly from his arm, the bones white and jagged. Rose took the grayed hand and the graying stump and aligned them. She closed her eyes. Power gathered in her hands, obscuring the hand and stump. Eli looked at me, seeing my reaction to her use of death energies.

I turned away, to the mist that veiled Audric. "Deactivate the amulet," I said. When the mist persisted, I said, my tone sharp as a blade, "By your vow to me, deactivate the amulet, Audric."

The mist transformed, revealing my senior champard. Covered in blood. I dropped beside Audric.

"Decided to make an appearance, did you, assassin?" Eli asked as he interposed himself between the mage who'd appeared out of nowhere and my exposed back. "Now that the danger is past?" Cheran didn't answer. We all knew him to be a coward.

Vaguely aware that the warriors who had protected the town were gathering around us, I slid my kris into the opening of Audric's shirt and slit it open. Buttons popped into the air, revealing Audric's chest. I couldn't help my gasp. Cheran eased himself to the street beside me and stared at the wound. The center was a puncture almost as large as my fist, looking much like a deep spear wound, bleeding steadily. Beyond the hole was a ridged ring, purpling. From the bleeding center, infection crawled, through the ring into the flesh beyond. A fast-acting toxin had been injected.

Cheran shook his head and rocked back to sit on his heels. "He's a goner," he said without thinking.

Eli kicked him, knocking the mage flat to the street. Cheran's hand banged against the old road and a concealed knife bounced free. "Help him, mage," Eli said, standing over the assassin. "Or you'll wish you had."

Cheran laughed, the tone mocking. A hand lifted toward his amulet necklace. There was an odd shift, as if time had undergone a sideways transition. Suddenly, Cheran was surrounded by EIH warriors, weapons unholstered, all pointing at Cheran's head.

"I said, help him," Eli growled. "Or I'll kill you where you lie." My champard's amber eyes were no longer laughing, but were dark with purpose. Hard with intent. A dozen handguns cocked. At least two shotguns racked shut.

"Can you help him?" I asked the assassin.

Options flickered through his eyes for a long moment. I ground my teeth, resisting the impulse to skewer him. Finally, Cheran said, "Can you not take it from my thoughts?" When I didn't answer, he shrugged and said, "Maybe I can help. Maybe not."

"Try or die, mage," Eli said.

Cheran sighed, sounding longsuffering, unafraid, almost bored. He rolled to his backside, legs stretched out in front of him, crossed at the ankles, his weight on his elbows slightly behind him. He looked relaxed, not as if he was looking down the barrels of the town's best fighters.

"I'll need an amulet from my necklace." He glanced down at his shirt buttoned over the necklace, and looked up at Eli. With a lazy half-smile, he said, "The amulet shaped like a leaf, looks like steel. You want to . . . draw it out for me?" The words were a challenge, the tone something more so. And there was something almost sexual about the way he sprawled. Teasing. While Audric died.

Rage blasted through me, a volcano of fury.

I heard the growling before I realized I had moved. I was lying across Cheran's body, my kris at his throat. The blade, still coated with the stinging blood of the dragonet, pierced his flesh. A thin, scarlet trickle ran down his neck. Cheran's eyes widened. He hadn't seen me move. Something told me my speed had been unusual, even for a mage, but I was too angry to care. I leaned in, so close my breath merged with his, my words emerging between clenched teeth. "If you can help him and you don't, I swear before the High Host I'll flay the flesh from your body one slow strip at a time and feed it to the town's dogs." My jaw ached with the words, my teeth grinding with purpose and the vow. I closed the remaining distance, so close our lips nearly touched. I whispered, "And then I'll cart your bleeding body up the mountain. And leave it at the mouth of the hellhole."

Cheran swallowed, the sound audible in the street. But his eyes were over my shoulder.

I shifted a bit and looked back. Rose stood behind me in a gap made by humans who cringed away from her. She was smiling gently, glowing with power. A prism of death energies scintillated about her, dangerous, deadly, promising much. Moving like the dancer she was, my twin knelt beside me.

"I healed your prophet," she said to me. "I did that for you. This one is much stronger." She leaned close, breathing in, tasting the energies of his life-force. "I can take his life and give it to Audric. I can see how it could be done." She put a trembling hand on Cheran's chest and licked her lips, trying to control her eagerness. "Let me do it," she whispered, the plea a breath of desire.

"I can heal him," Cheran said, breathless, his eyes wide brown pools. "Get her off me."

I remembered the cry of the human at the start of battle. *Get it off me!*

"Rose."

My sister's face twisted with regret. She eased back, moving slowly, sliding her hand along Cheran's body in a sensuous glide. "Someday, mage. Someday she won't protect you. And I'll take your life for my own."

Cheran rolled across the street and to the far side of Audric, seeking safety in distance. Rose laughed, the sound sending chills up my spine. Cheran ripped two amulets off his necklace. He dropped them into Audric's wound, saying, "Silver, gold, life and death; lead, tin, steel and nickel rare. Draw the poisons, heal the mule. Give him life for future use."

I didn't like the words "future use." It sounded almost as if Audric would be beholden. And that was not going to happen.

Cheran put his hands on the puncture, one atop the other. He pushed. Audric gasped and gagged, his body bucking with pain. Pus and foulness spat up from the wound. Cheran's hands began to darken. The assassin mage looked at me, fierce and vicious. "You owe me, mage," he spat. "You owe me for this pain." He doubled over and vomited onto the road.

"They both will live," my twin said, mournful. Rose drifted down the street, her thin dress ruffled by the chill wind, her bare arms and legs shimmering with might, warm with the lives of the recently dead. I shuddered, watching her.

Audric took my hand in his, tugging once to attract my attention. His palm was clammy but his grip was sure. Almost afraid, I looked into his eyes. "You are a fierce mistrend," he murmured, the words a compliment.

"I'm a better friend," I said.

His eyes softened. A ghost of a smile curled his full lips. "Yes. You are. You are indeed."

Not trusting myself to say the right words, afraid I'd screw it up by blurting out something stupid, I just squeezed his hand, my face tight. I gave him another of the *Healing* amulets that seemed to block pain so well. As an afterthought, I gave one to Cheran too. He clutched it tightly and his breathing smoothed.

"Don't think this makes us even. You owe me."

I shrugged. "Owing a coward is a small price to pay for Audric's life."

Ignoring the expression that crossed his face, I stood, gathered up my dropped weapons, and walked up the street. I had a train to catch. A train to New Orleans.

Our Lady of the Stones
Early Summer 105 PA / 2117 AD

Spike Y Jones

"And then Hombre Verde comes down from the sky . . ."

"No, crawls out of the ground."

". . . crawls out of the ground and hits him. *Bam!*"

"But Capitán América is stronger with his shield and stops Hombre Verde. And then he jumps on Hombre Verde. *Pow!*"

Maria López liked it when José came over to play with Enrique. Maria couldn't afford to buy a lot of toys for Riqi—there was just enough money for necessities and sometimes not even that—and José always brought some of his own toys with him.

Sighing, she turned back to preparing supper, the television playing quietly on the end of the counter.

"Araña Negro and Araña Rojo fly at el Capitán and knock him down."

Maria heard the clunk of plastic against plastic.

"And Sword Man chases them away before they can suck out his blood and eat his body."

She was bothered by the violence of their play, but the world was a violent place—especially now. The *noticias* weren't showing the video from Mineral City over and over again like they had been, but it still showed up at least once a day in some context.

Maria said a quick Hail Mary.

"And then a bunch of soldiers drive up and shoot Sword Man."

"So the Dragon flies up and kills the soldiers," José said, knocking over the soldiers before Enrique could even finish setting them up. "And then he kills the Spiders. And then he knocks over the house."

There was a scrape as a chair was shoved across the floor.

"But more soldiers—"

"The Dragon breathes at them and they die. And then the Dragon breaks the store. And then he breaks another house. And then he stamps on a truck. And then—"

"That's no fair. He can't break *everything*."

"Sure he can. He's the Dragon. Nobody can stop the Dragon."

The plastic-on-plastic noises continued, and Maria heard Riqi scramble around the room and then plop back down on the carpet.

"The Lady in Black steps out of the kirk and pulls out her sword and tells the Dragon to go away."

"The Dragon flies over the Lady in Black and stomps on the kirk," José replied.

"No he doesn't! The Lady is too fast for the Dragon, and she stabs him, and the Dragon falls down."

The Lady in Black? Maria didn't remember José having any girl dolls. Maybe it was something new.

"Stop cheating, Riqi!"

"And then she stabs him again and the Dragon dies."

"That's not what Padre Pedro said in kirk. He said that nothing was strong enough to beat the Dragon except the Most High and the seraphs!"

"Uh-uh. The Lady in Black is stronger than dragons. I saw it on TV."

"It's still cheating!"

"No it isn't!"

"Yes it is, Riqi. You cheated and you beat my best guy and I'm not playing with you anymore!"

"I didn't cheat, José. I saw it! And I don't want to play with you and your crummy toys!"

"They're not crummy!"

Maria emerged from the kitchen, wiping her hands on her apron, just as the boys started wrestling on the floor, scattering the assortment of Pre-Ap plastic *acciones* and a stuffed cloth dragon.

"Enrique Felipe López Rodriguez and José Antonio Gómez Gonzales, stop that this instant!"

The boys froze at the sound of her voice, then quickly separated. Good —she couldn't see any bruises or scrapes.

"What is this all about? Why are you destroying my house?"

José stood silently and wiped his nose with his sleeve. Enrique wouldn't raise his head to meet her glare.

"Riqi, what did you do?"

The boy slowly pointed at one of the figurines on the carpet, a black-clad woman with long, red hair and a silver sword.

Maria stepped over the mess to gently, reverently pick up the statuette she'd bought only a few days before.

"This is not a toy. Do you understand? It's not for play. This is Mami's *imagen*—serious business. It's time for you to go home now, José. And I'll deal with you later, Enrique."

Maria put the *estatua* back in its proper place in the shrine on the other side of the room, next to Our Lady of Guadalupe and the *Sagrado Corazon*. She'd offer a full rosary to the new Lady later this evening, but for now she lit a votive candle to ask for forgiveness after Riqi's rough handling.

Wings on Site
Summer 105 PA / 2117 AD

Faith Hunter

Vonn tossed the stub of his cigar into the creek, knowing that the kirk elder would smell the tobacco, and also knowing that the man could do nothing about his infringement. No one had seen him smoking. Scent and smoke weren't proof of guilt, and unless Scoggins wanted to search him for contraband, the elder had no case. Most elders had loosened the chains on personal habits for smoking and drinking, but Elder Scoggins was old school—hardline and unyielding. A real pain in the ass until you needed him on the battlefield. You get a soldier wounded or in trouble, and Elder Scoggins would dash in where seraphs feared to fly, and lay down cover fire until the soldier was safe. The men might hate his Scripture-spouting guts, but they respected Scoggins in every way that counted.

"Evening, Master Sergeant," Scoggins said.

Vonn grunted a hello and knelt to fill his canteen from the snowmelt stream. Icy water chilled his fingers, making them stiff when he tried to put the cap back on. Without asking, he lifted his hand and Scoggins placed his own canteen into Vonn's outstretched hand. Vonn filled it too, capped it, and handed it back before standing.

With a smile in his voice, Scoggins said, "You're a good man, Master Sergeant—despite your personal habits and lack of piety."

Vonn grunted again and shifted his rucksack to his other shoulder. "It'll be night soon. The kylen will be back with intel. Let's get the men into a circle and a fire started."

"Of course," Scoggins murmured. Vonn really hated that smug amusement.

Scoggins followed him up the steep hill to the clearing his patrol had staked out. Claire was talking to a group of men, standing on a fallen tree to bring her face nearly level with theirs. The tiny priestess had a beauty that was so perfect it was nearly unearthly, and—according to Scoggins—evil in its sensuality and seductive charms. If he went only by his men's reactions, Vonn might agree. The soldiers were focused on her like flies on honey. But Vonn didn't think the priestess was evil; he didn't think any neomage was inherently evil. In the Last War, they fought on the side of Light until the remnants of the Army tried to blow them up. He'd never been completely clear on who'd been on the side of evil in that little skirmish.

Claire looked over her shoulder at him and smiled, her cupid mouth curling up like a bow. Vonn lifted a finger in acknowledgment and fought down his own smile. At his side, Scoggins murmured something about not suffering a witch to live, and if they hadn't needed Claire's magics so much right now, Vonn might have worried about Scoggins murdering her in her sleep. But they did need her to find an entire platoon, and Scoggins would never kill anything or anyone who might save a soldier in danger.

The forty men they were hunting had been on routine patrol when they'd just up and vanished. Their commanding officer radioed in at dusk, seventy-two hours ago, and then . . . nothing. Nada. They'd had an assey with them, Sam Wong, and even he hadn't called in. All assey's carried satellite phones, so there was no way the men were out of range. If Investigator Wong wasn't checking in, then something bad had happened.

Vonn's men were standing on the last known coordinates of the missing platoon, and if Claire had her way, they'd camp tonight right here. Claire had taken a reading—whatever the saints that was—and said the lost men had slept comfortably here before moving on in the morning. She insisted that the platoon had decamped at dawn and headed east. The tracks suggested that she was right, and that his men would be safe here tonight.

Vonn knew that the priestess had layered reasons—political and personal—for agreeing to join them on this hunt, but he was pretty sure the biggest reason of them all was the presence of the kylen, though Eldratos never so much as looked at her. Claire touched her seraph stone and looked to the sky, waiting on the arrival of the kylen like a drunk waited on his next bottle. She was seraph-struck, for sure. But a lusting mage wasn't his problem. His men were.

"MacEachern," he said, "take two and gather deadfall wood. Myers, get a fire started. What the saints is wrong with you people? A pretty face turn your mind from duty? Who's got KP tonight? Simko killed a warren of rabbits with her sharpshooting, and I expect rabbit stew tonight, even if it is flavored with dehydrated-not-much-a-nothin'. Sundown's comin'. Get your as—backsides in gear."

The soldiers dispersed and Vonn was pleased to see that they didn't dawdle. He continued to cajole his platoon. "We got ten bunnies for the stewpot and I'm not of a mind to bite down on a bone. We got dehydrated carrots and dehydrated peas and dehydrated onions and let's hear it for the maker of the dinner!"

"Hail to the dehydrator!" his unit answered, laughing.

Scoggins had pursed his prissy lips the first time he heard the joke, but this time he just smiled. Maybe the elder was coming along after all. Claire's tinkling laugh joined the troops' and more than one man turned her way. Not good. No one, not a kirk elder, not an assey, not even an Enclave witchy woman, should be able to distract his patrol. But before he could come up with a response to the dangerous reaction, he heard the sound of air whistling through feathers overhead.

"Atten-hut! Wings on site!"

The kylen guiding Vonn's patrol landed with a sweep of flight feathers and folded his wings. Funny thing that. Somehow none of the troops had ever seen the kylen fly. They'd seen him *land* plenty of times, but never take off. There was a rumor of a video showing kylen soaring alongside seraphs in a mopping-up operation years after the Last War, but Vonn had never seen it or met anyone who had. He almost doubted that they could fly; the kylen's eighteen-foot wingspan was impressive, but a lot smaller than a seraph's. Still, he had to be coming down from somewhere. And the intel he'd gathered from above had been spot on so far.

This was the first time a first-gen kylen had been seen outside of a Realm of Light for generations. And Eldratos had military training, even boasting the rank of lieutenant, bestowed on him by some grateful, but now long-dead, general. Vonn wasn't sure why the High Host was interested in this one missing platoon, but whatever the reason was, he welcomed it. He had friends among the missing men. They all did.

And whatever minor discipline problems she might cause, Vonn was just glad to have the priestess along, too. She and Eldratos had magic, and that might be the only thing that allowed them to rescue the missing patrol. Well, that and the brand-spanking-new RPGs they carried. These models launched grenades packed with some newfangled explosives—something holy, built to destroy Darkness in any of its forms.

"As you were, men," Eldratos said, his voice so musical it was like bells ringing.

The men weren't what Vonn was worried about. The master sergeant saw the neomage raise a hand and grip her seraph stone so hard that her knuckles blanched white. Even with the stone to damp her mage heat, it was hard for the priestess to be in the presence of the kylen. Eldratos was beautiful in ways that made even the gorgeous Claire pale by comparison. He was nearly seven feet tall, with ebony skin, tightly curled black hair, and vivid blue eyes. His wings were the pure white of a swan. Vonn was totally straight, but he could see how the kylen's face and form would tempt any other-than-straight man. The thought made him uncomfortable, and Vonn turned so the kylen was to his side.

"Did you find the trail?"

"I did. But I also found the train." At Vonn's blank look, Eldratos touched his own seraph stone for a moment before dropping his hand. There was something almost tentative about the gesture. "A passenger and freight train is over the mountain, the tracks in front of it buried beneath tons of ice and rock. The Omega is with it; Darkness created the avalanche to stop her."

"Omega?"

"She who you call the consul-general. The battle mage."

"Holy sh—" Vonn cut short the expletive. "You mean Thorn St. Croix?" Eldratos nodded once. Vonn had heard of her. Every military man in the nation had heard of her, and had seen her fight Darkness on SNN. She was an amazing warrior.

Things fell into place in Vonn's mind. If Thorn St. Croix was here, and the Darkness was trying to stop her From getting somewhere, then maybe that Darkness had something to do with his missing platoon. Vonn pulled out a much-folded paper map. He knelt and spread it open on his knee. "We're here," he pointed," as near as I can say. We got railroad tracks here and here. Which one is St. Croix on?"

Eldratos pointed at a section of track that wound in a gorge between two nearly vertical mountain cliffs. He slid his finger over to the other side of one of the mountains. "And here are the tracks of your missing men, moving in this direction. The Omega prepares for battle. She does not know it, but she moves to fight the Darkness."

"Darkness?"

Eldratos nodded slowly. "I believe the Darkness took your soldiers."

"That's what I was afraid you'd say."

As shadows lengthened, Vonn marked the reference points and tried to figure out where the missing platoon had been going. As he worked, his troops secured the perimeter, set up camp, and fixed a meal. Securing the perimeter had meant putting out sensors that would alert them of anything that moved in the shadows beyond the fire. There would be no patrols tonight, as they'd all be inside a *Charmed Circle* provided by the priestess. It felt strange to depend on magic walls he couldn't see or smell, but mage-bought security was better than anything his men could provide with human senses. Instead, they'd pull shifts inside, keeping watch on the forest and monitoring the sensors from the safety of the mage circle.

Patrols with mages and the occasional kylen had their advantages, but some things just felt gut-wrong, like huddling inside instead of being out there on watch.

Vonn watched as Claire took a stick and started walking a circle, scratching it into the dirt around the clearing. Behind her walked a sharpshooter, Corporal Susan Simko, carrying a fifty-pound bag of salt, letting it dribble out of the bag at a slow, steady rate, into the small trench Claire left behind her. Vonn felt more comfortable assigning a female soldier to close duty with the priestess. The *Charmed Circle* would be huge to allow for so many people inside, but Claire was stronger than most mages, maybe stronger than St. Croix, and he trusted her to maintain a *Circle* big enough for them all.

And that reminded him. He tapped his com unit and said into the mic, "Mac."

"Here, sergeant," Specialist Michaela MacEachern answered.

"You should have enough deadwood to burn down Atlanta. Get your men back here. The mage is ready to close the *Circle*."

"Sarge, Malc found something. Maybe you better see this." MacEachern gave her coordinates and signed off. She sounded spooked, and Mac wasn't someone to get spooked easily.

Vonn thought about going alone, but he had the kylen, and so he walked to the winged warrior and stood at attention, waiting to be recognized. Eldratos was standing, his wings half-furled, his face and hands lifted to the sky, still as a statue, staring at the sunset. It was nearly the time for Jubilee and while most soldiers participated in the worship of the Most High at sunset back at base, few did while on active duty. Getting lost in the Jubilee meant taking one's eyes off possible danger—a way to get killed. Vonn wasn't religious himself at all, but he recognized the expression on Eldratos' face as pure passion and true fervor, the zeal of the believer. It might be easier for the kylen; *he* might have actually seen the Most High. Scoggins stood to the rear of the kylen, his own eyes closed, his mouth moving in praise.

When the moment passed, Eldratos dropped his hands, snapped his wings shut, and turned to Vonn. "Yes, human?"

"My men have found something, sir."

Eldratos cocked his head and nodded once. "Let us see this *something*."

Vonn ordered a squad to prepare to move out and told Claire to hold off on setting the *Circle*. She didn't like it, but she complied. The men's weapons and night-vision gear ready, Vonn moved into the trees, Eldratos on his heels. Scoggins called out a prayer asking for protection for them all, and Vonn nodded at the elder, appreciative of the fervor of the man's belief, even as he found it difficult to feel such zeal himself.

It was nearly pitch black when they reached MacEachern's work detail. They were twitchy, hyper-alert, looking out over the woods and even overhead. Vonn saw instantly what the problem was. He'd seen pictures of the assey, Sam Wong, and the head on a pike was his. What little was left of the body scattered about the tiny clearing was torn to shreds; it was a safe bet that Wong had been eaten.

Eldratos sniffed, his eyes and nose searching over the nearby woods. "Spawn," he murmured. Vonn picked up a bone, a femur, he thought. There were teeth marks on it.

"There's more, sir," the specialist said. "This way." She led them down a narrow trail to a low ditch. In the bottom of it were two more men—or rather, the remains of two men. Not much left but bones and scraps of bloody cloth. Soldiers. Also eaten.

MacEachern said, "We found where we think they're coming from. A hole in the ground, maybe an entrance to an old mine. About two clicks that way." She pointed.

Vonn recalled the map and the points of reference he'd marked on it. He said to Eldratos. "Recommendation, sir. Let's put the men to bed and secure the mage circle. Take a look at the mine site in the morning when spawn are sleeping and the troops are fresh. Close it permanently."

"Your recommendation is wise. So be it," the kylen said.

"Back to camp. Double time," Vonn said.

"But, Sarge, the men . . ."

"You collected their dog tags?" When MacEachern nodded, Vonn went on. "We'll come back for what's left of the bodies after we deal with the problem. Let's get back to camp for now. Good work, Mac."

"Thank you, Sergeant."

Back in the clearing, Vonn counted his men and nodded to the witchy woman. With a snap of her fingers, she closed the *Charmed Circle*, and shut out all danger. They were safe—for now.

But there were too many strange things happening, all close together. There was a missing patrol and men eaten by spawn. A first-gen kylen had asked to lead his men. A licensed witchy woman—a priestess, no less—had asked to join the rescue. Thorn St. Croix was only a mountain over. The mine site they were going to close was between his camp and the tracks the battle mage was trapped on. No way was all that a coincidence.

Tears of Taharial
Summer 105 PA / 2117 AD

Faith Hunter

GARRICK'S TAKE

The seraph was perched high on the hilltop, staring into the hellhole entrance far above them. Garrick's parents had told him about seraphs, and his grandparents. He'd seen them on TV—when it was working. But he had never hoped to see one in person. This one was called Raziel, and he had scarlet hair and wings, with teal beneath, in the place where wing and human-shaped arm met. He had red irises in a tawny-skinned face. His jaw could have been carved from marble, it was so sharp.

Garrick watched as the seraph unfurled his wings and lifted from the mountain top. The seraph circled the sky several times before diving toward the earth. He back-winged, touched down on a huge stone that towered over the clearing, and snapped the wings closed. With the motion, his scent wafted down the hillside and through the clearing, like honey and chocolate, and Garrick closed his eyes to breathe in the scent of Heaven. When he opened them again, the seraph had tilted his head, his feathers catching the sunlight, glistening almost as bright as the red-gold armor that sheathed his human-shaped legs, arms, and chest. A sword appeared in his hand, so fast Garrick didn't see him draw it, the seraph steel blade glistening and dangerous.

Some called this seraph the chief of the supreme mysteries, one of the archangelic governors, and the angel of caves, caverns, and places of the dark, which made stone his element to call. Others said he was a herald, blowing a trumpet when the Most High came to Earth—or would if the Most High ever came so low. And he was considered the author of the Book of the Angel Raziel, though he had never confirmed it.

Only soldiers and humans on the edges of what was left of civilization saw seraphs these days, and then not often—unless a mage called mage-in-dire to protect himself from humans.

The dark-skinned Audric was a mule, an evil, immoral, half-breed, the result of a mating between a bespelled, captive human and a mage. Or so Garrick had always been taught. But this one seemed anything but debauched. He went about his duties as a bodyguard of Thorn St. Croix with attention to detail, but that was all. Unlike all her other companions, he showed no emotion toward her. He seemed neither a friend nor an enemy of the mage, just someone who was there to do a job and nothing more.

Garrick wasn't prejudiced against mules—or neomages neither, not like his parents were. But he had no reason to trust them either. They were licentious and sinful and went into rut like animals, mating with anyone or anything that moved, especially seraphs, who were messengers of the Most High, but were also easily tempted, according to the histories. And this seraph was here because the new battle mage had called him, yet they weren't indulging in sin.

None of this made sense to him. And the strangeness made him want to learn more.

Thorn St. Croix stood beside the massive war horses. They were both saddled and ready for riding, seeming unconcerned by the seraph who had all the humans so on edge.

The mage was dressed for battle in an outfit made for war, torn and bloodied leather, with weapons in loops and pockets, and over it all a cloak. Her red hair was braided back and up in a tight bun, with a knife hilt visible at the nape of her neck.

The mule was dressed far better, in leather armor the color of blood— the color of the angel's wings. When the mage stepped close, he caught her knee and tossed her up. "My Mistrend, you go into battle wearing your old dobok," he said. "May this champard know why?"

Thorn took the reins in hand and looked at the mule. "I'm saving all the pretty stuff for the priestess at Enclave. Even the battle clothes."

The mule shook his head, swung up onto his horse and checked his weapons: several swords and a huge gun that held some resemblance to a rocket launcher. Audric called to the seraph. "I am yours to beck and call," he shouted, his voice both a challenge and a pact, "my blood and bone and sinew."

Garrick's mouth dropped open. Now he knew why the mule had good armor. He was bound to the angel. *And* to the mage. And *none* of them were in rut. He had never heard of such a thing, and he knew his kirk elder would never believe it. Not ever.

The mule continued, "With sword and shield, in battle dire, I follow your behest. Never to fail, never to falter. For the length of my life."

The seraph, Raziel, laughed and dropped from the cliff, wings spread open their full twenty-four-foot span, shadowing them all before he landed. "My servant, you are a joy to take into battle." The seraph looked at Thorn then, and his face softened. "My mage, I am yours to command."

Garrick's mouth couldn't drop any farther. He had never, ever, not once, even in fiction, heard of a seraph placing himself under the command of a mage. But this one just had. *Seraph stones!* He wished he had a camera, a Pre-Ap one that could zoom in for close-ups and record sound too!

The train's conductor stepped close and held out a sword to Garrick. "A bunch of us are going in. You can come too, if you want." He counted on his fingers. "That makes eight of us all told, I think, and the mage said she would try to keep you alive."

Garrick took the sword, wordless with delight. He was going to battle! With a seraph! No one back home would believe him!

"You stay close to the mage," the conductor said. "And close your mouth, boy, before flies swarm in."

The little girl stepped off the train. He'd never really gotten close to her before, since the workers didn't interact much with the passengers. A tiny thing—she couldn't be more than ten. But she wore jewelry an adult might wear: a carved stone cat on a thong necklace, and a clasp shaped like an angel wing pinned to her tunic.

"Call your flames, Ciana," Thorn said to the child.

The little girl looked at Raziel and smiled. And the angel smiled back at her. "We go into battle glorious," he shouted, "with Mole Man's progeny at our back!"

"Battle glorious," Thorn muttered, her scarred face pulled into a frown.

The girl held out her arm, something clasped in her hand. She said "Yeehee" something or other. She repeated it, and seven globes of fire popped into the air. Garrick nearly dropped his sword. These were flames of the High Host. A human had called them and they just . . . appeared.

"Three and three and one, I greet thee," the mage said, sounding all formal. "If you will, three to lead and light the way, three to harass the spawn and the Darkness as they attack us, and one to me."

The flames rose and twirled, leaving bright blue plasma trails in the air. They divided and spun away in two groups of three, one group straight up the mountain toward the hellhole, while another three formed a whirling circle of fire in front of the mage. The last flame moved to the back of the big horse and hovered there. The mage didn't look directly at them and Garrick looked away too, blinking away the bright lights that had burned into his eyes.

The flames had done what the mage had asked.

Garrick felt awe and fear building inside his chest, emotions tangled together, leaving him confused and breathless. He crossed himself, the action something his grandfather had done in times of danger.

Thorn St. Croix looked around at the small clearing, and down the length of the stopped train. She lifted her head and raised her voice, saying, "It's only fair that you know why we ride into battle, underground, into the hellhole, a place where no sane being would trespass. The avalanche that stopped the train's progress was not caused by nature. It stinks of Darkness and the blood of human, kylen, and mage. If we do nothing but continue to shovel and melt the snow, night will fall, and the Darkness will emerge. And we will all be dinner to the spawn." She smiled at the men clustered around the train. "Some of you look like you might even be tasty." The men laughed, most of them.

"Whyn't you jist do what you did when you melted the snow caps on the mountains?" Eford called out. He was one of the men not laughing, and Garrick could almost feel the hatred rolling off him in waves. Eford had never hidden his distrust of anything mage-ish, but this felt more like a taunt.

"You call out all the power of Heaven and we kin jist be on our way."

The mage turned to him and stared, and Eford was too brave or maybe too stupid to look away. "I don't have access to that . . . that energy. Not anymore," Thorn said. She looked embarrassed, and the angel—the seraph—laughed. It sounded like bells tinkling. They knew something that Garrick didn't, like an inside joke. But then, they probably knew a lot of stuff he didn't.

She raised her voice again. "We go into the hellhole, after the power that caused us to stall here. We go into the hellhole to free the prisoners, the humans and any mages who wish to be saved—to free the kylen and the watcher—to wage war and engage in battle in the name of the Most High."

But to Garrick, she didn't look happy about heading them into the hellhole. More like resigned, and maybe even a little angry.

"When we get to the entrance, all of you stay close to me. I'll activate a *Shield* that will make any spawn who happen to be awake unable to scent us. You'll stay close and hold position until I drop the *Shield*. Then it'll likely be hand-to-hand." Her horse danced under her, and the mage rode the motion with ease, despite looking like a child perched on the massive beast.

From a pocket St. Croix pulled out several small stones. She tossed one to each of the men who'd volunteered to fight with her. Garrick snagged his out of the air and looked at it. It was polished stone, like something he might have skipped across a pond when he was a child. "These are *Healing* amulets. If you're injured, press it into the wound. Bind it in, if you can. But be quick about it: You fall, spawn will be on you in an instant."

Garrick carefully tucked the rock into his chest pocket. He had a mage stone—a real honest-to-the-Most-High mage stone. His mom would never believe it!

AUDRIC'S TAKE

They were going into a hellhole to battle Darkness. Again. He had hoped that leaving the mountains of Carolina and going to the New Orleans Enclave would free him for a while from the horror of battle. But that wasn't going to happen; not while Thorn St. Croix was near. Darkness was determined to kill the little mage, and it seemed she had strong feelings against it as well.

Audric, his heartbeat steady, his breathing deep and even, wheeled Clyde up the hill, the big animal moving with a smooth pace and muscular strength. The Clydesdale had never been ridden into battle, and he had no idea how the horse would react to the smells of the hellhole as they grew near. Most animals were terrified of the scent of blood, brimstone, noxious fumes, and old death. He hoped the *Calming* amulet Thorn had given him would be enough to keep the animal quiet.

Behind him, he felt more than heard his seraph take to the air. The connection between them was penetrating and compulsory, binding his thoughts and actions, his intent and deeds. Almost any other of the second unforeseen would have been ecstatic at being bound as war-partner to the winged warrior Raziel. Audric, however, was still grieving the loss of his love, Rupert, and that grief shrouded his soul like a lead blanket, leaving him unable to care, even about combat. He adjusted his swords and armor. Perhaps he would die in battle and go to join Rupert, wherever he was in the afterlife.

"You will not die today, my companion," the seraph said.

"I am yours to command," Audric said, submerging his grief deep inside, into the dark of his soul. "I am yours to beck and call, my blood and bone and sinew. With sword and shield, in battle dire, I'll follow your behest. Never to fail, never to falter. For the length of my life."

From overhead, Raziel laughed at Audric's morose tone, his voice ringing. He called out, "I will answer your call, guard you beneath my wings, and carry you into the Light at the end of your days." The seraph swept up and back down, wings spread in a long glide. "Though some will find the Light by nightfall, this battle will not be your end. Nor mine. Nor the little mage's."

Audric shuddered. *Some would die.* But then, someone always died in battle.

The smell of brimstone and sulfur stung his nose. They were close to the hellhole, above the snowline, and Audric dismounted, to crunch on ice. Eli swung down from the horse Thorn had commandeered from an indignant passenger on the train. Audric hobbled the horses. They'd be able to paw through the thin ice and eat the winter grass, would have ice-melt to drink. And with Thorn's amulets hanging from their saddle horns, they'd remain calm until their riders returned.

Eli glanced at him, his eyes speculative and tense. The human loved Thorn, and would protect her when Audric's battle-tie to the seraph might draw him from Thorn's side during combat. Eli would stand by her no matter what. He was a good companion to have on this foray, although Audric would never say that aloud.

The ride had been without event, but for the humans slipping and sliding on snow. And now they stood at the opening into the darkness. The flames danced inside the cave opening, moving as if excited. Other flames whirled over Thorn, as if awaiting orders, and the one lone flame seemed to rest on the air behind her. They all hummed, static-crackling notes in minor keys, as if singing or speaking to one another. And perhaps they were. Who could know? With the High Host, most anything was possible.

Thorn turned, her back to the hellhole, the black entrance framing her. She threw back her cloak, revealing the scarlet lining, torn and stained and ripped by claws. Spawn claws. Her face caught the light, her scars shining white against her pale pink, glowing skin. She lifted her eyes to the seraph on an outcropping of stone overhead, the pose making her look both small and stalwart. His little mage was learning the use of the dramatic to capture and hold the attention and loyalty of humans. Had he not forgotten how to smile, his lips might have curled up in pride.

Thorn pulled an amulet from her pocket and tied it onto her amulet necklace, now worn outside her clothing, in full view of humans. "This amulet is charged with a moving *Shield*, one that will allow us to move over terrain, will allow bullets out and air in. It will keep the Dark at bay. But if you step outside its walls, you can't get back inside. You'll be on your own, and it isn't likely any of us will risk our lives to rescue anyone that stupid."

"You got another one of those amulets, consul-general?"

The rough voice came from the treeline.

Audric drew his sword and whirled to the rear, all in one motion, to see a group of men dressed in Army camo. And a kylen in a distant tree, his wings furled and his scent both seraphic and mage—and strong; far stronger than Thaddeus Bartholomew. Could he be a second- or first-generation kylen? Audric had never seen a first-gen. He wasn't certain that anyone alive ever had.

Standing on the ground below the kylen was a woman, tiny as Thorn herself, dressed in silks and gauze far too thin and insubstantial for the cold. A priestess. One he knew. Audric nearly swore.

Claire wore an amulet belt of carved wood figures—leaves, flowers, various animals—tied around her waist; the Earth mage with her charms. Her left wrist was adorned with her visa. She was beautiful. And deadly. She had lain with him during a long-ago mage heat, and he had satisfied her demands. When the heat subsided, he had left her. It was an egregious insult to leave a mage-lover without being sent away. Her eyes narrowed as she recognized him, but she didn't speak.

"Raziel," the ebony-skinned kylen in the tree called out. "By blood and fire, in battle and praise, in the River of Time and without, I am yours to command, my brother-father."

Raziel nodded. "The mage will lead us into battle dire."

Claire's head lifted and she started to smile, thinking the honor hers.

"Eldratos, acknowledge the consul-general," Raziel said, "Thorn St. Croix." The kylen spread his wings and dropped from his tree, gliding toward Thorn. He lit on the earth with seraphic grace.

Claire's smile died, and the look she shot Thorn was murderous. Audric would have to keep an eye on her. He distrusted everything about Claire, from her petty jealousy and fierce temper, to her intense self-worship, to her preference for sexual violence. That violent streak permeated every aspect of her life, and was one of the more treacherous things about her, making her brutal, savage, and sadistic.

"'Omega mage,' I have been called," Thorn said softly, her voice not carrying to the humans nor to Claire. "Yet I ask, not demand; I beg, not command. Will you help in this battle?"

The kylen bowed his head. "I am yours to command."

"Yourssss to command," the flames said, the words like the explosion of gases, the hum of electricity, and the ringing of heavy brass. "Yours."

"Always and forever, in the River of Time and beyond, yours," Raziel said.

"*Tears of Taharial*," Thorn murmured. And none of the assembled host commented on the curse.

"My men," Eldratos said, pointing. Thorn turned to watch the newcomers, the humans tramping across the snow. "We followed the tracks of spawn who'd attacked a military platoon to a small entrance on the other side of the slope face. They took men captive. U.S. Army bootprints were mixed in with the spawn-prints."

"They took human prisoners?" Thorn murmured. "How long ago?"

"Two—perhaps three days," the kylen said.

"We would have followed them in at that entrance," the soldier who'd first spoken when they came out of the trees said, "but one of my men tripped a line. The mountain came down over the opening."

"I felt the tremor in the earth," Thorn said. "I'm Thorn St. Croix." She held out her hand and the soldier took her tiny one in his battle-toughened paw.

"The battle mage," the grizzled soldier said, "Master Sergeant Vonn, ma'am. Big fan here of your battle against the Dark. My team and I spent two weeks watching the footage on SNN. Pretty amazing."

Audric was amused as Thorn turned red under her mage glow. All she had been through and she still blushed at the oddest times.

"Ma'am," Vonn said, still holding her hand. "My men and I would really appreciate the protection of a moving *Shield*. Our mage can do a lot of things, but she isn't a battle mage."

Audric would have missed Claire's reaction had he not been watching for it. She gripped an amulet, her eyes narrowing for an instant in fury before smoothing to calculated neutrality. Claire had the canny, crafty mind of a predator trapping prey. Thorn was in danger. He knew it.

"I will help in any and every way I can, Master Sergeant," Thorn said.

Audric shifted his body to face the priestess, and stared, catching Claire's eyes as he walked across the frozen snow to her. When he was close, he leaned down and said, "If something happens to my mistrend, and I track it to you, I will make certain that the seraph knows."

"Who are you to speak to me in such a manner?" she hissed.

"I am your death if you mis-step."

THORN'S TAKE

I looked back at my champards, Eli and Audric. I'd left the others at the train, to mount a last-ditch defense should the Darkness get past us and attack the humans there. Ciana wasn't happy at being left behind, but she accepted the necessity. Before we departed, she placed her hand on my brow in what was clearly a blessing, and I'd felt the imprint of her small, warm palm on my forehead for hours. I touched the place now—long cooled, but holding the promise of her love for me. From there, my hand moved to my amulet necklace, and the *Shield* talisman that hung from it.

I knew my amulet didn't have enough power to protect and cover all the humans with us, but I could draw power from the stone of the mountain and store it in the empty amulets I carried just for that purpose. I could—if I wanted to risk contamination from the Darkness taint.

I had deliberately not used any of my mage gifts up until now, not wanting to see the Dark power. It often physically hurt for me see so much Darkness and I . . . well, I was so tired of fighting the energy ranged against us. I knew that was foolish. I knew that, but it didn't make it any easier to mind skim the mountain.

I moved away from the soldiers and found a stone outcropping jutting from the snow. The top was rounded and wide enough for my backside. I leaped to the top and sat, crossed my legs yogi-fashion. Between my thighs, I piled all the empty amulets and the one holding the moving *Shield*. I closed my eyes and opened my mage sight.

Around me the energies of snow and frigid air glared at me, looking pale and dull, green, gray, and the soft lavender shade of old bruises—the hues of mold and fungi and dead things. The leafless trees were likewise sickly looking. Not because they were tainted with Darkness, but because I was a Stone mage and only the energies of stone were truly beautiful to my mage sight.

Bracing myself, I turned my attention to the hellhole and the energies blasting from it. The trampled snow at the entrance was sicklier yellow-tinted gray, speaking of sulfur and brimstone and disease. Splatters of black and deepest purple surrounded the stone maw, a brownish, mustard-yellow under-glow indicating the power moving like maggots through the rock. Below the sparkling energies was a heavy thrumming power, almost a sound, almost a vibration, almost pain, but not quite.

I knew by looking with mage sight that the major Darkness nesting in the lair was not Stone-linked. His was an Air power. He had tried to weave protections into the rock, and perhaps had Dark Stone mages adding incantations to reinforce his workings, but they were poor at best, and dangerous at worst. No wonder half the mountain had crashed down when the soldiers tripped the wire. The stone was riddled with cracks and fissures. It was an unholy mess. If it tried to come down while we were inside, it would crash on top of us. So, while it felt strange (and was probably stupid) to reinforce an enemy's stronghold, I did just that.

I sent my power creeping out in fingers of intent, to slide into the fractures, propping up the roofs of caverns, sealing stalactites in place, bracing tunnels. It was dangerous on several levels, mostly because I couldn't use my own power. To keep from being noticed, I had to draw on the power of the Dark itself and curl it back on the stone, shifting, adjusting, sealing, and restoring. I had to move slowly, which was tiring. And I was taking on some of the Darkness, which was . . . tempting. All that power, there for the taking. I could defeat my enemy with its own workings and its own might. I could. If I was willing to become something not much better than it was. I could feel the Darkness clinging to me, a slimy, acidic second skin, burning like nettles and fire ants.

But now I had a pretty good map of the tunnels to get us into the upper levels of the lair. And I knew how to get out if we had to make a run for it.

Before I pulled my conscious mind out of the hellhole, I took a steadying breath and prepared to open a mind skim too. I'd never heard of anyone else who could use a blended scan, and neither had Cheran Jones or Audric, though the seraphs had a name for it, omega sight, so it must not've been unique to me.

The blended scan rocked me, a nauseating vertigo that left me sick and sweating. I didn't get nearly as sick using the scan as I used to, but the scan itself wasn't the only thing making me ill. The stink of rot and Darkness slammed into me, the reek of the reptilian evil lurking deep within the mountain. I took a shallow breath, parsing the different energy elements of it all, knowing that it wasn't really smell I was scenting, but the signature of the hellhole and its owner—and the blood of a watcher and a kylen, sickly sweet and rancid from days of torture, and fresh and copious from today's cruelty. My stomach refused to settle, and I knew that I'd be some time recovering. But now I also knew the position and matrix of the conjures that guarded the tunnels.

It was going to be easy getting in. About twenty feet in past the entrance, though, the tunnel narrowed and a spiderweb of *Shield* energies was laced across the opening. On the other side of the web the tunnel branched and branched again. Working alone, it would take time to break the Dark *Shield*, and whichever of us did the work of dissecting and dismantling it would be there alone. Which meant that once it dropped we'd be attacked.

Of course, I could allow the pretty little priestess access to my mind, creating a circle and letting her work with and through me. That would speed up. Or I could merge with Raziel again. But neither was something I wanted. Being raised alone, away from the Enclave of my birth, I wasn't skilled at joint conjuring. And I wasn't myself after merging with Raziel.

I dropped the blended scan and opened my eyes. And nearly fell off my rock. Claire was standing about six inches from me, her spread hands to either side of my head and a look of intense concentration on her face. I slapped her hands away and bounded from the stone, drawing my sword and a *Shield* amulet. My face must've looked fierce, because she slammed a *Shield* of her own in place. It glowed a greenish gold and melted the snow in a circle around her.

"Audric?" I said, not taking my eyes from her. The name came out a growl and I drew a second sword.

"I could do nothing, my mistrend. She is a priestess."

"You ever do that again—" I started.

"What were you doing?" Claire demanded. "You were using something new. *Doing* something new."

"—I'll cut you in two," I finished. "Do you understand?"

Claire lifted her chin, her shoulders going back stiffly. "You could try. I am not a battle mage, but I am not lacking in skills."

"Do *not* touch me." I wanted to add, "you little witch," but didn't. I resheathed my swords and dropped the *Shield*, turning my back on her. I heard her gasp, and I figured she wasn't used to being dismissed as unimportant. I strode across the ice to my seraph—not that I'd call him that aloud. He watched me, his eyes warm in welcome.

"Raziel," I said, "there's a spiderweb-style trap about twenty feet in. Can you see it?"

The seraph turned his gaze to the tunnel and a moment later said, "The Dark have shared their defensive and offensive workings. We have fought this before, in the hellhole above your town. Beyond the web are other workings and something dead. And two who must be rescued."

"Yeah. That's what I got. Can you break it alone?"

"No. The kylen and I can tear it apart, if he is willing." He looked at Eldratos. "My brother-son, will you work with me?"

"Yes, my brother-father. But we will be incapacitated while we work. Will your mage protect us and battle the Darkness that will attack when the *Shield* falls?"

"I will." I said.

"She will," Raziel said at the same time.

So much for me being able to speak on my own. I raised my voice. "Audric, will you see to the placement of men so they're protected under a *Shield*?" I looked up at the sky to gauge the amount of daylight we had left. Never enough, even if we were going in at dawn. But there was a watcher and a kylen down there; I wasn't going to leave them down there another night.

"Vonn," I called, and the soldier jogged up, looking light on his feet, even with forty or fifty pounds of gear on his back. I picked up a stick and drew in the snow, making a sketch map of the upper tunnels as I remembered them from my scan. "We're going in. Once the seraphs and kylen blow the web-trap away, it'll be hand-to-hand fighting. What major armament do you carry?"

"In addition to our personal arms, we've got one SMAW rocket launcher and a new-model ARC-DK, Dragon Killer. The SMAW fires standard 83mm rocket rounds and the DK uses the new AIMs—Artificial Intelligence Missiles filled with seraph steel fléchettes and frags."

"Can any of them shut down a tunnel, say one of the branchings that we don't want to leave open behind us?"

"No problem, ma'am. But it might bring down the roof of the tunnel we're in," he said with a grin.

I shook my head. "We don't want to bury ourselves or our retreat. Raziel? I strengthened the tunnel as best I could. Can you keep the stone above us from collapsing?"

"Of course, my mage."

"Okay. Then, Vonn, we need these three tunnels closed off," I pointed on the map in the snow. They were the ones with no scent of seraph or kylen, and the strongest reek of devil-spawn and Darkness. "And that's just to get us in the door."

"Can do, ma'am."

"Thank you. And these are for your men." I pulled the rest of my *Healing* amulets out of a pocket. "One stone for each soldier. If they get injured, they can press it with a thumb and the energies stored inside will stop bleeding, decrease the chance of shock, and shore up immune defenses."

Vonn took the amulets with a small smile. "These things are worth their weight in gold back at base. Thank you, ma'am."

"If we find ourselves in dangerous fumes . . ." I started.

Vonn held up a gas mask. "We got that covered, ma'am."

I handed him two more amulets. These were roughly faceted and polished labrodorite. "These are small traveling *Shields*. If someone has to be taken back to the surface, two soldiers can fit under one. But that's all I have. Use them at your discretion."

The smile that lit Vonn's face warmed me so much that I added, "Whether you use them or not, keep them when we're done. And the *Healing* amulets too. They can be recharged by any Stone mage."

Vonn gave orders to his troops, then gathered the train's volunteers at the cavern opening to explain how we would enter the hellhole. With the soldiers present, we wouldn't need to take the untrained men into the Darkness's lair. That meant the kid, Garrick, would remain on the surface, safe, along with his boss, the fifty-year-old geezer. They'd've been a liability in the hellhole, but might actually do some good on the surface, shooting anything that tried to escape or that tried to block our escape. The railroad employees weren't happy at being left on the surface, thinking that battle against Darkness was some kind of heroic experience and not the blood and guts and gore it actually was. They grumbled, but agreed to follow Vonn's orders.

I looked for the prickly, spoiled priestess, and wasn't surprised to see her sitting on a log off by herself, stiff-shouldered and shivering, even with the *Warm-Me* incantation she was using. I sighed. She should have brought winter clothes, but most Enclave-raised mages had no sense about outside weather, and they were too dependent on amulets and creation energy to be practical.

Claire wasn't much older than I was, but she was by far less experienced. And as the political creature I now was, instead of swatting her across the back of the head, I needed to unruffle her feathers. If I could. I went to her and bent into a squat, bringing my head below hers. "I can't do this without you," I lied.

Her head lifted, her nose in the air. She didn't look at me, but stared off into the trees. "You are a battle mage—the only rogue mage ever found who wasn't torn apart by terrified humans or put down like a rabid dog by the kirk—the only mage to have a seraph who comes when you call—the first mage to have a seraph stone. You don't *need* me."

"Fine. We *can* do it alone. But if you add your *Shield* to mine, it will help cement your relationship with the soldiers—and the kylen."

Claire's eyes widened. "They are forbidden."

"I noticed. But they *are* fascinating."

Claire turned to stare at Eldratos. She unconsciously gripped the seraph stone hanging from her belt." Yes," she murmured. "They are."

I waited, and after her eyes had drunk their fill of the beautiful kylen she said, "I will help you."

"Thank you." I held out my *Shield* amulet to her and watched as she closed her eyes, studying its energies and the working it contained.

She tilted her head and murmured, "Interesting." She pulled up one amulet from among those hanging from her belt, a well-worn wooden carving of a babe in a manger. My eyebrows rose. I would never have taken the woman for a Christian. She studied the amulets closely, aligned them carefully, and touched the wood to the stone once. Even with mage sight off, I could see how the energies aligned. "Done," she said and handed mine back to me.

"Nice work," I said, and let my brows rise again when she blushed. Now that was weird. "You'll need to stay within fifteen feet of me when we get inside the hellhole."

Her shoulders stiffened again. "I am well aware of the parameters of my own working."

I sighed and left her, calling Vonn. "Ready when you are."

We stood at the entrance to the hellhole in a tight grouping, the untrained and poorly armed humans left at the entrance as guards, under the command of a single corporal. Claire and I held our *Shield* amulets, ready to thumb them on. The soldiers assumed a formation that would fit within the confines of the overlapping *Shields* when we activated them, moving with weapons at ready. They kept their weapons aimed outward, but I was still nervous. If they fired before the *Shields* dropped, the bullets would ricochet inside the *Shields*, and I wasn't wearing a flak jacket. Vonn nodded to me and I activated my mage sight and stared into the hellhole.

"Flames," I said, not knowing if they needed reminding, but not taking chances, "I ask, not demand, that you join in this fight."

The flames bobbed up and down and spun in dizzying circles of light too bright to look at directly. I turned my head and stepped inside the entrance. The flames shot ahead in two groups of three, with one flame at my back, staying close but out of my line of sight, as if trying not to blind me. Behind me I heard a female soldier mutter, "Saints' balls. She really *can* make them do things."

Raziel and Eldratos stepped forward, and when they were far enough ahead I said, softly, "Claire? Now, please." We pressed our amulets and the merged *Shield* flickered on with a tiny electric jolt. The air was noticeably warmer inside the hellhole, and the stench of sulfur, rot, and old blood was much stronger. The soldiers pulled gas masks over their faces. I thumbed on an amulet with a new conjure that would block the worst of the fumes. From the corner of my eye, I saw Claire do the same and wondered how she knew to make one; I had only recently figured it out myself. But that question vanished as the darkness of the cavern closed in on us.

In their threes, the flames darted all around, testing the boundaries of the entrance, and skirting around the soldiers, who started when they came too close.

Behind the seraph and kylen, we moved forward as one unit, like a many-legged insect whose body shape was determined by the environment, flowing toward the web of energies that protected the lair. The soldiers guarded our backs as Raziel and Eldratos stood side-by-side and pulled their swords. The seraph steel cut through the Dark magic spell as easily as it might have butter. The flames darted through and danced in the shadows. The one at my shoulder buzzed with delight.

"So not fair," I muttered. The last time I'd tangled with this type of construct, it had nearly killed Raziel and me, and that was saying something when a seraph could be brought down by a working, no matter how advanced.

Raziel must have heard, because he laughed and looked back at me. "We have studied the web that trapped the cherub. We learned much. My sword is now proof against it and all similar workings of the Dark. But I hear an echo in the deeps. An alarm has been sounded, my mage. We must hurry."

"Move," Vonn said.

We raced ahead, the flames and seraph leading the way, until we reached the first of the side-passages I wanted brought down. Raziel raised his arms. With mage sight, I followed the movement of his seraph energies as he shored up the ceiling directly above us. As he worked, the flames flashed down the stone corridors and back, sizzling with distaste at whatever they found.

Raziel nodded to me through the *Shield*. The roof over our heads wouldn't fall.

Turning to Vonn, I pointed at each of the tunnel openings. The soldiers with the rocket launchers took up position, aiming up at the tunnel roofs. We thumbed off our *Shields*.

Claire covered her ears; Audric, Eli, and I followed suit—the soldiers had earpieces built into their helmets both for communication and for protection. On Vonn's silent count of three, the SMAW and the Dragon Killer both fired. Even through the protection of my palms, the sound was astounding, a vibration that thudded through my feet. The rumble that followed brought down two tunnel roofs, showering us with dust and debris. If our location had been a secret, that was over.

The flames seemed to like the destruction and they darted forward to test the new rock barricades.

The soldiers quickly reloaded, and the SMAW fired again, taking out the third tunnel. The weapon was loaded again, even as Vonn shouted into his mic over the rumbling, "Regroup!" The entire platoon moved in and Claire and I thumbed our *Shields* back on, covering us mortals with mage energies. The two groups of flames moved out ahead, leading the way.

The tunnel sloped down and narrowed. The air quality got increasingly worse, and tears gathered in my eyes from the stench of chemicals and decaying flesh. We passed five more tunnels and the flames investigated each. Though it left us temporarily unprotected, we snapped off the *Shields* each time so I could scent-search for our quarry. Watching the flames, I stood for a moment before each tunnel opening, flipping from mage sight to mind skim and back. I didn't want to try a blended scan; I couldn't afford to be weakened, even for a moment.

I smelled only Darkness in each of the tunnels, and the flames seemed to agree, zipping around, buzzing with that peculiar sound that meant disgust. I had Vonn blow the first few tunnels, but on the fifth one I smelled something else close by. The flames seemed to burn a brighter blue as they raced down it. And they didn't come back. The flame by my ear crackled with excitement.

"Kylen," I said, breathing deeply of the scent.

"My brother is wounded," Eldratos said.

I reached for the *Shield* amulet. And the attack hit. A wave of devil-spawn rushed at us from a side-tunnel just ahead, flowing over floor and walls and even the ceiling like water over stone, thousands of them, squealing and cawing, their raucous cries grating and deafening in the echoing space. It was too late to use the *Shield*. If I raised it, they'd be inside the conjure's radius with us, and the soldiers' guns would be almost as dangerous to use as the spawn were themselves. And while I'd been thinking that through, my hand had reflexively drawn my sword and cleaved through three of them. I let the *Shield* amulet swing free on its thong and drew a short sword with my left hand, flowing into the cat stance.

The soldiers on either side of me opened fire with automatic weapons as I took down a half-dozen more, the big rat-like creatures falling to become victims of the ravening appetites of their kin. Eldratos and Raziel danced straight into the wave of spawn, swords slicing. Eli took up a place at my back, his weapons firing with steady determination, his short-sword beheading any wounded spawn that raced behind me. Audric, drawn by his battle-tie, worked his way through the melee until he stood behind Raziel, facing outward to form an impenetrable triangle with Eldratos, his blades a whir of motion and splattering gore.

We killed maybe fifty in the first minute of fighting, my flesh burning where it was exposed to the splatter of spawn blood, my ears ringing with concussive blasts of our firepower. Another fifty fell in the next half minute. But even with the spawn stopping to feast on their dead, it wasn't going to be enough. We were going to be dinner.

Faster than I'd ever seen one move, a big spawn leaped over the dead bodies of his brethren and launched at me. By instinct, I raised my left arm to cut him from the air, but he seemed to adjust the trajectory of his leap to the side in midair. And his teeth latched onto my forearm. The pain was razor-sharp and burning. I felt my mage-brittle bones snap like twigs. I went down to one knee. More spawn swarmed me. I screamed.

Light brighter than the sun filled the cavern. The spawn shrieked, the sound so piercing my eardrums fluttered with pain. Fire raced down the tunnel. The spawn biting me fell away in flames, its flesh consumed in the space of two heartbeats. Before I dropped to the ground to shield myself, I was pretty sure I saw its bones roasting. The air burned; I couldn't even take a breath. And then it was gone, leaving only the stench of cooked spawn and moaning humans. I blinked in the sudden dark.

Eldratos stood over me, one leg to either side, his wings furled so that they brushed my cheek, the one with all the scars. I shuddered with pain and cradled my arm. The kylen bent over me and reached down to take my broken bones in both of his hands. I hissed as he straightened them, the tiny grinding and clicking of fractured bones making my heart skip a beat. I might have screamed but for the blast of healing he sent into me. Burning and icy, it shocked through my arm, and I *felt* the bones heal. The pain slid away.

"Tears of Taharial," I hissed, jerking my arm away.

"He does weep for us all," Eldratos said.

"Yeah. Um, thanks," I said. I had no idea what he meant, but tested my arm by picking up my small sword lying in the ashes of crispy critter. The hilt was warm to my hand, but not hot.

"Are you well, my mistrend?" Audric asked.

"Peachy," I said, "thanks to the winged wonder here. What did you do?"

Eldratos smiled, and it wasn't exactly a peaceful, heavenly smile. It had an edge of darkness to it that made me wonder if killing anything with life was harder on the beings of Light than I previously knew. "I am not certain, mage of Raziel," he said. "I drew upon you. And upon your wheels."

I swallowed hard. "I don't have any wheels. Only cherubs have wheels."

"So you say."

Vonn said, "Sorry to break up your little confab here, but we need to get a move on."

I shook my head and pointed down the open tunnel. "That way. Kylen close by—injured." Claire and I reactivated our *Shields* and we moved out together. I noticed that several of the soldiers had quickly applied pressure bandages to wounds and activated their *Healing* charms to deal with spawn bites and claw scrapes. And no one had died. I turned my attention to the tunnel, its irregular walls illuminated by flames' light.

"How far ahead?" I whispered to the flame at my shoulder, not knowing if it could speak in human language.

"Fooollooow." Then the flame zipped ahead and disappeared into a cell sealed by doors made of demon iron. I could feel the bars' icy cold leaching the warmth from the air. When I looked at the cell door with mage sight, it was covered with a woven net of energies, lines of force that zig-zagged back and forth across the opening. The cell entrance was warded with something I didn't recognize, cooked up by the Dark.

Raziel was just ahead, and I lifted a hand, touching his flight feathers. He understood without words. "I see it, my mage. This is another new thing. The Darkness has learned how to create that which is new, which has never before been known. Only mankind may create that which is new. Only mankind was gifted with imagination by the Most High. Not the Light. And not the Dark. This is . . ."

"Troubling," Eldratos murmured, finishing his thought. "Troubling."

The two members of the High Host studied the construct and I let my mage sight go. Which allowed me to see beyond the spell into the rough cell. I nearly hissed in shock. The kylen lying on the cell floor was naked and crusted over with blood, his back looking like raw meat. His wings were gone. They had been severed close to the shoulder. And he lay on the wings. There was so much blood coating them that it took me a long, horrified moment to figure out that the wings had once been white, the pure white of a dove. The seven flames were working on the kylen, zipping into and out of his body, which they did when they killed Darkness or when they healed beings of the Light.

One flame zizzed back through the bars and hovered slightly above my head, hissing and spitting sparks. "Hurrrrrryyy. He faaaailssss."

I didn't know what that meant exactly for a creature that was probably as immortal as the seraphs, but I also didn't need to find out. "Raziel?"

He turned to me and held out a hand, his scarlet irises seeming to glow in the dark tunnel. "Join with my brother-son and me. We will destroy this working together."

"Ummm." It wasn't the most informative response I'd ever made.

"Trust," Raziel said. "Trust." He smiled that smile that made my heart race and my knees wobble and my seraph stone grow hot to the touch as it tried to block the mage heat trying to rise. I didn't reply, but sheathed my short sword and placed my hand in his outstretched palm. His flesh was warm and smooth and just touching him made my toes curl and things low in my belly heat and grow heavy. Thankfully, I wasn't expected to clasp Eldratos' hand too, as Raziel took it in his.

Instantly we were in Otherspace, the world there bright as day, and the others we fought with were gone; yet we still stood in the tunnel, the cell bars glowing like black sparks and living shadows before us. I looked around, seeing that I was dressed as I often was in this place: in scarlet and black chain-mail and articulated plate. The hand Raziel clasped was wearing a black glove that looked like leather but felt like metal. In my free hand was a sword I'd never seen before. Here in Otherspace, weapons and clothes were symbolic of a person's state of mind and spirit, and I had no idea what a glowing seraph steel blade with a blue light of sparkling energy at its tip and along its edge might mean. The symbolic sword had a gold-plated crossguard—or solid gold; I couldn't tell—and a hilt wrapped in what felt like dragon skin. Just feeling it through the glove made me remember what fighting them had been like, and my toes curled in my boots.

"Use the gem, my mage," Raziel said.

I flipped the sword and studied the glowing blue sapphire on the pommel. Then I studied the web of energies on the dark bars in front of me. In the center was a clear space just big enough for the stone. "Usually a blade is better for fighting Darkness," I said, "but this does look promising." I steadied the blade between my arm and side and pressed the pommel into the space.

Heat and light blasted out and I was thrown back, my hand wrenched from Raziel's. And I was back in the real world—just in time to hit the stone wall behind me. "Seraph stones," I gasped, or thought I gasped. With the world swimming and rocking before me, I wasn't certain of anything. Except that the barred door had blown open and Raziel and Eldratos were inside kneeling beside the tortured kylen.

"We are here, my brother," Eldratos said. "You are finally safe."

I was still trying to get my bearings as Eli and Vonn helped me to my feet. Eli pulled me under the protection of his arm and holstered and sheathed his weapons, his hands and eyes moving down my back and limbs, ostensibly checking my fragile bones for breaks. Holding my swords away from him, I stopped his hands, watching. "Look," I whispered. In the space between one heartbeat and the next, the two kylen had disappeared.

"No," Claire whispered. "Not yet . . ."

Raziel stood and smiled at me. "They are now in a Realm, my mage. You have saved another. The Host sing of you and your exploits."

I didn't know what to say to that, so I just kept my mouth shut. Which was a good thing, as a flame darted up to me and tried to say something. It was mostly just the "Zzzzzzssss" of its excitement.

"Slow down," I said.

The flame bounced up and down a moment before it stilled, hanging in the air before me. I kept my eyes to the side to preserve my vision but bent in close to hear it say, "A watcher issss here. Closssse. Come."

It darted away and I followed, Raziel and Eli and Audric on my heels. When we found him, the sight was more appalling than what we'd just seen. The Dark liked cutting off the wings of creatures of Light, but this one had been given special attention. Most of the flesh on his back and shoulders had been peeled back, exposing blood-clotted muscle and viscera. His thighs and upper arms had been chewed on, leaving little but bone. He was healing, but only slowly. The stench suggested that he had been here a long, long time. I blinked at the sight, not able to tell what body part was what with this one. Without thinking, I flipped the sword and jammed it into the network of the working separating us from the prisoner.

I woke up an hour later, lying on something warm and wonderful smelling, like caramel. "Raziel," I murmured, but my lips didn't want to work right.

"Do not speak, my mage. You suffered greatly from the release of the energies. You were foolish," I tried to figure out how to react to that, but a moment later he added, "but very brave."

"Wrong sword," I managed.

I felt the chuckle in his chest beneath my ear. "Yes. Indeed. But I have healed you and brought you to the surface. The others follow with mages and humans. Both your warriors and those they rescued have suffered, some greatly. I will wait here and heal them, if you'd like."

That sounded like a personal favor to me so I nodded. "Thank you."

"And then I will fly you back to your steel conveyance and the others of your champards."

I perked up at that, but Raziel placed his large hand on my head and stroked down my back. I sighed with ease, as pain I didn't even recognize I'd been fighting vanished. Either I slept or it was only an instant later when I heard the screams of the wounded and the shouted commands of the soldiers making it back to the surface. Raziel held me as the humans from the train raced forward to help and to fight off the hundreds of spawn that were chasing them.

It was always amazing to watch the ordinary people close with the spawn and hack them to pieces until there were none left. I didn't like lying back in safety and watching while others suffered and fought, but when I tried to move, the pain of my injuries sent shock waves through me. This time, I had no choice. And eventually I slept again.

The next time I awoke it was to the movement of the train, the slightly misaligned wheels making a clackety-clickety-clackety beneath me. I smelled kylen and human and mage, and opened my eyes to find myself in the large bed, sleeping, Ciana in my arms, her father on her far side facing me, his eyes closed in sleep. A kylen cradled me at my back: Thad once again ignored by the seraph, not stolen away to a Realm of Light. I didn't understand it, but I welcomed it.

It was night, the car lit only by a mage light that hovered over the shoulder of Cheran Jones, who sat in a chair reading, his bunk folded against the far wall.

Eli, his forehead bearing stitches from a wound I didn't remember him receiving, lay on a cot on the floor, one hand curled beneath his cheek. When I recovered my energy, I could offer to heal his wound so that it wouldn't even leave a mark, but I hoped he'd refuse me. The scar on his brow wasn't disfiguring. If anything, it made him look more rakish and dashing, and would give him one more thing to talk about with the ladies.

A hammock swayed in the corner, Audric's leg hanging over one side. He was watching me, his eyes dark and fierce in the dim light. Uncertain, I smiled at him, feeling my lips tremble. For a moment he didn't respond, as dour and unapproachable as he had been ever since Rupert's sacrifice. Then he inclined his head, the merest hint of acknowledgment. Maybe we could make this relationship work yet. Maybe.

I sighed, nuzzled Ciana, and closed my eyes. We were safe again. This time.

Rolling Stone
Summer 105 PA / 2117 AD

Lucienne Diver

I gave my knee a jolt as I got to the part of my story where the daywalker grabbed the little girl. Fiona O'Connor shrieked and jumped off my lap, making all the other kids scream as well. She recovered quickly and rounded on me with seven-year-old indignation, her eyes snapping, an expression that meant nothing to me before I met the freckled menace. I wouldn't normally put the fear of Darkness into a child so young, but Fiona was a cheeky little thing, capable, I feared, of just about anything, including wandering into a Darkling pit out of sheer curiosity. She reminded me of me as a child.

"You did that on purpose!" Fiona accused, fists jammed onto her narrow hips.

"Did I?" I asked, giving her my best innocent look. But she put me to shame. I'd seen her smile like a cherub while smearing honey cake into her brother's hair. "You mean, like this?" My voice rose into a roar as I leapt from my seat on the lip of the town well, gathered up my walking stick and pretended to swipe at the children, who screamed in delighted mock fear and ran to their parents standing on the fringes. Listening. Smiling. In some cases readying a coin or two for me, Aoife Cleary, traveling talespinner . . . and more, though that was strictly need-to-know.

I smiled, brushed at the seat of my coat with frost-stiff fingers, and pulled a hat from my pocket to pass. I didn't dare take the one from my head; I was half frozen already.

When the hat appeared, more than one person ghosted away to avoid paying, but it was one man in particular who caught my eye, as he'd meant to. He tipped his head just barely toward one of a handful of public houses still open in Kilkenny and moved quickly along. I lost sight of him as I put my back to Elder Doolan, who was hurrying from across the square to once again lecture me—a wee girlie who clearly needed a man's hand—about the secular nature of my tales. I'd been informed on numerous occasions that if I put the fear of anything into the children, it should be the wrath of God the Victorious, not the Darkness, which, he believed, was no threat to the Virtuous . . . always proclaimed with a capital V.

If his belief had any basis in reality, I'd have more patience with his point of view. But the powers of Darkness fought the seraphs themselves. They'd hardly balk at children and self-righteous churchman. I was not going to spread pretty lies to keep his people in line. But I was happy to encourage a healthy fear of things that went bump in the night. Or even the day. News had reached even here about the daywalker who'd crawled out of a den in Carolina, in America. They'd been nearly legendary before this latest sighting.

But here in Ireland, we thrived on our myths and legends. Stories of the sidhe told of magical beings with the power to lure and glamour and compel. Were they really so different from the neomages, the seraphs? Were the baobhan sidhe, stunning fae who lulled mortals with their singing and then sucked their blood through needle-like nails, so unlike night- and day-walkers? Had the old tales been myth or prophecy?

Heresy. That's what Elder Doolan would say. Suggesting that the armies of God bore any resemblance to old pagan tales would earn me a branding at best, or more likely a stoning.

The Catholic priests and missionaries who'd first come to Ireland had done their best to stamp out the old religion and transform its tales to fit their theology. Later, the Protestant Brits had done their all to wipe out the Catholics, destroying churches and monasteries, enforcing Anglicanism as the state religion and making it illegal to speak Gaelic or, practically, to be Irish at all.

But we were a stubborn people. We held fast. And I had seen both too much and too little during my time in Enclave to believe in Elder Doolan's God.

Hence my meeting with Whit Lahey. I wasn't committed to the Earth Invasion Heretics. My opinions were too complex, and I wasn't much of a joiner. But my mind was open, and their money spent as well as any other. Being an itinerant storyteller gave me all the freedom a girl could want, but it didn't exactly provide. Not a living wage. That came from special deliveries—information, packages—not all of them approved by the Administration of the ArchSeraph. But not all under-the-table, either. Not with mail service only intermittent and glaciers making more of the countryside impassable by the year.

Elder Doolan got waylaid by a rawboned woman I didn't recognize, and I used her distraction to get away, barely glancing at my hat as it came back to me holding a mere pittance. Possibly enough for a meal and a pint, if I wasn't too picky about the quality.

I found Whit exactly where I expected to, at a small table at the back of the public room, his back to the wall. He was nursing a hot cuppa, and as I sat, I reached for it without asking—not to sip, but simply to wrap my still-gloved hands around. He relinquished the mug with a wry grin and signaled for another. I gave an additional signal that there should be a tipple in it. I'd trade Whit's mug back to him when it came. I needed something stronger than tea to warm my blood.

"So," I said, meeting Whit's gaze across the table. In the low light of the taproom, his eyes were nearly black. Ages out in the elements had carved lines into his face like the glacier-swept grikes of the Burren, but they worked for him. They gave him character. "What do you have for me?"

His lips quirked, as though he was about to say something completely unrelated to the package I was to carry for him, but then my tea arrived, the vapor rising from it carrying the distinct tang of whiskey, and I pushed his mug back to him. I raised mine to my nose even before my lips, inhaling the scent, letting the steam begin to thaw my face. I closed my eyes as I drank. Pure heaven.

When I set down my cup and opened my eyes again, the moment had passed. Rather than take his mug, both of Whit's hands were hidden beneath the table, and I felt something nudge at my leg. I lowered a hand to take it from him but it was bulkier and heavier than I'd expected. Reluctantly, I took the package in both hands and transferred it to the satchel hidden beneath my jacket. It just barely fit. The flap would close but not fasten.

"For the Widow Reilly at GtV Repairs in Kerry," he said, giving me a meaningful look. "No one else."

"Got it," I answered. "Mule train leaves tomorrow. I'm leaving with it. Any message?"

"She'll know."

He folded some money behind the salt and pepper shakers before rising to leave, pulling a woolen cap down over his head and raising the collar of his coat. That wad of bills was more than enough to cover his drink. Enough to cover my fee, I hoped. Not that I could check it right now with potential witnesses all around. I grabbed the money, stuffed it into one of my pockets and signaled for the server, hunger gnawing at my insides. The drink had done me good, but trying to stay warm in the biting temperatures burned calories that I needed to replace.

I spotted the kylen as I approached the muster point the next morning. Even with his glow dampened, even turned away so that I couldn't see his unearthly beauty, I could read the signs. The man who was not a man was tall and broad, at least at the shoulders, his coat bulky to accommodate the wings I was sure were hidden beneath. His long, copper-blond hair was gathered into a ponytail with a leather cord, his head bare in defiance of the cold. But it was the power that rolled off of him in waves that truly gave him away.

And put me in grave danger. There was no reason for a kylen, not even second or third generation, to be outside the Realms of Light. Not unless he was on a mission of some kind . . . like hunting down EIH sympathizers.

I nearly turned back to town. I could, potentially, wait for another mule train, but there was no telling when the next might be leaving. Possibly not until Liam and his riders returned from this trip. And recovered. I wasn't crazy enough to strike out on my own across the icy landscape, and I couldn't afford a private guide or guard. It wasn't so bad here in Kilkenny, but the glaciers that had once covered the Burren menaced the landscape once again. They hadn't reached all the way to Kerry, but it was still several days journey on treacherous footing. No sane person braved it alone.

Then the kylen turned and spotted me, and I was caught in his gaze like a fly in amber. His eyes were ice-green with darker rims encircling them and possibly even flecks of gold at their center. I tried not to study them. I tried to tear my gaze away, but it was no good.

I couldn't turn back now. It would be remarked. I would give myself away.

He nodded at me, merely acknowledgment, but my heart raced and my . . . well, if I could ride on the wings of my libido right now, there'd be no need for a mule train.

I nodded back, trying for neutrality. I was pretty certain I accomplished at least that much. I'd learned stoicism during my formative years in Enclave, having to hide what I thought of the arrogant neomages who tried to order me around, though it was my parents who worked there and not me. As soon as I was old enough to enter service, I got out.

To make matters worse, Elder Doolan and his wife bustled up, loaded with packs, clearly set to join the mule train. The glint in the elder's eye as he caught sight of me said that he looked forward to delivering his aborted lecture of the evening before. I wondered if setting off alone was truly as foolhardy as I feared.

Beside the Doolans and the kylen, there were Liam and his outriders, both of whom I knew from travels past—Mad Molly, who came by her name honestly, and Ronan, who was always trying to get me to share his bed "for warmth." On the colder treks, I'd even considered it. I enjoyed his company well enough and, if I was truthful, the breadth of his shoulders and knowing spark in his eyes. But I knew men like Ronan, and if he got what he wanted once, he'd expect it to be available whenever he liked. As my livelihood depended on travel and Liam's mule train was one of my only options, it was best not to start anything. I could do without complications . . . or stoning, which with the Doolans along seemed a likely thing.

There was a family with us as well—a woman, two men who looked to be brothers, and two children, one a babe in arms, who seemed desperate to escape her carry sling . . . or his; it was hard to tell all bundled as he—or she—was. The other child hid behind his mother's legs, peering up at the kylen with stunningly big eyes framed by dark lashes. The kylen noticed the boy's regard and the ice of those green eyes seemed to melt. A smile cracked his face. The boy reddened and ducked back behind his mother, peeping from her other side seconds later.

The kylen pretended not to notice, but I saw the quirk of his lips. He had a sense of humor, then. That did not at all help my libido.

Ronan sidled up to me as I was making nice with my mule and cinching up my saddlebags. Whit's package was strapped to my body, no longer in my messenger bag, but in a pack between my shoulder blades. I'd done my best to redistribute the weight without actually opening the package, but still I looked like I had a hump . . . or wings hidden underneath my coat.

No one, though, was going to mistake me for seraph spawn. I was all angles —no more flesh than would coat my bones. I had cheekbones that were an angel's envy, I'd give myself that. They were sharp enough to cut. Everything I had came to points, from the widow's peak of my stark black hair to my arched brows to my vaulted ears.

"So, that's the way it flows, does it, lass?" Ronan asked, nodding toward the kylen. "You know, if your motor gets running and you need to burn off some steam . . ."

I looked up into those dancing eyes of his. As tall as I was, Ronan had me by a good five inches, at least. "Ronan, you silver-tongued devil. You certainly know how to sweet-talk a girl."

He didn't look the least chastened. "You've managed to resist all of my charms so far. I thought I'd try a new approach."

I laughed, and Ronan's leer turned into a grin. That was another thing I liked about him—he never took rejections to heart.

"Ah, me lad," I said, pouring it on thick, "how could I possibly end our merry chase?"

"I have a few ideas," he said, but he left then with a wink and a nod, ignoring Liam's scowl as he got back to work.

It was a well-organized train, and it wasn't long before we were on our way. Too brief a time before the life and warmth of Kilkenny was behind us and what lay before us was nothing but the road, nearly choked off by the tall, unruly weeds that seemed to survive the frosts even when nothing else did. There was thistle, as always—hearty, like the people of Ireland. There was also meadow grass as tall as a man, and groundsel, nettle, and the tall, yellow-tipped stalks of mayweed. It was a prickly riot of color that we stayed well clear of. The mules might be tempted by the thistle, but our weeds had the habit of biting back.

We pushed through beyond sunset to get to the campground the mule-skinner had picked for the night. It was nothing more than a series of lean-tos, really, arranged in a semi-circle around a central fire pit. Stacked wood and kindling were stored inside one of the structures, covered over by a tarp and obscured by a dusting of snow that had blown in. Liam assigned the lean-tos while Ronan and Mad Molly went about clearing the fire pit and building the fire.

We ended the night around that fire—Liam, Ronan, Molly, me, and Flynn and Aidan, the men from the young family. The rest had turned in as soon as their plates were cleaned. Elder Doolan had stayed awhile, as though to chaperone, but disappeared somewhere during my tale of the gypsy and the fox. Aside from my children's stories, it was the tamest I knew, and as soon as he left I shucked it aside for a livelier tale. Ronan passed around a flask of good Irish whiskey, loosening Liam's tongue enough to regale us with stories of the last mule train and the battle of wills between one mule and the fool of a boy riding him. That one's trip to Kerry might very well be one way, since he'd have trouble sitting a mule again after the chunk the last had taken out of his bum.

I turned in only after my laughter turned to yawns.

That night I dreamt of blood and madness.

At first it was disjointed images—claws and teeth, red and black, flashes of light, the clang of steel, the rending of flesh, screams. Flashes of pain. Fabric tearing away, flesh with it.

I thrashed in my sleep, aware deep down that it *was* sleep, a dream. Still, my body reacted as if it was real, jerking to throw off the nightmare. I tried to force myself to surface, to break free of the visions, but something powerful kept pulling me down, a sick, dark horror that sucked at me like a bog. I was trapped, and the more I struggled, the deeper I fell.

The flashes resolved into images. Cinder-red eyes belonged to an unnaturally white face on which the veins stood out like ink spills. There was a terrible beauty to the angles of the face and the knife-point cut of the chin, but it was the fangs that riveted me. Serrated like shark teeth and flashing toward a throat . . . a *child's* throat. The little boy with the big eyes, now rolling in terror, the whites revealed all around. The scream had been his, cut off by the blackened claws that trapped him.

Something came at me inhumanly fast as I faced off with the nightwalker. I could see a glowing blade in my hand. I had just time to whirl before an impossible monstrosity was on top of me, spraying black spittle that burned on contact.

There was a flash, another scream, and I woke, sweat freezing on my face.

With a pair of eyes staring into mine.

I screamed and jerked back, away from those eyes, but I was trapped in my bedroll like a butterfly thrashing in its cocoon. My heart beat so hard I thought it would burst.

"You sense it too," said the voice that went with those eyes. "What did you see?"

In my terror, it took me seconds to realize the eyes I was staring into were pale green rather than red, and while they glowed, it was with the warmth of the sun or, given the color, the sun reflected off the moon. Kylen eyes. My heart gave a great kick and then settled, still beating just as fast but no longer as hard.

"You scared the shite out of me," I spat at him, yanking myself free of his gaze and trying to kick loose from my bedroll. The adrenaline flooding my system insisted there was still danger, and I wanted to be free, just in case.

"What did you see?" he repeated.

"Nightwalker. Spawn. Danger." *A child.*

"You know about the attacks—"

"Up *north.* We're supposed to be safe here. What would the Darkness want in this godforsaken place?"

The kylen stared at me intently, and for a moment I feared he'd lash out at me for my heresy. The powers of Light took those things seriously. Some—Elder Doolan most assuredly—believed that blasphemy was like a beacon to the Dark. I swallowed hard.

"What do *we* want with this place?" he asked, his voice as cold as the wind whipping around outside the scant shelter, blowing snow into the kylen's face—which he ignored.

"Nothing. This is just a waystation."

"And so—"

Mad Molly in her bedroll beside me cried out, "Baba noose!" or something equally nonsensical, and flung an arm out, hitting the kylen in the side. He didn't so much as flinch. He *did* look up, but it wasn't Molly who snagged his attention. It had gone from my face to the foot of my bedroll. A sick feeling rolled over me, clenching my gut. I knew what lay there. My pack. I was afraid of what I might see when I followed his gaze.

My bedroll was sturdy canvas lined with thick wool, and yet through the protective layers, something within glowed. I'd pushed Whit's package down to the foot of the bedroll where no one could possibly get at it without alerting me. Every time I stretched, the obstruction was a reminder and reassurance. There was nothing reassuring about the eerie red light.

"Your pack is glowing," the kylen said, deadpan.

"I can see that."

There were numerous reasons something in a pack might glow, but not to this extent. I thought fast. "I have an amulet that flares in the presence of the Dark. I'd say my dream isn't our only warning. And you're up and about. You must have sensed something."

He gave me a hard look, not buying my explanation for a second, and started to pull at my bedroll.

"Hey!" I said, loudly enough that Mad Molly snorted in her sleep. Some protection she was. "Stop!"

I had my knobbed walking stick just beyond the rolled blanket I used for a pillow, but I didn't want to start a fight I couldn't win. My father had taught me *bataireacht*—Irish stick-fighting—practically from the time I could walk, but as nimble as I was, I knew myself no match for kylen-speed. He'd have me disabled or dead by the time I could kick free of my bedroll.

So I wouldn't.

I tightened my core, gathered my legs, my pack flapping like dead weight at the base of my bedroll and lashed out with it, catching him under the chin with the heavy pack. His head flew back, but his reflexes were like lighting, and he caught my legs in his arms, trapping me in an awkward and vulnerable position.

Our eyes met and his suddenly went wide. His arms tightened around my legs in shock, and I looked beyond him to see Mad Molly, awake, her eyes dancing with gleeful menace.

"Let. Her. Go," Molly said. She sounded dangerous, like she fervently hoped he'd ignore the command so she could have some fun. Fun. With a *kylen*.

He growled.

"Carrick," she snapped out, "I'm not playing. If you've got an issue, you take it up with Liam. But you don't lay hands on any member of this train."

"She's got contraband," he said.

"Do you have proof?"

"How can I prove it if I can't look in her pack?"

Molly was right behind him. With kylen reflexes, he could almost certainly have shaken her off, so either she had a blade aimed at a particularly sensitive area or he wasn't as concerned as he looked.

"All right, Molly," Liam said, his deceptively quiet, absurdly deep voice coming out of the darkness to our right. The fire had been banked to keep from drawing notice. "I think he's gotten the message. In fact, I think *everyone* has gotten the message. Whole camp is awake . . . except maybe the Missus Doolan, who sleeps like the dead."

He fixed a hard-eyed stare on Carrick, who was still frozen at the point of Molly's blade. Or maybe it was just his regular kylen stillness. The powers of Light often reminded me of birds of prey—statues one minute, part of the landscape, silent and deadly the next, sweeping in for a kill you might never see coming, might never feel until your head was looking back on the rest of your body. "Carrick, just because we're away from civilization doesn't mean we're uncivilized. If you have a warrant, serve it. If you have a problem, come to me. Otherwise . . ."

I looked around. Sure enough, we had an audience. The eyes of the boy, Tom, flashed in the moonlight like a cat's.

Carrick bristled, seeming to grow larger. Then he took a deep breath and released it, exhaling his aggression.

"Apologies," he said when he'd drawn breath again. He didn't bother to make it sound convincing.

Liam didn't seem to care. He nodded tersely. "If everyone is up, we might as well get an early start. Long day today."

"Yes!" cried a voice into the sudden silence. Mature. Female. Sounding like she was in the throes of passion. "Oh, yes!"

"Maeve!" came an answering cry. "Maeve, wake up. For seraphs' sake, everyone is watching."

It was followed by a smack that carried in the chill air.

Liam moved almost mage-fast to jump in before another blow could fall, catching Elder Doolan by the wrist as his arm started to arc again. The elder turned on Liam, nostrils flaring with righteous anger. He ripped his wrist out of Liam's hand, and for a tense moment it seemed they would come to blows.

Then Maeve sat up, clutching her blankets to herself in fear of the two men rearing over her. Liam left them to themselves now that Maeve was awake and Doolan had no excuse to strike her again, but I wasn't so sure that would stop him.

Carrick moved and my attention snapped back to him. He took one look at the base of my bedroll, no longer glowing, and glowered back at me before pushing himself to standing. He strode angrily off the way we'd come the previous day.

Molly was now busily rolling her bedding into a tight bundle, humming flatly to herself to tune out the fight starting in the Doolan lean-to. I heard "blasphemy" and "loose woman," and I vowed to keep watch. The righteous seemed able to justify whatever action they chose to take, to wrap it up in Scripture, ignoring the parts that didn't suit, and present it as the moral high ground.

We didn't need trouble within our little group. We had enough to be wary of outside. I didn't assume for a second that the fact that my satchel no longer shone meant the danger had passed. In fact, I was pretty certain that Maeve's fevered dream and mine, the kylen's restlessness, and the glow all pointed to the same thing: Darkness was near.

I needed to find out what was in the package I carried. But not now, while everyone was watching.

Instead of giving in to my curiosity, I kicked free of my bedroll and stalked off in the direction the kylen had gone—not because I was eager for another encounter, but because the trampled ground was the best for what I had in mind. I needed to practice with my bata, my stick, to be ready for whatever came and to work off some of the tension that made me liable to spark like a live wire.

Carrick must have had the same idea. He was already there, moving through the forms of savage blade, his weapon gleaming in the pre-dawn glow. In motion, the kylen was a thing of deadly beauty. It was all I could do to shut him out as I sank into my own starting stance well out of range of his sword.

Bataireacht was not elegant like Carrick's savage blade . . . or like any martial art. It hadn't been codified or spiritualized. It wasn't practiced by monks or warriors. The bata, or shillelagh, was a weapon of the street. And it was a weapon of dissidents, like me. When the English made it illegal for the Irish to carry weapons, the bata was the only one left to us. Merely a walking stick. Nothing to see here. And yet deadly in the right hands.

I began as I'd been taught, holding my knobbed stick with its metal reinforced bulb over one shoulder to start, hand a third of the way up the shaft. I centered myself, slowed my breathing, and began—first a lunge and strike, stepping forward with my right foot as I slashed with my stick toward my opponent's temple. Then a quick backswing, aiming for the carotid on the other side, twisting my whole body with each blow for maximum force. Next, the shaft in a two-handed grip and a powerful jab with the slim base straight for my imaginary opponent's solar plexus. As quick as thought, the bata was up again over my shoulder, this time in a hanging guard, defending against an envisioned blow from behind. Then a pivot and swing to take on that attacker, a blow to the knee with the metal knob, meant to shatter bone.

I swung, blocked, pivoted, attacked, moving between one- and two-handed holds as I imagined the opponent against me, seeing my father there as he had been so many times, knowing his moves like I knew my own.

When I circled back to the beginning, I started again. Faster this time. And faster the next, until I was flying. No time, no room for thought; only movement, instinct, muscle memory. It was the closest I ever came to feeling the divine.

I held my final pose, stick in both hands after using each end to strike at my foe, not truly ready to let go of my adrenaline high but knowing other things awaited me. My body thrummed. My heart and breathing raced. I worked on calming them as I became aware again of my surroundings, of the kylen nearby, watching me, his own practice ended and his blade sheathed.

I met his gaze, still feeling powerful and energized, fully ready to take him on if it came to that, though I knew that confidence to be misplaced. He gave me a nod and even a bit of a bow, and when he raised his head, his eyes were glowing. "You are good. Even impressive," he said. "Ever work with a blade?"

I tried to ignore the way my body thrummed at his praise and focused on the question at hand. "Some."

When I'd told my parents that I would be leaving, my father insisted on teaching me a variation on *bataireacht*, one that used a blade in my free hand, but a knife, not a full sword. Not anything close to Carrick's savage blade. I wondered whether to say so. If he was truly my enemy, keeping the secret might someday give me the element of surprise. Might save my life.

"I'm standard-issue human," I said, looking him dead in the eyes. It was not a confession. Unlike the neomages and others, I did not for a second equate this with *lesser*. "I was never offered sword training."

"You grew up in Enclave," he said, not a question, but a revelation.

"Yes. My parents worked there. I schooled there. And then I left."

Carrick grunted, and I had no idea what to make of that. It didn't seem as though seraph spawn should do anything so . . . human. "I will teach you, if you'd like."

I stared at him. "Why?"

"Because we are at war. Because the Dark are on our heels. If your skills are any indication, you are a warrior born. You have the footwork, and the muscles already developed. The blade is not so different from the cudgel."

"I don't have a blade to practice with," I said, but it was a weak objection. I wanted what he offered, the chance to train with a kylen. It was a once-in-a-lifetime opportunity.

"I'll arrange it," he said, and then turned and walked away as though it had all been decided, my acceptance assumed. Not wrongly, but the arrogance of it still left me grinding my teeth.

A quarter hour later, Liam, Molly, and Ronan had everyone set up with camp breakfast—pressed oatcakes that tasted like barely-sweetened sawdust. By the time we finished eating, they'd saddled the mules and were ready to go. Maeve Doolan seemed pinched—more pinched even than usual—and wouldn't meet anyone's gaze, least of all her husband's.

I seemed to have acquired my own personal kylen. I couldn't shake him. All day Carrick rode beside or just behind me. Every time I looked, his gaze was on me—or off in the distance, watching for trouble.

I couldn't blame him there. That uneasy feeling from my nightmare stayed with me all day, and I scanned the landscape too, determined not to be caught unaware. It was hard to keep up the hypervigilance, though, especially after a disturbed night, and after a while I was looking for a distraction. Or a nap. I couldn't afford either, but chose the lesser of two evils.

"What are you doing outside the Realms?" I asked the kylen finally.

He turned my way, and again I thought of a raptor sighting in on his prey.

He didn't answer right away, and when he did, it was to return a question for a question. "Why did you leave the Enclave?"

I shook my head and gave him a wry smile. "I asked you first."

He scanned the horizon again before turning back to me. "So you did."

I sighed and debated whether it was worth continuing the attempt at conversation. Maybe if I showed him mine. My cheeks heated at the thought. I'd meant it metaphorically, but apparently my mind had jumped straight to a more carnal interpretation.

"My parents were in service to Enclave," I said finally. "I was not."

"You weren't happy there?"

"I wasn't myself. There were expectations," I said, surprised when the words wanted to flow. "Not expectations that I would make something of myself—not do great things, or at least important things like a neomage, but that I would fetch or cook or cobble as my parents did."

"And you wanted—"

"Something more."

"What?" he pushed.

If my cheeks burned now it was with frustration. "I don't *know*. You don't need to know where you fit in to know where you don't."

"Fair enough," he said, releasing me from his raptor's gaze.

I felt relief and loss all at once. I still didn't know where I belonged, unless it was on the road. The title of an old Pre-Ap song had always stuck with me: "Like a Rolling Stone." That was me.

"What about you?" I asked. "Why are you with this mule train? Is it related to the Dark attacks? Are we in danger?" I would not ask, *Does it have anything to do with me?*

"Carrick!" Liam cried out, raising his usually quiet voice to carry. "Molly and Ronan are going to ride out, scout the land ahead. Can I count on you to help me guard the train while they're away?"

I wondered whether he really needed the help or whether he thought he was saving me from interrogation. After all, daylight was the safest time—not that it did my anxiety any good to know that.

The kylen gave me a stonefaced nod, and rode up to speak with Liam. I couldn't tell how he felt about being interrupted. He seemed perfectly capable of diverting my inquiries without any help.

The kylen then dropped to the back of the train where Ronan usually rode. It gave me breathing room, but also nothing to divert me from my worry. Something was coming. I knew it. Carrick knew it. And, from the sound of things, Maeve Doolan knew it too, at least on some level.

By nightfall my nerves were drawn to the breaking point. I set down my bedroll, but didn't open it. I wouldn't be sleeping tonight. What I really wanted was to sneak away, to explore what Whit Lahey had given me, and whether it could be calling the Dark. I'd rather lose my commission than my life. If the EIH felt the contents of the package important enough, they could come back for it. Although leaving it out here undefended . . . no, the Darkness was likely to get to it before the EIH, and nothing that drew the Dark meant any good for humanity.

I was no hero, but neither was I someone who let bad things happen.

I startled when a body suddenly appeared before me, blocking the fading light. Molly belly-laughed at my reaction. "Wool-gathering, eh?" she asked. "I shouldn't wonder. He's worth a daydream or ten."

"Who?" I asked, honestly baffled at that moment.

"Why, the kylen, of course. I've seen how you look at each other."

"Like he wants to drag me away in chains?"

Molly looked at me like *I* was crazy, her head cocked as if she might understand me better from that angle. "Sure, chains."

"What did you see out there today?" I asked.

No one had said and Ronan hadn't once today tried to get inside my clothes. It was ominous.

The amusement leached from Molly's face along with all the color. "Blood," she said.

"Way out here? Deer? Wild pigs?" I asked.

"Maybe."

"But you don't think so."

"Who says I don't?"

"Molly, I'm a storyteller. I know when someone's telling a tale."

She chewed on her chapped bottom lip. It must have hurt, but she didn't seem to notice. In the end, all she did was shake her head and turn away, hoping to put me off by giving me her back and starting her preparations for our second night.

"Remains? Drag marks?" I pushed. And then, because it slipped out even though I didn't really want to know, "Bodies?"

She shot me a look that said everything. She'd seen things she couldn't unsee and wasn't about to relive.

I gasped in a breath, then another, trying to convince my chest to expand, to take it in.

"Another mule train? Have any been reported missing?" I asked.

She'd turned back to her bedroll, and at first I thought she wasn't going to answer me. Then, quietly, she said, "Not that we've heard of . . . yet. We'd never have come out else."

The breath I'd taken gushed out of me. We'd been riding for two days. It would be two days more to Kerry. We were as far as we could get from help, from sending or receiving news—unless Carrick had some way to send messages or unless Liam sent out a rider, leaving the mule train one guard short and that rider totally unprotected. He wasn't going to do that.

"I'll . . . be back," I told Molly.

I grabbed up my pack and ventured out, checking first to see that Carrick was occupied and wouldn't follow. Tom, the boy who'd been watching him since we started, must have finally gotten brave enough to approach. He stood now with Carrick, who was showing off his sword and, very slowly, the first moves of his kata. Katie, the boy's mother, stood close by, alternately watching in concern and cooing to the baby in her arms.

With the kylen occupied, I crept into the brush that screened the sides of our path. The weeds caught at me as I went, probably depositing seed pods and prickles I'd have to pick out later. I stopped when the high grass enclosed me entirely and then turned back to face the way I'd come, so that the swaying brush would give away anyone who might approach. Unavoidably, I'd left a trail that was easy enough to follow.

Satisfied that I was alone, I brought my pack around to the front of my body and released the flap. If the contents were still glowing, I couldn't see it. I pulled the package out of the satchel, marveling again at its weight. The contents shifted awkwardly inside the oilcloth wrappings. So not one thing then, but several. I squatted so that I could lay the package across my thighs and began gently to unwrap it. There was more shifting and sliding as I loosened the contents, almost as if they were alive, as if I was unswaddling a baby who was about to burst free.

And then I twitched aside a fold of the oilcloth and something fell to the ground: a shard of metal, light-suckingly dark. Dead. Infernal. One side of the shard had obviously been worked, honed to a fine edge that was the only part of the former blade that gleamed, as though whatever blood it had last shed still clung wetly at the edges. The other side showed stress fractures from having been shattered.

I let it lie where it had fallen for a moment, and peeled back another fold of the oilcloth to reveal the other half of the weapon—the hilt and the lower part of the blade. A demon iron sword. I knew it not because I'd ever seen one, but because I'd heard about them in my collecting of tales. I knew they were nearly unbreakable. Something major must have happened to this one.

How would the EIH have come by a broken demon iron blade? And why would they want it? Unless . . . well, unless they didn't trust the Light any more than the Dark. They didn't believe the seraphs were angels or that they had anything like mankind's best interests at heart. They'd seek out things that gave them a fighting chance if it came to open rebellion.

I didn't know whether the metal would scorch me or how much of its power the demon iron retained, but I wasn't willing to touch it directly and find out. I refolded the oilcloth over the hilt and carefully moved it aside.

The package hadn't yet revealed all its secrets. There'd been too much shifting for just the Dark blade. The next layer revealed an amulet, as night-dark as the blade, but with a sheen, possibly obsidian, carved in the shape of a dragon curled around a mottled green stone with a blotch of crimson off-center, irregular tendrils radiating out from it like blood spatter. Blood-stone? The snapped remains of a leather cord that had once held it around a neck were coiled with the amulet.

I started to reach for it. It was so beautiful, and I wanted to trace the carving of the scales, the intricate detail of the dragon's whiskers. The artist had even thought to carve texture into the multitude of tiny claws. Com-pared to the dragon, the bloodstone looked so smooth, so satiny. As I watched, the red inclusion in the center of the stone began to glow, igniting the green around it as well. I felt warmth, like I was standing too close to a fire. Or just close enough. I wanted to touch it—

I heard the swishing of the meadow grass as something approached, and had just enough time to fold the oilcloth back over the amulet and broken blade and shove the whole bundle back into my pack. I closed the flap and slid the strap around so the pack was behind me, cutting off the glow of the amulet with my body. Hiding it.

Protecting it? No! That felt dirty. Wrong. These were infernal artifacts. Surely no good could come of them.

Carrick burst through the brush just as I got everything squared away, gaze shooting around as though he expected to find trouble.

I crossed my arms and glared as he got to me. "Well, this would have been awkward if I'd been answering a call of nature."

"Liam has a place sectioned off for that," he answered, unfazed.

"Maybe it was in use," I said. "Maybe I couldn't wait."

He looked straight into my eyes, and I expected a glare, but his ice-green gaze glittered differently, strangely, as if he didn't trust that he'd found me so innocently standing in a field. I couldn't exactly blame him.

"I brought you a sword," he said, though not as if he was ready to sur-render it to me. "Come, where we have more room."

And less chance of ambush. He didn't have to say it.

I sighed. In that single breath I considered and discarded the idea of re-fusing. There was no way I'd have the chance to sneak off again and ex-plore the rest of what I carried, not now that I had his attention. Best to keep it diverted.

Also, I was oddly excited about the chance to watch him again at savage blade. I knew I shouldn't be. He was the enemy. Well, not truly. I didn't *have* enemies. I hadn't chosen a side. But as a representative of the Realms in some way he had yet to confirm, and with me carrying contraband for the EIH, he was as close to an enemy as I had. Certainly he was not my friend.

Carrick pulled a sword from a sheath behind his back and offered it to me hilt first. It was plain—utilitarian—and yet strangely beautiful. If there was an imperfection, I couldn't spot it.

"Mage steel," he told me. "My second best, but it will do."

As though I would argue that the blade offered was unworthy of me.

I slid my pack to the ground and pushed it off to the side where it wouldn't trip me up. I'd have felt better keeping it close, but it would have put me off-balance and gotten in my way. Carrick checked my grip on the hilt, but didn't correct it. He showed me how to stand, how to hold the sword in my dominant hand, fingers just so. He didn't have to do anything about my feet. I knew how to position them for maximum flexibility of motion, how to turn into my strikes. Immediately we moved on to attacks, lunges, guards. I caught on quickly, my borrowed sword slicing the air, nearly singing. It was probably my imagination that I felt a tingle, a connection straight through the hilt and into my hand, zipping through my arm and up my body. It might have been adrenaline, endorphins, Carrick's nearness—

Then we heard little Tom's scream.

We froze for only a second and then took off as though the hounds of Hell were nipping at our heels. I swept up my pack without a pause as I ran full out back toward camp. My heart hammered in my chest at the thought of something happening to the boy with the big eyes who'd watched Carrick so worshipfully.

Carrick reached the edge of the campsite first and stopped. I came up fast behind him and barely swerved in time to avoid crashing into his back. We faced a maddened Maeve Doolan holding the terrified boy to her chest, an already bloody knife at his throat. The others were arrayed around the two of them, Katie crying and begging, the men with her exchanging dangerous looks as though silently plotting to take Maeve down. But crazy came with its own kind of strength, and I feared for Tom's life. Especially if Maeve had already tasted blood, as I feared from the knife and the sight of the boots splayed behind her, which I recognized as Mad Molly's. I wanted to run to her but didn't dare set Maeve off.

"Don't hurt him," Katie wailed. "Let him be. Please. He's no harm to anyone. He's only five."

"A fitting sacrifice then," Maeve hissed. "Innocent." There was no sanity in her eyes. She was clearly in the thrall of someone or something—likely whatever had invaded her dreams.

I shot Carrick a sidelong glance, wondering what to do, whether he had a plan, whether his magic—but he was looking at my pack; I presumed that meant it was glowing again.

I yanked it around to the front of me to see, and it attracted Maeve's attention as well.

"You have it with you!" she cried. "Give it to me! Give it here and I'll let the boy go."

Beside me, Carrick shook his head just slightly, but enough for the boy's mother to see. Katie cried out, dropping to her knees at his feet.

I had a second to decide whether I dared trade the amulet and whatever else my pack held for the boy. On the one hand, Tom's life was easily worth anything I had. But if the contents of my pack could be used to take thousands of other lives—I couldn't let it fall into the hands of Maeve and whatever controlled her.

To buy time, I reached into my bag for the wrapped package, which warmed my hands almost to burning. I held the glowing oilcloth out to Maeve. If she stepped up for it, Carrick could strike her down, but she was too smart for that.

"Fetch it for me," she told Tom, moving her knife out of the way and shoving him forward, point pressed to his back.

Tom shrieked and instead of going for the package, ran for his mother. Maeve lunged after him, but Carrick was suddenly in her way, swinging his mighty blade down to cut her neck to sternum, the seraph steel slicing through her flesh as if it was mist. Maeve's mouth opened, her eyes wide in surprise. And then she fell to the ground, lifeless. Katie held her son to her, pressing his face into her shoulder so that he couldn't see, as much as he tried to wriggle around.

She raised accusing eyes to me. "*You*. She was after what *you* had. *You're* the cause of all of this."

I looked immediately to Carrick. If he too thought I was the cause, I was as dead as Maeve. I'd just seen proof of how swift and merciless kylen could be when dispensing justice.

"Show us," he said. His sword swung my way, dripping with Maeve's blood. "And do it quickly. Maeve was touched. Whatever she served will come itself, now that its tool has been dispatched."

I thought of the other mule train and Molly's haunted look. Dark forces might have come with or without me, but if I carried a lodestone . . .

I didn't argue.

I set the oilcloth on the ground and unrolled it. Carrick hissed when the demon iron was revealed and let out the last of his air when I reached the amulet.

"Spiritstone," he said on the exhale, his gaze riveted to the red glow at the heart of the stone. "I've heard of these, but I've never seen . . ."

I looked at him, questioningly, and he explained. "A stone that holds the concentrated essence, the spirit, of something. Terrible to trap any being that way."

"Even your enemies?" For my part, I couldn't imagine anything that constrained the feral force of a dragon to be a bad thing.

He didn't answer, and I hurried to reveal the rest, careful not to touch the spiritstone with my bare hands.

The package held two more amulets. One was a great cloudy green stone embedded in the broken end of a staff. Jade? Aventurine? I was no expert in these things. The other was a pendant of clear stone that immediately caught and held the light from the moon. Neither affected me the way the infernal artifacts had. They didn't sicken or burn or attract me.

Confirming that these were something other, Carrick reached for the moonstone, which glowed brighter the closer he came, nearly blinding as he wrapped his fingers around it.

"Where did you get these?" he asked, not taking his eyes from the glow.

Artifacts of the Dark and the Light. At a guess taken from some battle-field—but what battle? There'd been reports of attacks in the north, but were they worse than had been reported? Were we humans being kept in the dark? Carrick had mentioned a war. I'd thought he meant the eternal struggle, but what if he meant something much more immediate?

And how on Earth had Whit gotten his hands on these things? What did he know?

"I'm just a courier," I said, but it sounded weak even to me.

Carrick spared a glance for me. "Not anymore. Something's coming. We both sense it. You will fight or you will die."

He looked to the rest of the group, making sure to meet everyone's eyes, even those of Elder Doolan, who had collapsed into a heap by the body of his wife, slack-faced with shock. "That goes for you all. You will fight or you will die."

Carrick turned to me. "I'd have a word with you." I didn't take it for a suggestion.

"Can I check on Molly while we talk?"

"What—" Liam started.

Carrick cut him off. "Make sure that all are armed. Form a perimeter around the children. I'll be right with you."

If he'd had a free hand, Carrick might have dragged me off. Instead, he gestured with his sword for me to put the artifacts back in my pack, and then herded me in Molly's direction. She wasn't moving. Not a twitch. She was on her stomach, arms splayed, laying as she'd fallen. The slant of the lean-to cut off the light, so at first I had hope she might still be alive. Knocked out but breathing. That hope died when I reached out to her and my hand came away covered in blood that had blended with the deep brown of her coat. It was everywhere. I turned her over to be certain, but I knew the truth even before I saw it in her open, lifeless eyes. Maeve had knifed her in the back. Molly'd never had a chance.

My heart ached. My fault—all my fault.

I turned to Carrick. "What do you need? How can I help?"

"The spiritstone. Have you touched it?"

"No."

"Do it. Now." His gaze burned into mine.

Reluctantly, I pulled the oilcloth out of my pack, partially unwrapped it. The spiritstone stared up at me from the cloth, its red heart pulsing. I swallowed hard before I took it in one hand. It was hot, which was not a surprise, but it was also heavier than expected, and I knew why the package with only a single broken sword and three amulets had weighed on me.

"It doesn't burn you?" he asked.

"Not . . . much." I answered, afraid of what that meant for my soul.

Maybe only that I hadn't chosen a side, though that was about to change. The stone's heat burrowed into me, but it didn't burn. For now.

"Good. When the forces come, you will activate it."

"How? What?"

"A drop of your blood and it will answer to your call."

I wasn't sure I wanted it to, but Carrick had already moved on, reaching for the final amulet, the green stone. He held it for a moment with his eyes closed. "Simple *Illumination* conjure," he said. "Not yet spent. We'll put this near the children in the center. The light will be at our backs, blinding to our enemies. Their eyes aren't meant for it. Little enough advantage, but we'll take what we can."

And he was off, stalking toward the others and issuing orders like a general commanding his troops. I said a brief prayer over Molly before the amulet in my hand scorched me to silence. I tucked it into a pocket and turned back toward the others.

Liam had made sure everyone was armed. Even Katie brandished a hog-butchering knife she must have carried with her, the look of a warrior about her. She would die before she let anything get to her kids. Carrick had the adults—Katie, Flynn and Aiden, Elder Doolan, Ronan, and Liam—arrayed in a circle that he cut through to plant the broken end of the staff with the green stone in the ground.

He called to Tom, and when the boy stepped forward, Carrick took off his coat and handed it to him as though to a squire. Tom's eyes widened, as did mine, I'm sure, at the sight of Carrick's wings unfurling. Gorgeous wings, starting white as alabaster at the top and transitioning to dove grey in the center on to charcoal at the tips. Or more accurately, some iridescent form of gray, as the colors seemed to shift, there and then gone in an instant, like the changing black of a raven's wing.

Then he gave Tom the very important task of triggering the amulet. The responsibility seemed to push back the boy's fear. His shoulders squared, his jaw jutted out in determination and he gave a single brave nod.

Carrick caught my eye and I caught my breath as we joined the circle protecting the children and our camp. I held the mage steel blade in the hand that would usually hold my knife, the spiritstone in the other, with my bata tucked into the belt at my waist within ready reach.

There we stood, tense, waiting.

"Your amulet," I whispered, meaning the moonstone he held. "What does it do?"

"Moon madness," he answered, without taking his gaze from the darkness surrounding us. "Stay well to my side."

After a few minutes a shiver of warning went through me, despite the heat of the amulet I held. Carrick's stone flared in his hand, and I knew. He cried out for Tom to trigger the *Illumination* amulet and suddenly our enemies were upon us.

Light flared at our backs, and before us I heard a hissing and howling in reaction, a gnashing of teeth and claws that was nothing to the horror of seeing our enemies revealed—an entire army of dragonets, each a chimera of parts, each more grotesque than the next. One with a hag's head, stringy black hair sparse across it, with a jaw that unhinged to reveal viper's teeth and a body that owed more to mosquito than man. Another with a tail like a flail with multiple strands, each barbed. Others looked more like insects or scorpions, with segmented bodies and too many legs, or eerily saurian, with pointed snouts full of bladed teeth. So many I couldn't take them all in. And behind them stood a nightwalker, cadaverously thin and bone white, one hand up to shield red-glowing eyes that watered in pain and burned with malice.

We were outnumbered. Whether it was their aura or my body's own response, fear took hold of me, wrapping itself around my heart and squeezing. The stone in my hand pulsed in time with my heart's frantic beating. I didn't waste the reminder.

Blood. I tipped the blade toward my hand, giving just a tiny nick to my thumb where I held it poised above the amulet. As the first drop of blood struck it, the spiritstone bucked in my hand and then the obsidian . . . moved. The carved eyes flared, and it uncoiled, rippling, growing, becoming less and less opaque as it did. As soon as it was large enough, it unhinged its jaw and swallowed the stone at its center, at which point it exploded up into the air, becoming a dragon of shadow, huge and menacing, dripping darkness. So many legs, like a giant millipede, two sets of bat wings. One head, with a spined ridge running from the apex of its head down the entire length of its body. The stuff of nightmares.

The nightwalker cried for his army to charge before my shadow dragon could reach full size. I thrust my hand forward the way I would release a hawk, calling in voice and mind for the shadow beast to attack the Dark army. It struck at the front line, coming up with a dragonet trapped in its teeth and another caught in its many legs.

The rest of the creatures boiled toward us. Beside me, Carrick thrust forward his own amulet and called out a word in a language I couldn't understand. The moonstone flared brighter than the moon itself, sending out a pulse of power that swept the horde. Those caught in the pulse turned on each other instantly—ripping, tearing, biting, rending.

But others reached us. I shoved the remains of the amulet down my shirt, in case it needed to be in contact with my skin for me to stay in control, and used my freed hand to grab my bata. In a second I was fully engaged—bashing, thrusting, swinging, breaking. My sword was less familiar and mostly a defense at first, deflecting blows, keeping my opponents at blade length. All around me were cries of power and pain.

"Again!" I cried to the shadow dragon, not sure whether to direct it with words or will. There'd been no time to learn.

A bladed beak snapped at my neck, and I threw all my weight into an overhand swing, bringing the metal end of my bata down on the beak with a crack so great it bounced the beast's head off the ground. But another attack was already coming in from my left, pincers snapping together.

Instinctively, I swung the sword to counter the new menace, the way of it coming more naturally to me now. The flat of the blade knocked the pincers aside before they could pierce me, but the first creature had recovered. Its beak was caved in where I'd beaten it, a painful-looking set of cracks radiating outward, but it didn't stop the creature from coming. It struck at me, lighting fast, its beak easily as sharp as my blade. I had to dive and roll beneath the other's pincers as they swung back at me, coming up on the other side and straight to my feet, both weapons at the ready. I became a dervish—whirling, slashing, cracking, never in the same spot from one second to the next to confound the dragonets' deadly aim.

The shadow dragon swept back and forth across the field as I fought, doing devastation with each pass. Beside me, Carrick was a maelstrom of motion, but I couldn't spare a glance to marvel. A third dragonet was circling now, more behind it. I had to finish the first two before I was overwhelmed.

The pincers came at me again, but this time I leapt into the air, landing on top of them just long enough to propel myself even higher, up onto the other beast. I'd been aiming for its head, but only got as far as its oversized beak. I landed hard, and the beast reared back. I started to slide and thrust my sword down deep into the beak to hold myself in place. The dragonet gave a strangled squawk, and I hung on to the sword hilt for dear life as it thrashed back and forth, trying to dislodge me.

The pincers came for me again, the dragonet deaf to its fellow's agony. I gave up my hold on the embedded sword to slide away, letting the pincers smash into the other creature with a crack that I hoped would finish it off. I hit the ground rolling, coming up beneath the second dragonet with just my bata. There was a seam in the beast's lower shell, and I aimed for it, pounding away with the head of my bata until it cracked like a crab's carapace. The creature fell back, but I chased it down, beating it with my metal-tipped stick until it started to waver. It was going to come crashing down.

I dove out from beneath the dragonet as it collapsed, catching my boot under its bulk. I kicked hard to get free just as something raked my back, opening fiery furrows in it. I twisted to see a new dragonet with claws the size of meat hooks coming for me. I was trying desperately to free the bata trapped underneath me when a cry I felt more than heard split the night. The shadow dragon jetted back over the battlefield to sweep up the taloned monstrosity in its maw and carry it away. Maybe my spilled blood had called it.

A horrible laugh brought me abruptly and painfully to my feet—and face-to-face with the blood-red eyes of the nightwalker. His skin glowed ghoul-white in the light of the *Illumination* spell. He smiled as he saw me, but there was nothing of joy in it. Or mirth. Or sanity. I slashed at him, but he was inhumanly fast, twisted and changed by the blood he'd taken from his Dark master. He knocked my bata aside as if it was nothing and latched ragged claws around my neck to lift me off the ground. I felt the amulet I'd hidden away slide out as my shirt came untucked. Panicked, I cried for help, but only managed a gurgle.

Of all people, Elder Doolan was suddenly there, lunging at the creature, swinging a sword inexpertly. The nightwalker lashed out with his free hand, throwing out a wave of force, and the elder flew back, leaving a gap in the protective circle we'd formed around the kids. I swung and kicked and bashed, desperate to get to them, but the nightwalker was armored and I had no leverage. I frantically pried at the fingers around my throat, but it was like trying to bend steel. His claws only dug deeper. I called on my blood to bring the shadow dragon back around, but with the amulet now on the ground at my feet, it wouldn't respond to me.

The others were all locked in battles to the death. I was on my own.

Going against every instinct, I dropped my weapon and stopped clawing at the nightwalker's hands around my neck. Instead, I shot my hands toward those burning eyes, gouging with my thumbs, ignoring the squishy, horrible feel of his eyeballs giving way and the blistering acid of his blood. The creature howled and dropped me.

Hitting the ground, I rolled for the bata and came up with it in both hands, shoving the bulbed end up under his chin, snapping his head back. Then, while he was vulnerable, I thrust the pointed tip straight into the soft, unprotected hollow at the base of his throat, hard enough to drive the tip an inch into his flesh. He made an awful sound. Worse when I yanked the bata free, twisting to the side to avoid his fountaining blood, but not quite fast enough.

A spray of it burned across half of my face, caustic as acid. I screamed and clawed at it with my free hand, trying to wipe it away, but only rubbing it in. I reached for the ground, praying not all the snow had been trampled and came up with a handful of dirt more than anything, but I scrubbed it on my face regardless. The grit stung but cooled the burn to an almost bearable level.

I blinked away the tears and dirt just in time to take out the legs and bash in the skull of a dragonet making a grab for me with needle-like fingers and then looked around for more danger. I found Liam dispatching a creature that looked like a spider-cricket mix, and Carrick bisecting a dragonet with a single massive swipe. When it was done, he strode to the nightwalker and delivered the coup-de-grace.

It took me a moment to realize that the battlefield lay nearly still. Two of our own were dead. Whatever attack the nightwalker had thrown at Elder Doolan, he never got up from it. And Flynn, one of the two men in the family group, had fallen. I had to glance away or be sick. He'd been gnawed, with barely enough left behind to bury.

Little Tom cried suddenly, "Mama!" and I turned, fearing the worst, but Katie was still standing, if only just, a great gash across her stomach and one arm hanging uselessly at her side. She dropped her butcher knife from the other hand and caught Tom with it as he ran to her, the *Illumination* spell dying just as he reached her, dropping the battlefield, mercifully, into darkness . . . at least until our eyes readjusted to the moonlight.

The shadow dragon wheeling in the sky gave a shriek and faded away, as though it needed light for its shadow. I saw a thin trail of vapor being sucked toward a spot on the ground where I'd dropped the amulet in my fight with the nightwalker, the dragon's essence returning to its prison. I swept the ground for the amulet, knowing I was close when I felt the burn. *Burn* this time, no gentle heat. I grabbed the spiritstone and pocketed it as quickly as I could. I didn't dare leave it behind for the Dark.

Carrick was watching me when I straightened. "Do you have healing?" I asked him.

"I have amulets," he said, and I breathed a sigh of relief. Kylen magic could be unreliable, but stored spells should be safe. We would be okay, those of us who remained.

Carrick took the *Healing* amulets from inside his jacket—round, nearly translucent stones in braided silver settings. I wondered if they were moonstones as well, and if he had an affinity for them. But I didn't ask. He handed the amulets to Liam to deal out and held me back as I'd have gone to help the wounded as well.

"I'll be confiscating your artifacts," he said, holding my gaze. "You won't make your delivery."

I forgot about my burns and injuries as a chill seized my heart. Did he blame me for the attack? If I was going to die, I wanted a moment to make my peace.

"Is that all?" I asked, afraid of his answer.

"You will accompany me on my mission and then back to the Enclave. You are wasted here."

"*Enclave?*" I said faintly, surprised to feel a small twinge of longing, not for the place so much as for my family. I hadn't seen ma and da since leaving.

"Whatever else you may be," Carrick said, "you are a warrior. I think you should be properly trained."

Enclaves did have human soldiers: some champards, fighting side-by-side with mages, and others working as security. I'd never considered that life. Not if it meant staying. But if I could have another life—missions like Carrick, taking the fight to the Dark rather than waiting for it to come . . .

"What *is* your mission?" I asked, not ready to accede to what was clearly more order than suggestion. Not yet ready to give in. To go back.

I had avoided ties, restrictions, and servitude for so long. I'd wandered, but I'd never found my place. Never found my purpose. As much as I enjoyed tale-telling, I only knew peace when I was practicing with my bata, losing myself in the movement and the strength and the power. I was only truly at peace when I could step outside myself, stop thinking and *do*.

"I was sent to hunt the monsters threatening travelers," Carrick said, "to dispatch any nests."

"Alone?" I asked.

"Will I be alone?" He looked deeply into my eyes and my heart tried to beat its way out of my chest.

The question hung between us, needing an answer. When I'd left Enclave, I'd been running from something rather than running to, but it didn't have to be that way. If the Dark was encroaching on us like glaciers on the Burren, if there was truly a war where I was needed . . . Maybe the reason I'd never found a place was that I was destined for wherever battle would take me. Maybe it was time to stop telling tales and start living them.

The glimmer of pre-dawn started in the east, as though the sun rose with my new awareness.

"No," I said. "You won't be alone."

The words didn't even stick in my craw.

Lions and Tigers and Monkeys, Oh My!
Mid-Summer 105 PA / 2117 AD

Faith Hunter

The train's passage was slow, because some of the wheels were damaged when a landslide of snow-loosened scree hit the train broadside. We spent two days stranded, while my least favorite Steel mage tried to fix them. And even after Cheran Jones got them mostly straight, the train only moved at half speed to allow the still-warped wheels to roll.

We were going to be late at the New Orleans Enclave. I figured that would irritate the priestess, but she wasn't my best buddy, so I wasn't too concerned by the political implications. In fact, by showing up on my own timetable, they might think I was making a statement about my independence.

Claire, the mage who could provide us with a good excuse for tardiness —something along the lines of, "Thorn and her warriors spent two days fighting Darkness . . . underground . . . on the way"—wasn't on the train with us. And she probably wouldn't help anyway unless she found a way to make it benefit her. So, independence it was. Again.

We'd left the mountains behind and reached the Gulf Coast, with its humidity and heat. I'd lived in the mountains so long that I'd forgotten the miserable heat. Even a mini-ice age couldn't cool off a Louisiana summer. I'd also forgotten the animals down south, the original wildlife and the new ones—the zoo animals and farm animals set free after the end of the world and their descendants.

In the mountains the wildlife was mostly the same as it'd always been. We had moose, elk, deer, wild cattle, bison, boars, wild horses, roving bands of dogs, wolves, snow leopards. Raptors of every kind. Trout, salmon, and small-mouth bass in the icy rivers. Bobcats and lynx were common. Probably more of all of them than there'd been in centuries, but that's because there were fewer people to hunt them, fewer fences, fewer highways.

In the temperate zone between the interior glaciers and the south coast, the critters were changing. Herds of animals—and predators with plenty to eat—were being seen on military overflights, and by trackers and deadminers who were willing to brave the Dark for the possibility of profit. Immediately after the Plagues and wars had killed so many people, domestic cattle had roamed free in huge herds. But as the weather turned harsher and winter took over more and more of the year, hardier plains bison, survivors of the last ice age, made a comeback. Now they numbered in the millions, were bigger, meaner, and took whatever grazing grounds they wanted. The wolves that hunted them were taller than me at the shoulder, looking like the dire wolves of the last ice age. But at least they were still normal animals.

The Gulf Coast and the Deep South were something else. The ecology was so varied it hurt the eyes, ears, and nose—a kaleidoscope of sensory impressions. Rare animals were becoming more common. Monkeys were everywhere in the trees, fighting for space with multi-colored parrots. Gators had grown to amazing lengths, as had the pythons, boas, rattlers, water moccasins, and anacondas. Scientists had counted dozens of species of primates that now thrived in the wild, including mandrills, chimpanzees, gibbons, and over thirty species of African and American monkeys, if you included the new ones.

With creation energy running rampant, and with so few of their own kind to choose from, some of the zoo animals had begun to mate outside of their own kind, creating new species. There were gorillas and chimps producing gorilpanzees, squirrel monkeys and spider monkeys making spiquerrls, lemurs and gibbons making lebons. And it wasn't just the primates that were cross-breeding. Tigers, lions, tigons, and ligers were now at the top of the North American food chain. Below them were pumas, leopards, jaguars, cheetahs, and pumapards, pumuars, jagupards, cheepards, and every mixture in between. Rumor had it that you could find animal-*spawn* crossbreeds far south of the border.

I stood in the space between the moving cars, watching the morning landscape unfold before me, trying to find a moment of peace before my bickering champards got up. The men were unused to the cramped quarters of the train and the forced inactivity and if I didn't get some time away from them I was going to teach them all some sword play—with bare blades, mage speed, and a dose of pique.

Outside, standing between the jostling cars, I could smell the salt of the Gulf of Mexico. I heard a family of howler monkeys miles before I caught sight of them between the hundred-year-old trees, screaming and cavorting, performing high-altitude gymnastics. As I watched, I could feel some of the tension leave my spine.

The sounds and smells—and the monkeys—said "home" to me, a home I hadn't seen since I was fourteen, a home that had gone on without me, changing and evolving and becoming different. It would never be the safe haven it had been for me before I lost my parents as a child; not even the safe haven it had been while Lolo, the Enclave priestess—and my grandmother, if only I'd known it at the time—raised me and my sister Rose. It would now be a political hotspot, a place of adult intrigue and mage power games.

We'd be there soon, and I'd have to start acting like the new consul-general of Mineral City. Once in Enclave, they'd expect me to dress like a proper female mage, exposing my body in silks and gauze and tassels, because that's the way things were done. I'd have to start speaking like a politically trained mage, as well as a battle-hardened warrior. I'd be wearing weapons every moment of every day, including some hidden ones, and I'd have to find a way not to draw my sword every time a New Orleans mage stared at my scars and judged my every movement and word. Self-control wasn't my strongest character trait.

I closed my eyes—and popped them open at a faint thump from above. A tiny Capuchin monkey was hanging from the train car roof by his back feet, swinging, his two-toned coat catching the sunlight, his white-ringed eyes watching me. Then he opened his mouth and howled, Just a little howl, but such a deep tone from such a small monkey; it reverberated through me. Not a Capuchin, then: a howlpuchin. I laughed and wished for a crust of bread or a piece of fruit to give him, if just to shut him up before he woke up the whole train.

Even as I had the thought, the car door opened and Ciana slipped through, her mouth opened in an O of delight. She was holding a sliver of apple and staring at the monkey.

"Can I give it to him?" she asked.

"Sure. Be careful to hold only the tip and extend the apple itself out or he'll grab your hand and won't let go. I had that happen to me when I was about your age, I guess. It scared me to death!"

Ciana pinched the apple slice between her fingertips and held it out. The monkey swung near and ripped it from her fingers, swung back, let go of the roof, and executed an amazing triple flip, to land on a tree limb flashing past. Ciana screamed, "Wow! Did you see that?"

"Yeah," I said, my face softening in a smile, "I saw."

Pan-Elemental
Late Summer 105 PA / 2117 AD

Faith Hunter

Drayson braced his arms on the stone wall, unable to draw power from the cave itself and pass it into his tattoos. The conjure for resilience, drawn in swirls and lines like brecciated jasper across his shoulders and down his back—his oldest and most powerful ink—could stop the pain, but activating that spell now would interfere with his master's current work. His muscles trembled as he leaned into the stone, and his master, the dragon Jesreael, stepped back, waiting until the spasm eased. Jesreael had cast a spell to keep Drayson alive while the dragon worked, but anything more than that use of power might interfere. And if Drayson survived, pain would forever be his companion.

Jesreael had experimented in the past at tattooing River conjures onto Stone mages, Stone spells onto Air mages, Sea spells onto River mages, but even before the designs had been completed, the mages' bodies had begun rejecting those foreign magics, causing their skin to painfully slough off within hours—sometimes fatally. The dragon could probably have found a use for such short-lived magic weapons, but he'd had something bigger in mind.

These new spells were something different, a new working created by Jesreael solely for this unique Dark mage. Drayson's mutated flesh—and only *his* flesh—could accept the workings, and that only with great pain. The spells were worked with the dragon's blood and the inks blended with one of his scales, ground to powder. Between those and the mage's special skin, these tattoos might just be permanent, despite being antithetical to the Stone mage's element.

His master had been putting the blood-ink in place for hours now, and soon the dragon's strength would flow to all those spells crafted into Drayson's body. *Soon . . . so soon. Only a little more pain.*

Along with the conjures common to Stone mages, picked out in inks made from sapphire and agate, granite and schist, in mountain-scapes and faceted gems on his body, Drayson now had many other spells: a hawk in flight, created from feathers and pulverized sky-blue kyanite; a full moon shining on still water, made of silver and ground up moonstone that had lain exposed, charging for the three days of a full moon's light; weapons, armor, and shields of all sorts, in inks of crushed bloodstone and raw iron ore.

Now Jesreael's needles, finer than the width of an incubus hair, flew across Drayson's flesh, pounding steadily beneath his skin, completing the scene of a towering wave, the blues and greens of the powdered kyanite and labradorite (mixed with saltwater and dragon blood) crashing across his abdomen. Normally saltwater would drain a Stone mage of power, but this tattoo was designed to protect Drayson from this elemental allergen—and possibly allow him to draw on the ocean itself for power.

The Sea conjure finished, the dragon barely paused before dipping a new blade into the last pot of pigment. The needles danced, creating a complicated network of vines and leaves, an Earth image, filling in spaces between the mage's existing tattoos. This pigment was composed of fresh green ferns gathered by Dark Earth mages from above ground—another elemental allergen.

The vine was the lynchpin, allowing his master's blood to flow through him, his master's power to flow through his tattoos, as vital fluids flowed through a plant's stem, connecting and powering the conjure tattoos of all the foreign elements, making Drayson the first pan-elemental mage in history—if the elemental allergens didn't rip him apart.

Drayson took a breath as the torture became a hammering spike. Jesreael laughed. "You are strong, my son, stronger than I thought possible so soon in my breeding program. Unique now, but a precursor of what is to come."

"I am yours to command," Drayson said through clenched teeth, "in all things."

"This, my children," Jesreael said to the Dark mages sitting on the stone floor at his feet, "is the weapon that will allow us to begin the siege of the gilded cage built by the seraphs and the Light."

After only a few more minutes, the dragon announced, "It is done," and released the spell that had been sustaining Drayson against the elemental allergens as the dragon worked. A wave of nausea seized the Dark mage, as the foreign elements began burning his skin from the inside. The experiment had failed. At least Jesreael was a merciful master; he would quickly destroy Drayson and the mage's agony would be short-lived.

Then Jesreael spoke again. "You are mine. My strength is yours"—not destruction, but a spell linking dragon and mage. The other mages sang notes harmonizing with their liege's voice. Drayson inhaled the magic in his master's breath, felt the gift of power from the Earth mage nearest, from the River and Sea mages, the Air and Metal mages, from his brother Stone mages, and from the Moon mage at the edge of the gathering. He could feel the creation energy flowing into him, a rush of power that made his breath catch.

The fire under his skin died down and his mage glow increased in strength, illuminating the cavern.

Four days later, Drayson, dressed in human clothing, waited at the depot for the train carrying the mage, Thorn St. Croix.

Kraken Conquered
Late Summer 105 PA / 2117 AD

Faith Hunter

Standing at the back of the train car, I looked over the dome of the Enclave. It looked as if a huge, amber crystal bowl had been upended over the French Quarter of New Orleans. Bands of darker material, perhaps heavenly metals, held it in place, rising to a central pillar capped with a gleaming, golden fleur-de-lis. It was the sort of beauty someone with a soul might expect to see in the heavens, in an afterlife. The massive dome covered the Quarter, downstream over Faubourg Marigny and parts of Tremé/Lafitte, and upstream all the way to Lafayette Square.

When it appeared, the first Enclave in the world to be set in place by seraphs, it had blocked the Mississippi River, forcing its waters to cut a new bed through the alluvial soil and the remains of cities to the west of the dome. I hadn't seen the gilded prison of my home since I left it, smuggled out wrapped in a rug, when I was fourteen.

Enclaves were rare, made by seraphs, the angels of Heaven, to keep neo-mages safe from humans. Or so it was said. Maybe it was to protect them from us.

The dome glowed with power in the early evening, a scintillating rainbow light blasting out, the visual spectrum of power itself. I had never seen it in person from this side. I'd been unconscious when I was carried out of Enclave more than a decade ago, taken into the human population to save my life. From inside, it had looked like cut crystal, and reflected back the blues and greens and yellows of mages within conjuring.

The light from inside the car angled out and Eli took his place to my left, smelling of horse and hay and sweet-feed. The train clackety-clacked over the rails, as it had for weeks. He didn't speak. He just stood there, available if I needed him. Silent, if silence was what I wanted. As a human, he shouldn't know what I needed at any time, not nearly as much as some of my other champards, but he always did. He always knew.

Softly, he said, "You look beautiful, mistrend. You look beautiful in a ball gown or in fighting leathers. You look beautiful fresh from the shower or covered in the blood of battle. And more importantly, you look powerful. *That* is what they will respect. That is what they will respond to. To them, power is the greatest beauty of all."

I laughed and the notes were harsh, strangled. My few friends and enemies in the Enclave would think many things of me when I went back inside. Beauty would not be one.

I am Thorn St. Croix, once rogue mage, returning to the Enclave of my birth, with my twin, Rose. I could feel her inside the train car. She was like a splotch of death in space itself, a touch of chaos, like the faint scent of explosives, blasting cap in place, ready for destruction, death, and ruin. All while sitting in a corner, reading a book. The skin along my spine tightened with fear. Fear of my own sister.

This trip had multiple purposes but my main goals were two: to force the priestess to parley and provide me with a permanent visa, so that I could remain in the human world; and to discover a way to cure death magics once they'd taken hold of a mage. If I failed, I'd end up a prisoner inside the gorgeous, brilliant dome, or on the run, in hiding, as I'd spent most of the last decade. And my only sister would become a mass murderer before I had to kill her to stop her.

I looked down at my hands, resting on the painted wood railing at the back of the car, seeing the glow of scars on one. *You look beautiful, mistrend* . . . Lies. Unlike the expectation of mages in Enclave, unlike the best of the best, I wasn't soft, beautiful, young, or idealistic, as I had once been. I was battle-scarred and damaged, had been broken and put back to together— more than once by a seraph of the Most High. My skin was pearled and shining with blemishes of healed flesh on my left hand, my cheek, my throat, and a dozen other places. I glimmered like mages and glowed with mage scars, testament of war. Yet I carried a shadowy stain of darkness on my side where a Major Darkness had claimed me.

"You. Are. *Lovely*," Eli said again, with emphasis. "And even if others see only the scars and not the beauty and strength, your power makes them pause. You are more than any other mage. A Stone mage *and* a battle mage. And you are the consul-general of the Battle Station Consulate of Mineral City, Carolina. Never forget that, Thorn." Then he added with a touch of the mischief I'd come to love, "And you're a *celebrity*."

I smiled and shook my head, letting my breath flow from me. My consulate sat on the edge of civilization in the Appalachian Mountains. It was the last bastion of safety between the reign of Darkness in the frozen peaks and glaciers and the reign of human civilization. "A general by default," I said, wryly.

"Nevertheless. You held your land in the face of Leviathan."

Leviathan was the name of one of the most powerful forms of Darkness, a dragon of true might. To defeat it, I had broken a sacred vow and allowed my best friend to die. And Rose had taken his death energies to save us. If that was discovered, we would be anathema to Enclave.

There were other things that made me different. I could, rarely, join minds with my own seraph, Raziel, the chief of the supreme mysteries, an angel of secrets, and an archangelic governor. Together, we could enter the River of Time and change events that were about to happen, or had just happened. Not that I had told others about that. It was unheard of. Possibly deadly to me if I did it again.

Worse, I was also an omega mage. I was hard, edged like a blade, strong and brittle as stone, and powerful beyond most other mages. I could command seraphs in battle. Omega mages died for their presumption at commanding seraphs to act. I probably had a life expectancy of days. And Rose? She was a death mage. Together, we were a weapon not seen in . . . forever. Omega mage and death mage. Together, it seemed that we had begun to fulfill the prophecy uttered at our birth: *A Rose by any Other Name will still draw Blood.*

My greatest fear was that there was still a purpose left undone, something that the Most High (if He existed) wanted us to accomplish. And that accomplishment would mean our deaths. And the deaths of those I loved.

I laughed softly, the acrid sound blending with the clacking. I tightened my fists on the railing, letting the wood burn through me, painfully binding me to the here-and-now. As a Stone mage, wood can be hazardous to me. The healed skin of my left hand glowed brightly at the contact of the allergen. My prime glowed as well, protecting me.

If I failed at my goals, my sister and I would suffer or die, my champards would suffer and die, and my seraph might go to war against the mages. That last wasn't likely, but . . . my fear said it was possible. And terrifying.

It was dead dark when the engine and remaining cars clacked away along the tracks that paralleled old Highway 90. It left my two cars on the spur line set aside for commuter cars, sleeper cars, and personally owned cars like mine. Well, like Cheran's. I had claimed the cars for the consulate and he hadn't disagreed. Much. Cheran Jones was another champard, though a bit unwillingly in his case.

Eli again at my side, I stared into the night, the nearly full moon brightening everything for him, and mage sight allowing me to see far more than a human. In the distance, uptown, I could see the lights of New Orleans, the parts that humans had returned to after the Last War. Homes and businesses had been expanded over the last decade into what had once been the Garden and Warehouse Districts, the land protected from attack by the Darkness under the faintly glowing power of one of the strongest wards in the world. Human New Orleans might not like mages, but her citizens made use of their abilities. And in exchange for the ward, the mages received transportation, shipping, legal and trade assistance, and imports of perishables, raw stone, and ores.

Thanks to the Enclave, New Orleans was a hub of trade, shipping, money, and magic.

The train car door opened behind us. "Orders, mistrend?" Audric asked. His tone was cold as steel in winter and I didn't turn to see him. The lamps threw his shadow across the ground beyond, massive shoulders, rounded bald head. A death lay between us, a sacrifice that had pierced us both. The friendship that should exist between champard and mistrend had died with Rupert.

As had my self-worth. I had sworn before the Most High (if He existed), promising that I would give my own life in exchange for Rupert's, that I would die by own hand rather than kill one of those I guarded. I had vowed it to the Most High by His unspeakable Name. And I was foresworn.

"I'll go to the inn," I said without turning, "and check us in. You unload the horses and bring them. They can use the exercise. We should be safe enough within the city ward."

"And Thadd?" Audric asked.

Thaddeus' wings were going to be a problem. They had proved impossible for him to glamour, they were large enough that they trailed on the ground behind him, and kylen were creatures of tremendous interest to humans and mages alike. He would attract attention no matter where he went, and eventually that attention would bring seraphs who'd take him to a Realm of Light forever. I sighed. Audric knew what to do. "Put him on one of the horses and give him a cloak. And stop being such an ass."

He ignored my comment. "And your power sink?"

We'd brought four, two hundred-pound rocks packed in dirt, in crates, in the stall car. They would need to be taken to the cardinal points of whatever acreage I chose as my temporary embassy grounds. Their placement and the raising of my flag were diplomatic declarations meant to confuse the priestess of Enclave and her advisors. They might be interpreted as declarations of war against her personally. Or they might be a declaration that I had my own power sink—which I did—and that I was setting myself up as a separate nation, outside of Enclave—which I might have to do in the end. Such a thing had never been done, and would be in violation of the edict that all mages must wear what were essentially tracking devices, tied to their home Enclave. I had one now, one with a time limit built in. When it went out of date, I would be forced to other, untried measures. Or the boulders might be a declaration of personal insanity that put all of New Orleans outside of Enclave in danger. Or a combination of all three. Either way, I was declaring total independence from the priestess. Whatever she and her advisors thought, my actions would keep them guessing and give me time to establish myself here.

The massive stones would need to be buried as soon as possible, so that light and air couldn't touch them. Once in place, I could use them to anchor a ward, as well as provide power. And since they came from the earth near my power sink at home, I could use them to link to the power stored there.

"Leave them for now," I said. "We're all tired. Let's sleep in real beds that don't rattle and shake."

"As my mistrend commands." He backed away, into the train car. I kept my eyes on the horizon, but inside I ached at the loss of our friendship. It felt as if I bled.

When he was gone, I pried my hands from the railing and accepted Eli's assistance to the ground. The trip had been eventful and I was exhausted. I wasn't expected to make an entrance in Enclave for several days, maybe for several weeks, once the Enclave rulers had a chance to see my new quarters, power sink, and flag. My champards would be negotiating with the priestess and her council and acting sly and amused and haughty while I established myself and threw wrenches into the process by my actions. We had rooms set aside in the St. Charles Inn, a short distance from the spur line track.

From the train car, Rose called, "Thorn, wait! I'm coming!" I felt Eli tense, a fast reaction, quickly gone. My champards feared my sister. She tossed down her reticule and stepped to the ground. She was wearing pink silk with heavy embroidery, which she could use to store creation energy for her Earth magery. She was using her birth element again. I hoped that the power of death would begin to fade.

She hefted her bags and I pulled my longsword from its sheath, just in case I was wrong about our safety for the walk. As we strolled toward the buildings that comprised the city and port of New Orleans, Rose added, "Lucas and Ciana said they'd be along shortly. Seraph stones! It's good to be home!"

I didn't reply. As a child, I had never been outside of the dome. As an adult, New Orleans had become a familiar place to her. Nothing was familiar to me.

Eli murmured, "You should let me shoot him."

I chuckled. He was talking about Audric, and we'd had this half-serious/half-joking discussion more than once. "Tempting sometimes. But I'm his mistrend. I'm still his friend even when he isn't mine. And besides, we might need him. He has friends inside, friends who *might* know the priestess and who *will* know her staff."

"I still should shoot him," Eli grumbled, his words cut off by a rumbling train. For all his claim to want to kill his fellow champard, he was the most thoughtful of them all. Of course, part of that was his desire to bed me. I hadn't chosen to accept any of my champards as bedmate. Having a kylen as champard and the threat of death to me should I give in to mage heat and sleep with him had kept me chaste with all of them. "Or at least hit him with a big stick," he finished, trying to make me laugh. I managed a smile.

Eli adjusted my reticule. He was carrying all my luggage, including my large weapons case. We'd have to hire servants soon to do the mundane and housekeeping tasks. No visiting priestess or royalty or whatever I might become should be seen with only one servant. It simply wasn't *done*.

There wasn't much left of the old city between Lafayette Square and the old expressway. Now there was the new railroad, terminal, warehouses, the entrance to the warded city, and the gas station with its pay phone, the one used by mages when they needed to make calls to the human world. The banks of the Mississippi were close, as was the Gulf of Mexico, and I could smell the power of water on the air, a natural toxin to me. I drew on mage sight to see the sickly greenish-yellow of its energies.

I could also hear the screams of prey as minor, water-borne Darkness crawled from the river in search of food. There was no way to keep these creatures away. Some few always managed to find a way to swim or float in on the currents, do some dreadful thing to local wildlife, and disappear. Mage power kept the larger things at bay and protected the humans of New Orleans. When I was growing up, there had been regular training missions for the second unforeseen, when large numbers of fighters would leave Enclave and wipe out the minor Darkness. I had no idea if the current priestess had kept up the policies of the previous one.

The screams got loud, high pitched, as something wild died in the night. I wanted to be back in Mineral City.

At the ornate ward-gate, I presented my visa and papers to the soldiers who guarded the only entrance through the ward after sunset, and informed them that my champards would be following shortly. I was several days early, but the uniformed humans were eager to provide me access and would have tales to tell in the morning about the sight of the rogue mage who fought with seraphs.

Once inside the ward of uptown New Orleans, the scent of coffee, to-bacco, and food assailed us and Rose breathed deeply, the rose quartz focal on her chest moving with her ribcage when she groaned with delight. It was moments like this that made me believe she could be saved. The city smelled wonderful, even to a dedicated vegetarian like me. The scents were spicy, meaty, and cooked in grease. The entrance was prestigious, with repaved streets and new construction, most of which had been built from the blasted remains of older, Pre-Ap buildings. Mage lights kept the streets well-lit and people were everywhere in the safe confines of the ward, eating, drinking, partying—a lifestyle unknown to me. Here there was little influ-ence of the orthodoxy, the citizens reputedly having thrown them out when the kirk tried to stop a Mardi Gras celebration long ago.

Only a block into the city, we walked the roundabout on St. Charles. The ancient roundabout was surrounded by restaurants and pubs and even a playhouse, as the ward-gate and the nearby inn were focal points of city life. Trade made its entrances and exits through the main gate, mule trains and miners, diplomats and envoys hoping to negotiate with the mages came and went from here. And it was part of the party life of the city, so in-grained that even the orthodoxy in uptown had not been able to eradicate it totally.

The St. Charles Inn was a few steps off the roundabout on a side street, composed of two old churches that had been combined and converted to living spaces. The amalgamation of the buildings had resulted in a mish-mash of architectural styles, brick and stone, with tiled roofs, one curved side, two turrets, a bell tower, and a garden space.

Many buildings in the area had been devastated in the Last War, but the blended churches stood strong. The once-sacred ground had been turned to other uses in Pre-Ap times, de-sanctified as museums, playhouses, and such, and the stone of the structure had been painted over and protected from the elements for over a century. I had hoped it might be possible to combine the old stone with my boulders for a bigger power sink. We took the walkway to the inn's entrance and I let my hand trail across the stone. I felt the buzz of latent power. *This is good.* I drew upon it to restore my own exhausted state before walking inside.

The inn had our two, three-bedroom suites set aside, with living space and beds for us all. And, most importantly, bathrooms with hot and cold running water. And real toilets.

Eli checked us in, a servant drew baths for Rose and me, and Eli placed a dozen fist-sized, charged stones in my water. Stones to protect me from the water allergen. Then he left, returning to the train to bring the others.

Once alone, alone for the first time in weeks, I locked the door. With the earth-salt from my reticule, I poured a narrow ring of protection around the tub, peeled the sticky clothes from my body, placed my amulet necklace on the small table by the tub, and sank into the steamy heated water for a long-overdue scrub and soak. The heat soothed the puckered, pale scars that traced up my limbs, and warmth seeped into my bones, easing their ache.

The water cooled. Dripping onto the floor, I reached for an amulet, dropped it into the water, and released a *Heating* spell, the power in the stone warming the water fast. I'd needed something to do on the long trip, so I'd stepped out to collect likely rocks every time the train stopped, and made conjure amulets of them. It had been that or shooting someone. Amulets were more productive, and now I had all sorts of helpful stones in my suitcase as well as the fully charged necklace.

I heard my champards come in, voices muffled. Smelled the meal they ordered. Felt the vibrations as they moved around and settled. Heard Rose as she joined them, chattering. I got out and dried off and plaited my clean, wet, scarlet hair. It had been damaged over the last months, but had grown out fast. I dressed in nightclothes and a robe, though it was summer in the Deep South and the rooms were warm. And still my champards were lively.

I opened the door and stood in the shadows of the main room, watching, silent. Audric, Thadd, Rose, and Eli were playing cards, some fast-paced game with lots of shouting. There were bottles of beer on the table, and spicy scents in the air.

Ciana, the child of my soul, curled beneath a blanket on a sofa, eating ice cream, her mouth ringed with chocolate. Lucas, my ex-husband, had a book open on his knees, telling her about the school she would be attending. A fire blazed merrily in the fireplace.

It warmed my heart to see them having fun. Together. Even Rose, who was losing badly and didn't seem to care. My sister was beautiful tonight, all her glamours stripped away, glowing with mage-light.

The evil suspicion raced through me that she had killed and drained someone to glow with such power. She wouldn't. She had sworn. At the thought, my hunger fled. I closed the door and crawled beneath the coverlet to sleep.

~

I was wakened by the sound of fists thundering on the inn's door. Heard voices, then quiet whispers outside my room. Some of my champards were unwilling to wake me; others felt I needed to be informed of whatever had occurred. "I'm awake," I called out.

Lucas opened the door and said into the crack, "Thorn, there are two mu— two second unforeseen at the registration desk. They're asking to be hired on."

I thought for a moment, and drew on the visa, just in case the seraphic intelligence within it had an opinion. Oddly, it did. *Presentation to the Enclave Council will be formal. There is security in numbers.*

I said, "Audric, do we need the numbers?"

"Numbers will enhance the esteem of the consul-general of the Battle Station Consulate of Mineral City," he said formally.

If they swear to my senior champard, is that enough, or do they have to swear to me? I asked the visa.

Instantly it replied. *If they are to be paid servants, then to the senior. If they are to become champards, then to the consul-general.* The visa was unusually cooperative tonight. I wondered if it was because I was so close to the Enclave. I still didn't know much about mage visas. The seraphic artifacts weren't powered by Enclaves, nor by the wearer. Perhaps they received some power from the seraphs, or from a self-contained infinite power source in a Realm of Light. Or perhaps from the Most High himself. However they were powered, mine was taking some energy from the ambient power of Enclave and I felt its might on my skin.

"Audric, as senior champard, you may accept their vows of allegiance," I said.

"As my mistrend decrees." The door closed.

Audric was still grieving. But at some point we would be in front of the council. I hoped by then that he'd be less hostile. His icy tone was unlikely to inspire confidence in the council at a time when I needed them to respect me. Fear me. Yes. Fear would keep me safer than respect or even love.

I dropped my head back to the pillow. It was damp and I palmed a *Drying* charm to dry both hair and pillow. And a *Warming* one to heat my feet. It was summer, but cold snaps still occurred when the winds blew strong off the glaciers, in some places only six hundred miles to the north. These temps in the forties were chilling even through the mage-spelled panes of window glass—mages created built-in failures for everything sold to humans, so they'd eventually have to come back to us to buy more. Tomorrow it might be in the eighties again, or even the nineties, the humidity even higher, but for tonight it was unseasonably chilly.

As the sheets warmed, I thought again about having more people around me. And the boulders I had brought. And the church stones. Using all that rock might allow me a suitable power sink without drawing on the one below the Enclave, maybe even without going blooey. Having that independent might be essential to my bargaining power and any future plans we might define.

Just before daybreak, I rose, dressed, tied my amulet necklace around my waist like a belt, put others in my pockets. I tried to be quiet, but woke several of my champards, and we ate breakfast in the common room together—boiled eggs, French toast, oatmeal, and fresh honey for me, while the others dined on various fried and spiced meats.

Thadd informed me, "Audric rented a carriage large enough for us all, so your creation energy doesn't cause an El-car to go on the fritz." Though his seraphic scent was muted beneath the power of the seraph stones we both wore, he smelled of caramel, vanilla, brown sugar, and ginger, the scent mélange like a candy shop. His jovial eyes were the greenish-blue of the ocean in spring, long red hair curled over his brow, and his red-gold beard was clipped short. He'd let his hair and beard grow when he realized he would never again work as a detective with Carolina State Law Enforcement.

My champards had lost so much fighting Darkness, but today Eli's amber eyes glinted with mischief. "Our Thorn can take out anything electronic or mechanical."

Audric's full lips shone with honey as he said, "Clyde looked at the harness and then at me and kicked the stall. I don't think they want to be hitched to the carriage."

"I hear that the city fathers got the old trolley up and running," Eli said. "Never been on a trolley."

"Streetcar," Audric said, sounding more relaxed than in weeks. "Locals call it a streetcar. Never a trolley."

I listened to them banter and gibe, and felt some of the misery of the last years fall away.

When we were done, we left the inn and Audric brought the carriage around. The Friesian and the Clydesdale looked odd together in harness, but the mismatched animals were just another level of disguise. No one would expect a mage to have mismatched horses, not in New Orleans where all mages were unfailingly wealthy—or at least the ones allowed in public.

Together, we left the warded city, Audric, Eli, Thadd and I. I wasn't appearing as the CG, so I wore a simple dress and leggings with boots, a scarf over my hair, my sword sheathed at my hip but no fighting leathers. It was freeing to not be the only mage in town, to have no responsibilities, and to know that the lives of everyone in a hundred miles did *not* depend on me. The strange freedom made me even more introspective than usual. Even with the newness and excitement of being back in New Orleans, I couldn't seem to find the energy to be chatty. Chatty wasn't my nature.

As we rode, I took in the sights. Three parks planted around the entry to the city's ward-gate were abundantly green. The streets were free of potholes and perfectly straight. Black cast iron was abundant in street lights, benches, and ornate streetcar stops. Mage magic had been used well and often here. I wondered what the city fathers were trading for it.

By daylight, New Orleans' unique scents had softened. The smell of horse, salt water from the Gulf, the iron-like scent of the Mississippi River, rotting vegetation, fish, coffee, and cooking was everywhere. No smell of ice sheets. No scent of stone or pine. It was so different from the scents of home, even different from the places we had traveled through to get here. It was also different from the life I had lived as a child in the confines of Enclave. It left me unsettled and the men seemed to understand, engaging in their usual banter without me, enjoying the pale sunlight of the early day.

We left Thadd at the railyard to finish unpacking the train while Audric departed on foot to run errands, restock our supplies, and listen to the locals. We needed intel and humans carried gossip from Enclave daily.

Eli and I took the carriage the short distance to the banks of the Mississippi. There were tracks in the sand, and I remembered the screams in the night. Darkness had crawled from the waters, attacked, and eaten, leaving the decomposing, ravaged remains of wild boar. Homer tossed his head, his black mane flying, feet prancing in distress at the stench of Darkness and blood. "Eeeeasy. Whoa," Eli murmured to the horses. The carriage slowed to a stop.

According to Pre-Ap maps, the Mississippi had once carried less water during spring melt and flood seasons than she did now, and her east bank had been much farther to the west on the other side of a levee. Now New Orleans stopped at Magazine Street, while across the river, Algiers, Federal City, and McDonough had been wiped away by floods before the construction of the Enclave. Now floods were held back by water mages, which was a much more successful means of controlling rampaging waters than earthen dikes and levees. Now conjures kept the Mississippi in its new banks, leaving a wide sandy shore between river and Enclave.

A permanent, preset circle had been burned into the sand, scorched to glass by Sun mages. The twenty-four foot circle incorporated stone, air bubbles, moonstones, and greenery frozen as if in amber. It was beautiful, a glistening greened brilliance. The circle was covered by a lesser, but permanent ward, with protected entrances direct to the Enclave dome itself safe from Darkness, water, and humans, easily available for use by any mage.

I leapt from the carriage to the sand. Eli followed, carrying a bag of my own salt, mined from below ground. He stood watch as I studied the ward in mage sight to get a feel how it was put together. It had a simple on-off mechanism. With a touch the ward fell. I walked the circled and then poured the precious salt into place.

I sat at the center, on the dry sand, and thumbed a stone fish on my amulet necklace, opening a portable ward before I let down my defenses. Satisfied, I went to work. I needed to see how the mage conjure that created and powered the city ward was set up, how power reached from the Enclave to the ward, where and how the port was protected, how the Enclave itself was protected, and a dozen other things. Mostly to see if the visa would allow me to draw power from the power sink far below ground in bedrock, just in case my own power sink was not enough to protect me from the priestess.

That was my first goal and I was successful. For now at least, the power of Enclave was accessible to me. I followed the creation energy links deep into the earth, running through the water, flashing through the air, followed them, learning them, figuring out how I might use them.

Hours later, feeling refreshed, I opened my eyes to see Eli surrounded by dozens of second unforeseen. The men and women were rough-looking, people who clearly lived on the outskirts of society. Perhaps even pirates. The river was known to be ruled by brigands in small skiffs who took what they could steal from smaller merchants, always hiding from what was left of the Navy. Dangerous, elusive. Yet no one except Eli had drawn a weapon. His old six-shooter was aimed at the group, though it was hard to cover so many with so little.

I stood, smoothed my skirts, and dropped my circle. "Is there a problem," I said, making it statement. But the visa took it upon itself to boom the words, so they sounded like a challenge. Almost as one, the interlopers turned toward me. Eli didn't shoot, and I thought that was a good omen.

One woman, smaller than the others, took a single step to me and bowed. She had dark-copper skin and kinky hair, an upturned nose, and for some reason reminded me of Lolo, though perhaps only because I missed the old priestess so much. She wore shirt and trousers, held up by suspenders, and mud-covered boots. She was armed to the teeth.

"My name is Zoeheret, second unforeseen," she said. "We wish negotiations with the consul-general's champards."

I realized they didn't know me, not with my scars glamoured and wearing a dress instead of a dobok. SNN had most often captured me in fighting gear, not in the garb of a shopkeeper and jewelry maker. From the scabbard at my side, I drew my weapon and stepped into the goose stance, the sword held two-handed, blade high. The pink quartz pommel caught the noon sun and blazed, as did the visa and my prime amulet. "I'm listening."

Eli sighed, a theatrical sound, and holstered his gun. "Woman. I tried to protect your privacy."

"*You* are the consul-general?" She sounded unbelieving. I dropped my glamour, letting my scars shimmer. Stepped toward her, toward Eli, forcing them back. But Zoeheret fell to her knees in the sand. "The second unforeseen have been awaiting your army. We are yours to command."

"Well blow it out Gabriel's shorts," I swore. Eli laughed with an *I told you so*, tone. Because her words sounded like prophecy. Prophecy always meant battle and death and I was so very tired of both. "Can you fight?" I asked, strangling my emotional reaction to her words.

"We are trained in savage-blade and savage-chi." She nodded to two mountainous men. "Clemet and Clovis are especially skilled. We are fast, strong, and loyal. Will you have us?"

"Fine." I lowered my blade. "I accept your allegiance, as warriors and employees. I have enough champards and most of them are completely without manners." Eli laughed.

Back at the carriage, I divided them into four groups and sent them to seek Audric, sending a note with Zoeheret. With their help, Audric could get the two hundred-pound stones into place at cardinal points quickly. It was a good use of time and money. And an army of second unforeseen seemed like a good thing to have around.

Satisfied with the work and the things I had learned, I let Eli take me to a late lunch at a bistro that served a vegetarian peanut-and-filé gumbo, better than anything I had tasted in the last decade. Served with fresh bread and a glass of wine, it was fabulous. Sitting in the warm sun, in a public place, under glamour, ensuring that no one knew me, was even better.

But while we were away, things happened.

Near sunset, we returned and Audric met me at the inn's door, his dark-skinned face scowling, long furrows on either side of his mouth. "The priestess," he said before I could speak, "sent a mage with a missive, demanding you attend her."

"Oh!" It came out breathless.

"That *mage*," he snarled, "threatened, postured, made demands that you appear, and was dumbfounded when no one could make it happen."

I looked around the foyer to find no strange mage, just three of the inn's staff, watching with overly curious eyes. I should take this upstairs. "Where is he?" I asked, worrying about rumors. The priestess should not have summoned me until I was scheduled to appear.

"He's gone," Audric growled, the tone deeper.

"Good," I said, pushing past him to the stairs.

"Thorn!" he thundered.

That tone snapped me out of my slightly sunburned and happy mood. I stopped, one foot on the stairs, one hand on the banister.

"You will not turn your back on me! You did not inform the priestess that we had arrived, which was a *foolish* political mistake. It's *irresponsible* to incite the most powerful mage on the coast!"

I didn't move. The silence in the registration area was absolute for a dozen heartbeats and then I heard the sound of running feet as the staff disappeared. I realized that my glamour had slipped; my neomage attributes were glowing. And I was . . . furious. Because this was not about the priestess or a importunate mage. *Foolish. Irresponsible.* This was about *Rupert.*

Slowly, I turned to my senior champard, my body glimmering with mage might. Unconsciously, I drew on the stones of the old churches. "What did you say?" I whispered, my words a breath of sound.

"I said you were *stupid.*"

My body blazed. My visa woke up, confused, as if it had been sleeping. "Just like I was *stupid* when Rupert died? Rupert, who was my *best friend* long before he was your lover?" I stepped toward him, balanced, rooted in the earth, in the bedrock so far below the surface. My prime and every defensive amulet had warmed, ready to be activated, their heat growing against my waist where the necklace was tied. "Rupert, who was beyond all but the healing power of a *seraph*?" My eyes blazed, but when I spoke it was less than a breath. "Rupert, whose blood will *stain my soul*, if I have one, until I stand before the High Host?"

"You will not," he rumbled, "bring Rupert Stanhope into this!"

"Rupert Stanhope *is* this! He is all of this!" My hand flashed back and forth between us. "Nothing that is now would be so if not for his life, his love, and his death." Tears burst from my eyes at the last word and flowed down my face. Audric's skin went darker with rage, veins bulging. I clenched my fists to keep from striking him. "Rupert is gone," I whispered through a tight throat, made worse by the scarred tissues there. "Both our pledges are foresworn."

Audric took an unwitting step back. "I will keep my vow to you," he said.

I quoted, "'I will hold you in the highest regard, and I will serve you and train you to the best of my ability. I will dress you for battle, and should you die by the sword, I will dress you for burial. All that, I swear.' *That pledge?* The sworn *regard* that allowed you to call me *stupid?* Made you attempt to shame me in front of our friends? Well, you didn't shame me, Audric. You shamed only yourself. And Rupert. You shamed him too." I turned and swept past him and up to my room.

I was halfway there when the alarms sounded.

I stopped, not sure what it meant, the hooting blaring sound, and then I knew. Darkness. Something was attacking. With mage speed, I raced to my room and threw off my clothing, pulling on skin-tight undergarments and slithering into the new dobok. I hadn't worn the new leathers yet. We had picked them up in Birmingham, where a group of licensed mages had opened a leather shop specializing in fighting leathers. The armor tingled against my flesh, the creation energies worked into them by Earth mages, defensive conjures that protected against the claws, fangs, and saliva of minor Darkness. They were black as night, conjured to form to my body, and they slid onto me like a second skin.

My door opened and Audric entered without knocking. He too was dressed in new fighting leathers. Boots came to his knees, battle cloak on his shoulders, armed for war. Moving almost at combat speed, he shook out my battle cloak and buckled it in place around me, slammed weapons into the various sheaths, then tied my amulet necklace in a new configuration around my chest.

Without meeting my eyes, he asked, "Have I been so horrible?"

"A total ass," I said.

He tucked more amulets into the special pockets that kept each in place. "I miss him," he said softly. "There is a hole in my heart where he once lived." I sobbed and he took a cloth, wiping my face where a day in the open had chapped it. He met my eyes, waiting to see how I might respond.

"You had accomplished so much else, saved so many others. My heart did not accept what my intellect knew—that there was no other choice."

My throat closed up again and my reply was strangled. "I couldn't save him."

"I know. And I . . . accept that."

"So easily? After that . . . um . . ."

"Contretemps in the lobby? It's been . . ." he waggled his head side to side, the bald pate catching the lamplight, "coming to me for some time. That . . . *discussion* was the slap in the face I needed."

"Just to be clear, you gave yourself the slap."

"Indeed." He smiled and tucked the cloth with my tears into a pocket in my dobok. "Let us go forth and fight Darkness, my mistrend."

Laughter sputtered out. "Sure. It's what we battle mages do."

My champards—all except Ciana, who was placed in the care of Lucas, Zoeheret and three of her handpicked second unforeseen—met in the otherwise empty registration area. Clemet and Clovis joined us. We all wore black leathers, new, all alike except for four of us. The new second unforeseen wore spelled cloth, rough and coarse. Eli's leathers had been designed with a Western flare, embossed all over with roses and thorns. Rose had no need of protective leathers. She was Death Itself. She met my eyes from across the room, holding me still with her gaze. "If I go too far, stop me," she said.

She meant kill her. Kill her if she killed one of us. I nodded slowly, and my visa blazed as if in witness. "I so swear." My champards echoed around me, "I so swear."

The possibility of losing Rose as I had lost Rupert weighed on my mind, feeling as if an avalanche had buried me. I stood wrapped in thought until Eli discreetly cleared his throat, bringing me back to the present. Straightening my shoulders, I walked through my team and out into the night.

Audric stopped us, standing in the moonlight, and pointed at four of the biggest second unforeseen. "You were with me when we brought in the crates. You were with us when we marked the cardinal points around the inn." They looked puzzled but nodded. "Bury each stone at the exact place we marked. Exact place. Understand?" They nodded again. Audric was choosing my embassy land. The inn's staff and owners would be ticked off, but other than that, it was a good choice.

"Bury them fast," I said. "Accurately, but fast. And then get away. I'll charge them remotely."

The four blinked, taking in what I was saying. Their knowledge of Enclave politics told them exactly what I was doing and their part in it. "Yes, ma'am," the smallest of them said. "And we'll light a fire at the ward wall when it's done. It can be seen from the shore."

"Why are we going to the shore?" I asked.

"That's where the Darkness comes."

I nodded and stepped outside. The city was locked down. No one and nothing moved, the streets were deserted; not so much as a stray cat could be seen. No lights brightened windows. The only sound was the eerie, hooting alarm. The ward was up, a ghostly aura rising in an arc to a central point. The ward-gate was empty, vacated by the soldiers who were supposed to keep watch, which wasn't a surprise, considering the pile of dead devil-spawn just beyond the gate. There were hundreds more feasting on the dead, a writhing mass of ripping fangs and tearing claws, and still more Darkness converging from the river. "Moving ward," I said and we gathered close. I thumbed on the portable ward and it passed over me in a wash of dull light. "Stay close."

Weapons drawn, we moved through the ward-gate and crawled over dead spawn. Squealing spawn tore the flesh from the bones of the dead. Spawn are always hungry. *Always.* The live ones didn't even look up as the ward moved them out of the way. I had learned a lot about imbued amulets and had added silence, muted scent patterns, and forgetfulness to my ward's protections.

In the distance, the Enclave dome was blazing bright as a sun, the moon rising over it. Powering it. It was the first day of the three-day full moon. Moon mages were the most powerful creatures on the face of the Earth for three days out of twenty-eight. Their ability to collect and use creation energy then rivaled even a seraph's. Working together, they could bring down a flight of dragons.

Even with multiple mages working, excess creation energy reflected off the dome, dropping through a converter conjure that allowed all mages to draw from the energy, and flooding into the power sink far below ground. The Enclave power sink was overflowing, which meant that no one would notice me using it. "Stop," I whispered. I gripped my prime, seeking out all stone in the vicinity that hadn't been claimed as a power sink by another mage. There were four locations, buildings all made of stone, all available for my use, but none of them storing power. "I need a minute."

"*Here?*" Cheran demanded. Eli did something that made the Steel mage grunt in pain, but I was too busy with the trails of power below ground to pay attention.

"There is a light in the city," Audric said with approval. "The boulders have been buried."

I sank to my backside on the street and spread my awareness, finding a trail of converted Moon power to siphon off and into the power sink at the inn and at each of the four empty sinks in the old city. It was difficult to establish a continuous flow, one with a timer that would shut the flow down when the moon set, but I might have succeeded. Partially.

"Thorn!" Cheran hissed. "They scent us."

I opened my eyes to see my ward ringed by spawn, four as large as good-sized boars, red eyes glowing, their magics foul to my mage sight. Rose pressed close, her skin touching mine, close enough for her thoughts to reach me had the thought pathway not been sealed. I patted her shoulder, standing. "Let's see where they're coming from."

"You throw the best parties," Eli said. Thadd laughed, the tones seraphic. Cheran cursed. The hired second unforeseen nodded at Audric, blades held ready.

We moved toward the Enclave at an angle, until we saw the shore of the Mississippi. Its waters were thrashing with spawn. Thousands crawled out of the river, squealing with hunger. They were climbing the bodies of their dead, up the city's ward walls. Cheran Jones cursed.

Someone must have moved too far from me, because the ward sputtered, flashed, and closed. Our commingled scents hit the spawn. Their screams and stink hit us. As one, the spawn lifted their noses into the air and shifted position. Attacked.

My champards circled me, blades flashing silver in the moonlight. The corpses piled up. Not one spawn stopped to feast. That told me this attack was more than coincidental. It was directed at us. As blood flew, Rose began to glow, absorbing the energies.

Swords swinging, Audric shouted. "Pull back!"

"Where?" Thadd asked, his seraphic might blazing. "There's a mountain of spawn at the city. And the Enclave won't let us in."

As blood spattered, the acidity blistering our skin, I drew on the pooling energies and managed to raise another ward. It was weak, but it was enough. Spawn were trapped on both sides, and my fighters dispatched the ones inside, leaving bloody sand beneath our feet. Rose blazed, so full of death-power she was drunk and laughing.

Through the swirling waters and swimming spawn, I spotted something dark beneath the surface, glowing with sickly energies, reddish-yellow with purple undertones. "Audric!" I called and pointed.

Whatever they were, they were big. They spanned the river surface, rising from the deeps. Tentacled, with massive central heads/bodies, these Darkness were eight-armed, green-skinned, with bumps and ridges on the surfaces of their deep-toned tentacles. The skin on the underside of the arms was whitish and smooth with round mouths, each with a single spur-tooth. Each head was centered with a single eye, platter sized, oval and glossy. The underside of the heads was both maw and claws.

"Kraken," Audric ground out. "It's been nearly fifty years since they attacked last. They threaten the Enclave."

From Enclave's fleur-de-lis power blasted, the shimmering silver of moonstones and icicles, a burning might that scored lines of black death across the krakens, severing tentacles. *An energy weapon.* The creatures thrashed, flailing, heaving themselves ashore. Toward Enclave.

We were trapped here and my champards were no match for such creatures. I shouldn't have answered the alarms.

One kraken turned to us. Three limbs snaked high and slammed down, just missing us. Sand sprayed. Dead spawn smashed against the ward. It wavered. "Thorn!" Thadd shouted.

Suddenly all the stones in New Orleans were fully charged, and I poured power from them into my ward. The closest tentacle thumped high and landed only a foot away. Then it curled closer and wrapped slowly around the ward. The suckers pressed close on the energies. The mouths began to feed.

The kraken had the ability to absorb the energies of the ward conjure. This was not good. My ward thinned. I could feel the loss in my bones and pulled harder on my power sinks.

The ward wavered. A tentacle coiled in. I reached for more power. Clemet and Clovis rushed the tentacle. Hacked and tore into it. Caustic blood splattered. Faster than I could follow with human sight, the suckers opened and spat bursts of darkness. Clemet fell. I got a partial ward back up, but a second tentacle wrapped around Clemet and pulled him away. A smear of blood marred the sand. Rose absorbed his death energies and laughed. Cheran cursed, "Bones of watchers!"

Clovis fell at my feet, his body riddled with darts, each pouring poison into him. I struggled to close the ward overhead, but a small section remained open, like the puckered top of a bag. The suckers drew off more power. I hit my knees as creation energy raced through me, straight to them. I was nothing more than a conduit. The kraken was stealing the creation energy in my power sinks through me.

It reached a tentacle up and through the top of the ward. Audric severed it, splashing us with caustic blood, and the squirming flesh fell inside with us. Rose knelt and touched the tentacle, pulling its death inside her, petting it as it died. Clovis's eyes went wide and he dragged himself as far from Rose as the ward allowed.

Another tentacle struggled into the top. Through a space in the straining muscles of the kraken, I caught a glimpse of the Enclave. Krakens had wrapped themselves around the dome. More than a dozen of the Dark monsters. Though their flesh was scorched, they seemed able to ignore the blasts of defensive light that stabbed from the dome-top.

With a sound like thunder, the Enclave dome cracked.

The energies of the dome flickered, as if the mages powering it were stunned into immobility. It seemed the entire world went still.

A second crack sounded.

A final kraken pulled itself from the river. Massive beyond belief, as large as Enclave itself. It called out, a sound like an oboe if the instrument were the size of a freight train. It rattled my ward with might. River waters rushed in before the beast like a tsunami, engulfing the ward. Water poured through the hole at the top. Drenching us. My power faded at the contact.

The huge beast shoved the smaller creatures away and wrapped its tentacles around the dome. Beneath it, the light of Enclave went dark.

A third crack sounded, shaking the ground. The lesser krakens on the beach stared across the sand to the Enclave and their leader, making slurping sounds but standing immobile.

I dragged power in and closed the ward. I was shaking, fingers white on the sand. I didn't know when I had fallen. My amulets were sapped, nearly empty.

A fourth crack sounded, the sands shifting beneath us. Over the distance, we could hear the screams of mages from inside. Enclave was about to fall. They were calling mage in dire, but . . . seraphs weren't coming to help. The huge kraken had power of its own. Had it stopped the call? Was no one hearing it?

Rose watched. She was cradling a severed tentacle. In mage sight, the cut flesh glowed with her death energies. And so did the creature it had come from. The kraken released its hold on my ward, its remaining tentacles waving in the air, Slowly, it moved aside. Rose met my eyes, a look on her face that might have been ecstasy. And I realized what was happening: My twin was making the smaller kraken go away.

"Rose?" I whispered.

"My death energies can merge with the energies of the kraken," she said. "I can . . . take it."

"What—what does that even mean?"

"I can control it. I think I can control all of them. I just need the blood of the big one."

"So let's get the lady close to the Big Bad Ugly," Eli said.

Audric lifted me to my feet. "You are exhausted."

I nodded, holding on. "I can walk."

Thadd lifted Clovis onto his back, cradling the second unforeseen between his wings. "Leave me. I'm dying," the man said.

"No." Thadd said no more.

I pushed at the ward and it began to move again. "Stay close," I murmured, as Audric steadied my steps. "There are more spawn."

The small kraken drove itself across the shore before us, clearing the way.

A fifth crack sounded. It seemed to echo forever. Spawn raced over my ward, fought to get inside. Still we moved toward the Darkness ahead. Finally we were there, the smaller beast, still bigger than a Pre-Ap bus, beside us, snuggling close, like a cat might.

"Okay," I said. "I can drop the ward for five seconds. In that time, you need to get your blood and get back inside. The rest of us will be killing spawn."

Rose just laughed, which made no sense. But I was too tired to care.

I dropped the ward. Rose sped the few feet and stabbed with her knife. Blood pulsed over her hand. Her death energies slammed into the blood and . . . Rose took control of the kraken. Her death energies swelled and flooded through it, greenish and brown and sick shades of death.

Around me, my champards were fighting. "Thorn!" Thadd shouted. "Raise the ward!" But I just watched as the behemoth dropped a tentacle tip down and Rose stepped onto it.

"Rose!" I screamed.

"Thorn! Now! Or we all die!" Thadd shouted.

The huge kraken raised Rose to his maw. Set her on its tongue. A dome

—just like Enclave but smaller—opened around Rose.

Almost as one, the krakens slipped away beneath the crashing waves, taking Rose and her dome with them.

"Rose," I whispered.

"Thorn!"

I thumbed the amulets, raising the ward. Spawn ran squealing after the krakens, into the water. Ignoring us. It took half an hour for the army of Darkness to vanish.

The night grew still.

Black.

Silent.

The Enclave's dome was dark for the first time since it was raised by the seraphs of the Most High seventy-seven years ago. Cracks zigged and zagged across its surface. Time passed and then a faint glow began as Moon mages pulled power from the sky and began to mend it.

We stood, beneath my ward. None of us were certain what to do.

The huge gateway into Enclave slid open. Pale light filtered out. People walked into the night. The priestess of Enclave and an armed entourage stepped out. Walked to us. I dropped my ward and my champards arrayed themselves around me. Audric threw his cloak around Thadd and took Clovis's dead weight.

The priestess smoldered with power and beauty. She stopped in front of me. We took each other's measure. The breeze blew across us warmly. Waves lapped at the shore.

"Enclave thanks you for your help," she said, grudgingly.

"The consul-general accepts your thanks," Audric said before I could reply.

"Our people will . . . schedule talks," she said, her power brilliant in the night.

And I realized that the priestess hadn't seen Rose's actions or her disappearance. The priestess thought that my power defeated the krakens.

"Yes," Audric said. "That is acceptable to us."

The priestess of Enclave turned and walked back inside the dome. And shut the door.

We had won. For now.

About the Authors

FAITH HUNTER is the NYT and USAToday bestselling author of the Jane Yellowrock series, the Soulwood series and the Rogue Mage series. She collects orchids and animal skulls, loves the rain, and writes fantasy. She likes to cook soup and bake homemade bread, and go to the shooting range to hone her skills. She also kayaks easy whitewater rivers, edits the occasional anthology, and drinks a lot of tea. Some days she's a lady. Some days she ain't.

For more info please visit: www.faithhunter.net, www.gwenhunter.com and www.magicalwords.net. To keep up with her, like her fan page at Facebook: https://www.facebook.com/official.faith.hunter

MISTY MASSEY is the author of MAD KESTREL, a rollicking adventure of magic on the high seas (Tor), KESTREL'S VOYAGES, a collection of short stories featuring those rambunctious pirates (Amazon), and the upcoming KESTREL'S DANCE (Lore Seekers Press). She is a co-editor of THE WEIRD WILD WEST (Espec) and LAWLESS LANDS (Falstaff Books), and a founding member of Magical Words, the well-known blog for and about writers (magicalwords.net). When she's not writing, Misty studies Middle Eastern Dance and performs at regional events as the opportunities arise.

You can keep up with what Misty's doing at mistymassey.com, Facebook, and Twitter.

LOU J BERGER lives in Denver, Colorado with his high-school crush, three kids, two Sheltie dogs and a kink-tailed cat with a hidden agenda. He began writing short stories just shy of his fortieth birthday and has been published in a variety of venues. A member of the Science Fiction and Fantasy Writers of America, he is now working on his first novel.

His author website is www.LouJBerger.com.
Follow him on the following social media platforms:
Twitter: WriterLJBerger
Facebook: https://www.facebook.com/AuthorLouJBerger/

KEN SCHRADER is a science fiction and fantasy writer, a shameless geek, a fan of the Oxford comma, and makes housing decisions based upon the space available for bookshelves. Ken loves music of (almost) all kinds, books, the big sky off his front porch, *Star Wars, Firefly*, Blind Guardian (to which he writes almost exclusively), star gazing, jasmine tea, and the smell of rain on the air. Ken lives in Michigan, is co-owned by several dogs (especially the border collie), and is one of the rare breed of folk that enjoys mowing the lawn.

Visit his website at www.ken-schrader.com

Or follow him on Twitter @kenschrader4882

Or find him on Facebook at https://www.facebook.com/ken.schrader

SPIKE Y JONES is a long-haired, tie-dye-wearing Canadian editor, writer, and trained philosopher. There not being a lot of money in philosophy, he's concentrated his energies on his other talents.

As a writer, Spike's work has ranged from write-ups of *Dungeons & Dragons* monsters in the '80s all the way to stories about different sorts of monsters in this collection three decades later.

As an editor, Spike started by editing a presidential campaign game in 1992, and now in his day job edits 2016 presidential campaign transcripts. Rogue Mage: TRIALS and Rogue Mage: TRIBULATIONS are the first short-story anthologies he's edited.

DIANA PHARAOH FRANCIS was born, lived, and is not dead yet. She writes fantasy stories with much adventure, romance, and danger. She's owned by two corgis, has two children and a husband, likes rocks, geocaching, knotting up yarn, baking bread, Victorian England, and Monty Python. She can often be found cackling madly over her keyboard.

CHRISTINA STILES is an award-winning freelance tabletop roleplaying game writer, editor, and developer from South Carolina, who occasionally tries her hand at fiction and game publishing. She is the developer and co-author of THE ROGUE MAGE RPG: Roleplaying in the World of Faith Hunter, and her current project is the MEDUSA GUIDE FOR GAMER GIRLS. She teaches game-writing and critical thinking as an English professor at Winthrop University in Rock Hill, SC.

Christina can be reached at https://www.facebook.com/christina.stiles1 or on Twitter at @koboldminion7

TAMSIN L. SILVER is a writer of urban and historical fantasy. Originally from Michigan, Tamsin currently lives in New York City. She holds a BA in Theatre and Secondary Education, with a minor in Creative Writing and Shakespeare, from Winthrop University. She's also taught both middle and high school drama, and run two award-winning theater companies. She loves her dog, cat, swimming, Wild West history, and visiting New Mexico.

You can learn more about her web series, books, short stories, and social media links by visiting her website, www.tamsinsilver.com.

MELISSA McARTHUR is a master swordswoman, a world-renowned traveler, and lover of all things bookish. One of these things is actually true. When she isn't saving the world one word at a time, she's busy lecturing university students on parenthetical citations and torturing authors with her red pen.

She can be found at any of the following cyber places:
Web: www.melissamcarthur.net
Facebook: www.facebook.com/melissamcarthurwrites
Twitter: www.twitter.com/mcarthur_me
Goodreads: www.goodreads.com/melissamcarthurwrites

JEAN RABE is the author of three dozen novels and a hundred or so short stories. When she isn't writing, which isn't often, she tosses tennis balls to her cadre of dogs, visits museums, and plays wargames. Visit her on the web at: www.jeanrabe.com

LUCIENNE DIVER is the author of the *Vamped* young adult series (think *Clueless* meets *Buffy*) and the *Latter-Day Olympians* urban fantasy series from Samhain, which Long and Short Reviews called "a clever mix of Janet Evanovich and Rick Riordan." Her short stories have appeared in the KICKING IT anthology edited by Faith Hunter and Kalayna Price (Roc Books), the STRIP-MAULED and FANGS FOR THE MAMMARIES anthologies edited by Esther Friesner (Baen Books) and her essay "Abuse" was published in DEAR BULLY: 70 Authors Tell Their Stories (Harper-Collins). Her young adult thriller, FAULTLINES, is a new release from Bella Rosa Books.

More information can be found on her website:
http://www.luciennediver.com/

www.ingramcontent.com/pod-product-compliance
Lightning Source LLC
Chambersburg PA
CBHW031103030726
47496CB00002BA/350